SETTLEMENT

Ann Birch

RENDEZVOUS
PRESS

Cover design by Emma Dolan
Author photo by Studio Anka

Le Conseil des Arts | The Canada Council
du Canada | for the Arts

We acknowledge the support of the Canada Council for the Arts for our publishing program. We acknowledge the financial support of the Government of Canada through the Canada Book Fund for our publishing activities.

RendezVous Press
an imprint of Napoleon & Company
Toronto, Ontario, Canada
www.napoleonandcompany.com

Printed in Canada

14 13 12 11 10   5 4 3 2 1

Library and Archives Canada Cataloguing in Publication

Birch, Ann
        Settlement / Ann Birch.

ISBN 978-1-926607-04-7

        I. Title.

PS8603.I725S48 2020   C813'.6   C2010-904985-3

This book is dedicated to

Martha Lee Lawrence
John Harvey Lawrence
and
Hugh John Lawrence

remembering
"the lamb white days"

Part One

Winter Studies

PROLOGUE

York, 1817

The duellists and their seconds agreed to spend the night of July 17 in Elmsley's barn just north of the town. No one would think of looking for members of York's élite in such a place. There they would be able to hide from magistrates or family members who might try to put a stop to the wretched affair.

Sam Jarvis and his friend, Henry Boulton, arrived first and climbed up into the loft, where they could stay clear of the pigs and the worst of the stink. There they found a thick bed of hay. Sam cleaned his pistol, and they lay down to try to get some rest.

"How did I get myself into this mess?" Sam said. "Ridout is just a bloody-minded fool. Eighteen years old. And I'm twenty-five and should have known better."

"He insulted your father, didn't he? What else could you do?" Boulton gave a loud yawn. "People will give you credit for defending your family's honour. But we've been over all this before, so shut up about it. Please."

"The pity is, he reminds me of myself at his age. Remember those two Mohawks I almost killed over that squaw I fancied? I'd have gone to prison if Mr. Strachan hadn't persuaded the magistrate to drop charges."

"You might as well address all these remarks to the pigs, Jarvis. I'm not listening. I've got to get some sleep, and you should do the same."

They had scarcely settled when the barn door opened and John Ridout and his second, James Small, arrived.

"Just like your old man and your whole bloody family, Jarvis," Ridout said, coming to the foot of the ladder and shouting up at them. "Take the best spot and expect anyone who's not part of your tight little circle to fend for themselves."

Boulton put his hand on Sam's arm. "Leave it, Jarvis. It'll all be settled at dawn."

Sam could hear the curses of the two men below—even over the snorting of the pigs. Eventually they found an empty stall and banged the door shut. The barn grew dark. There was no moon, and the pelting rain leaked through the boards overhead, making an incessant pinging sound on the bare floor in a corner of the loft. Sam lay awake, his nostrils filled with the stink of pig shit, his ears assailed by the rain and Boulton's snores. Finally, just before dawn, he climbed down the ladder and went into the barnyard.

It would all be over before Elmsley's farmhand made his morning rounds. Boulton and Small had checked that out. Nevertheless, Sam upturned a pail over the head of a rooster he noticed strutting about the yard. If it couldn't get its neck up to crow, it couldn't give off alarms to wake the man up.

Too bad someone had not put a pail over Ridout's head the day he'd burst into Sam's father's office and accused the old man of evading his creditors. "Transferred all your land holdings to that son of yours," he'd said, pointing to Sam, who had come into the office to help his father. "Now my family will never get back the money you owe us." Sam's father, who had gout, hobbled towards Ridout, supporting himself on a crutch the family carpenter had made for him.

"You've got an almighty nerve," Ridout said and shook his fist in the old man's face. The lout seemed ignorant of the fact that Sam's father had unloaded on him all the huge debts charged against those land holdings. "You'll pay them off, son," he'd said as they signed the papers, "and I can die in peace."

· The clerks in the office were witnesses to the elder Jarvis's humiliation.

Boulton was right. Any decent man would protect a father's

reputation: that was duty. And duty was the fabric of decency. Sam had grabbed Ridout by the back of his coat and booted him out the door.

Later that day, in full view of everyone on King Street, including the drunks in front of the taverns, Ridout had hit Sam with a cane and injured his hand. Then the scoundrel had sent his friend, Small, to Sam's house with a challenge to a duel.

Sam walked over the field where the duel was to take place, whacking at the burdocks with his walking stick. Where was his blame in all this? He had done what any good son would have done, damn it.

At daybreak, the other three men emerged into the drizzle. Sam went back to the barn to get his pistol from the loft. Then they counted off eight paces in opposite directions, so that when Sam and Ridout turned to face each other, they were only fifty feet apart. Because Ridout was short-sighted, the four of them had previously agreed to this concession, the usual distance being twelve paces. Then Sam noticed that they were between two large tree stumps. He shouted, "We must pick a new spot!"

Small shook his head in disbelief. "A new spot? What are you talking about?"

"Getting cold feet, are you?" Ridout said.

"Because the stumps make it too easy to sight my pistol quickly."

Well, he'd done the decent thing. If he died on this miserable morning, people would at least have to acknowledge his fair play.

They chose another field that was clear of stumps and once more took their eight paces. "I'll give the count," Henry Boulton said. "It will be 'one...two... three... fire'!"

The duellists turned, raised their pistols to shoulder height, and waited. Boulton called out from a safe distance. Sam could hear him clearly. "One...two—"

But he got no further.

John Ridout fired on the count of two.

His bullet missed Sam. The boy did not seem to know what he

had done. He stood there, his pistol smoking, crying over and over, "Have I hurt you, Jarvis?"

Sam could not answer. He had dropped to his knees in response to the sound of the shot, and his heart was pounding so hard he thought it would break through his chest. He could not believe he was still alive. Then came an anger so huge he could not contain it. Kill the bastard. Kill him.

Small and Boulton rushed from opposite sides of the field to huddle together in the rain.

"Jarvis, you must comply with the duelling code and return the fire," Small said finally.

"And Ridout must not have the chance to reload," Boulton said. "The scum has broken all the rules of fair play."

"Agreed." This comment came from Small, who seemed ashamed now to be his friend's second.

So Sam and Ridout marked out their paces for the third time. Turned. Faced each other. Ridout raised his empty pistol to shoulder level. Perhaps it was a pitiful attempt at bravado, but the gesture renewed Sam's fading rage. He remembered his terror. He fired.

The bullet tore into Ridout's right shoulder, knocking him backwards. Sam threw his pistol to the ground and ran towards him. The jugular vein had burst open. Blood was everywhere. Pools of it leaked onto Ridout's waistcoat, spattered onto the weeds, soaked the ground under him. "What have I done? What have I done?" cried Sam, his rage spent. The only response was a moan. Then silence.

"He's dead, Jarvis. Let's get the hell out of here." Boulton pulled him away. "Nothing to be done. We've got to get out. Now."

The three men ran. Like rats. And all the way through the bush back into town, Sam said, over and over, "I fired on an unarmed boy. May God forgive me."

ONE

Toronto, 1836

Sam Jarvis woke in the dark, stuffy pit of his four-poster bed. He drew back the curtains that encircled him. A pale half-moon shone through the lace curtains, illuminating the china drink-warmer on the table beside his bed. He took off the lid. The candle at the base had burnt out, but the tea laced with whiskey was still warm. He drank it down in one gulp, then lighted a candle and moved out into the hallway.

He tiptoed past the bedroom of his daughters, the chamber of his eldest sons, and the nursery with its three small inmates, and reached his wife's room at the end of the hall. He lifted the latch, gave a slight push, and found resistance. He tapped his knuckles lightly against its smooth walnut surface. "Mary, Mary?"

No answer. He knocked again. "Mary, let me in!"

A door down the hallway opened, and a slim little figure in a pink nightdress appeared. "What is it, Papa?"

"Go back to bed, Ellen," he said. "I just want to see how your mother is."

As he said this, Mary's door opened an inch. He glimpsed a strip of her white gown and her bare toes. "Come in if you must," she whispered as he squeezed by her.

She stepped up onto the bed and moved over to the far side to make room for him. He pulled the curtains around them.

"Why was your door locked, Mary? You know I like to visit sometimes. Is it too much to ask you to let me in without waking up the children in the process?"

"Sam..." She moved towards him. He could smell the rosehip soap she used when she washed her hair. "I'm worn out. I cannot sleep with you again. I'm forty years old. If I found myself in the family way again, I don't know what I might do." He heard her sobs. "Men can't understand."

He put his hand on her breast and felt her pull away.

"I've tried to tell you before, but...I'd rather be left alone..." She rubbed her hot, wet cheek against his chest.

They'd married shortly after his trial for the murder of John Ridout. William Powell had been the judge. Murder among gentlemen—one joker's definition of duelling—sometimes went unpunished, especially if one's future father-in-law sat on King's Bench. He and Mary had hoped for happiness, like any newlyweds. They had not reckoned on the tragedy that had occurred nine months after their union.

He, too, could not forget the screams from the bedchamber that went on hour after hour while he sat in the hallway. And then the silence, and the doctor calling him inside to look at a small blue-skinned corpse. He'd wanted to comfort Mary, but the sight of his dead son made him sick, and he'd had to puke into the basin with all the bloody cloths.

There had been nine more births within sixteen years of marriage. She said men couldn't understand. But remembering that stillborn child, then the small son who died in the first year of his life, and all that terrible pain, those screams...well, yes, he could understand why Mary locked her bedroom door. He sighed, reached for her hand and held it. "Don't worry, my dear, I will not come to your bedchamber again until I have seen Dr. Widmer. He can advise me. I hear there are devices a man can use."

He could hear her intake of breath. "But surely, Sam, such... devices...are against God's will."

His head throbbed. Damn, damn. He'd offered to cover his prick with sheep's gut, and she tried to give him a lecture on God's will.

He listened to her sobs for a minute. "Sleep in your narrow bed without worry, my dear." He climbed down and tiptoed back to his own room. She might come around in a few days. She usually did. He was off for his annual moose hunt tomorrow, anyway. And perhaps Dr. Widmer would have the sheep's gut coverings by the time he got back. "They're expensive," he had told Sam. But Sam had so many debts, what was an extra bill? Widmer could always have another piece of Sam's land if he desired.

He rose late the next morning. It mattered little when he got to the block of offices that flanked the new Parliament Building. No one cared. Deputy Provincial Secretary: an impressive title for a job that involved paper-shuffling. The pay was not bad, but not enough to cover his father's debts and his own as well. Perhaps the new governor would come through with a promotion. He had an ego that could be stroked.

Mary was in the breakfast room. He got himself a cup of coffee from the sideboard and sat opposite her.

"Damn it, Mary—"

"Excuse me, sir." The maid came into the breakfast room carrying a platter of poached eggs. She slipped three onto his plate, two onto Mary's, and set the rest on the sideboard. While she was checking to see if there was still enough coffee in the urn, he dipped his bread in the eggs and put a large piece into his mouth.

"Disgusting," he said and spat the dripping mess into his napkin. "Can a man not get a decent breakfast in his own house? These eggs are bad." He threw the napkin onto the floor.

"If you please, sir, I tested them this morning in cold water. I did, sir. Cook says if they're fresh, they sink to the bottom. If they're rotten, they float. And sink they did, sir. I swear it."

"Don't argue. Take Mr. Jarvis's plate to the kitchen and bring him some rashers of bacon."

The maid picked up the napkin from the floor, set it on Sam's plate, and hurried off with it.

He watched Mary pick at her eggs, then push them to the side of her plate. They drank their coffee in silence, listening to the sounds of their daughters and the little ones belowstairs, enjoying the attentions of Cook and their expensive but excellent new governess, Miss Siddons. The maid came in again with bacon and fresh-baked rolls, set them at his place, and clumped down the kitchen stairs.

Mary stared down at the uneaten eggs on her plate. The case clock chimed nine times. As if recalled to life, she rose, gathering her shawl around her. It was a cashmere shawl in a soft shade of green that set off her pink cheeks. He had bought it for her from a merchant on King Street, and the bloodsucker kept reminding him of its cost in the quarterly bills that arrived.

The maid came back into the room. She picked up Mary's plate and headed for the door. Then she turned and came back to the table.

"What is it?"

"Please, sir. I need..."

"Need? What?"

"My wages."

"You'll get them, damn it. Now leave me in peace."

He sat at the table for a few minutes after she left. The bacon grease congealed on his plate. He picked up his cup of coffee. The dregs were lukewarm and bitter.

TWO

Sam and Jacob Snake portaged past the Narrows between Lake Simcoe and Lake Couchiching, where the Indians had driven stakes into the water to trap fish. Carrying the eighty-pound canoe and their gear, they walked along the bank for a half a mile.

At a turn in the well-worn path, they came upon Sir Francis Bond Head and his official entourage. They were making an inspection of the huge Indian encampment which the previous governor had established. The new man was small in stature with a large head of pretty grey curls. Sam had met him twice before at official functions in Toronto.

"Surprised to see you in such a godforsaken spot, Jarvis," he said. "Colborne left me with a mess here which I'll have to sort out. Too many savages in one place. Bound to be trouble."

"May I present my friend and guide, Jacob Snake?"

No response from Sir Francis. He looked down, seemingly more interested in counting the coloured studs on his frilly shirt than in acknowledging the introduction.

After a pause, Sam said, "Please excuse us, sir. You have much on your mind, and Jacob and I have a trek to accomplish before we make camp. Tomorrow we go moose hunting."

They tipped the canoe over their heads again and trudged onwards until they were able to put their craft into Lake Couchiching, north of the Narrows. They reached their campsite just after sunset.

"Sorry about the Governor," Sam said, as they pulled the canoe up on shore. Actually, he was more embarrassed and angry than sorry. "Savages" indeed. The nerve of the man. Why did these British upstarts have such a sense of superiority?

Jacob laughed. "Perhaps he is afraid of losing his buttons."

"Probably wanted to show us he can count to ten."

They lugged their gear to an open spot in the bush and threw down the fish they had caught en route.

"I start the fire, Nehkik. You gut the fish. We have a good supper." Jacob took out his tinder-box and with one deft swipe of the metal pieces, he got a spark going to light the tiny shreds of paper in the bottom of the box. Then he dipped a spill into the burning bits and transferred the flame to the dried moss heaped on the logs he'd already prepared. Sam had watched this procedure many times in his fishing and hunting expeditions with Jacob and was always amazed at the Indian's dexterity. He had tried to use the tinder-box himself but never achieved anything beyond scraped knuckles.

Sam turned to his own task and soon had several bass ready for the pan. Jacob made strong tea and bannock, and they settled down with tin plates and bone cutlery to an excellent meal.

"You know, Jacob, sometimes when I'm at the Governor's banquets in Toronto, sawing my way through a tough steak and talking to a corseted matron, I yearn for a meal of fish with you, taken in the peace of a fall evening like this one." He gestured at the harvest moon rising behind his friend.

"Pardon me, Nehkik, what is this 'corseted matron' you speak of?"

"A fat white woman who pulls in her waist with..." Sam found himself unable to describe the heavy material stiffened with whalebones and tied together with laces. "Imagine a wide band of deerskin so tight around your middle that you cannot breathe. Then you will understand 'corset.'"

"So because the lady cannot breathe, you must do all the talking."

"That's about it, Jacob, though I never before realized this was why white women have no conversation."

After rinsing their plates in the lake water, they sat in silence, smoking their pipes. They were both tired. It had been a long day, so instead of making a couch from balsam tips, they simply rolled up in the comfortable stink of their bearskins and fell into a sound sleep.

About four o'clock, Sam jolted awake. Loud snuffles and grunts came from the bushes beside his bed. Jacob wakened too. He seized a tin plate and beat a tattoo on it with a fork, shouting something in his own language. The marauder—perhaps a bear enticed by the scent of their sleep-covers—lumbered off into the darkness, and just as quickly, Jacob lay back again and fell asleep.

But Sam stayed awake, staring up at the full moon. Gradually the darkness faded, and Jacob still snored softly. Finally, Sam tapped him on the shoulder. "Shall we call now?"

"Maybe," Jacob said, then added, "or maybe wait."

"Damn it, Jacob, why can't you answer a simple question outright? It's going to be a perfect dawn. Why don't we use it?"

There was no answer, only the sound of his companion's deep breathing.

It was utterly still, the sort of day that Jacob had once told him was necessary for moose calling. Of all the deer family, Jacob said, the bull moose had the keenest sense of smell. When he heard a call, he would circle downwind to get a scent of the animal beckoning him. If there was even a breath of wind, he would know that the caller was not the one he wanted as a mate.

Rifle in hand, Sam climbed a tall pine tree nearby. Two-thirds of the way up, he found a thick branch that provided a comfortable perch. There he waited. Sunrise came gradually. The stars and moon faded, and the pale light deepened into the pink and red that herald the warmth of the sun. The light glanced off his rifle, illuminating the silver inlays on the walnut stock and the barrel with its engraving of the serpent in the apple tree. It had belonged to his grandfather.

Suddenly the peace was shattered by wild, diabolical cries. Shocked out of his reverie, Sam clutched the branch of the pine tree to stop himself from pitching to the ground. He turned and saw Jacob grinning at him from a perch in an adjacent pine tree. "Nehkik, I call the moose now," he said.

He put to his mouth a cone-shaped horn of birchbark, about a foot and a half in length, and fashioned like a speaking trumpet.

The sound coming from this instrument was the primal call of the moose to her mate.

They waited in silence for upwards of fifteen minutes. Then Jacob tried again. Then another fifteen-minute silence. And so it went, for more than an hour, while the branch on which Sam stood pressed into his moccasined feet and the cold crept through his buckskin jacket and took possession of his body.

A movement in the next pine tree caught his attention. Jacob lowered the horn and held his forefinger to his mouth, signalling quiet. Then he pointed in the direction of the marsh. They inched their way down the tree, careful to be perfectly silent, both aware that a bull moose had uncannily acute hearing. On that clear, still morning, the slightest sound would announce their presence.

They started for the open space the Chippewas called Lake of Spirits. It had once probably been a lake of some three miles in breadth, but now it was a marshland filled with rushes on which the moose liked to feed. At intervals across its width, there were high, dry patches of treed land that were once islands. They waded through the marsh, making their way to one of these islands, where they lay down on pine needles and waited. The sun was higher in the sky now, and Sam welcomed its warmth on his wet legs. He dozed.

Snuffling noises like the breathing of a large animal brought him to his senses. Jacob had the large end of the birchbark horn in the water, and he was blowing through the small end to make bubbling sounds like an animal drinking. Then, smiling at Sam, he put his fingers over the small end, filled the horn with water, and held it aloft. In a moment or two, he removed his fingers, and a stream of water coursed back into the swamp.

It was an old trick. "Sounds like a cow moose pissing," Jacob had once told him.

Scrambling back up onto the grass, Jacob waited with Sam, who watched the horizon with his telescope. It was only a moment or two before Jacob whispered, "Moose comes over the barren," his word for the marshy land they had waded through. Sam threw down his scope and picked up his rifle.

And suddenly there it was, at least ten feet tall, and against the sun, its black bulk and huge antlers made it seem like a monster from some ancient folktale. It evidently sensed danger, for the bristles stood high on its shoulders.

Sam readied his rifle for a shot. He had the animal in his sights. Then, into his head flashed an image of Ridout, arm raised.

"Fire!" yelled Jacob.

The animal lunged towards him, eyes rolling and mouth drooling, hooves stirring ripples in the water, its bulk blocking out the sun. It would crush him. Sam dropped his rifle, covered his head with his arms, stopped breathing.

But in that hopeless instant, Jacob discharged his rifle. The animal staggered and crashed to the ground, four feet from Sam.

Cradling his firearm, Jacob crept towards the beast. A shudder rippled through its hide, and it was still.

"Aim for the head," Jacob said. "When the brain dies, spirit leaves."

"You saved my life," Sam said. He took deep breaths, afraid that if he said more, he'd make an ass of himself. Cry like a baby.

In its last charge, the moose had propelled itself upwards from the marsh onto the dry oasis, so they did not have to lever the body to a place where they could work easily on its carcass. With the knives that Jacob produced from a deerskin pouch, they were able to get right down to the task of skinning and gutting.

Sam paused to sharpen his knife on a whetstone. "I promised my small son a fine set of antlers for the nursery."

"Then I sever the antlers," Jacob said, "so they do not break."

The sun was hot as they worked, and Sam's hands grew tired from hacking at the flesh. "Don't think I can stand this much longer, Jacob."

"Think, my friend. You work hard now, and I give you a reward: one grilled kidney when we carve him up." He smiled and shook a bloody finger at Sam. "No work, no reward, white man."

Sam laughed, forgetting his fatigue for a minute. "Now I understand why my fine white friends call you folk savages."

They resumed their work, stopping only when they heard the sound of splashing. Looking up, they saw five Indian men crossing the marsh towards them.

"We hear rifle shots," they said. "We come to help."

"Just in time," Jacob said. "Poor old white friend here is worn out. Let us go back to the camp and eat first. Then we leave him to smoke pipe while red men do the work."

So they took some pieces of meat from the carcass and slopped back through the marsh to the place where he and Jacob had slept the night before. Jacob got a good fire going, and they impaled the moose meat on sharpened sticks and set it to roast.

"For you, my friend," Jacob said, handing him a choice piece of the kidneys.

"Ah, so I get my reward after all. Thank you. Roasted moose kidneys with salt, a cup of strong tea and sugar, a hard biscuit: it's a feast for King William himself." They munched in silence.

Jacob looked at the sun. "Time to get to work."

"Poor old white friend will help you," Sam said. "I'll take my pipe and smoke while we work." He turned to the other Indians. "Let us work well together, and at the end of the day, we shall divide the moose among us."

The sun was low in the sky when they finished carving up the carcass and smoking some of the pieces. There were several hundred pounds of meat. Sam saved a portion for his family, and the other men took their fair share and departed, single file, down the narrow bush trail.

"A good day, Nehkik," said Jacob that evening as they sat at the campfire. Jacob had grilled two moose steaks in the coals and filled their tin cups with scalding tea.

"A good day, Jacob." Sam set down his tin plate and sighed. "Tomorrow, alas, we must start our voyage south." Back to paper-shuffling. Back to his debts, to the insatiable demands of his large family. Back to Mary, who no longer wanted him in her bed. And goodbye to promotion now that the new Gov had seen him consorting with a "savage".

They made themselves comfortable beds of dried bracken and tender balsam tips and lay down for a sound sleep. They rose at dawn and loaded their canoe in preparation for the trip.

"I'm going for a swim," Sam said. "Just a few minutes' more respite before we launch the canoe."

Taking off his clothes, he swam out into the cool lake waters, his destination a small island a few hundred yards off shore. "You swim like an otter," Jacob had told him once long ago. "So I call you 'Nehkik.'" It was one of the few compliments he had ever received from his Indian friend, though they had known each other from childhood, when his parents had struck a friendship with Jacob's Chippewa grandparents.

He climbed up on the rocks of the little island and looked back at Jacob, who waved to him from the shore, then disappeared into the bush.

His fingers cupped around his mouth, Sam called out, "WOOOOO!" And again, "WOOOO!"

A few minutes elapsed. He called again, "WOOOO!"

Then Jacob reappeared on the shore. He'd strapped the moose antlers to his head somehow, perhaps with the beaded sash he wore on his buckskin jacket. "WOOOO!" he called back.

Laughing, Sam dived from a rock back into the chill waters and headed for shore.

THREE

Anna's husband must have known that she had arrived in Toronto. At this time of year, there was but one steamboat a day from Niagara, and this vessel had been the last to make the crossing till spring. But he had not come to meet her. She stood alone on the dock, her trunk and portmanteau beside her on the slush-covered planks. The bay had nearly frozen over, and three feet of snow lined the shore, blowing into her face. The other passengers had already commandeered cabs or rushed into the waiting arms of family and friends. What to do next?

In the one letter she had received from Robert weeks ago, he had mentioned a pretty little house he was building with a view of the lake. Where was it? Would it have a hot fire? An obliging maid to serve a tasty dinner? She looked up towards the town, a dingy place of frame and log buildings against the dark gleam of a pine forest.

On the street facing the bay was a tavern towards which a man in a greatcoat and top hat appeared to be heading. She saw him pause to look out towards the lake and the departing steamboat. Then, seeing her alone on the wharf, he moved towards her.

"Help you, ma'am?" He removed his hat and bowed.

He had friendly blue eyes that looked straight at her. Not a young man, middle-aged like herself. Up close, she could see that his coat was well-cut superfine and his gloves, good leather. Evidently a man of stature.

"I'm Anna Jameson. I expected my husband to meet me here, but something must have delayed him."

"Mrs. Jameson? Ah, you are the Attorney-General's wife. Welcome to Toronto. The town has been expecting you to arrive." He smiled. "Do not look surprised. You will soon find that there are no secrets in this place. I'm Sam Jarvis. At your service, ma'am."

In an instant he had hailed a two-horse wagon on runners, driven by a red-cheeked yokel who made no effort to help. Two swings of Mr. Jarvis's arm, and her luggage was aboard. Then he steadied her up the step to a wooden plank which served as a seat.

"No. 1, Bishop's Block, Newgate Street," he said to the driver, slipping a coin into his outstretched hand. And to Anna, "He'll get you there safely. Good day to you. Undoubtedly we shall meet again soon. I look forward to it."

They went west along the street bordering the harbour. It was called Palace Street. What a misnomer! She saw one ugly church, St. James by name, without tower or steeple, and some low government offices of red brick. There seemed to be taverns everywhere, but not a single bookseller's shop. The snow pelted into her face as they moved through dreary, miry ways, largely solitary because of the storm. It was strangely quiet, the horses' hooves muffled in the falling snow. Eventually, the wagon stopped—not in front of a pretty little house—but beside one of five forlorn-looking brick row houses, on a desolate street.

The driver set Anna's luggage by the front door, leaving her to climb down from the seat by herself. She watched him drive off. Across the road she noticed a wretched little shanty and a poor half-starved cow, up to its knees in a snowdrift. She ploughed through the snow and banged on the knocker of the brick house.

The sturdy, grey-haired woman who opened the door looked half surprised, half alarmed to see her. But she straightened her apron and curtsied.

"Come in, ma'am. I be Mrs. Hawkins. I fear we have not finished redding up for your arrival. We supposed the boat might be slow coming through that slushy water." She led Anna up a creaking, uncarpeted staircase. At the top she called out to a small wiry man, evidently her husband. He lugged Anna's baggage up the stairs and slung it into a room where the bed was unmade, and the bedding and towels were piled upon the mattress. The fires were out. Everything was as cold and comfortless as the outdoors.

Anna looked into another room made dingy by hideous wallpaper of creeping vines. There was a pine dining table, six chairs and a buffet. She tried to envisage a fine supper party in this room. There was a Coalport dinner service that looked usable on the buffet, and perhaps Robert would spend money to repaper the walls. She lost herself for a moment in reverie; then she noticed that Mrs. Hawkins was concealing something behind her apron. She smelled spirits on the woman's breath.

"Has Mr. Jameson said when he will arrive home?"

"No, ma'am. It be eight o'clock most days, though he never do say for sure."

She suspected that the manservant had also been drinking. The decanter of brandy on the buffet was half empty and had no stopper. Tired as she was, she held out her hand to the woman.

"Give me the stopper. Better still, put it back where it belongs. Make your husband and yourself a strong cup of tea and bring one to the bedchamber for me also. Then I expect you to get the fires lighted, these rooms made ready, and the meal preparation under way. When I've had my tea, I will go for a walk. I expect everything to be in order when I come back."

The tea was scalding, and she felt better after drinking it. It was now the middle of the afternoon, and already the light through the dirty windows seemed darker. She made haste to put on her heavy outerwear and went down the stairs, but as she moved towards the door, the servant came running with gaiters and two strange-looking wooden soles mounted on iron oval rings. "These be for the outdoors, ma'am."

Anna put on the canvas gaiters. She could see that they would provide warmth and protection from the slush. Then Mrs. Hawkins showed her how to put on the things she called "pattens". They raised Anna's shoes an inch from the ground, and they made a clanking sound when she moved forward. "You'll not be noticing it in the snow, ma'am," the woman assured her.

But when Anna tried to walk down the street, she found it

necessary to adopt a kind of waddle, feet far apart, to compensate for the extra width of the pattens. An urchin pointed at her and laughed. Suddenly she was tired, more tired than she had ever been in her life. She turned back to the house, shook off the pattens in the front hall and removed the gaiters. She took her coat and went upstairs.

In the drawing room across the hall from the dining room, she found one comfortable armchair beside a Pembroke table piled high with newspapers. Perhaps it might be a good idea to find out the news in this wretched place, she thought, and took the top paper from the pile. But the headlines blurred in front of her, and her eyes closed.

As she drifted into sleep, she could hear the servants' voices.

"Thought we'd say good riddance to her for an hour."

"At least she be asleep. But not for long, I'll warrant. 'Meal preparation', that's a new one. I've got to be finding my recipe book."

"Shake a leg, woman. Or we'll have our walking papers."

A striking clock woke Anna up. She felt much warmer, almost too warm under her coat. The housekeeper and her husband had evidently applied themselves to their labours while she slept. Fires had been lit in each of the fireplaces, and her bedchamber was in order, though there was little in the way of real comfort. Perhaps there were merchants who would supply comfortable chairs or bookcases for her volumes.

The woman brought hot water to Anna's room, set the pitcher down with a thump, and left, muttering something about recipes. Anna removed her travel-stained clothing and washed herself in the basin. She had kept a new silk dress for the reunion with her husband, and she took it from her trunk. It was of two pieces, with a close-fitting bodice and a full, pleated skirt. The sleeves were narrow at the shoulders and wide at the wrists, and when she raised her arms, the sleeves fell back to show to advantage her white wrists and arms.

While she waited for Robert, she looked around the house.

She found a rough pine table in an unused bedchamber and had the manservant put it in her room. At least she now had a desk of sorts. She unpacked some of her books and her drawing materials and spread them out on its surface.

The case clock in the drawing room struck eight, then eight thirty. The door opened. Anna moved into the hallway to greet her spouse. For a moment she stood, unable to speak, seeing afresh after three years' separation his tall, elegant form, his curly hair and large brown eyes, the right one with a slight strabismus.

"My dear," he said, extending his fingers so that they brushed her sleeve. "I am happy to see you looking so well." He smiled.

"I am glad to see you in evident health and good spirits, too, Robert." She raised her arms to embrace him, but he was already removing his coat with the help of Hawkins. There was a long pause. The servants hovered. "Go belowstairs," Anna said to them, "and bring up our dinner."

"I see you have already taken charge, Anna. I fear I am too tired at the end of the day to give instructions. Hawkins and his wife provide a dish of gruel and a decanter of wine." Robert threw his coat onto a chair. "Let us move into the drawing room."

He took the comfortable armchair for himself, and she perched opposite him in a straight-backed Windsor chair. He looked her over. "How strange it seems to have you with me again, Anna."

"If I may borrow a phrase I overheard from one of the boat passengers today, 'Where the deuce were you when I was freezing my balls off on that blasted wharf?'"

"I am sorry, my dear. I had hoped to be there. But at the last moment, His Majesty's representative, Sir Francis Bond Head, requested my presence at Government House for coffee. I foresee an opportunity for advancement to Vice-Chancellor of the Province—if the winds are favourable. If one hopes for promotion, one cannot be too assiduous in attendance when the Governor summons. Such are the realities of life in this place." He paused, his attention diverted by a newspaper beside his chair.

"But why did you not send someone to meet me? Why did you leave me to stand on that freezing wharf dependent on the kindness of a stranger?"

"Ah, that *was* an oversight for which I must beg your pardon. But apart from my dereliction of duty, I trust your voyage was satisfactory? Not too many impediments to your comfort?"

"I have been two months in transit. I shall spare you the details. Except to say that surely Franklin's charting of the Arctic seaboard was scarcely more arduous than my trek across the Atlantic to this godforsaken town. But I survived, Robert. I thank you for asking."

Her husband smiled. "Still the jokester, dear Anna. We must talk further at dinner."

He picked up the newspaper that had engaged his interest and began reading. Anna counted slowly to ten in English, French, and German. Then she closed her eyes for a few moments, trying to shut out of her vision the strangling vines on the wallpaper and the snow collecting on the inner ledge of the ill-fitting window.

"Dinner, master." Mrs. Hawkins set a platter of sausages and a dish of boiled potatoes on the buffet. "And I made a nice bread pudding for you, ma'am, in honour of your homecoming."

"One of my favourite things. Thank you. That will be a treat."

The woman smiled, her lined face transformed into prettiness. She went again belowstairs.

Robert forked sausages onto his plate. "Sir Francis asked me to extend a welcome to you. He said that he looks forward to meeting you at the soirées at Government House. Lady Head arrives in a few weeks."

"One of the men I spoke to today on the boat from Niagara called His Lordship a nincompoop. Was he right?"

"I can have no opinions. And I must caution you, Anna. While you are here, I ask you to keep clear of any expression of contention."

"While I am here? What do you mean, Robert? You see this as a temporary arrangement, do you?"

"Please do not pounce on a stray phrase. Of course, I want you to stay."

"I know you need me to lend credence to your pretence to have a normal married life. That's what you had in mind when you asked me to come across the sea. But I have nonetheless hoped for more. Some warmth of welcome. Some sympathetic discourse." She laid down her fork and pushed her plate away.

"You are right, Anna. I want to rise from Attorney-General to Vice-Chancellor of the Province. You are an essential part of my plan. We must try to get on together. I shall do my best to be a good husband. But I doubt, my dear Anna, that you have come across the sea solely for altruistic reasons."

"So let us lay down our cards. In the twelve years we have been married, we have lived apart for almost eight years, and during all that time, I have been reliant on my own resources as an author, but—"

"Ah yes. You want money."

"The writing business is uncertain at best. I have been lucky with my books so far, but who knows how long the reading public will stay with me. So here it is, Robert. I shall need three hundred pounds a year to maintain myself and to provide for my parents and my unmarried sisters. My poor father has suffered a stroke."

"Three hundred pounds!" Robert's normal pallor disappeared under a pulsing wave of crimson.

"You will be able to afford it. I learned some facts before I left England. The salary of the Attorney-General is twelve hundred pounds a year including fees; the salary of the Vice-Chancellor is twelve hundred a year, not including fees. Your income will more than double. You'll be a rich man. I ask for a mere three hundred."

"Never. But as long as you stay with me, I shall give you an allowance suited to your status as Chancellor's wife. Some of that may certainly be dispatched to your family. If you leave, you are on your own."

Robert poured another glass of wine, then another and another. Anna spooned some of the bread pudding onto her plate. The rest of the meal passed in silence.

As they parted for the night, Robert stopped outside his bedchamber. "I promised you a pleasant little house, Anna. Alas, it is not ready. The carpenters and bricklayers took a month off for the hunting season. You can't hurry the hoi polloi in this town."

"Never mind. This place is just fine. The street is no doubt named after London's best prison."

"Would you like me to come to your bedchamber for a while?"

"Perhaps we are both too tired. Let us rest for tonight."

In her bedchamber, Anna found that Mrs. Hawkins had left two flickering candles. By their light, she removed her dress. Her husband had not noticed her white arms and hands in the new gown. Perhaps he had once found her physically attractive, but that had been long ago.

She remembered his letters during their courtship. They had been delightful, full of warmth and passion. She had fallen in love with those fine words on that beautiful linen-fibre paper. But whenever they met in person, his conversation was strained and impersonal. She had broken off their engagement once, then changed her mind. If he had not been successful and well connected, would she have married him, knowing his cold, reserved demeanour?

Her friend Ottilie von Goethe had asked her once if their marriage had been consummated. Yes, it had been consummated. A grim word, but the right word. It suggested the completion of sexual congress without any of the joy or desire a married woman had a right to expect. In the early days, there had been caresses which had led to gropings and perfunctory encounters, but there had been no northern lights, no shooting stars.

Once she had found on his desk a poem of fourteen lines written to him by Samuel Taylor Coleridge's son, Hartley. In length, it seemed to be a sonnet, but she remembered the unorthodox rhyming couplet which formed its beginning. And the even stranger content:

Thou art my dearest love. O Rob! Sans thee,
A vast and woeful wasteland my life would be.

"How dare you poke into my private correspondence?" Robert had said, coming into the room as she held the poem in her hand. She had put it aside hastily, but now, as she remembered it, she recognized a truth she had long tried to suppress.

She took from her portmanteau the pocket of otter fur that Ottilie had given her on a fine summer morning in Vienna, as they drank coffee in lodgings overlooking the gardens of Schönbrunn Palace. She held its softness against her cheek now, feeling its warmth and a hint of Ottilie's scent.

"It's so pleasant, so pretty," she had said to her friend, "but what is it?"

"It's a foot muff, my dear Anna. I understand there will be a frozen lake in that faraway place to which you seem determined to go. No doubt when you are there you will travel in a calèche all by yourself with only the horse to talk to. Keep your poor cold toes tucked inside the muff while you discuss oats and harness."

Sitting down now at the pine table that must serve as a desk, she put her cold toes into the warm fur. Perhaps she could find release by recording her day's disappointments in her journal. Better still, she would write a letter to Ottilie. She would begin, "Dearest Ottilie: Here in this forsaken outpost, by that frozen lake you warned me about in July, I long for your overflowing high spirits and *joie de vivre*."

She took the inkwell from the top of the bureau and set it on the table. Then she saw that the ink had a thin layer of ice over it.

FOUR

In his bedchamber, Sam Jarvis dressed for dinner at Government House. Mary came in to help him attach the collar and cuffs to his dress shirt and to brush his top hat. "I am looking forward to this dinner," she said. "It will save me from an evening with Mama and Eliza. They are stitching petticoats for the bazaar for the poor—utterly, utterly boring."

"No doubt your sister would have some gossip. Has she met Mrs. Jameson?"

"Not yet. Some of the ladies intended to call today and leave their cards. Eliza has heard that she has written some popular books. And she carries a Spanish guitar and a stiletto wherever she goes. She also is apparently great friends with a man named... named... Go Thee, who wrote about the Devil."

"I met her briefly on the wharf the other day and summoned a cab for her."

"Oh, Sam, why didn't you tell me? What does she look like?"

"Not as pretty as you, my dear." Though, indeed, he did not especially like the immense sleeves of Mary's dress which closed with a tight-fitting cuff. No doubt it was the current style, but it made her arms look grotesque.

"A new face will be welcome in this town," Mary said. "If nothing else, the lady will furnish us with new sources of scandal, provided the stories that preceded her are true. Do you think she'll be there tonight?

"Possibly, but do not suppose that the Governor's affair will be any livelier than your sewing circle. Sir Francis will be sure to bore us again with his tales of exploits in Argentina. There are times when I wish that his horse had fallen over a cliff in the Andes and—"

"Sam, you must keep on the man's good side. No arguments with him or anyone else, please. And put yourself forward for promotion if you have the chance to speak to him personally." She reached up and patted his shoulder.

"You're singing the same old refrain, Mary. I don't need to be told what to do. I know that I've got to get a promotion. I've heard he's looking for someone to 'control the savages'—that's what he calls them."

"What an opportunity, dear Sam! Surely you can play up your friendship with Jacob Snake."

"Not sure he wants someone who has an Indian friend. But I mean to do what I can. Otherwise, I may end up in debtors' prison. And believe me, a four months' lockup in 1817 was more than enough for one lifetime."

"I've been thinking. We could discharge Miss Siddons. After all, twenty-five pounds would go a long way towards settling our debts with the butcher and the baker." She attempted a laugh. "And the candlestick maker."

"The girls must be educated. I don't care what it costs. Do you want them to grow up like your sister, dependent on the goodwill of relatives? Accepting handouts in return for labour in the kitchen and the sickroom?"

"But the girls will marry, will they not? They need only to be educated to fill that capacity. My sister is a plain woman, but the girls are pretty. There will be men who—"

"We can sell them to. Is that what you want?"

"Is that why you married me? In return for my father letting you off on the murder charge?"

For a moment he could not speak. He could only feel the pulse in his head and his face growing redder and redder. "Murder, Mary? Is that what you think? Do you truly believe I murdered Ridout?"

She moved towards him then, wrapping her arms around his waist. "Oh, Sam, forgive me, forgive me. I say these things when we quarrel. Of course, I don't mean them."

He looked at his knuckles, white and clenched. He took a deep breath, sat down on the bench in front of the pier glass and spread his hands on his knees.

"Now, Mary, you will remember that the children are my responsibility as well as yours. Our sons are at a fine school. But there is very little education for girls in this town. That is why Miss Siddons is so necessary. Hang the expense."

"But Eliza and I could teach them drawing and stitchery skills. I could ask her to—"

"Stitchery and drawing be damned. Let us be clear. I will not have the girls wasting their lives making hair bracelets and watercolour daubs of the peony patch. As for your sister, what could she teach them except the pleasures of laudanum and whiskey? I don't blame her, mind you, she must do something to relieve the tedium of her life."

Mary started to cry. ""Hair...hair...bracelets, Sam. You can be so cruel. Say what you want about Eliza. She has her faults, as do we all. But that remark about hair bracelets. Why do you bring up poor little Eddie? He's part of every waking memory. I don't need your sarcasm to make it worse."

Their small son, Eddie, had died in 1828, only one year old, and Mary cut off all his beautiful red hair just before his burial. Then she had spent days making a bracelet from it. He could not bear to look at her when she wore it, and she had finally put the thing away somewhere.

"I shouldn't have mentioned it."

But what the hell. She'd had the nerve to mention his trial for murder. It had happened almost two decades ago. And he had been exonerated. How dare she suggest that he'd made some deal with her father, Chief Justice Powell?

"I'm sorry, Sam, so sorry."

He reached for her hand. It was cold, though her small, delicate face was flushed. "Let us think of the advantages of well-educated daughters. Why just last week, Ellen treated me to a dissertation on our three political parties, the Radicals, the Tories, and the Wigs, as she called them."

Mary wiped her face with her lace handkerchief. He watched as she struggled to smile. "Oh, Sam, do you think she will want to stay with the gentlemen for port and cigars when we have a supper party?"

"Undoubtedly. I expect they will be greatly enlightened by her views on the Wigs."

He rose, leaned over her shoulders, and put his face against her cheek. "We shall say no more about discharging Miss Siddons."

Mary took his new fur-lined greatcoat from the wardrobe and draped it over his shoulders. It was a fine piece of tailoring, and in it he felt like a millionaire, perhaps John Jacob Astor or one of those other New York men he read about in the American newspapers that arrived at his office downtown. "Clothes make the man," his mother had often said when she'd urged his father to spend more and more on outward trifles, and it was a proverb Sam found himself remembering too often these days when he looked at his tailor's account.

He and Mary went out the front door onto the wide verandah and down to the phaeton which had drawn up to the steps. John, the coachman, whipped up the horses, and they slipped down the long gravel driveway past the lawns and gardens now covered in snow. Pretty they were as they gleamed in the moonlight, but lovelier by far in summer and fall.

Government House, located at King and Simcoe Streets, was a two-storey frame house in the Georgian style with shutters and an attractive portico. Not as handsome as his own house, though, Sam noted.

John pulled the horses to a halt. "Elmsley House, sir."

"Government House, man. Why do you persist in calling it Elmsley House?"

The house had once belonged to Chief Justice Elmsley, who had also owned the farm and field north of the town where Sam had killed John Ridout. He still could not bear to hear the name.

The footman in the front hall took their coats, and they entered the drawing room. The new Lieutenant-Governor came forward to greet them. "Welcome, Jarvis, and welcome to your good wife." He gave a nod in Mary's direction and called to a hired waiter whom Sam recognized as a corporal from the garrison. "Have some rum punch."

Sir Francis gestured towards two vacant chairs. As Sam went to sit down, he noticed the Governor standing on his tiptoes to look at himself in the mirror over the mantelpiece. What did the man find to admire? Certainly not the beaky nose or tiny figure. Perhaps it was his large head of luxurious curls? Any girl would be proud of them, Sam reflected, as he turned to talk to the Attorney-General, Robert Jameson, who perched on the beechwood settee beside Sam's chair. Here was a man whom the mirror would declare "fairest of all".

"And how does Mrs. Jameson like her new abode?" Sam asked.

"She is used to the comforts of large drawing rooms in London, Paris, and Vienna. I fear there will be a period of adjustment. But why don't you ask the lady herself?" He called to his wife, who had taken a chair near the fireplace. "Anna, come here. This gentleman would like to meet you." Jameson stumbled to his feet to give his seat to his wife. In the process he set his punch glass on the Pembroke table, spilling some of its contents over the polished surface. The hovering waiter moved in to mop up the puddle with the napkin he had over his arm. "Better get some barley water into me," Jameson said, as he suppressed a hiccough and walked off.

"I have met Mr. Jarvis before. And this is Mrs. Jarvis? I am happy to meet you." As the lady stretched out her arm to greet them, Sam noticed how her dress sleeve was moulded to her slender arm and ended in a wide cuff that fell back to display a delicate wrist with a pretty pink topaz bracelet. She sat down on one side of him in the chair her husband had vacated, while Mary sat on the other.

Before Sam could say more, the room fell silent as Sir Francis raised his voice and launched into one of the familiar anecdotes about his career as a mining supervisor in South America. "...and as I may have told you before..."

"Yes indeed, many times," Sam whispered into Mary's ear. She gave him a dig in the ribs with her elbow, but from the corner of his eye, he noticed Mrs. Jameson's smile.

"The natives there called me—"

"Galloping Head!" This epithet was shouted by Sir Francis's son, the schoolboy Henry Head, who had somehow escaped from his studies and come unannounced into the drawing room. "Tell them about your wild ride from Buenos Aires, Papa!"

"And now shall we have twenty minutes of the inevitable?" Mrs. Jameson whispered, leaning towards Sam so that he could smell her lavender fragrance. He took another cup of rum punch from the waiter's tray.

Sir Francis's story went on and on, and the men were tipsy by the time the dinner gong sounded. Jameson weaved about as he made his way to the dining room, and Sam had to steady himself on the chair backs as he looked at the card which indicated his place at table.

It was a good spread: squash and apple soup, a fine roast turkey stuffed with oysters, a huge cured ham, roast potatoes, carrots, a cut-glass crystal bowl of peaches and pears in a heavy syrup, and excellent berry pie. Sam was glad of the food. He felt his head clearing as he ate. He had to stay sober if he were to make a favourable impression on Sir Francis. When was he to have his opportunity? So far the talk at the table had been of the state of the roads along the St. Lawrence River.

Henry Boulton, the man who had been Sam's second in the duel, monopolized the conversation, as he always did. He had three topics: roads, politics and the price of wine. This night his theme seemed to be "My Late Visit to the Eastern Townships". He waved his knife about as he complained of one of the bridges: "The planks were so loose, so rotten, and so crazy, that every moment I thought that my expensive new carriage and spirited thoroughbreds would fall through."

"It would have been a great loss if you had fallen with them." Sam hoped he'd made the remark in a neutral tone that no one at the table could take issue with. But Mary pressed her foot into his ankle.

The women remained silent for most of the meal. Then, over the berry pie, Mrs. Jameson spoke up. "As a newcomer to the town, I must ask your advice on what to read. There seem to be a great many newspapers, though from what I understand, there are very few books. But one must read something. I have perused the *Toronto Patriot* and cannot say that I enjoy its content. What do you think of the *Constitution*? Much livelier, if I can judge from the two copies I've read."

There were groans about the table. Henry Boulton gave a loud belch and covered his mouth with his napkin. The ladies brought out their fans, and Mrs. John Beverley Robinson, wife of the Chief Justice, inhaled the vapours from her vinaigrette.

"I fear I have said something amiss," Mrs. Jameson said, though she did not look at all contrite.

"Dear lady," the Chief Justice replied, "you have been here only two days. You cannot know that the editor of this paper, William Lyon Mackenzie by name, is a viper and a demon. In the vile pages of his rag, he has abused everyone in this town, even my dear departed mother."

"In the brief weeks I have held this post, Mackenzie has even seen fit to print the foulest rumours about me, His Majesty's represenative," the Governor said. "Believe this, I intend to do whatever is in my power to scotch the viper. And I will depend on each and every one of you, loyal servants of the Crown, to support my cause."

"Hear! Hear!" The gentlemen beat their fists upon the table, and the ladies, at a signal from Mrs. Robinson, rose to take their tea in the drawing room.

Mrs. Jameson hovered in the archway, looking back at the dining table. "Perhaps I might stay for a few minutes to hear the discussion about this man? I know so little about the politics of the town."

"By all means, Mrs. Jameson," Sir Francis said. "Instead of 'Shall we join the ladies?' we now have a lady asking, 'Shall I join the gents?' Most unusual, but I say, 'Welcome, dear lady'." He pulled out a chair for her.

The manservant removed the cloth, leaving the mahogany surface bare. He passed cigars, and the gentlemen settled to their glasses of port, bowls of walnuts and wedges of Stilton cheese. As an afterthought, the man found a stick of barley sugar in one of the drawers in a small table and gave it to Mrs. Jameson.

Boulton slumped down into his chair, while Jameson's glassy stare seemed locked with the protruberant eyes of King William, who looked down from his portrait above the sideboard.

In the brief lull that followed, Robinson spoke. "Has your lordship heard of Jarvis's attack on the reptile?"

"I have heard something, to be sure. But I would most willingly hear it all again from your own lips, Jarvis." Sir Francis pushed back his chair and stuck his tiny feet and short legs straight out in front of him.

Sam had expected to work in a word or two about the Indians, but the conversation had gone off on a tangent. Well, so be it. Wasn't there a line somewhere for this moment? Ah yes, he had it. "The readiness is all."

"It was almost ten years ago, sir, and the *Colonial Advocate* had printed the vilest slander against Governor Maitland—"

"Excuse me, Mr. Jarvis. The *Colonial Advocate*?"

Sam looked across the table at Mrs. Jameson. "That was the name of Mackenzie's former paper, ma'am." He turned his attention back to Sir Francis. "He didn't stop with Governor Maitland. He attacked all the people whom the Governor appointed to the Legislative Council. 'Obsequious, cringing, worshippers of power' was what he called them. Indeed, sir, he implied that it was patronage, not merit, that prompted these appointments. In doing so, he struck at the very manhood of our society."

"There wasn't a decent household in this town that went uncontaminated by his pestilence," Robinson said. Sam remembered Mackenzie's snide revelation that Robinson's mother had once kept a common ale-house.

"Continue, Jarvis," Sir Francis said. "I am eager to hear it all."

"Well, sir, in early June, 1826, I found myself the leader of a band of angry men heading towards Mackenzie's print shop. We knew that he was away in Lewiston—getting an extension on his debts, no doubt—and that his foreman had left early for his daily binge at Simpson's Hotel. We armed ourselves with clubs and sticks and pieces of cordwood, and we were united in a single purpose—"

"To destroy the demon's presses!" This from Henry Boulton. Fists thumped on the table.

"We smashed open the office door, pulled down the press, then went for the cabinets. We emptied the type cases and strewed them in the yard and garden. We kicked to bits a frame filled with type, ready no doubt for the printing of another piece of slander. We twisted and tossed aside the thin brass strips that held together the pieces of lead. Some of my friends even carried three or four of the type cases across the road and flung them into the bay."

"Admirable, my dear Jarvis," Sir Francis said.

"That day we were gods." Sam smiled, remembering the exhilaration of the moment. Mrs. Jameson's blue eyes locked with his. She did not smile.

"But this superhuman effort did not quell the rogue?" Sir Francis asked.

"He launched a civil suit which did not go well for me."

"I'm not surprised," the lady said.

What was that supposed to mean?

Sam continued. "The jury was a passel of low-born farmers and one Irish shopkeeper who sympathized with the scoundrel. They had the gall to tout the virtues of unrestrained freedom of speech."

"But who was in the judge's seat?" Sir Francis said. "Surely he could have spoken to the jury on your behalf?"

"I had the affliction of William Campbell, unfortunately the only member of the upper class whom Mackenzie had not slandered in his paper."

"And?" Sir Francis pulled in his feet and sat upright in his chair.

"They brought in a verdict in Mackenzie's favour, awarding him a settlement of six hundred and twenty-five pounds."

Sir Francis sucked in his breath. "I cannot believe it."

"Yes, it is true. And with this ridiculous boost to his coffers, he was able to pay off his debts, buy a new press and type cases, and put himself back in business."

"The bastard!" Boulton shouted, knocking over his wineglass at the same time. "Whoops," he added, "apologies to the lady."

John Beverley Robinson spoke. "I must tell you, Sir Francis, that Jarvis had to mortgage a parcel of land to help pay the fine." He stood up, placed a hand on the edge of the table to steady himself. "May I propose a toast, sir?"

"By all means, Robinson."

"Then let us drink to Sam Jarvis for his heroic leadership in the attempt to quell Mackenzie and his press." There was a clinking of glasses and a chorus of "To Sam" and "To Jarvis." People always listened to Robinson. As Chief Justice, he got respect.

"And do I have the word of everyone here?" the Governor asked. "We will stay united in our resolve to oppose the scoundrel?"

The men staggered to their feet. "Down with Mackenzie!"

Boulton fell backwards, upsetting his chair.

"I shall join the ladies now," Mrs. Jameson said, rising. "This has been most edifying. I thank you for including me."

Her departure precipitated a flurry of activity. Jameson and Boulton went straight for the pisspot behind the screen. The butler set fresh decanters of port on the table. Sam drank his fill, confident that he had acquitted himself well.

At the end of the evening, as he and Mary took their leave at the front door, the Governor moved in close to him and said, "That was an impressive act you told me about this evening. I play fair, Jarvis. Merit must be rewarded." He shook Sam's hand and, taking the fur-lined coat from the footman, helped him into it.

"I do believe, my dearest husband, that you are on the Governor's roster for promotions," Mary said as they climbed into the phaeton. She took his hand and snuggled close to him.

Sam looked up at the stars in the quiet, clear night sky, and reviewed all the details he had not included in his heroic story, a story he had told so often that it had become more fiction than fact. He had not destroyed Mackenzie's print shop out of any exalted sense of righting a wrong. He didn't give a damn about Robinson's mother. Or that Mackenzie had called Lady Sarah Maitland, the former governor's wife, a "titled strumpet".

No. The inciting words had been those applied to him. "A murderer," Mackenzie had written. And said of his father-in-law, Chief Justice Powell, that his hands had "caressed a murderer". Everyone had read those words. He had heard them spat at him oustide taverns in King Street.

He wanted to forget that Mackenzie's small son had come downstairs from his grandmother's room above the shop to try to stop the destruction. That one of the plunderers had struck the boy. That the child had stood there, helplessly listening to their curses against his father. That throughout the ransacking of the print shop, they could hear the boy's sobs and the screams of the old woman upstairs. He hated to think of that part of it. He had not dared to tell Mary everything.

And the financial loss he suffered had not been quite as large as Robinson had implied, for Sir Peregrine Maitland had authorized the collection of money to help defray the huge fine. And Maitland had even rewarded him with the title of Deputy Secretary of Upper Canada, a useless position, true, but one that brought in a steady income. He remembered, too, that Mackenzie in the pages of his rag had called this sinecure "newly invented".

He realized that his wife had said something to him. "Sorry, my dear." He turned to her.

"I asked your opinion of Mrs. Jameson."

"Courageous, I thought. It's probably the first time in the history of the town that a woman has sat with the gentlemen over port and cigars."

"Oh, Sam, surely she did not smoke—"

"No, but she took in the whole scene and stored it away in that head of hers. I wish you could have seen those blue eyes studying everyone around that table. There's bound to be a chapter about this evening in one of her books."

"Imagine bringing up the subject of newspapers at a dinner table. So unfeminine, I thought. But let's forget about her. Let's think about our future."

FIVE

The next morning, the maidservant brought a cup of chamomile tea to Sam's bedchamber. He drank it as he dressed, and his stomach felt better. It was that godawful port which the Governor served, perhaps in an effort to cut the costs of Government House.

As he passed the door of his daughters' room, on his way to breakfast, he could hear Emily's sobs and Miss Siddons' calm, well-modulated voice. He stopped outside the closed door to listen. "There, there, child, dry your tears and let us plan something happy for this day. Shall we go along King Street and see what the merchants have in their windows for Christmas? Then we can compare prices and draw up a list of best buys for your Mama."

The woman understood the need for diversion. Really, she was worth every penny of her wages. But still he could hear Emily's sobs. What childish tragedy could have so rent his little girl's heart?

He knocked on the door. Miss Siddons answered. Over her head, he could see Emily sitting on the bed. Her face was flushed and her eyes red.

"Papa, oh Papa, my lovely hens are..." More sobs.

"Emily's pets have died, sir. A fox got into the chicken coop and killed them all. We found out from Cook when we went down for breakfast. The c-a-d-a-v-e-r-s are still in the henhouse, she said."

Oh dear. Emily and her sisters went out every morning to collect eggs and to feed the hens. He sat down on the bed beside Emily and put his arms around her. "Let us go out to the coop and give them a decent burial. You may pick some of those pretty purple chrysanthemums from the conservatory to put on their graves. Or any of the other flowers there. Whatever you want, dear."

"And perhaps we could read something appropriate for the occasion," Miss Siddons said. She picked up a Bible from the top of the bureau. "Ellen and Charlotte and I will come along for the service. Let us all get our coats and mittens on."

Sam went downstairs to get his coat and boots from the front hall. "We're having a funeral service for the hens," he called out to Mary, who was in the breakfast room. "Complete with passages from King James. Come along."

She came into the hall. "Oh really, Sam. Do you not think it absurd—perhaps even sacrilegious—to read scripture over the carcass of a hen?"

"I don't give a damn about sacrilege at the moment. Come or don't come."

He looked up the staircase as his daughters clattered down. Emily had stopped crying, and Ellen was smiling. Miss Siddons followed close behind, holding tight to Charlotte's hand. As Mary saw the funeral procession advance, she sighed and pulled her heavy coat off the hall tree.

In the conservatory, Emily selected some pink coneflowers, and they set off for the hencoop. It was beyond the stables, where Sam stopped to enlist the help of John, the coachman, who took down two spades from hooks on the wall. Then Sam emptied the contents of a pine toolbox onto the ground and put the box under his arm. On they went, over the bridge across the burn, past the now leafless hazelnut woods, and beyond the smoke shed. Finally, just as Charlotte was begging Sam to carry her, they reached the large brick henhouse.

They could see the fox's bloody tracks in the fresh-fallen snow, and when they opened the door, they saw grey and white feathers and blood everywhere. Emily started to cry again as she looked at the carcasses. The few frightened pullets that had survived the massacre squawked on the roost.

"Pick out your favourite hens, darling," Sam said, "and we shall put them into this box for separate burial."

Emily walked about, looked at each dead hen, then picked

up two bedraggled grey and white bodies. They were not much mutilated. Perhaps they had died of fright.

"Here they are, Papa. Happy and Merry." She held them out to him, and he placed them gently, side by side, in the toolbox.

"I remember now. We got them last Christmas, did we not? And their names were Merry Christmas and Happy New Year. But how did you recognize them among the others, dear?"

"By their faces, of course, Papa."

"Of course. I should have known that."

Then Miss Siddons read from Psalm 84. "Yea, the sparrow hath found her an house, and Happy and Merry a nest where they may lay their eggs, O Lord of hosts, my King and my God." Sam began to wish that his wife had stayed in the breakfast room.

"Amen," they all chorused. Except for Mary.

John and Sam dug a trench in the floor of the henhouse. The ground had not frozen and they made short work of their task. Emily laid the toolbox in the grave, and the other two girls gathered up the remaining corpses and put them to rest in the earth. Miss Siddons gave the words of committal: "Earth to earth, ashes to ashes, dust to dust, in sure and certain hope of the Resurrection."

Sam filled in the trench, and Emily placed the coneflowers in a pickle jar on the fresh grave.

It was altogether a happier group of little girls that began the march back to the house, stopping from time to time to throw snowballs. Miss Siddons joined in the game, while Sam and Mary and the coachman trudged ahead.

"Resurrection for a bunch of squawking hens? Really, Sam, that was a bit too much."

"More likely for them, I'd say, than for some of the people I've seen buried recently."

He was glad to hear her laugh.

At the stable door, Sam waved goodbye to his family and Miss Siddons. "Got some business to clean up here," he said. When they were out of earshot, he turned to the coachman. "Get me one of the rifles."

He set off back to the henhouse and beyond it into the wild bush. The snow was not deep, and the trail was easy to follow, even though some of the blood had washed off in the snow. When the footprints disappeared into the hollow of a huge, dying oak tree, he stopped and lay down on the ground to wait.

It was a long wait. His fingers grew numb, and the snow melting under him made his whole chest and the front of his legs wet. How long was it? An hour? Two hours? He dared not move to pull out his pocket watch.

Then a black snout appeared and disappeared. Then a hiatus of a minute or two or three. Then the whole head and forelegs. Sam pulled the trigger. A blast of shot, and the creature lay dead.

He pulled the fox from its lair and laid the carcass on the snow. It was a large vixen with a beautiful tail, which he cut off. Perhaps the skin could be treated and a fur collar made for Emily. He left the rest of the bloody mess beside its lair—the Indians who sometimes came through the property from the lake would probably pick up the pelt—and began the trek home.

As he trudged on through the snow, he made up his mind to buy more chickens at the market on Saturday. Emily could come with him and pick out the ones she liked. She would then have new pets to care for, and he would have fresh eggs for his breakfast.

It was only as he sighted the rear entrance to his house that he considered what he had done. There were surely cubs in that hole in the old oak tree. Without their mother, they would die.

The vixen had tried in the only way she knew to feed her family. To care for their young: that was the lot of all creatures on God's earth, man or beast. It was his own biggest responsibility. Perhaps it was something the fine Mrs. Jameson would not understand, playing the role of fine lady to her fine husband. Nothing on *her* mind but the big decision of what newspaper to read.

He looked down at the bit of fur in his hand. It seemed diminished and pathetic. With the butt of his rifle, he scooped a hole in the midden at the back of the house and put the tail into it.

SIX

Mrs. Powell had extended an invitation for afternoon tea, and Anna's driver, Hawkins, took her east along King Street to York Street. She had grown accustomed to touring the town daily to leave cards or to visit people who had called on her in her first days in her new residence.

But she could not get used to the cold that bit her nose and made her forehead ache. Only her feet were comfortable, warmed by the foot muff her friend Ottilie had given her before she'd left Europe. As they slid along the snow-covered streets, she huddled inside the buffalo robes that Hawkins had piled over her.

"Mrs. Powell's house, just ahead, ma'am," he said, then she heard a loud "Damnit, you bastard!" as they narrowly missed a careening conveyance pulled by two huge oxen. It was not really a sleigh at all, only a large board platform raised upon runners, and heaped with logs held on by a few upright poles tied at the top with a rope.

"Apologies, ma'am, but the rogue nearly hit us."

"I can't believe what I'm seeing, Hawkins. Are those really frozen reindeer lashed to the top of that pile of logs?" But already the sleigh—if it could be called that—had plunged a hundred feet down the road as Hawkins pulled up in front of the Powell residence.

It was a white frame house with a wide front porch two storeys high, which gave the place the look of a hotel. Hawkins pulled the buffalo robes off her and helped her descend. "Back in an hour, ma'am," he said.

The maidservant waited while Anna shed coat, gaiters, hat, lined gloves, and unwound from her neck the warm knit scarf that Mrs. Hawkins had produced from somewhere. In the drawing room, she met Mrs. Powell, her daughter Eliza, and a girl of perhaps sixteen or seventeen whom Mrs. Powell introduced as "my granddaughter, Sophia." Anna was also glad to see Mary Jarvis, the pretty and pleasant wife of the man who had garnered so much praise for an act of vandalism. And there was a woman called Mrs. Fitzgibbon, a smiling lady of perhaps sixty, who wore a dove-grey dress with a fine piece of lace at her neck.

"Mr. Jameson introduced me to your husband, Colonel Fitzgibbon," Anna said, curtseying. "A great hero of the War of 1812, so everyone tells me, though he himself denies everything. I'm summoning my courage to ask him to take me for a ride on the lake in his cutter." She'd found out that these were the fancy sleighs, drawn by one horse, in which the officers from the garrison raced each other over the ice.

"Perhaps it would be more fitting to go with your husband," Mrs. Powell said. "In this small world, ladies must be ever vigilant to avoid gossip."

Mrs. Fitzgibbon laughed. "Dear Mrs. Powell, Mrs. Jameson must go with Fitz. He loves to show off his fine horse and his excellent driving skills. She will have the ride of her life."

"Perhaps you would tell him how privileged I'd be to have that ride?" Anna smiled at Mrs. Fitzgibbon, then, remembering her manners, turned to her hostess. "Your house has an admirable location."

"Humph," the old woman muttered. She was swathed in widow's weeds from head to foot, though Anna knew that her husband, Chief Justice William Powell, had died over two years before. "When it was built, it did indeed occupy a prestigious site commanding an excellent view of the lake. Now, Eliza and I must put up with the commercial district that has grown around us, including that dreadful place." She gestured in the direction of the British Coffee House which they could see from the front window.

"Ah yes, my husband says it is a place where a gentleman can get middling ale and vile beer and where one can meet the famous— perhaps infamous—William Lyon Mackenzie," Anna said.

A silence ensued. At such moments, as Anna had already

discovered during her visits, someone would mention the weather. So she said, "I have never been so cold. When I looked at the thermometer an hour ago, it stood at eighteen degrees below zero. A glass of water by my bedside was a solid mass of ice this morning."

Anna's hostess looked at her over the top of her little round spectacles. "In a well-regulated household, such things should not happen, Mrs. Jameson. You must speak to your staff."

There was another pause while a maidservant, noticeably pregnant, set down rolled fish-paste sandwiches and the raisin-filled scones that were the staple of Toronto tea parties. Derby cakes, they were called. "You probably notice my maid has done those things which she ought not to have done," Mrs. Powell said, waiting until the girl had departed, but not bothering to lower her voice. "No husband, of course, and any day now I expect to have to support the child as well as the mother."

She poured tea from an engraved silver pot. "I have been named Honorary Patroness of the Bazaar for the Poor," she told Anna. "You have perhaps heard that I am lending my name to the event until Lady Head feels able to assume her responsibilities after her long journey from England."

"Indeed."

"And may we look for your assistance in sewing for the bazaar?"

"I must decline. I have no needle skills. My interests are writing and translating, sketching and engraving." Anna turned to the granddaughter seated beside her on the sofa. The girl was looking at her small hand on which glittered a large sapphire ring. "And what are your interests, my dear?"

"Sophia is to be married this summer. Her 'interests', as you call them, are in embroidering petticoats and hemming sheets."

"And I am helping her," Eliza said. Her face was flushed and her voice too loud.

"After your marriage, your husband's welfare must of course be paramount among your concerns, my dear Sophia," her grandmother said. "I saw that Mr. Powell's breakfast was always up to snuff. He had to have fresh bread with a good dollop of butter to start the new day. I went to the kitchen at four thirty each morning to see that Cook had fired up the bake oven in time to make the loaves. It was one of my most important wifely duties, for I—and indeed my whole family—knew that Mr. Powell's digestion at breakfast determined the course of the day thereafter."

Anna choked on a piece of Derby cake but recovered in time to give her full attention to the ensuing dissertation on "The Management of Husbands".

"Lead up to difficult topics gradually and make sure you have his full attention when you speak," Mrs. Powell asserted. "Once you are married, dear"—at this point she rapped her silver spoon against the teapot—"you will find that your husband's interests are no longer entirely centred on you."

Anna said, "Inevitably, his mind will be distracted by important issues like the quality of his wine and the reading of his newspaper." She was beginning to enjoy herself.

"Very true," Mary Jarvis added. "But nevertheless, Sophia, one has a reasonable chance at happiness in marriage if one does not expect too much of it."

"I do not think this is a subject for levity, Mary—and Mrs. Jameson. Married ladies can always give useful advice." Mrs. Powell shook her head vigorously, and two sausage curls popped out from her black cap.

"Oh, Mama," Mrs. Jarvis said, "what's wrong with a laugh?"

Sophia got up from the sofa, her face very red. "You're making fun of me. I'm going to my room."

Mrs. Fitzgibbon put out her hand and touched the girl's sleeve. "Please, sit down, my dear, while I tell you the loveliest story I know about marriage." Reassured, Sophia smiled and resumed her seat.

"During the War of 1812, there was a brave captain stationed at Queenston Heights. One day he went to his commanding officer, General Sheaffe, and asked for leave of absence to go to Kingston.

"The general said, 'No, captain, your country needs you here. We expect another invasion from those damned Yankees within hours.'

"So the captain spoke up, 'Sir, you command me on the

battlefield, but you cannot command me in the affairs of the heart. If you give me leave, I will be back in three days. But if you refuse me, I will go to Kingston anyway. There is a little girl there that I love, and if I can marry her before I am killed, she will have the pension of a captain's widow.'

"General Sheaffe got out his musical snuff box, as he always did when anyone crossed him. He snuffed deeply, sneezed three times, then he said, 'Leave of absence granted.'

"So the captain mounted his horse, rode one hundred and fifty miles in an exceedingly short time, married his little girl, and returned on the following day to his duties, and to fight another battle.

"And he lived, Sophia, to be the father of a fine family of four brave sons and one gentle daughter. And he and I love each other as much as we did all those years ago."

"I envy you, Mrs. Fitzgibbon," Anna said. "You married a man of spirit, and you have been happy. How many married people can claim such bliss?"

Sophia took a cambric handkerchief from her cuff and dabbed her eyes.

The maid came in again, this time with a decanter of sherry, which she poured into six crystal glasses. Anna noticed that Eliza downed hers in a gulp and reached again for the decanter. Mrs. Powell moved the sherry out of her reach, setting it on a small table beside her chair and keeping her hand on it.

"Your local engraver, Mr. Tazewell, has been a great help in the preparation of ten etchings for my American publisher," Anna said, seeking a diversion. "It took me twenty days to complete them, and now I must find a courier who will take my plates to New York."

"Why, ma'am, there is no need to worry," Mrs. Powell said. "I can assure you that I sent twelve place settings of Coalport to my brother in New York, and not a cup was smashed."

"Coalport, Mrs. Powell?" Then Anna realized that she had not made herself clear. "Not china. The plates are glass, and I make my etchings upon them."

Eliza laughed too loudly. "Oh, Mama, you are so...so...funny."

The old woman's face flushed. Anna took a pencil and paper from her reticule. "But fine china and glass are not unalike, are they? Both need careful handling. My dear ma'am, if you will be so kind as to give me the name of your courier, I shall send him a note and see what he thinks can be done with my engravings."

Anna and Mrs. Jarvis left at the same time and stood together for a minute in the street as they waited for their sleighs to arrive. "Mama is greatly worried over Sophia, Mrs. Jameson. My brother has little interest in his family, and his wife is...is indifferent as well. That's why Mama goes on about the rules of marriage. She thinks by laying down the law on the management of husbands, she can forestall catastrophe. Her other granddaughter, my niece Elizabeth, has just run off with a military man, leaving her two small daughters to the mercy of their violent father. I fear for their safety."

"I can understand a woman fleeing from abuse, Mrs. Jarvis. But forgive my ignorance. Why does she not take the little ones with her?"

"Because the courts in Upper Canada always assign the custody of the children to their father. Even if he can scarcely remember their names. Oh, ma'am, you who have no children must find it hard to understand the burdens women bear in this world."

"I am not completely ignorant of women's burdens."

"Have you heard it said that marriage is a nine-month preparation for death? That was my own experience with a still-born son. And then little Eddie died at one year of age. But I have eight living children. And fortunately, a kind husband. But even if he beat me black and blue every day of my life, as Elizabeth's husband did, I would not—could not—abandon my children."

Anna took Mrs. Jarvis's gloved hand in hers. "My dear, in some respects, I *am* fortunate in my own married life. I am free to pursue my own life and my own happiness."

Their sleighs pulled up to the curb, and they said farewell. Yes, thought Anna, as the sleigh headed back to Newgate Street, there may be fates worse than my unhappy marriage. If I had children to worry about, I'd have to stick with Robert.

SEVEN

L ead up to difficult subjects gradually, and make sure you have
your husband's full attention when you speak." Mrs. Powell's
comments came to mind as Anna sat across from her husband at
breakfast.

"If you are to advance yourself, Robert, we must entertain. And
since there are few theatres, ditto for clubs, we must provide an
occasion where people can meet and talk. Put yourself forward,
and you will find promotion."

He folded his paper and cast it aside. He poured himself a cup
of coffee and one for her. He leaned towards her, his brown eyes
intent on her face. "And what ideas do you have, Anna?"

"We will have a levee here on New Year's Day and invite all the
most influential gentlemen in the town—and their wives—to visit
and partake of excellent food and drink. I am told that the levee
is the most important occasion in the holiday season. It will be an
opportunity to show yourself to advantage."

"In this town, it is a 'gentlemen only' function."

"No, no. We must ask the wives as well. There is a good deal of
gossip over the Derby cakes and tea. So what better way to spread
the word about our 'happy marriage'?"

"Gentlemen only, Anna. We must not flout convention."
Robert looked at his surroundings. "But these rented rooms
are hardly suitable. And Mrs. Hawkins is hardly capable of
providing good—"

"Have you not noticed how your meals have improved since
my arrival?" She pointed to the crumbs and smears on her
husband's plate. "You appear to enjoy Mrs. Hawkins's marmalade
on your biscuits." She did not tell him that the woman had made

it with eight pounds of imported Seville oranges and two cones of the most expensive sugar that the grocer offered. "Indeed," she continued, "I find that Mrs. Hawkins has a fund of recipes that you, in your bachelor state, have never required. The servants are the least of our problems."

"What, then, is needed?"

"Your *carte blanche* to have the principal rooms repapered, and some comfortable chairs purchased. For the walls, when they are ready, I can furnish some sketches I have made since my arrival. Mr. Tazewell will frame them for a small outlay and provide some pleasant lithographs of his own for additional decoration. It will all cost you a modest outlay, yes, but the results will be worth it."

Her husband stared beyond her at the peeling wallpaper and the sparsely furnished room. His lips opened and closed, as if he were doing sums in his head.

"Order whatever is necessary."

"Leave it to me. Meanwhile, I shall get the invitations out."

"No invitations. The gentlemen of the town make the rounds of the best houses without formality." He consulted his pocket watch and rose. "You are right, Anna. Any expenditure that will facilitate my appointment as Chancellor will be entirely worthwhile. I confess to the desire to leave my name in history books as the first Chancellor of Upper Canada."

"Amen to that. You shall be bound up in a book of jurisprudence. I say this from my heart."

"Have your little joke, my dear. But I take it as a compliment." He paused as he put on his coat and top hat. "And I must tell you that you have evidently made a favourable impression on Sam Jarvis and his good wife. They have invited us for Christmas dinner. It may be diverting, though I hope we are not subjected to all those children. At any rate—with some reservations, mind you—I accepted."

From the front window, Anna watched Robert stride across the street on his way to the courtroom. It had been a satisfactory breakfast hour.

She turned away from the window, laughing to herself. In the space of a mere three weeks in this outpost, she had become everything of which Mrs. Powell would approve. She would sit down now while the moment was fresh in her mind and write to Ottilie von Goethe. Her friend would be amused to hear of her metamorphosis into a, a—what would Ottilie call it?—*eine biedere Hausfrau.*

But the inkwell was not on the table in her bedchamber. She pulled the bell for Mrs. Hawkins. The woman was there in an instant, wearing a clean apron and a modest, grey-striped dress. "Ink, if you please."

"Right away, ma'am. I be just this moment warming the inkwell on the hearth. I looked to it while you and the master was at breakfast. The ink was froze solid."

"Well done, Mrs. Hawkins, thank you."

"What is all this writing about, ma'am?"

Anna was beginning to enjoy the Canadian servant, if Mrs. Hawkins could be considered typical of the serving classes. In England, they did what they were told without question. Here, they spoke up.

"I've decided to write a book about Toronto. My title will be, I believe, *Winter Studies in Upper Canada.*"

"Oh, ma'am, there be so much to write on that subject. It will be a heavy book."

"So much? Really? I find very little so far to write about. But I do have an observation to make that I must set down as soon as you've warmed the ink. 'One day of a Canadian winter is only distinguishable from another by the degrees of the thermometer.'"

Mrs. Hawkins put a finger to her chin in the manner of Anna's London editor. "Perhaps it be clever, ma'am. I do not set myself to judge. But it also be what every newcomer says of this country."

"Really?"

"You must get out and about, ma'am. Watch the savages catch their fish from holes on the ice. Go to the falls at Niagara. Have a ride in one of them fancy cutters and a race on the lake. There be nothing like falling into a soft snowbank. You won't be getting that thrill in one of them fine places you come from."

"I am going for a ride on the ice soon with Colonel Fitzgibbon. What do you think of that, Mrs. Hawkins?"

The woman clapped her hands.

"I hope not to be one of those stereotyped Englishwomen you speak of. I am making progress. Indeed, I have even got used to the smell of people."

"Smell, ma'am?" Mrs. Hawkins's fingers touched her chin again.

"I couldn't figure it out at first. Now I know it's from the layers of buffalo robes that everyone piles over themselves when they go out in their sleighs. There is also a ranker, wilder smell—especially from the officers at the garrison. The source of that one eluded me for a while. Now I have discovered it comes from the bearskins they prefer. But an assiduous washing down with lavender soap at the end of the day removes the stink, I've discovered."

Mrs. Hawkins left the room without further comment and returned in a minute with the inkwell, which she set down on Anna's table without asking as she usually did, "Anything else, ma'am?"

She did not close the door as she left—was it an intentional omission?—and Anna could hear her comment to her husband, "Just when I be getting to like her, she turns into Lady Snob."

EIGHT

By noon on Christmas Day, the drawing room at Hazelburn was filled to bursting with Sam, Mary, their eight children, and invited guests.

"Into the breakfast room, everyone," Sam announced over the din of voices.

"For Bag and Stick!"

"Bag and Stick!"

It had been Mary's idea to invite Jameson and his wife. "I think Mrs. Jameson may feel lonely in this new environment," she'd said. "I didn't like her much when I first met her, but she grows on one." He'd agreed. It was always a good idea to keep in with the Attorney-General. And Dr. Widmer and his wife would probably enjoy meeting the much-talked-of authoress.

But now Jameson looked quite put out by the shrieks from the children. "I think I'll just have to be an old stick myself and decline, if no one minds."

"Not at all," Sam said, pouring a glass of sherry for his guest and pointing him to a comfortable chair. He noticed that Mrs. Jameson had joined the young people in the breakfast room.

"And I," Sam's mother added, "shall be an old bag and sit here in comfort by the fire and work on my embroidery. Please do not feel you must talk to me, Mr. Jameson. I shall be counting stitches."

"I decline as well," Mrs. Powell said. "Instead of getting knocked about and putting my back out, Sam, I shall go belowstairs and instruct your cook on the heating of my bread sauce."

So without the two old bags and the old stick, Sam went into the breakfast room.

The furniture had been pushed into corners, the china stowed safely away, and the centre of the room left bare for the game. Sam suspended a paper bag filled with sweets from a string tied to the chandelier. First he blindfolded his five oldest children and Mary. Then the rest of them: Mrs. Jameson, Dr. and Mrs. Widmer, and his sister-in-law, Eliza.

"Everyone know the rules?"

Everyone did.

"And Caroline, Charlotte, Charlie and I will make sure that the players spin like dervishes until they are quite dizzy. That way no one can cheat."

Mrs. Jameson, as guest of honour, went first. She spun round and round and round. Then five-year-old Charlotte put a stick into her hand. She swung it towards the centre of the room, striking out three times as the rules permitted, but failing to hit the paper bag.

"You're out!" Charlie said. The lady retired to a corner of the room and took off her blindfold.

Next came Mrs. Widmer. She seemed dizzy enough, but as she went round and round, she managed to fall into Sam in such a way that her plump bosom pressed against him.

"Watch out, Papa," little Caroline said, "the lady's titties keep bumping you."

"I'm next." Mary moved into the centre of the room and gave Mrs. Widmer a dig in the ribs with her elbow. "Whoops, excuse me," she said. "I can't see a thing." Then she twirled around and around, and, when Charlotte handed her a stick, she aimed straight for the bag, giving it such a wallop that the paper tore and the candies scattered far and wide.

Everyone took off their blindfolds and went for the candy. The adults and the older children let the little ones discover the best pieces first. Sam noticed that Mrs. Jameson dropped one of her candies directly in front of Charlie's small arm.

Mary found a piece that had skipped under the buffet in the corner. She unwrapped it and popped it into her mouth. "Yum, marzipan. My favourite!"

Sam pulled her under the mistletoe in the hallway. He kissed her sticky lips. "Merry Christmas, my dear," he said while the children and guests looked on and applauded.

"Don't forget to pluck a berry from the mistletoe, Papa!" yelled William and George.

"And now," Sam said, "it's time to see—"

"What St. Nicholas brought!" Charlie ran towards the staircase, followed by Caroline and Charlotte. "When he came down Papa's chimbly!"

"Wait, my darlings," Sam said. "Let us get the rules straight first. The three of you must go with your big brothers and sisters. William, George and Sam, you are in charge. You will get all the stockings down from the hooks over the fireplace. You must be very careful of the fire."

The adults settled into their chairs in the drawing room, and Sam poured sherry for everyone. Mrs. Powell reappeared from belowstairs, saying, "I think Cook understands what must be done. My dear Mary, you can't be too careful with bread sauce."

The shouts from Sam's bedchamber made them all smile. "Only three of them still believe in St. Nicholas," Sam said, "but everyone gets a red felt stocking."

"And this year, the older boys had a good idea," Mary said. "They took a horseshoe from the stable and made reindeer tracks in the snow. So they've all been outdoors this morning to see them. And imagine, just beyond the big red oak in our back garden, the tracks stopped."

"Where the reindeer flew off into the sky, of course," Mrs. Jameson said.

Mary laughed. "And the little ones stared upwards as if they might still spot those coursers going back to the Northland."

"It's all so much happier than when I was a child," Mrs. Jameson said, "and the mummers appeared at the front door in strange disguises—I remember monsters and devils—and scared my sisters and me with intrusive questions about our behaviour during the year. My answers were never good enough to satisfy them."

There was a clatter of footsteps on the staircase, and the

children reappeared, each with a bulging red felt stocking. They emptied out the contents onto the floor. Each stocking had an orange which Mary had bought from Mr. Wood's store. Then a packet of shortbread—"I gave the recipe to St. Nicholas," Sam's mother said to the guests—then a small box of candied ginger, walnut halves, and dried sweet apples and dates. Finally, on top, the wrapped wooden gifts made by Mr. Ross, carpenter and undertaker. This year, Mary had ordered a box for Sam Jr.'s treasures, and wagons, marionettes and dollies for the younger children.

"Miss Siddons has a party for you all in the nursery now," Sam said. "Off you go and enjoy it while we have dinner."

"Oh Papa, Miss Siddons has a puzzle for us, too," Ellen said. "It's General Washington on his white stallion, and if Emily and I can put it together in an hour, she'll give us a prize."

The dinner gong sounded then, and the adults went into the dining room, where Cook and her helper had set out the roast goose, cranberry-orange relish, brussels sprouts and whipped potatoes. Sam carved, and Mrs. Powell spooned liberal portions of bread sauce onto everyone's plates, whether they wanted it or not. The manservant James poured the wine.

Sam sat down. "It's a happy day for me, too. Sir Francis Bond Head told me yesterday that I am the new Superintendent of Indian Affairs."

"Bravo, Jarvis," Widmer said.

Jameson raised his glass. "Well done."

"More money, I take it," Mrs. Widmer said. "It will be welcome with all those children."

Mary's mother set down her knife and fork and picked up the monocle she brought to parties. It dangled on a chain around her neck. Conversation stopped while she affixed the glass to her right eye and stared at Mrs. Widmer as though she were some strange beetle that had taken up residence under the carpet. "Mr. Jarvis's finances are surely his private concern, ma'am."

Sam downed his wine in a gulp, and James, who hovered by the sideboard, refilled his glass. Sam smiled at his mother-in-law. "As you undoubtedly know, ma'am, Dr. Widmer has for many years held the mortgages on my properties. My improved finances may indeed be of interest to him."

Beneath the starched linen tablecloth—as he said this—he felt a gentle pressure on his left foot. Certainly not Mary. She was at the other end of the table. It was, of course, the Widmer woman. He leapt to his feet and picked up the large spoon beside the goose. "Did I remember to give everyone stuffing?"

"Are you too hot, Sam?" Mary said. "Your face is very red."

"My son is an excellent choice for the post," his mother was saying in her gentle voice. "He even has an Indian name, you know, given to him by his friend, grandson of a Chippewa chieftain, whom my dear late husband and I knew when we lived at Niagara."

Mrs. Jameson leaned forward. "How wonderful! Oh, Mr. Jarvis, I hope you will introduce me to some Indians. It would be a welcome diversion. But much more than that. It would provide material for my book on Upper Canada."

Mrs. Widmer giggled. "I'd better behave, or I'll find myself described in Chapter One: 'Indians and Other Savages in the New World'."

No one laughed.

The ceremony of the plum pudding came next. James brought it in, alight in the blue flame of the whiskey which Cook had drizzled over it. Mary cut substantial pieces for everyone, pouring the rum sauce liberally over each serving.

"How many sides has a plum pudding?" Dr. Widmer asked. No one pretended to know, though the joke was an old one.

"Two: inside and outside." In the polite laughter that followed, Sam was able to move his foot well out of reach of Mrs. Widmer's.

After dinner, the cloth was whisked away, and Dr. Widmer, the Attorney-General and Sam filled their glasses with port and passed round the walnuts and nutcracker while the ladies retired to the drawing room. Soon Sam could hear Eliza at the pianoforte banging out something from Mozart. She had the touch of a cow moose.

"Mary has taken a liking to your good wife, Jameson."

"Ah yes, I had hoped that Anna would make friends. I have not been much in society myself, as you may know, but she has taken me in hand and pushes me here and there." Jameson poured another glass of port, downed it in a gulp, and having made this effort at conversation, slumped in his chair and closed his eyes.

The doctor cracked a nut and popped the meat into his mouth. "It is kind of you to invite us to Christmas each year, Jarvis. These feast days are dull when you have no children around to brighten them."

"You've done me many a good turn over the years, Widmer." Sam looked over at Jameson. His head was tilted, and his mouth had fallen slightly open. In a softer voice, he added, "I have not forgotten your help when I needed it."

A slight frown deepened the wrinkles of Widmer's pale forehead. "I sometimes think of that poor young man. But I know he instigated the whole thing." Widmer cracked open another nut. "Whatever happened, Jarvis, it's water under the bridge."

Water under the bridge, yes, but Sam would never forget that bloody corpse. Or his subsequent lie in the courtroom when he'd stated that Ridout had lived long enough to offer his forgiveness. Widmer, who'd been the coroner, had said it was possible the death had not been instant.

Sam poured himself another glass of port and avoided the doctor's gaze. They sat for a while in silence. Then Sam looked at his pocket watch. "Time to join the ladies. Shall we take our port and see what they're up to?"

The scraping of their chairs awoke Jameson. "Sorry, gentlemen. Worked too late last night."

Eliza was still at the pianoforte. Sam's mother and mother-in-law sat at opposite ends of the settee where they were intent on their embroidery, Mary and Mrs. Jameson played cribbage, and Mrs. Widmer had positioned herself in the hallway under the mistletoe. She smiled at the men as they came from the dining room.

"Which of you will be the lucky man?" She looked at Sam. Her bodice had slipped down on one side, exposing an expanse of plump white shoulder.

"I am the lucky person, of course, my dear," Widmer said as Sam and Jameson hurried by her. Jameson joined the cribbage players, and Sam took a seat between the old ladies. Out of the corner of his eye, he could see that the perfunctory kiss was already over. Widmer plucked a berry from the mistletoe.

Miss Siddons appeared in the archway of the drawing room with Caroline, Charlotte, Charlie and the older girls. "The little ones want to go out and look at the reindeer tracks again," she said. "I shall take them, and Emily and Ellen will finish their puzzle upstairs."

"I have a small gift for your schoolroom," Mrs. Jameson said, rising from the cribbage table and making her way over to the governess. From her reticule, she brought out a small book.

"A dictionary?" Miss Siddons looked at the cover and turned the pages. "And written by you, ma'am?"

"It was my first book—I was twenty-one when I compiled it—and it is the one I'm proudest of. I was a governess then, and I published it for the small boys I taught. It has four thousand words that children may meet in conversation or in the books they read."

Miss Siddons showed the book to Emily and Ellen. "We are honoured. We shall use it in our compositions tomorrow." Sam was glad that his girls looked as pleased as their governess.

Sam Jr., William and George came in. Their voices were rather loud. Perhaps they were nervous, or—more likely—they had been sampling the bottle of whiskey Sam kept in the top drawer of the chiffonier in his bedchamber. "Who'd like to see Papa's antlers?"

Most of the guests looked mystified. "Papa's horns?" said Mrs. Widmer. "It would be a treat to see those." She winked at Sam.

"Antlers, Mrs. Widmer. From a moose that I shot in October on a hunting trip with my Indian friend."

"With a span of nearly six feet," Mary said, "and not a point broken."

"And you have them somewhere on display?" Mrs. Jameson asked. "I should love to see them."

"They are worth a look, I assure you. Mary took them down to King Street to Mr. Ross, carpenter, coffin-maker and undertaker."

"I don't understand, Mr. Jarvis. What did this Mr. Ross do with them?"

"He mounted them on a fine piece of black walnut, then he came to the house and put them up on a wall in the nursery. They are magnificent. But after all, Mr. Ross's motto is—"

"WE SHOW YOUR LOVED ONES TO ADVANTAGE!" The boys shouted this at full voice. Everyone laughed.

Sam left the boys to do the honours and stayed in the drawing room with Mary, Eliza, and the mothers. It was a relief to be rid of Mrs. Widmer for a few minutes.

Mid-afternoon, when the guests had reassembled, Mrs. Powell yawned and roused herself from her stitchery. "Come, Eliza, I told our coachman to be here at two thirty, and it is already past the time."

It was the signal for everyone's departure.

In the hallway Mrs. Powell saw the mistletoe and paused under it. "Dear Mr. Powell always enjoyed trying to catch me." She sighed. "How the years have passed." Sam noticed a smear of grease down the plain black bodice of her gown, no doubt from the bread sauce.

Sam put his arm around her waist. "May I have the honour, ma'am?" He planted a kiss on her whiskery cheek and felt her stiff body relax for a minute. Then he released her and plucked a berry from the wreath.

"Dear Mr. Jarvis, it is now my turn," Mrs. Widmer said, coming up close behind the old woman.

"Look at the wreath, Mrs. Widmer." Mrs. Powell turned and gathered up the folds of her dress. "You must surely know the traditions of Yuletide. All philandering must stop once the last berry has been removed. Mr. Jarvis cannot oblige. There are no more berries."

"No more berries, you say? Ah, but there are!" Mrs. Widmer lifted up a loop of greenery and pointed to one remaining berry. Then she moved in close to Sam, shutting her eyes and turning her mouth up towards him.

Mary pushed in front of her guest. "My turn then, ma'am. Wives have precedence on such occasions. If it's the last berry, it's mine."

So Sam leaned down and kissed his wife, aware as he did so of Mrs. Jameson's blue eyes fixed upon him.

The guests trooped towards the coat tree and the pile of scarves, gloves, gaiters, pattens, boots and muffs stowed at the entrance. Sam caught a glimpse of a shapely leg as Mrs. Jameson bent over for a moment to button her canvas gaiters.

He and Mary stood at the door to wave goodbye to their guests. The sleigh bells were still ringing in their ears when Mary slammed the door and turned to him. "That woman is intolerable, Sam."

"Widmer was one of the reasons I wasn't hanged, Mary. Have you thought about what we owe the man?"

"Oh Sam, you don't find her attractive, do you? And what did she mean by 'Papa's horns'? Does that have some ribald connotation?"

"To answer your questions briefly. 'No,' and, 'No idea.' Now let's go and see what the children are up to."

NINE

"Please, sir..." Sam looked up from his newspaper to see Cook standing in the doorway of the breakfast room. Her arms were covered in flour, and her face was flushed, probably from the heat of the bake oven.

"What is it?"

"There be a savage come to the kitchen door, sir. He wants to see you. He says he won't wait outside and now he be seated on a chair by my fire warming hisself. What am I to do, sir?"

"Go back belowstairs. I will be there directly."

Sometimes the Indians did not follow white man's rules. Sam remembered John Beverley Robinson's story of a native man who had come into his wife's bedchamber after she had delivered one of their sons. He looked at the babe in its rocking cradle beside the bed, stroked its head and departed through the imposing front door. Had the man perhaps remembered a wigwam on the site of the Robinson mansion?

Sam descended the narrow staircase. The kitchen was dark, lit only by the open hearth, and he squinted into the gloom at the tall, thin man seated by the fire, who rose to greet him.

"Nehkik," a familiar voice said. "May you walk well in the New Year. I bring gifts to lighten your journey." Jacob pointed to a deerskin sling on the floor by a chair.

"Jacob!" Sam rushed forward. He hugged the Indian and threw his arms around his tri-coloured blanket coat, while trying to avoid stepping on his heavy moccasins. "What are you doing here, friend?"

And right away, as his arms touched Jacob's bony frame, he knew something was wrong. He stepped back. Jacob's eyes glittered and his cheekbones and chin protruded from the sunken skin of his face. There were black smudges on his cheeks.

"Are you ill?"

"Hungry, Nehkik. I am in Toronto with my father, Chief Snake, and my friend, Elijah White Deer. We come by snowshoe across the lake and south to town. It has been a long journey. We go today to speak to the Governor, to ask for blankets and food. We camp for three nights with Mississauga friends by the big lake. Then we go north again."

"Bring bread and butter, cheese, ham and tea," Sam said to Cook, who watched them from behind the broad oak table. "And be quick about it." And turning to Jacob, he added, "You will stay, please, Jacob. Here you will have a warm bed and plenty of food, and you can rest and grow strong again." It was hard to keep his voice steady as he stared at the emaciated figure of his friend.

"No, I thank you, Nehkik. I must go back to my family soon. They are hungry."

Cook set a plateful of food in front of Jacob. "Sit here close to the fire," Sam said, "and say no more until you have eaten."

"First, I give gifts." Jacob opened his sling and brought out the objects, each wrapped in deerskin. "This for your lady," he said, uncovering a pretty fan of dyed fishskin. Next came four pairs of beaded moccasins for the boys, four cornhusk dolls for the little girls, and last, a piece of polished, weighted wood, which Sam viewed with delight.

"A snowsnake! Oh, that will be fun. I'll take my sons out on the ice one of these fine days. But where are your father and your friend?"

"They find a fox carcass back there." He gestured in the direction of the henhouse. "They scrape it clean now and take it home when we go."

Then Jacob reached out and pulled the plate of food in front of him. From a beaded pouch around his neck, he took out a small bone-handled knife and a lead fork and set them beside the plate. Though he probably had not eaten for some time, he cut his ham carefully, slipped slices of cheese between the bread, and chewed each morsel slowly. The lines on his face smoothed out. At last, he set down his empty cup.

"Now, Jacob, you must have a pipe with me and tell me your story. I want to know why you have been hungry in this land of deer and moose." Sam took two pipes from the rack near the cupboards and passed a pouch of tobacco to his friend. He filled his own pipe, tamped down the tobacco, lit it and puffed. Jacob did the same.

Cook pushed open the small window beside the hearth. A blast of icy air blew in. Sam turned to her, "Close the window, damn it. If you don't like the pipe smoke, go sit in the scullery." And out she went, banging the kitchen door behind her.

"Now, Jacob..."

"I tell you once before about the Governor. Not this new Governor, but the one who comes before..." He paused and took another puff on his pipe.

"Governor Colborne. Yes, I remember." Colborne had ordered three Indian bands from different islands in Lake Simcoe to move north to the Narrows and live together. There, so Colborne reasoned, he could monitor the Indians' movements more closely. But then he grew frightened of the "threat", as he called it, of all those "savages" in one place. Some of the Indians had moved back to Lake Simcoe, with Colborne's blessing.

"All that moving back and forth, it is disaster, Nehkik. When we move to the Narrows, we leave behind crops on the land. But we do not worry, there are many moose at the Narrows, so we have plenty to eat. But when we go back home again to Snake Island, we find nothing but weeds. Nothing to eat there but mushrooms and berries."

"But there is game, is there not? Do you not have moose there, too?"

"Many white men settle on the lake, shoot deer, shoot moose, shoot partridge. A moon ago, old white man points a rifle at me when he sees me stalk deer. 'Go away, savage,' he says, 'this is my land and my deer.'"

"Like Windigo," Sam said, remembering the story Jacob had told him on one of their hunting trips. Windigo was the cannibal hunter with a heart of ice, tall as a towering white pine, who ate every living creature that walked upon the earth. "Himself only for himself," was Windigo's cry.

"Yes, like Windigo."

They sat in silence for a few minutes. Jacob was a quiet man, and he and Sam had often sat by their campfire in the wilderness for hours, each deep in his own thoughts. Now, glancing at his friend as he smoked, Sam noticed the black marks on his face. They were not the dirt that came from a long trek across country, but something quite different.

"The black paint on your cheeks, Jacob—you are in mourning? Who has died?"

"My wife."

And now in his voice there was such sorrow mixed with anger that Sam was at first afraid to question him further. He got up and poked at the fire. He wound up the clock jack and set the roast of beef turning once more in the hastener.

"And your children, friend?" he said finally, as he remembered that Jacob had once mentioned two small girls, perhaps four and five years of age, and two boys of nine and twelve.

"With the grandmother. But she is old and sick, too. She is a good woman, does what she can..." Jacob tapped the contents of his pipe onto the empty plate and stood up. "But children need a mother." He looked at Sam, one man to another. "And I need a wife."

"You and I have had good times together, Jacob. I will go with you this day and talk to our new Governor. I will tell him of the plight of your people and ask what can be done. Do not despair."

Jacob smiled. It deepened the lines in his sunken face, yet his eyes shone in the gloom. "I tell my father, Chief Snake. I say to him, 'Maybe Nehkik can help.'" Jacob took Sam's hand in his long bony fingers. "May the Great Spirit who rules our world guard and protect you."

As Jacob moved towards the kitchen door, Sam suddenly

remembered Mrs. Jameson's request. "Jacob," he said, "I have a friend who is writing a book on Upper Canada. She wants to let Europeans know about the life of the country's original inhabitants. Would you, your father, and your friend consider spending an hour with her now? She would offer some food, if I asked her, and we should still have plenty of time to see the Governor."

"Yes, Nehkik."

Sam got into his coat and the moccasins which Jacob had given him months ago. He and his friend put on their snowshoes and moved into the pine trees behind the house. As they went forward, their tracks disappeared in the swirling snow.

TEN

Anna sat at the pine table in her bedchamber rereading the letter she had written to Ottilie von Goethe. Perhaps it was the type of letter that Mrs. Hawkins would label "Written by Lady Snob", but Anna thought it was clever, exactly the sort of thing her friend would enjoy. After all, Ottilie, in her free-spirited way, was always on the search for a new man in her life.

Dearest Ottilie:

Are you growing weary of your lover, le beau Charles? Do you yearn for a new objet d'amour? Come here, my dear, and I will present you with an Indian chief.

He will be tall and muscular, and you will grow accustomed to the stink of his sweat and the filth of his deerskin leggings. He will be a man of few words, and those he speaks, you will not understand. So you will not have to converse with him, nor will there be tiresome preliminaries to your love-making. He will simply throw you over his broad shoulders and carry you off to his wigwam deep in the pine forest. On a comfortable mat of boughs and branches, he will make you his very own... squaw.

There will be household tasks you must learn, of course, but these will be easy. You must skin a bear or two to make a warm covering for the nuptial mat. You must snare a rabbit, skin and gut it, and boil it over your campfire into a tasty stew. He may need a gallon of cheap whiskey each day, but that you can bargain for from a greasy trader.

When your handsome chief tires of you, or you of him, there will be no lingering heartache. He will strike off your

*head with his tomahawk. Or you may do likewise. White
man's courts will pay no heed. Indians have their own marital
customs and their own solutions for dissension.*

*When I contemplate my marriage to Mr. Jameson, I may
envy you. We have our meals on a table, but I hear only the
clink of the stopper on the wine decanter and the rustle of
his newspaper. Sometimes I long for a bear to skin. Or a
tomahawk to wield.*

*I have asked the Superintendent of Indian Affairs—a rather
good-looking white man—to bring some of his Chippewa
charges to meet me. So far he has not complied, but if he does,
I shall pick the perfect specimen for you. In the summer I travel
into the Canadian wilderness, where I shall find out more, and
pass on my wisdom to you.*

From your loving friend cum marriage broker,
Anna

She gave the letter to Hawkins to post. Somewhat to her
surprise, she had discovered on one of her walks about town that
there *was* a post office. She had heard so much from her European
friends about the backwardness of Canada. This office was in fact
an imposing three-storey red brick structure in the Georgian style.
Hawkins told her that the postmaster had to pay for staff, fuel and
candles from his own pocket, and she suspected that he rolled
some of the letters he received into spills to light his hearth fires.
Who could blame him? Few of the populace could afford to pay
the postage on the letters addressed to them, and there were piles
of unclaimed correspondence. She had seen how one old man
abused the system. He claimed he could not read, had asked the
postmaster to read the letter to him, then said, "Don't know none
of the folk mentioned. Won't pay for nothing that's not mine."

She sat down then to do the translations of the German essays
she had brought with her. She had just finished the second essay
and started on the third when Mrs. Hawkins interrupted.

"Come quick, ma'am, there be people here to see you."

She thought immediately of another dreary encounter with Mrs. Powell and her daughter Eliza. She was in Toronto to promote Robert's social reputation, true, and she should probably be pleasant to them, but enough was enough. "Can you invent a plausible excuse, Mrs. Hawkins? I have three hours of study before me as you can see." She gestured at the books on the table.

"But I think you be interested in these people, ma'am, if I may say so."

"Not Mrs. Powell then? Nor yet Mrs. Robinson or Mrs. Widmer?"

Mrs. Hawkins laughed. "No indeed, ma'am. Mrs. Powell and them would have nought to do with these ones. Three of them, anyways. Three be savages and one be Mr. Jarvis, the Indian keeper." Mrs. Hawkins's cheeks were flushed with excitement. She flapped the skirt of her apron. "Oh, ma'am, to think of real savages in our new-papered drawing room. Do they sit upon chairs, ma'am?"

"Let them decide. I shall be there directly. And please get a meal ready for them. Anything you can come up with in a hurry."

As soon as the door closed, Anna ran to her bureau, pulled open the top drawer, and found exactly what she was looking for, a bag of blue wampum. She hooked it onto the belt of her skirt.

In the entrance to the drawing room, Mr. Jarvis stood, ready to make the introductions. The Indians were in file behind him.

"May I present Chief Snake, ma'am?" he said, and gestured to a tall man in a red blanket coat and leggings. Fastened to the Indian's grey braids was a long black plume which dangled behind one ear. The Chief bowed.

"And Jacob Snake, his son." This was a younger man in a tri-coloured blanket coat with a pretty beaded pouch that hung around his neck. His cheeks were daubed with black paint.

"And Elijah White Deer." Elijah smiled and pointed at the bag fastened to Anna's belt. He said something in his native language.

"The Chief and Elijah don't speak English, and I, alas, speak no Chippewa. Jacob will translate," Mr. Jarvis said.

"Elijah pays you a compliment, ma'am. He says he likes the wampum bag which you wear on your belt."

"Please tell him, 'thank you'. The wife of the New York Governor gave it to me while I was in New York City on my way here. And please say that I too am impressed by the strings of blue wampum on Chief Snake's neck. And that in a minute or two, my housekeeper will serve breakfast."

All this was translated; everyone smiled and bowed. Anna noticed that Mr. Jarvis seemed especially pleased with her offer of breakfast. Then they moved into the drawing room where the Indians went directly to the fireplace. Elijah took the bellows and pumped up the fire to rich red flames. There the three men stood, backs to the burning logs, obviously enjoying the warmth.

Anna exchanged a few inanities about the weather with Mr. Jarvis. The Indians made no attempt to talk, yet they seemed perfectly at ease.

Mrs. Hawkins came into the dining room with a tray of cold meat, bread and beer. Everyone moved towards the table. At first the Indians tried to use the knife and fork that had been placed at each setting, but then they took out their own knives from the deerskin slings that they wore across their shoulders. Apart from a tendency to impale the ham on the end of these knives, their manners were good.

"Their restraint is remarkable," Mr. Jarvis said, speaking quietly into Anna's ear, "especially when one considers how hungry they must be." In a normal voice, he added, "We are on our way to the Governor to ask for rations of food and a supply of blankets. My companions have walked over the snow a distance of eighty miles, and not one of them has eaten for two days."

"You forget, Nehkik, that I have an excellent meal with you this morning." Jacob Snake took a clean, but much worn, square of cotton from his beaded pouch and wrapped his bread and meat in it. He paused for a moment, looked at Anna, who nodded approval, and continued his folding of the cloth around the food. He passed his tankard of beer to his father, Chief Snake.

Anna turned her attention back to Mr. Jarvis. "I have some questions to ask while I have you here with your party. But I am fearful of giving offence through my ignorance."

"I am happy," Jacob said, overhearing her comment. "Not often does white man show an interest in our ways."

So she asked about the making of the beautiful porcupine-quill baskets she had seen in the local shops, about their sacred scrolls, about the use of birchbark in their canoes, about their attitude to the white settlers, and about whether they were forced to take Christian oaths in a courtroom. While Jacob responded, he turned occasionally to speak to his father in his own language, apparently to check the veracity of his comments to her. The old man seemed pleased to take part in the discussion.

"And I must caution you, ma'am," Mr. Jarvis said, "not to lump all Indians together under one category, as so many people do. There is as much difference between the customs and language of, let us say, the Chippewa and Mohawk nations, as there is between the French and the English."

He looked at his pocket watch and rose, laying his hand on Anna's arm and drawing her aside. "Time for our visit to the Governor. I do not know what our reception will be, and we must not keep the Great One waiting. Governor Colborne always looked on the natives as a problem to be solved, and I fear that our new man will be no better. Worse, in fact. I've heard that the common appellation bestowed upon him is Governor Bone Head." He smiled, and Anna noticed again the attractive dimple in his left cheek. "But of course, you must repeat nothing of what I say, especially to my wife, who worries about my lack of discretion." He shook hands. "Good day, ma'am. I hope you now have new insights. And perhaps I should tell you that Jacob is in mourning for his wife. That's why he has blackened his face."

In parting, Chief Snake said something to her which Jacob translated as, "The blessing of the Great Spirit be on you and your house." Elijah White Deer held out his hand to her, and in a moment's impulse, she unhooked her wampum bag from her belt and gave it to him. He held it aloft for a moment, smiled and put it immediately into his deerskin sling.

Last to leave was Jacob. Anna stretched out her right hand and touched his sleeve. "May you find happiness in the New Year."

"Thank you," Jacob said. "You and Nehkik are good people. Not often I find good white people. Only sometimes."

Who was Nehkik? Anna wondered. And then she remembered. It was Mr. Jarvis, of course. Jacob had called him by that name earlier. And this "Nehkik" had actually asked her to keep a secret from his wife. What was she to think of that?

Mrs. Hawkins came forward as soon as the front door closed behind the guests. "Oh, ma'am, it be so exciting. Never have I seen a savage inside a white man's house before. Only at the door when they swap salmon for butter."

"Perhaps we ought not to call them savages, Mrs. Hawkins. They were anything but savage in their demeanour and their manners at table." She thought of her silly letter to Ottilie. Perhaps she could get it back and tear it up. "Has your husband already gone to the post office with my letter?"

"Oh yes, ma'am, it most likely be on the mail sleigh for Kingston by now."

So the damage was done. She had made a few bad jokes at the expense of people she knew nothing about. She was as bad as Mrs. Powell with her ignorant attitude towards the serving classes. She remembered the woman's dismissive remarks about her maid's pregnancy. Well, she would correct herself in her next letter to Ottilie.

ELEVEN

On New Year's Day, Anna and Robert stood at the entrance to their drawing room and waited for the door knocker to sound. Robert pulled out his gold pocket watch several times, while Anna tried not to look at herself in the wide mirror which she had installed over the mantel.

Because Mrs. Hawkins did not know how to dress hair, Anna had fussed with curl papers to produce the ringlets that now clustered on her forehead. She would not have bothered with this silliness in Europe, but here in Toronto she wanted to achieve an utterly feminine look to persuade the gentlemen at the levee that she was the perfect little woman.

Robert, she was pleased to note, looked every inch the Attorney-General-soon-to-be-Chancellor, or so they both hoped. With his black morning coat and black cravat, he had donned a new pair of fine striped trousers and leather shoes with laces instead of buckles.

"You look well, Anna," Robert said, studying their images in the glass. "Not pretty, in the conventional sense of the word, but well enough. Your red dress might have been an unfortunate choice with your red hair, but happily it sets off your complexion to advantage."

"Qualified praise indeed, Robert, but I thank you. And how pleasant it would be if you could say something at least as commendatory about the house."

"An improvement, my dear, and well worth the considerable expenditure. But why are those ugly black buckets at the front door? I noticed them there before, but now that you've put down that new carpet, they stand out like pustules on a pretty face."

"They're fire buckets. Mrs. Hawkins said they can't be removed. It's the law, since there are no fire brigades in this place."

"But what on earth are they for?"

"When the church bells sound the knell for a fire, we take these buckets and run to the lake. Everyone must volunteer in these situations, apparently. Have you not heard this before, Robert?"

"Perhaps, but I doubt the magistrates can enforce participation. At any rate, I leave these things to the servants."

Anna had rented livery for Hawkins, and he seemed pleased with the effect. She'd heard him say to his wife earlier in the day, "We've moved up the ladder since the missus arrived." Now he stood by the front door, ready to take the visitors' coats and usher them up to the head of the stairs where she and Robert waited.

By noon, the door-knocker sounded like the drumming of a drunken Scotsman the evening after the parade. It was a strictly male affair, the idea being that the men of the town spent the day paying their respects to the ladies. By two o'clock, some forty gentlemen had come and gone. These were all young men in hordes—or was it herds?—of nine or ten at a time. They came in, bowed, sat down in the drawing room for two minutes, got up, bowed again, and left without saying a word or taking a bite of food. Most of them Anna had not seen before, and her husband made little attempt to introduce any of them to her.

He seemed much more interested in the seven or eight older men who arrived after the herds and who actually paid a visit of some duration. They were talking together now in the drawing room. She had been so happy to see Mr. Jarvis among them. He could keep a conversation going, something that her husband found difficult.

From the hallway, she watched Mr. Jarvis now talking easily to Archdeacon Strachan and Chief Justice John Beverley Robinson, who, she had discovered at the Governor's party, liked to lay down the law when he spoke. In addition she noticed Dr. Widmer—without his wife, fortunate for Mr. Jarvis, no doubt—and several members of the militia and the Legislative Council, and the lawyer,

Henry Boulton. Colonel Fitzgibbon was also in the group, and if she could get a private word with him, she would set a date for their sleigh ride on the lake.

As she came into the drawing room, Robert and the others rose. She took a seat in one of the smart walnut chairs she had purchased, facing the drawing room door so that she could greet any latecomer who came into the upper hallway. To her right was Colonel Fitzgibbon, and on her left, the Archdeacon.

"I understand you are a friend of Mr. Tazewell," the Archdeacon said to Anna.

"I have benefited from his help with some of my etchings. And he has supplied some wonderful pictures for my walls." She gestured to one she particularly liked, a scene of a family having a picnic on a grassy knoll which overlooked the Falls at Niagara.

"He has been of inestimable help with our educational system. Before he came to Toronto, we had no Greek grammars for our youth, because there were no printers here with fonts of Greek type. He had an ingenious solution to the problem. He printed a grammar by making lithographs of pages from an existing text."

Lawyer Boulton yawned and tapped his foot. Robert got up and refilled the man's glass from the decanter.

"You have a fine educational system for your sons," Anna said, as she looked about the room, "but I have always found it sad that both here and in England, there is very little education for girls."

Robert's well-shaped eyebrows contracted. The other men looked at their drinks and said nothing.

"And what do you think, sir?" she said, turning to Chief Justice Robinson. "Do you not often wish that the women of Toronto had pursuits other than child-rearing and household management?"

"I have four daughters, madam," he said, his nose wrinkling ever so little, as if he had just caught a whiff of an unemptied chamberpot. "I wish nothing more for them than that they should find suitable husbands and devote themselves to the care of their partners and their children. That is woman's lot, and I see no benefit in their having a knowledge of Greek, an ability to do algebra or a view of history. It does not signify what women think: they are not called upon to act or judge outside the purlieu of their household."

"Well put indeed, Robinson," Robert said, as several of the men in the room nodded their agreement. He gestured towards the dining room. "Anna, perhaps the gentlemen are ready for the fine meal you have ready."

"In a moment. First I must respond to the Chief Justice." She turned and leaned towards him. "You are entirely right, sir. Women in this town have no need of Greek, algebra, or history because... because it is in every man's interest to keep his wife and daughters ignorant. For when the horse and ass begin to think and argue, adieu to riding and driving."

There was a long pause while the gentlemen took this in. Then the Archdeacon and Colonel Fitzgibbon laughed. But the Chief Justice's face grew red, and her husband's redder.

From the corner of the room near the pianoforte, a pleasant baritone voice called out, "Bravo!" Anna looked at Mr. Jarvis. He smiled at her. He was so attractive in his well-cut frock coat and black silk vest. Suddenly she felt as if she'd like to reach out and touch his square chin, put her finger on that dimpled left cheek.

In the London society she knew so well, there were men whose real material of mind it was difficult to discover. Many had been so smoothed and polished down by society, or overlaid by the ornaments of education, that the coarse brick-work or rotten lath and plaster of their real being was covered over.

In this new country it was so much easier to tell at once the rough brick from the granite and marble.

Mr. Jarvis was fine granite indeed. One of those smoothed and polished men of British society would have viewed her comments about the horse and the ass as mere metaphorical flourish. Their "Brava!"—for they knew about feminine adjectives—would have been for her verbal wit, not for the truth behind it.

In this tiny community Mr. Jarvis stood out. She would undoubtedly meet him again and again. The prospect was titillating.

Robert's voice grated on her thoughts. "My dear, please see if our housekeeper is ready with food."

As she rose, she heard the front door close and footsteps on the stairs. She went into the hallway. A young man stood at the top of the staircase looking about him.

"Percy Ridout, at your service, ma'am. I am a clerk in Mr. Jameson's office." He bowed and smiled. He was a tall young man with lovely white teeth.

"I am happy to meet you."

"I fear I am late in arriving. I intended to come with some of my friends half an hour ago."

"I was almost giddy watching those young men appear and disappear, Mr. Ridout." Anna put her hand on his arm and drew him closer. "You must explain something. Why do the gentlemen— the young gentlemen—come into my drawing room, bow, sit down, wait exactly two minutes, then rise and bow themselves out of the room again without uttering a single syllable?"

Her guest looked down at his feet. His wind-burned face grew redder. He gave several "hmms" and "hems" and lapsed into silence.

"Please, Mr. Ridout, you must inform me of the customs of this new country."

"Well, ma'am, there is a contest..."

"A contest, sir? Tell me about it."

"To see how many houses they can visit in one day..."

"And the purpose of this bizarre contest?"

"Mead."

"Mead?"

"Mr. Bloor—you may have heard of him—has a brewery. He will give a prize of mead to the winner. Once, when he had taken a dram too much, he told me his recipe: fourteen pounds of honey, four gallons of water, ginger, two handfuls of dried elder flowers, and a large gravy spoon of fresh yeast. Excellent stuff it is, ma'am."

"Ah. That explains it. Drink is the great motivator in this land, is it not? Thank you, Mr. Ridout. But come in, come in. You must sample my housekeeper's excellent cranberry pie and rum punch—unfortunately we have no mead." She gestured towards the dining room, where Mrs. Hawkins, in a spotless white cap and apron, had laid out a first-class repast.

But as Mr. Percy Ridout followed her towards the table, she saw him draw out his pocket watch, look at it furtively, then tuck it into his vest.

"I have kept you back, have I not? You are in the competition with the other young men. Am I right?"

He blushed. "Yes, ma'am. But I would be glad to stay a few minutes and eat something."

"No obligation, sir. But tell me, how do the...uh...*competitors* keep track of how many levees they have attended?"

"The cards, ma'am. They collect the calling cards from each place they visit."

"Then let me mark on mine, 'forcibly detained by me, the undersigned Anna Jameson'. Will that do to explain why you have stayed here for five long minutes instead of two?"

She watched her guest wrestle with a decision. "Cranberry pie, Mrs. Jameson? I haven't had it since my dear old aunt used to make it. Lead on."

Anna took him into the dining room. "A large piece of pie for Mr. Ridout, please, Mrs. Hawkins."

He had just picked up a fork and a napkin, ready to enjoy the pastry, when he looked across into the drawing room. "Oh, Lord, I cannot stay." He set the plate down with a bang on the sideboard. "Sorry, so sorry..." He moved back into the hallway.

"What on earth is wrong, Mr. Ridout? You look quite agitated. For heaven's sake, explain."

"It is not your fault, ma'am. You have not been in this town long enough to understand."

"Understand? What?"

"That scoundrel Jarvis who sits in your drawing room surrounded by the Archdeacon and the Chief Justice is a murderer. In 1817, he shot my young cousin in cold blood, and now he sits in fashionable salons—unpunished and unrepentant."

Anna felt a sudden vertigo. She put her hand on the wall to steady herself. "Murderer, you say? Surely not, sir. Murderers are hanged."

"Not always. It was a duel. And he is a Jarvis. And the judge was his future father-in-law. And the judge's favourite daughter was in love with the brute." Mr. Ridout wiped his face with his sleeve and took a deep breath. "I was a small child at the time, and I have had to listen to the sorry tale all my life. I cannot get it out of my head."

Was there any truth in this? Obviously they could not talk further at the moment. "I understand why you must leave, Mr. Ridout. I am so sorry." She walked down the stairs with him.

Hawkins took her guest's coat from the hall tree. As he shrugged his shoulders into it, Anna said, "Will you wait for one moment?"

She went back up the staircase and into the dining room, where the gentlemen had just gathered. On the sideboard was the untouched plate of pie. She took a napkin and slid the pie onto it. Down at the front door again, she handed the pie to Mr. Ridout. "Perhaps you will let me know if Mrs. Hawkins's recipe is as successful as your aunt's?"

"You have been kind to me, Mrs. Jameson, in spite of my behaviour. No doubt you will hear the story of the duel. It is still talked about in many quarters. And now I bid you good day."

She watched his retreat down the front walk. Then, taking a deep breath, she went upstairs again to the dining room. The gentlemen were bent over the table, heaping their plates with cheese and fruit and cranberry pie and whipped cream.

The Archdeacon stopped to whisper in her ear. "Ah, Mrs. Jameson, you come from a world where female emancipation can be a topic for debate. Here, I am afraid, there is no discussion. But do not despair, you have shaken them. They will think about what you have said." He took a fork from the sideboard. "And now I must do justice to your excellent pie."

Back in the drawing room, there was talk about Mackenzie and his supporters ("pigs") and the roads ("fit for pigs"), but the focus was on the food. Anna could think of nothing but the young man's outburst. She was relieved when the guests rose, one by one, and made preparations to depart.

She followed them down the staircase and watched as Mr. Jarvis pulled his coat from the hook. It was a beautiful coat of grey superfine, lined with soft fur, perhaps from a fox. But now she could scarcely look at the fur without thinking of the trapped animal, its bloody carcass taken to the tanners for cleaning. In her mind's eye, there flashed the image of the Ridout boy's corpse.

"It has been a pleasure, ma'am," Mr. Jarvis was saying. "I shall tell Mary about your housekeeper's excellent pie."

And Colonel Fitzgibbon, who had just pulled on his gloves, said to her in a confidential whisper. "I shall take you for a drive on the lake this week, Mrs. Jameson. You have been stuffed up here too long. Some fresh air is always a treat." He grinned at her.

"A reasonably successful event, I believe," Robert said to Anna afterwards as she rearranged chairs in the drawing room. "You seem to have captivated the Archdeacon, Fitzgibbon and Jarvis, all influential men in the town. But at the same time, I fear you offended Chief Justice Robinson. Did I not make clear, Anna, that you must have no opinions while you are in this town?"

"I don't know what to think sometimes. Perhaps my opinions are all wrong, and I should just keep my mouth shut—the way you manage to."

"This is affecting humility, my dear. What has brought on this burst of self-doubt?"

Anna stacked some dirty dessert plates onto a tray.

"Well, Anna? I asked you a question."

"Finish off this rum punch, Robert, while I ask *you* a question." She waited while he spooned the dregs of the punch bowl into a crystal cup. "What is *your* opinion of Mr. Sam Jarvis?"

"A war hero, a member of a founding family of Upper Canada, and a crusader against the indecency of the vulgar press, in the opinion of the Tories. A rogue who murdered a young boy in cold blood, in the opinion of the Whigs. A renegade and violator of the democratic ideal of freedom of the press, in the opinion of the Radicals." He drained the cup in one long swallow.

Anna sighed. "Perhaps you did not hear me. I asked what is your opinion of Sam Jarvis?"

"I have no opinion. Outsiders like myself who seek promotion in this small town can have no opinion. I agree with everyone; especially with those whom I may be speaking to at the moment."

"But you allow the man into our house. We go to his place for dinner. You must like him."

"The Tories are in the ascendancy now, my dear Anna. Therefore, at the moment, I am one of them. And if they approve of Sam Jarvis, I am with them."

She left him pouring the leftover wine from the decanter into his glass and went to her room. She was too tired to say one more word.

TWELVE

Anna looked at the case clock in her drawing room. Just after one o'clock. In an hour, Colonel Fitzgibbon would arrive to take her out on the lake in his cariole. But first she had to prepare herself.

"Everything be on the bed ready, ma'am," Mrs. Hawkins told her, coming into the room. "Hawkins has given you his wool socks, gloves and comfies. For certain, you be warm enough."

"I shall see, Mrs. Hawkins. Please thank your husband for his contributions." Whatever "comfies" were.

She soon found out. Across the width of her bed was a red flannel one-piece undergarment with long sleeves and a trap door at the back. When she considered the position of that trap door, she burst into laughter.

"Very convenient, but I fear of little use. At least in my circumstances."

Mrs. Hawkins giggled. Then she said, making stitching motions with her right hand, "Invented them myself and sewed them too, so I did."

Anna took off her outer layers and pulled on the invention over her wool knickers and corset. Hawkins was a short man, so the "comfies" were just the right length. The sleeves, however, were too long, but her housekeeper rolled them back to the right length and tacked them in place with her needle and thread. Next came two pairs of heavy lisle stockings, two plain petticoats, and a new skirt and bodice of heavy serge. She tugged on fur-trimmed boots. Then she pulled Hawkins's socks on over her boots.

By the time Mrs. Hawkins helped her into a flannel overcoat with a double cape collar for warmth, she was ready. So she thought.

"Not yet, ma'am, you must put on this linen cap under your

bonnet for extra warmth. And don't you forget them extra gloves. Pull them on over your own."

The gloves were large, but Anna slipped her hands into them and felt the warmth of sheepskin. "Oh, Mrs. Hawkins, these are lovely. Be sure to thank your husband. What would I do without these additions from his wardrobe?"

Her world had certainly changed in the space of a month. In Britain or Europe, her literary coterie would gather for tea in the afternoon. The talk might be of her actress friend, Fanny Kemble, and her new role as Juliet. Or perhaps Anna would give Thomas Carlyle her views on Michelangelo's Virgin, which she had seen in the Tribune gallery. "Harsh and unfeminine with muscular, masculine arms, my idea of a washerwoman!" she might say, and Carlyle would laugh. "Oh, Mrs. Jameson, how noble of the artist to immortalize the working classes! And think of it, over two centuries before the French Revolution!" Then he might belch or spit into his handkerchief—he had a nasty ulcer—and no one would care. There would not be a Mrs. Powell in the whole group to criticize his social gaffes.

In this new world, she had Colonel Fitzgibbon, a hero of the War of 1812 against the Americans, a man with a *superflu de vie.* "Everyone seems to like him," Robert said when she told him about the afternoon excursion.

"You, too, I gather. Amazing. No 'in the opinion of the Tories, in the opinion of the Whigs, in the opinion of the Radicals'?"

"I have no idea what you're babbling about, Anna."

Colonel Fitzgibbon arrived with military promptness. He had on a strange rough grey fur hat from which dangled a striped tail. She had seen these hats in the town before, but could not identify the animal that supplied the raw material.

"A varmint hat, we call it, Mrs. Jameson. It's made from a raccoon. They are about the size of a small dog, and you can find them any evening behind the taverns licking up the..." He blushed and continued. "Step right up here, if you please. Allow me to help you."

His sleigh, he told her, was properly called a cariole. It was like a phaeton mounted on high runners. His horse, Brigadier, was a large, spirited steed with a shiny brown coat and four white stockings. It stayed perfectly still while Fitzgibbon helped Anna up into the passenger seat and covered her with bearskins.

Most of the military men used bearskins in their sleighs. She had, at first, been disconcerted by the faces of these beasts looking down at her, their ears, snouts and snarling teeth carefully preserved by the taxidermist, but now she scarcely noticed them.

Once the Colonel took the reins, his steed plunged at top speed straight down Bear Street towards the lake. The upper part of the cariole swayed in an alarming way. "It seems unstable," Anna said, trying not to whimper.

"Indeed, ma'am, it takes considerable skill to drive it, and we overturn at least once every quarter of an hour, but that is part of the fun. Be assured that once we get out on the lake, the snowdrifts will cushion us against accident."

Anna struggled to keep her mind off the disaster that seemed inevitable. Surely all those layers would protect her. But what about her head? That, after all, would have to be her stock in trade if Robert did not come through with the allowance she hoped eventually to extract from him. "Are there truly bears in the middle of town, Colonel?"

"Well, ma'am, Lawyer Boulton, who tells a good story, especially when he has taken a bottle of claret all to himself, says that once upon a time, his sleigh with his two fine steeds, Wellington and Napoleon, encountered a huge bear—undoubtedly a grizzly—at the foot of this street. They—the horses, that is— reared up on their hind legs, neighed in what he calls 'a fearsome way', and chased that bear right down to the edge of the lake where it disappeared into the frozen swamp..."

"Never to be seen again? And everyone lived happily, bear-free, for ever after?"

"Aye, ma'am. You have met Mr. Boulton."

"Indeed, sir. A wonderful storyteller, as you say." They both laughed, and Anna felt calmer.

By this time they were out on the snow-covered lake. Several officers from the garrison in handsome carioles were chasing each other across the expanse in a madcap way. Anna saw one especially beautiful sleigh done up in red and gold paint, with a fine black stallion in front. Bundled in bearskins were a man and a boy. She did not immediately recognize them, but she noticed that the Colonel's cheeks had grown pinker and pinker, from the cold or excitement, she didn't know.

"It's the Governor and his son, Henry," he told her. "They're so full of themselves with that horse and cariole. By god, I'm going to show them what old Brigadier can do. Giddap, boy." And he touched his whip to Brigadier's flank. "Hang on, ma'am!"

In a moment they had overtaken the Governor's cariole. "Race you to where that tree is stuck into the snow!" the Colonel yelled, pointing at an evergreen branch farther out on the lake. Sir Francis responded by whipping up his horse. In a moment the two sleighs were careening across the lake. Anna could feel her breath sucked out of her by the wind and cold. The Governor's horse was nose to nose with Brigadier. Fitzgibbon touched his whip to the horse's flank again. Brigadier responded. Sir Francis's steed dropped behind a half length.

Then, a sudden unexpected rise of snow, and Anna flew through the air like one of St. Nicholas's reindeer, landing with a scarcely perceptible thump in a snowdrift.

It was not at all like what she had feared. The snow enveloped her, keeping her spine and head safe from the icy surface of the lake. She had had no time to prepare herself for the fall, and her limbs were completely relaxed. She lay on her back, laughing.

She could hear whinnying, shouts, muffled thuds. Then two faces looked down at her: one, pink, aquiline-nosed, blue-eyed; the other—well, all she noticed were the brown teeth, the legacy of too many cigars. The Colonel and the Governor, of course.

"Mrs. Jameson! You are—"

"Perfectly well, I thank you. What a lark!"

Then they all laughed, and she caught a whiff of Sir Francis's brown breath. The Colonel pulled her upright. She shook the snow from her clothes, and they all climbed back up into their sleighs. And off they went again. Sometimes they confronted more hills of snow where the wind had whipped it into drifts. Anna began to anticipate the sudden lurch of the rise, the drop on the other side. She began to admire the dexterity of the Colonel's gloved hands on the rein, the gentle way he guided Brigadier this way and that, the horse's keen response to every tug and touch of rein and whip. She forgot about Robert, silent behind his newspaper, about the snow-lined boredom of her days, about her narrow, lonely bed.

And then the race was over. The Colonel and Brigadier had won "by a nose", as the Colonel said to her as he stepped down from the cariole to shake the Governor's hand.

"I suppose we must congratulate you, Fitzgibbon." Sir Francis looked positively pouty, like a small child whose favourite spinning top had been taken from him. His son Henry seemed ready to burst into tears.

"Not at all, sir. If you had not kindly stopped when I upset Mrs. Jameson, you might have been back at Government House by now enjoying a cup of hot rum punch. And speaking of which," the Colonel pulled out a silver flask from somewhere in the recesses of his greatcoat, "have a nip of this. It will warm you up." Ever the old campaign soldier, ready for anything, he took out from another pocket of his capacious garment three tiny silver cups and poured whiskey for Sir Francis, Henry and Anna herself, while he drank from the flask.

Anna enjoyed the fiery drink. It went straight down and warmed her. She squinted into the sun. From the west, three figures on snowshoes approached. One carried a shovel. Fitzgibbon recognized them first and waved. "Jarvis, come over here," he called.

They waited while the three men came closer. Besides Mr. Jarvis, Anna could see a fair-haired boy, the eldest son, and a tall brown-skinned man whose face was smeared with black paint. Jacob Snake.

"So Jarvis has one of the savages with him, has he?" the Governor said. "I made a good decision when I appointed him to the Indian post. He seems to know what goes on in their minds, at least as far as a white man can understand these people."

Mr. Jarvis bowed to her and made the introductions to the Colonel and Sir Francis. "My son, Sam, and my friend, Jacob Snake. Jacob has given us this." He pulled from his pack a piece of polished wood about two feet in length and three-quarters of an inch thick. It was flat on one side and curved on the other with a rounded end that resembled the head of a snake, complete with eyes incised into it and a crosscut to mark the mouth.

"It's a snowsnake. We have cleared some snow away where the drifts are light, and we intend to have a small, informal competition to see who can shoot it the farthest down the ice. But I fear Jacob will win. He always does."

"I teach Nehkik some new..." Jacob paused, searched for the right word, and tried again. "I teach Nehkik some new... manoeuvres."

"So, as you see, we have a heavy afternoon of education ahead of us. And you undoubtedly wish to get back to a warm fire." Mr. Jarvis shook hands with the Governor and the Colonel and shouldered the shovel again. "I am glad to see you, Mrs. Jameson. It is not often that the women of our town break loose from their domestic cares to enjoy a wild ride. And I see you are decked out for the realities of our climate. Good for you." He bowed.

As they were about to move off, Anna said, "Please, Jacob, will you teach me the manoeuvres as well? That is, if my driver will be kind enough to let me join in for a few minutes?" She looked up at the Colonel.

"By all means, ma'am. And I think I'll have a go myself."

Sir Francis and his son climbed back into their cariole, saluted to the Colonel and Anna, and drove off. The Colonel helped Anna back into the sleigh, then took Brigadier's reins and led him forward with the rest of the party for several hundred yards until they came to a long, narrow strip of ice which had been cleared with Mr. Jarvis's shovel. In the snow alongside the ice, there was a series of branches to mark distances.

Jacob demonstrated. He held the tapered end lightly with the thumb and forefinger of one hand while he balanced the stick with his other hand. Then he made a short run of several feet, bending and flipping the snake onto the ice in one smooth motion as he ran. It raced down the long strip of ice and came to a stop at the most distant branch.

"Remember, run fast, bend and flip while you run. I go down to the end of the track and slide the snake back to you. Then you try."

It seemed simple enough.

"Got to get rid of some of these layers," Anna said. She took off Hawkins's heavy socks so that her fur-lined boots would have some traction. Next came the fleece-lined gloves. Mr. Jarvis helped her out of the cumbersome flannel overcoat. But there were still the "comfies", the petticoats, the stockings, and the skirt and bodice. Modesty forbade their removal.

Perhaps it was the Colonel's whiskey. Or the cold air. At any rate, Anna ran as she had not run since she was ten years old. She even managed to launch the snowsnake down the ice before tumbling backwards into a snowbank. The snowsnake also tumbled into a snowbank, and it was several minutes before Jacob uncovered it and sent it shooting back down the ice to their starting point.

"Let me confer with Jacob, ma'am, and come up with a new manoeuvre that may work better," Mr. Jarvis said. After a brief conversation with his friend, he had some good advice. "Try this. With your left hand, hold up your skirts as you run. Keep only your right hand on the snake. When you feel the moment is right, bend over and shoot the snake, whoosh, down the ice. One hand will do it."

It worked. There was a round of applause from her companions.

They all had a turn, and another, and another. Jacob was, of course, the only one who managed to shoot the snake to the end of the raceway, but the rest of them got better and better with the practice. Only when the sun sank low in the sky did they stop.

Anna retrieved her surplus clothing, which she had piled into the sleigh. As Mr. Jarvis helped her back into her overcoat, she felt his cold fingers on the back of her neck. They sent a *frisson* down her spine. "You are shivering, Mrs. Jameson," he said. "Time for the Colonel to get you back to a warm hearth."

"I find it difficult to believe that Mr. Jarvis is a murderer," Anna said to the Colonel as he turned the sleigh towards town. "He is so affectionate with his son and so companionable with us all."

"You must not always believe what you hear in this town, ma'am. Especially when it comes from the mouths of the Ridout family. Oh, I saw Percy Ridout at your levee and have no doubt that he spread the venom of his poison."

"What he said is not true then?"

"Sam Jarvis shot the Ridout boy in a duel many years ago, it is true, but the jury declared it was a fair combat between two gentlemen."

"If two gentlemen agree to kill each other, it is, I suppose, lawful? Even desirable?"

The Colonel reached over and patted her shoulder. "It is always difficult to understand these things. As I see it, Samuel Peters Jarvis is one of the town's best men. I knew him first during the War of 1812 against the Yankee scoundrels. He was only twenty years old at the time, a lieutenant in the Third Regiment of York Militia, and he was the chosen one."

"The chosen one?"

"Aye. When our brave general, Sir Isaac Brock, fell mortally wounded at Queenston, a bullet in his heart, it was Lieutenant Jarvis who carried General Brock's battle plan to General Sheaffe. He rode through hell—and only those who have been in battle can understand hell—and he delivered that paper. It enabled us to take over nine hundred Yankee prisoners and a magnificent arsenal of arms. It was a moment of glory I will not soon forget."

"You sound almost—angry, Colonel Fitzgibbon. I have upset you."

"No, ma'am, it is not you. It is the notion—perpetrated by the likes of Percy Ridout—that Samuel Jarvis is nothing more than a murderer."

They were at that moment nearing a rough patch of snow and ice by the pier, and the Colonel turned his entire attention to his driving.

That evening at dinner, Anna spent the first and second courses diverting Robert with the story of carioling on the lake, her fun with the snowsnake, and Hawkins's thoughtful additions to her wardrobe.

"I am glad you had an enjoyable day, my dear," her husband said as Mrs. Hawkins removed the cloth and left them alone for their dessert of pound cake and coffee. He sounded almost as if he meant it. Then he added, "Your nose is very red. The glare from the snow can be quite devastating to the complexion."

"Excuse me, Robert. If you have nothing further to tell me, I shall leave you to enjoy your cigar and port."

She looked in the mirror above her bureau. Yes, her nose was red. She applied some of Mrs. Hawkins's ointment. It was a concoction of buds from an elder bush, simmered on the hearth—so her housekeeper told her—with a few "dollops" of butter. As she rubbed it into her skin, it cooled and soothed her. It was better by far than any of the concoctions on sale in London's fine shops. She would have Mrs. Hawkins write out her recipe and take it with her when she returned to Europe.

It had been a fine day—in spite of Robert's remark about her nose. Never again would she have more fun than she had had this day with the snowsnake. And Colonel Fitzgibbon had been kind. He had also given her a most interesting opinion of Mr. Jarvis.

Could a murderer be a good person? Perhaps...

She pulled the goosedown duvet up to her chin. The last sound she heard was her housekeeper's soft tread as she went into the dining room and drawing room to snuff out the flickering candles.

THIRTEEN

On the infrequent occasions when Mary managed to badger Sam into going to church, he always tried to go through the doors of St. James early, before the congregation arrived, or late, just as they were singing the first hymn. This Sunday, he planned "early", but one of the horses went lame, and by the time another was hitched up, his coachman managed to deliver Mary and him to the church just as the members of the congregation streamed through the front door.

He and Mary had passed through the outer door and were just about to enter the nave when he heard Mrs. Ridout's clear voice from behind him. "Murderer. Damned murderer. May you suffer every torture Hell has prepared for scum like you."

"Pay no attention, Sam. Keep moving."

He walked on, as Mary asked, but he could scarcely breathe. Then he felt a sharp poke in his back. He turned around to confront the wizened crone who had been John Ridout's mother. She came at him again, brandishing the metal-pointed parasol that served as cane and weapon.

"Back away, Mrs. Ridout, please."

"Murderer. Vile, contemptible murderer." Flecks of spittle spilled from her twisted mouth. The incoming congregation stopped in its tracks. And just inside the main door were Mr. and Mrs. Jameson. They had undoubtedly got an earful.

The crone gave him another poke, this time just below his heart. "I wish it were a bullet," she said.

He took a deep breath, but he had to force the words out. "You have forgotten a few things, Mrs. Ridout. It was your son who stirred things up in the first place by insulting my poor father. On the duelling ground, I remembered his bad eyesight and shortened the distance between us. Then he fired on the count of 'two' instead of 'three', an unforgivable breach of the duelling code." As Sam said these words, he glanced over the old woman's shoulder and noticed Mrs. Jameson's total attention.

"But you killed him in cold blood, knowing his pistol was empty. You are the Devil's spawn, you are."

"Mother, please." It was George Ridout. He came from inside the church just in time. "Allow me to escort you to your pew, and let us leave Mr. Jarvis in peace to contemplate his sins." He bowed to Mary, put his arm around his mother's shoulder and led her through the door of the nave.

Sam and Mary climbed the wooden stairs at the back of the church to their pew, the one Mary's family had kept after the death of Sam's father-in-law. The Powell pew was in the gallery immediately over the central entrance below. Chief Justice Powell had considered it the finest pew in the church. "It reminds me of my elevated position in court," he said once. "Below me are the barristers, attorneys, jurors, witnesses and common spectators." It was also, unfortunately, the most public pew in the church.

It was a long, narrow space with a high screen at the back to keep off the cold air. The screen and the pew itself were lined with a dark green cloth. It always seemed to Sam like a coffin for a tall man, and when he walked into it, he sometimes imagined that someone from behind might push the screen forward over the pew to make a perfect place of entombment.

He sat and looked straight ahead, fearful of the stares of the congregation below. The organ squawked, then squawked again, as though it were summoning its strength. Then the chords settled into a steady wheeze. As Sam reached for the book to find the first hymn, his hands trembled so much he could not turn the pages. Mary took his right hand in hers and held it in a tight grip.

He got through Bishop Ken's finest hymn, though it was one he would rather not have sung that particular morning:

> *Let all thy converse be sincere,*
> *Thy conscience as the noon-day clear;*
> *Think how all-seeing God thy ways*
> *And all thy secret thoughts surveys.*

It was at first a relief to kneel and bow his head for the General Confession, but those words, too, stabbed at him with more force than the old woman's parasol. "We have done those things which we ought not to have done," he intoned and thought, my god, why did I subject myself to this, I could have stayed in bed or walked through the oak woods behind the house or gone ice fishing on Grenadier Pond where no one, except the Indians, would have seen me. And they would not have judged me.

Then Archdeacon Strachan launched into one of his interminable sermons. The folk in the pews directly below the gallery fell asleep. Watching them, Sam remembered that night in Elmsley's barn, the snores of Boulton beside him in the loft and of Ridout and Small, who slept below in one of the stalls.

At the end of the service, he and Mary went out of the church by the vestry door, and escaped a further encounter with the Ridout clan. But their coachman had not been able to find a spot for the sleigh in front of the church, so he had parked it on the far side of the churchyard, and Sam and Mary had to pass by the tombstones that lined the pathway. At the end of it, facing them, so that avoidance was impossible, stood John Ridout's headstone.

"Look at it. Read those damned words."

"Please, Sam, let us try to forget—"

"Forget? Who can forget?" He pointed at the bottom lines of the long inscription chiselled into Ridout's stone: "'A Blight came, and he was consigned to an early grave on the 12th of July, 1817, aged 18.' I am that Blight, Mary, and I am immortalized on that stone. What a wonderful way for people to remember me! My children, my grandchildren, my great-grandchildren, will know that I was a murderer and—"

But he was talking to the air. Mary had started to run. She

was now several paces ahead. She signalled to John, who stepped down from his perch to help her into the sleigh. For a moment he thought she would tell the man to head home and leave him alone by the tombstone. He jumped up beside her.

"Dredge up that dreadful business again," she said, as the servant touched the horses' backs with his whip, "and your great-grandchildren—aye, and your great-great grandchildren—will know that I murdered *you*."

Sam had to laugh. The idea of his wife with a smoking pistol in her hand was too ludicrous. "Mrs. Ridout would be happy. She'd probably even attend your hanging."

On the sidewalk near the church were the Jamesons. Jameson bowed, and Mrs. Jameson waved and smiled.

And a moment later, as they moved along Palace Street, they passed the elegant sleigh carrying Sir Francis Bond Head and his aide-de-camp. Sir Francis lifted his beaver top hat in greeting.

"See," Mary said, "the Governor doesn't think of you as a Blight."

"No, he likes me because I tore Mackenzie's print shop apart. And that's another story that will chase me through my life. I remember hearing at school about the old-fashioned torture favoured by Queen Elizabeth—"

"Torture, Sam? What are you going on about now?"

"A certain weight was placed on the chest of the criminal, and increased gradually every day till the life and the heart were crushed together. Going to church today was like that. Don't ask me again to darken the doors of the place."

But as they picked up speed and moved towards Hazelburn, he remembered Mrs. Jameson's smile.

FOURTEEN

Since Anna's arrival in Toronto, Mrs. Hawkins had gotten into the habit of providing Sunday tea. Robert took another piece of her excellent gingerbread, and Anna poured him a third cup of tea. "We have some good moments, do we not, my dear?" he said, spreading butter thickly over his cake.

She thought about that. Singing hymns together was one of the few pastimes they both enjoyed. What else was there? Aloud, she said, "I find myself in total agreement with you about that hideous window of painted glass."

"It cost five hundred pounds, and the Archdeacon is very proud of it, so I am careful to keep my mouth shut when he goes on about it. But the bit of theatre with Mrs. Ridout and Sam Jarvis was rather good, I thought. One enjoys unusual moments like these from time to time."

"I felt sorry for both of them." The old woman's grief over her dead son was pitiable, but she also remembered the stricken look on Mr. Jarvis's face as he tried to defend himself. And his poor wife, trembling and ashen-faced, trying not to cry.

"I have a proposition that may please you, Anna. Campbell, a clerk of the assize, must leave for Niagara tomorrow to see his wife, who has just been delivered of a fine babe, so he tells me. He is thoroughly reliable and I thought..." He paused to spoon more sugar into his tea. "I thought you and I might accompany him, visit my friends, the Almas, and—"

"Oh, Robert, how perfect. And we can see the falls. It is exactly what I long for." And it would be an opportunity to spend time with Robert, to get him away from his newspapers and the daily grind. Perhaps they could still put things right.

At half past eight the next morning, Mr. Campbell banged the doorknocker. He was a smiling young man, as tall as Robert, with a long nose and eyes as dark as his bearskin cap. Even though he had tethered his horses to the hitching post, they nickered and pulled at their harness, as if anxious to be off. They were a nicely matched pair, dark grey in colour with shiny black manes.

"A very pretty sleigh," Anna said, "and a pair of fine horses."

"Thank you, ma'am. They'll take us to Niagara in short order. Three days at most. I'm so anxious to see the wee bairn. Let's get started," he said, helping her and Robert up into the sleigh and piling their luggage behind them. "I see you have your sketchbook and pencils at the ready," he added. "You'll find plenty to draw."

Three days. That meant two nights in inns along the route. Since rooms were scarce in these places, so she'd heard, and since Robert held the purse strings so tightly, they would have to share the same bedchamber for the first time since her arrival. That should prove interesting.

She wrapped her borrowed blanket round her. Mrs. Hawkins had woven it herself, and it was lambswool, dyed a rich red. Then Mr. Campbell heaped buffalo and bearskins about them, until they seemed absolutely buried in fur, every breath of cold air excluded.

They set off briskly. Mr. Campbell evidently knew the way, a good thing since the road was invisible. Anna could never in her wildest imaginings have conjured this Canadian winter. The sky was one white, whirling mass of starry flakes. The robes about them seemed covered in swansdown. She loved the silence, broken only by the tinkle of the sleighbells.

In an hour the snow had abated. Now she could just see the road, which seemed to run in a straight line with the dark pine forest on each side. Above them, a huge bald eagle soared on the wind currents. It followed them for miles before alighting on top of a pine, where it folded its great, wide wings and looked down upon them. She remembered Jupiter's eagle, the symbol of apotheosis after death. Perhaps on this trip—she dared to hope—she and Robert could find some sort of renewal.

From time to time, clearings appeared, spotted with charred

stumps and blasted trunks projecting from the snowdrifts. "What a battle these settlers wage with nature," she said.

Mr. Campbell laughed. "It's quite a fight, and the settlers seem to be winning. First they set fire to the trees. Then when they get enough space cleared for a cottage, they start the ringing process on the remaining trees."

"Ringing?"

"They cut a deep gash through the bark round the bole of the tree. It prevents the circulation of the sap, and by degrees the tree droops and dies."

Sometimes openings in the forest gave glimpses of Lake Ontario. Anna leaned forward again to talk to their driver. "Why is it not frozen?"

"Look at those dark waves, ma'am. Nothing can freeze up with that constant motion."

Robert remained silent. At first Anna thought he had fallen asleep under his robes. Then she heard him say, "Wasn't the silence wonderful when we first started out?" Not a question, nor yet a statement. Just one of his sneers.

Just when she was beginning to wish she had not had two cups of early morning coffee, Mr. Campbell pulled the sleigh to a stop at a settlement at the mouth of a little river. "Time for a break here," he said, pointing to an inn. "This place is Oakville, and we can have lunch and a bit of a respite."

The landlady showed Anna to a small room with a chamberpot and a table with ewer and basin. The water was cold, but there was soap and a clean towel. Refreshed, she joined her companions for strong, hot tea and slices of venison between thick wedges of fresh bread.

"Delicious," she said to the landlady.

"Plenty of deer come from the woods," the woman said. "The wolves drive them out, and we shoot them." She raised her left arm, sighted down an imaginary barrel and pulled a trigger with a motion of her right hand.

Anna was pleased to see that Robert paid for their driver's meal, and to judge by the landlady's delight, left a sizable *douceur* as well. He had enjoyed his food, evidently a good omen, as Mrs. Powell had pointed out during her advice on handling husbands.

Back in the sleigh for a long afternoon, Anna whiled away the time making sketches of the passing scene. It was so warm under the animal skins that she was able to take off the warm gloves she'd borrowed from Hawkins. She actually found several minutes to make her rapid pencil drawings before the cold crept back into her fingers.

At a place called Stony Creek, Mr. Campbell stopped at a log hut which had a wooden sign proclaiming HOTEL. "Seems unlikely," he said, "but I'll give it a lookover. It's time we stopped for the night."

In a minute he was back at the reins. "Disgusting. Everything dirty and everyone drunk. Our next hotel will be ten miles farther on in Beamsville. We'll have to keep moving."

It grew dark, and the snow fell thickly. It was again impossible to distinguish the sleigh-track. "It happens often," their driver reassured them. "I'm going to loosen the reins and leave the horses to their own instinct. It's the safest way."

"I hope you know what you're doing," Robert said.

After this, Anna remembered nothing distinctly. Perhaps she nodded off, awakening when she felt the sleigh begin to weave and rock. One of the runners had slid off the path. She heard Mr. Campbell's, "Damn!" and "Whoa!" But the horses plunged ahead. The sleigh rolled down an embankment, coming to rest against a tree trunk.

Something must have struck her head. For a moment she ceased to hear the ever-jangling sleigh bells. Then she gained consciousness to find the sleigh overturned and herself under it, half-smothered. She lay in the dark, as if in a coffin, and waited for Mr. Campbell or Robert to rescue her. But they did not come. She could hear them calling to her. They seemed to have no idea where she was. She grew panicky, knowing she might die if she did not take action.

She reached up and felt the wooden slab above her. Her first action must be to push the sleigh off herself. Her body seemed to be on a slant. She gave the wooden roof above her a mighty shove. Nothing happened. She tried again, pushing as hard as she could with her whole upper body. There was a creak and groan, and the sleigh rolled off her and down the embankment. As she emerged from under the snow, into the deep blackness of the forest, she looked up the hill and saw her two snow-covered companions floundering about, calling her name and trying to control the horses.

"Here I am."

"Thank god," Robert said, as the two men plunged down the embankment through the drifts. He pulled her towards him and wrapped her in a snowy embrace.

"We thought you had died in the upset."

His companion wiped his hand across his eyes and repeated, "Thank god. Thank god."

Anna looked up towards the top of the hill and pointed at a light in the distance.

"It's the chimney of the blacksmith's forge at Beamsville," Mr. Campbell said as he fought to keep himself from being pulled over by the plunging horses. "Two of us must stay here with the horses, and one must go for help."

"I'll go," Anna said, as one of the horses reared up, kicking with its front hoofs and pulling the second one along with it. "There's no alternative. You have a job here for two strong men. The light will be my beacon."

Waiting no longer, she started her scramble up the hill. She had no idea how long it took her to reach the top, but once there, she could see the light from the forge straight ahead between the two rows of pine forest. So she was on the road, at least, but the snow was up to her knees, and each step required superhuman effort. Just when she thought she could not push her tired legs another inch, the path became easier. Animals—wolves perhaps—had come through the snow and laid a rough track. Not bears, thank goodness; someone had told her they hibernated, but what would she do if she encountered a wolf pack? And what were those shadows ahead of her on the trail? Best to make a noise.

She began to sing, "If a body meet a body comin' through the rye", then the sheer idiocy of those words in this place made her laugh so hard, she braced herself for a moment against a tree as she caught her breath.

Much time passed, and she found herself at last at the forge, where the smith was hammering with might and main at a ploughshare. She stood at the door and called out to him, but the din was so great he heard nothing. She advanced into the red light of the fire, and finally he looked up, a great, hulking man with immense shoulders.

One sound only came from his broad toothless mouth. "AAARGH!"

"Help, please, I—"

"AAARGH!" He must have been deranged with shock at her sudden appearance, for he pointed his hammer at her as if she were some avenging angel come into his Inferno from above. She turned away in despair. No help to be had here. She thought of the men wrestling with the horses on the snowy embankment. No time to waste.

After some more scrabbling about in the darkness, she found herself in the village main street, where she saw a low log structure with a crude sign, Beamsville Inn. The pink-cheeked old woman who owned the place was the image of Anna's long-ago nurse. She welcomed Anna in, dispatched her sons at once to lend assistance, and in a few minutes, laid the supper table, took the bellows to the fire in the hearth, and set the victuals to fry on the griddle. In a little room with a comfortable-looking bed, she made Anna strip off her wet clothes, replacing them with her daughter's bodice, skirt and petticoats.

"Now, set you down, dearie, in that chair by the fire and keep warm. As soon as the menfolk arrive, we'll eat supper."

As Anna settled into the comfortable seat, she heard the sound of a lark. Instinctively she looked out the little front window into the night. "But there are no larks in Canada," she said aloud. Then she turned her head, and there it was, a tiny creature on its sod of turf in a small cage suspended on a hook from the ceiling. It trilled and warbled away, and she sat stock still in her chair, listening with her heart.

"Why are you crying, dearie?" The landlady glanced at her as she turned the fish on the gridiron. She took a napkin from the table and passed it to Anna.

"I don't know...I don't know what's come over me. I heard your bird's song, and suddenly I was in Ireland again, a small girl lying on my back on the hillside above my parents' summer home, watching the larks as they sang and soared over my head—watching, watching, watching—until they melted into the blue sky. And here I am, in this inn somewhere in the wild forests of Upper Canada, listening to that caged bird's song, lost, lost..." She took the napkin and wiped her eyes. "Oh, perhaps I've grown nostalgic because you remind me so much of my old nurse."

The landlady knelt by Anna's chair and took her hand in hers. "I, too, dearie, sometimes think of those beautiful green hills and tuneful birds and the folk I left behind. But I have been here for thirty years and more. My old man and my dear lost kiddies lie in the churchyard yonder. This is my home now, and a good one it is. I would not go back, even if the King himself asked me to."

"I am beginning to understand how one could love this country," Anna said. "I have seen and done things today which I could never have—"

She was interrupted by the arrival of Robert and Mr. Campbell. The landlady's sons took their coats and hung them by the hearth, and they all sat down to a meal of venison steaks, fried fish, hot cakes, cheese, coffee and whiskey punch. "Best food I've ever had," Robert said, ladling out another spoonful of punch.

The bedchamber seemed cold, and Anna snuggled against her husband. "A day to remember," she said as she kissed him. "I felt happy when you hugged me."

"Hugged you?" He seemed genuinely bewildered. "That was

Campbell. I thought at the time he took an unwarranted liberty.
But we were out of our minds with worry, I guess. And you were
undoubtedly half-mad with fear yourself after being trapped like that."

Had she imagined things as she wanted them to be? Or had he
regretted his show of emotion and was now denying everything?

"I'm tired, Anna. Dead tired from wrestling with those damn
horses. Just want to sleep. Sorry." In a moment, she heard his
breathing slow and deepen.

The next day slid by without mishap, and by late afternoon, they
had arrived at Niagara. "Or Newark," Mr. Campbell said. "It's had
its share of names. I'll see you safely to your friends' house, then be
off straight away to see my dear wife and babe. I'll call for you at
eight tomorrow morning."

Mr. John Lees Alma and his wife Emily had been English friends
of Robert's. Anna had visited them once or twice when she and
Robert were first married, and she was glad to meet them again
on this side of the water. Robert seemed so intent now on making
friends for political reasons. It was pleasant to know that he wanted
to seek out the Almas simply because he liked them.

They lived in a Georgian brick house just off the main street of the
town. Mr. Alma was now a prosperous merchant, and his *embonpoint*
was testimony of his success. Supper was served at a huge mahogany
table. The plates were heaped with food, and everything was brown
in colour, from the lukewarm soup with chunks of beef swimming in
grease to the thick slice of mutton covered with gravy, to the caramel
pudding with a viscous molasses sauce. Anna found herself thinking
longingly of the venison steaks she had enjoyed on the way.

"I imagine you're happy to have a decent meal after two days'
travel," Mr. Alma said, as he passed Anna and Robert another glass of
dark-brown sherry. "Now, drink up and enjoy our national pastime."

"Which is?" Anna asked.

"Inebriety."

Robert laughed, downed the contents of his glass and poured

more from the decanter at his right hand. "Let me now recite the national anthem," he said. "It applies to all immigrants to this country, you, me and the rest of them:

Men learn to drink, who never drank before;
And those who always drank, now drink the more."

Mrs. Alma rose from her place. "Perhaps it's time to leave the gentlemen to the national pastime." A plump little woman dressed in the latest fashion, she had a bustle so large that she might have hidden a down pillow under her dress. "Do come with me, Mrs. Jameson, and admire some of our new acquisitions."

Very proud she was of what she called her "Franklin stove" in the drawing room. It was set into the fireplace, "with its pipe let into the flue," she said, "and the opening of the fireplace bricked up around it, as you can see. A great improvement on the open hearth, to my mind."

"Yes, indeed," Anna said. "It must hold the heat so well."

"And now, I'll show you what we have in your bedchamber. You and Mr. Jameson will find it so convenient."

What on earth could that be? Anna wondered, passing through her mind the various items she and Robert might find 'convenient'. A bedwarmer to heat up their lovemaking? A tub big enough for a communal scrub? A lithograph of a Bacchanalian orgy?

The "convenience" was a fine maple chair, and with a flourish, Mrs. Alma lifted the hinged seat to disclose a chamberpot below.

"A commode chair," Anna said. "How...comfortable."

She was striving to find another adjective to describe this piece of furniture when she noticed on the wall beside it a framed pencil drawing of a small boy wearing an embroidered skin shirt and, on his curls, a fur cap with a tail dangling from it. He wore tiny moccasins, and on his sturdy little legs, buckskin breeches decorated with beaded sashes. The drawing was beautifully done, evidently by a master artist and...

"Who is this pretty child?" she asked as she moved closer to look at its fine details. She could see the artist's signature, Wm. Berczy, in beautiful copperplate. Below the sketch was a title. Nehkik. Surely not. She looked again. Yes, Nehkik.

"It's a likeness of Sam Jarvis as a five-year-old. You've probably met the man himself in Toronto."

"But what...? Why...do you have this picture?"

"The ladies at St. Mark's—the Church of England—had a bazaar recently to help the poor. Someone who knew the Jarvises when they lived here brought in the picture, which they'd purchased at an auction. William Jarvis worked for the Simcoes, I believe, something to do with land grants. He was a ne'er-do-well, by all accounts, and I gather the son is no better. But I liked the sketch, and Berczy's art may go up in value."

"I wonder why the boy is in Indian costume."

"It was the fashion then. Mrs. Simcoe liked the savages, had them about all the time, even had her own son dressed in buckskin." Mrs. Alma ran her hand over the arm of the commode chair and lifted the seat once more. "My husband has put in an order for several of these from Montreal. He expects to sell them all." She turned to Anna. "But tell me about Mr. Sam Jarvis. I have heard that he is a murderer and a renegade."

"I too have judged him severely, Mrs. Alma. But many people like him. My friend Colonel Fitzgibbon is one. Mr. Jarvis is a generous host and kind to his wife and children. I confess—now that I know him—that I myself like him."

Anna and her hostess went downstairs to have tea in the drawing room, where they were joined in an hour by the men, "rather the worse for wear," as Mr. Alma put it. "And now you must get to bed," he added. "Clumping around the falls in the dead of winter requires a good night's preparatory rest."

Their bed was high off the floor and Robert had some difficulty mounting it from the stepping stool. Once they were settled, Anna pulled the curtains around them, making a dark little nest of warmth and comfort.

Robert pulled up her nightdress and touched her nipples for a moment. Then he put his limp member against her pubis. As she reached down to caress it into life, she heard his deep breathing and a gentle snore. She lay on her back and let the tears stream unchecked down her cheeks and onto the pillow. "Alone, alone, all all alone!" Like the Mariner, she felt doomed.

Mr. Campbell called for them promptly at eight in the morning, and they set out briskly for the fourteen-mile ride to the falls. "I shall drop you at the inn which overlooks the cataracts," he said, "where you can spend the night after your sightseeing. Then in the morning, we start our return journey."

"But are we not to see your wife and this lovely new baby?"

"Oh, ma'am, do you mean it? I'd be so happy. It would not be a great inconvenience for you, because my house is a stone's throw from the inn. I could pick you up, take you there, show you the bairn and be back at your lodgings within two hours."

"For god's sake, Anna," said Robert into her ear. "We came all this way to waste time burbling over a baby?"

The road led them along the Niagara River and over the Queenston Heights. "Yonder is General Brock's memorial." Mr. Campbell pointed at a tall monument on the highest point of land.

Anna found herself thinking about her conversation with Colonel Fitzgibbon during the cariole ride. "Look, Robert," she said, pulling the blankets away from his face. "It's where Mr. Jarvis carried the battle plans to General Sheaffe after General Brock died."

"You seem to have impressive knowledge of these colonial wars, my dear. And you keep bringing up the subject of Sam Jarvis. Is he of special interest to you?"

"Yes, I find myself trying to fit all the parts of his life together." She told him of Mrs. Alma's drawing. "Sweet little boy, brave young soldier, vile murderer, vicious vandal, loyal husband and loving father."

"Quite the puzzle," Robert said and burrowed again under his bearskins.

When they were within four or five miles of their destination, Anna asked their driver to stop. "I want to listen to the roar of the cataracts. Oh, so many times I have heard of their vastness. They must make a tremendous noise."

They stopped. How calm it was! The sun shone, and the sky was without a cloud. How vast the glittering white waste and the dark forests! But how disappointing, too. Not a sound could she hear. Mr. Campbell touched his whip to the horses' flanks, and they were away again.

She nodded off at that juncture, and she was entirely unprepared for Mr. Campbell's sudden check of the horses and his shout, "The falls!" She looked upwards, still half asleep, expecting to see their immense height. Then she realized. Not up. Down. She must look *down* on them. There they were, two great cataracts in the midst of a flat plain. Merely a feature in the wide landscape.

She must have made some sort of noise—a sigh, a moan?—for Mr. Campbell turned from his driving to look at her. "You are disappointed, ma'am?"

"Oh, sir, forgive me. I have seen Niagara, the wonder of wonders, and felt—yes, disappointment!"

She scarcely heard Mr. Campbell's comforting comments, or Robert's conventional murmurings, "How impressive, quite beautiful." She tried not to cry. They went on to the Clifton Hotel where their driver left them at the front door. "I'll pick you up late this afternoon. You'll have plenty of time to do a tour, Mrs. Jameson. You may find it all seems more wondrous when you have had time to look around."

The hotel was a desolate place. Its open verandahs were covered in snow and hung round with icicles. Inside were forlorn empty rooms, broken windows and dusty dinner tables. The owners were huddled in a dirty little kitchen and seemed quite overcome with amazement to see visitors in the depth of winter.

Robert leaned down to speak into her ear. "We cannot stay here over night." Then he turned to the old man who stood before them, mouth agape. "Crampons, if you please. We are here to see the falls. Then we shall come back and have a cup of tea and a glass of whiskey, if you can manage that much."

Without Robert's foresight in ordering the crampons, they could not for a moment have kept their footing on the frozen surface of the snow. At Table Rock, the ground became even more unsettled and dangerous. As they walked, the snow beneath their feet slipped in masses from the bare rock, and the spray that fell on the rocks changed instantly into a smooth, glassy sheet of ice. Down came the dark-green waters, over the edge of the falls, bringing with them enormous blocks of ice. On the ledges and overhanging cliffs on each side huge icicles dangled, at least thirty feet in height, and thicker than the body of a man. Every tree branch fringing the rocks and ravines was an ice sculpture, and the spray from the cataracts had frozen into strange shapes, sometimes houses of glass, sometimes old men with long white beards.

Anna crept to the very edge of Table Rock and looked down. The boom of the falling ice and the torrent of water assailed her. For minutes she stood, her mind emptied of everything but the noise. The spray, cold against her cheeks, washed away her hot tears. She was scarcely aware of Robert pulling on her sleeve. "Good god, woman, come away! What are you thinking of?"

They returned to the hotel after their adventure and had barely time to drink the tea and whiskey before the ever-faithful Mr. Campbell appeared. He looked around at the filthy room in which they were seated. "My apologies. I had no idea... I have only seen the inside of this place in the summertime, when it is full of people. You cannot stay here. Let us go and see my wife and the wee fellow, then talk over what to do."

The Campbells' house was close by the falls. Mr. Campbell took Anna upstairs at once to see his wife and child. Mrs. Campbell was young and lovely with tendrils of curly hair slipping down her forehead. The bedchamber was a nest of warmth and comfort. Anna took the newborn child into her arms, and in a moment it fell asleep in her lap in spite of the roar of the falls nearby. "What a strange lullaby!" she said.

"We never notice it. Such is the force of custom."

"And the power of adaptation." But as Anna said this, she realized that there were circumstances to which she herself could never adapt.

Back in the drawing room, Robert seemed ready to accept Mr. Campbell's invitation to spend the night. As their host left the room to get the whiskey decanter from the dining room sideboard, Anna said, "To intrude on the Campbells at such a time is impossible."

"Equally impossible to have the man drive us back to the Almas and then come all the way back here. Don't be stupid."

It was by then nightfall, and Anna was forced to agree that they had no alternative but to stay. In the hastily prepared bedchamber to which a maid took them, they undressed in silence. In silence they climbed into bed, each lying on the extreme edge of the mattress, as far apart as they could manage without pitching forward onto the floor.

It was an uneventful trip home. There was nothing to distract Anna from the reality that faced her. At Newgate Street, Mrs. Hawkins met them at the front door.

"A nice supper be ready for you. Just take off them woollies right here, and my man will sort them out."

A nice supper it was: a roast fowl with apple stuffing, fried potatoes and a squash pie with whipped cream. Robert tucked into it with gusto. Anna tried to do it justice but finally pushed her plate away, the squash pie untouched.

Mrs. Hawkins collected the dishes, then she and her husband retired to their quarters belowstairs. Robert began to drink his port in earnest. "A pleasant interlude in the great white wilderness, was it not, my dear Anna?"

"It's dead, Robert."

"What are you talking about?"

"Our marriage. It is like those blighted trees we saw on our travels."

"I'm too tired to listen to your flights of fancy. Perhaps we can talk of it at another time."

"No, Robert. I must say what I have to say. It's been a slow death. I think it started the first week after our wedding. You remember those rooms we rented in London? On Tottenham Court Road? How on our first Sunday as man and wife, we set out to visit Hartley Coleridge? Because you told me you always had Sunday dinner with him?"

"You've held that against me, have you, all these years?"

"Think about it. Put yourself in my position—if you can. I wore my white dress, the one I'd bought for our wedding. It started to pour rain. I was cold and tired. I couldn't stop my teeth from rattling like castanets. I said to you, 'We must turn back, Robert.' And you said, 'Go back, then, be damned to you. I'll go by myself to Coleridge's.'"

"As I remember it, my dear Anna, you shouted at me, 'I'm not going one step farther.' And then you said, 'I should have listened to my father. He said it wouldn't work. He said you could never love a woman properly.' How do you think I felt to hear that in our first week of marriage?"

"I shouldn't have brought up the past. Let's concentrate on the here and now. I have finally realized what I was crying about when I stood on Table Rock. I was mourning the death of a marriage." She reached out and touched his arm. "There are two principal methods of killing trees in this country, according to Mr. Campbell. You can set fire to them. Or you can ring them, a slow death in which the vital juices cannot circulate and the tree droops and dies. Do you remember all that?"

"No doubt you have some point to make?"

"Just this. Like those trees, there are two ways in which a woman's heart may be killed—by passion and by prolonged sorrow. To my way of thinking, better by far the swift fiery death than this 'ringing'. Our marriage has taken twelve years to die, and this trip has shown me that we must now lay it to rest."

Robert took some gold coins from his pocket and jingled them in his hand. "We had an agreement. You remember the terms. You will stay until I get my promotion to Vice-Chancellor, and I will provide you with generous amounts of money as compensation. If you leave now, you receive nothing." He laid the coins in front of her. "Send these to your family. I can easily spare them at the moment. And your father and mother and sisters will undoubtedly welcome a New Year's emolument."

"Bribery, Robert, bribery." But she needed the money. The mails had been delayed again, and she had not received royalties from her British publishers. She swept the coins off the table and walked out of the room. At least there would be enough money now to pay for her father's medical expenses.

FIFTEEN

"I need a poem, Miss Siddons. A love poem for my wife. It's Valentine's Day tomorrow, you remember."

The governess sat behind a desk in the small library that led into the conservatory. "I'm not sure what you want from me, Mr. Jarvis." Her long nose grew red, and a mottled flush suffused her cheeks. "Perhaps, if I have time when I finish teaching the girls, I could help you compose something, but surely you do not wish my assistance with such a personal—"

Sam laughed. "I have no intention of becoming a poet. I want you to lend me a book in which I might find something suitable, that's all. I bought a lovely card—lace and red roses and pink hearts—from Rowsell's store, and there's a blank space inside into which I thought I might copy a poem."

Miss Siddons's nose returned to its normal sallow brown. She put aside the girls' exercises which she had been marking. She got up from behind the desk, and after some consideration of the shelves on the far wall, picked out a book. "You may find something in this one." It was a heavy black-covered tome entitled *Best Loved Poems*.

"Good heavens, Miss Siddons, you do not expect me to wade through that thing, do you?"

"Perhaps if I listed some of the best authors of love poetry, that might help?" Taking up the quill from the desk, she wrote the names of six or seven poets in her beautiful copperplate script. "You will find these writers in the index, and then it will be relatively simple to review their poems and find a suitable one."

Sam took her list in hand and went upstairs to his bedchamber, where he poured some hot rum from the drink warmer, propped himself up on pillows, and stretched out with the book.

He had paid scant attention to literature at the school in Cornwall to where his father had sent him—at great expense, so he always boasted. Archdeacon Strachan had been merely the Reverend Mr. Strachan in those days, but his Cornwall school had seen the education of all Toronto's present élite.

And I have paid for that education a hundred times over, Sam told himself, when I consider all the years of my life spent in wiping the slate clean of my father's debts.

He leafed through the poems. There was not one he recognized. The only love poem he knew was one his mother used to recite:

> *Love in my bosom like a bee*
> *Doth suck his sweet:*
> *Now with his wings he plays with me*
> *Now with his feet.*

That one certainly wouldn't be in this book. Well then, how about one of Shakespeare's sonnets? He turned the pages. Hmm. Too wordy, too difficult. The next poet on Miss Siddons's list was John Donne. He'd never heard of the man, but he looked at the first poem.

> *I can love both fair and brown;*
> *Her whom abundance melts, and her whom want betrays;*
> *Her who loves loneness best, and her who masks and plays.*

Incomprehensible.

He was just on the point of going downstairs to ask Miss Siddons's advice again when he read the third name on her list. Leigh Hunt. He'd give this person's poems a brief once-over. He flicked through the pages. Ah, the language seemed easier. There were two or three that might be possible, but then he found the perfect one. It was titled "Rondeau", whatever that meant. Mary wouldn't know either. He read the poem over again. Come to think of it, the first line would make an excellent title. Or maybe he could just call it "Kisses". The lines were simple, there was a rollicking rhyme, and it was short enough to fit on the blank page of the valentine.

He went to his desk, took up his quill and copied it, taking care with his script, and making one or two minor changes to fit Mary's tastes. Then he went downstairs to the breakfast room and tucked it in the space behind the coffee urn.

"Sam, my darling, darling Sam." These were the first words Sam heard as he went down for breakfast on Valentine's Day. Mary jumped from the chair she sat in and kissed him. "Oh, Sam, you wrote this especially for me, did you not? It is so beautiful, so beauti..." She burst into tears.

Well, who was he to destroy her illusion? He pulled her into his arms. They were in a tight embrace when the servant girl came in with some hot toast. Good timing. He was glad that Mary was pleased, but right now he was hungry.

So he tucked into his poached eggs and grilled kidneys, had three of Cook's fresh rolls and Seville orange marmalade, and two cups of coffee.

While he ate, Mary nibbled on toast. Then she pushed the uneaten bits to one side of her plate and took up his poem again. He had almost come to think of it as his.

She read it aloud in her sweetest voice.

> *Mary kissed me when we met,*
> *Jumping from the chair she sat in.*
> *Time, you thief! who love to get*
> *Sweets into your list, put that in.*
> *Say I'm weary, say I'm sad;*
> *Say that health and wealth have missed me:*
> *Say I'm growing old, but add—*
> *Mary kissed me!*

"And I remember, my dear Mary, a strange coincidence. When I came in this morning, you jumped from your chair and kissed me—"

"And you imagined that, didn't you, my darling husband? When you wrote the poem? Oh, I shall always, always keep it."

"And now, dear," Sam said, wiping the egg yolk from his lips with the linen napkin, "I do not have to rush to the office this morning." He took her hand in his. "Shall we?"

Mary went upstairs. Sam waited a few minutes, then followed. The upper hallway was quiet. The boys were in school. One of the servants had taken little Charlie out to make snow angels. Sam had seen them from the breakfast room window. And in the library, Miss Siddons, bless her, would be keeping the four girls busy.

He went into his bedchamber and took the sheep-gut covering from the top drawer of his bureau. He had used it once before, but it was still in good condition. Tucking it into his vest pocket, he went down the hallway to Mary's room.

At eight o'clock that evening, Sam descended the curved staircase in his new formal attire. He had ordered it from George Michie's shop on King Street. Michie had made him a fine claw-hammer coat in black superfine, and his trousers had the new pleated hip fullness.

"Just what them toffs are wearing now," the tailor assured him as he displayed the illustrations from a British fashion magazine. Fortunately, Sam could forget about the expense until the end of the month. In the meantime, he felt sure it would impress the guests at the St. Valentine's dinner he and Mary were hosting. Especially Sir Francis Bond Head. And, yes, Mrs. Jameson, who had, according to Mary, said that "people at parties in Toronto dress elegantly in the styles of a decade ago." She'd change her tune when she saw his rig.

"You look so handsome," Mary told him as she took his hand at the bottom of the steps. She herself looked pretty in a new red two-piece dress. She made a small curtsy. "Do you like it?"

"I love it, Little Red. It shows off your ankles."

There was no more opportunity for conversation. The footman, a corporal hired from the garrison for the evening, stood at the front door to await the arrival of the first guests. He had placed a chair nearby, ready for the ladies to sit on while they removed their boots.

Sam watched Mary from the doorway of the drawing room. She took a quick look around the room, straightened two of the paintings, plumped up a cushion or two, and opened the tea caddy to make sure there was plenty of tea for the ladies. "See, dear," she said, turning to him, "I have put your valentine on the back of the pianoforte. I want it there with us this evening."

By half past eight, everyone had assembled. The corporal passed sherry and whiskey. Colonel Fitzgibbon sat ramrod straight on the sofa, his wife beside him. She was a small, fragile old woman with blue eyes. Sam was amused to see that the Colonel's right leg pressed against Mrs. Fitzgibbon's left one. Obviously they still played out their wild romance of a generation earlier.

Facing them on another sofa were Attorney-General Jameson and Mrs. Jameson. They sat at opposite ends; a gap of three feet separated them. Sam thought Mrs. Jameson looked handsome in her gold satin dress. It was a colour that would have been disaster on his fair-haired Mary, but their guest's luminescent white skin and red hair were perfect for the buttery tones of the dress.

The other three guests sat in chairs close to the pianoforte. Chief Justice John Beverley Robinson had been Sam's chum at the Cornwall school, and he had a connection to Mary, too, having once been engaged to her sister Anne, who had died tragically at sea. Robinson's wife, Emma, was a boring woman whose cares centred on her husband and children. "As they should," Mary always said when he complained about her conversation. Still, Sam reflected, surely the woman could read a newspaper and find something to comment on besides the weather. "Terribly cold this year," he heard her say to Sir Francis Bond Head.

Sir Francis's wife had still not arrived from England, and Mary had worried about the unequal number at table. "We could always ask Eliza," she said. "She and Emma Robinson are good friends."

"Sorry, my dear," he'd said, "your sister's laudanum habit and her thumps upon the pianoforte are too much for me at times. Emma Robinson will be more than enough in the boring female department."

He waited until everyone finished one drink—Jameson, two— then he pressed the ivory button on the side of the fireplace. The maid rushed in. "Tell Miss Siddons that we are ready for her and the girls." Then, turning to his guests, he added, "Our governess has a special treat for Valentine's Day."

Miss Siddons entered the drawing room on cue, curtsied, and introduced the two young girls who accompanied her. Ellen, aged twelve, and Emily, ten, had their mother's fair hair and blue eyes, and were dressed in matching white dimity dresses and stockings, though Ellen had a pink satin sash around her waist and Emily, a blue one.

"Ellen and Emily will recite one of Shakespeare's finest love sonnets," Miss Siddons said. The girls stepped into the middle of the room.

"'Shall I compare thee to a summer's day?'" Ellen asked.

"'Thou art more lovely and more temperate,'" Emily responded.

And on they went to the end, in a duet that Miss Siddons had obviously carefully planned and rehearsed with them. At the end, the adults clapped. Mrs. Jameson beamed. "Charming." Then she said, "It's one of my two favourites. The other is number one hundred and sixteen. But of course, you will not know that one by heart."

"'Let me not to the marriage of true minds, /Admit impediments.' Can you do it for the lady?" Miss Siddons asked. Ellen and Emily nodded.

Sam had never been happier about the money spent on the girls' education. To the best of his knowledge, he had not read or heard the sonnet before, but he sat back and enjoyed its lines now. It made the poem he had copied onto the card for Mary seem shallow and facile.

The girls' clear treble voices were sweet and eloquent, and they split the last two lines between them in a way that showed Miss Siddons's careful coaching.

"'If this be error and upon me proved,'" Ellen said, pausing while Emily took it to its conclusion, "'I never writ, nor no man ever loved.'"

Mrs. Jameson pulled a handkerchief from her reticule and wiped her eyes. "Even Fanny Kemble could not have done it better," she said. "Miss Siddons, you have trained the girls so well."

"I liked that line about love being a fixed mark that tempests cannot shake," Mrs. Fitzgibbon said. She looked towards her husband, who squeezed her hand.

At that moment, little Charlie came into the drawing room, dinner gong in hand. Sam had given him the honours for that night, and he had practised whacking it most of the afternoon. His small face was flushed, and after he had half deafened them all, he asked, "Did I do that good, Papa?"

"Well done, indeed, Charlie. You have made us all long for dinner. And now, if you will go belowstairs with Miss Siddons and your sisters, Cook will give you all a Valentine treat."

The invited guests moved to their places at Sam's fine mahogany table, laid with his and Mary's best Duesbury Derby china in green and gold, accented by white linen napkins and a centrepiece of red carnations from the conservatory.

"Fresh flowers," Mrs. Jameson said, "I have been here for two months, and not one fresh flower have I seen. I have pined for a bouquet, but I have not thrown out enough hints to my husband, alas." She smiled at Jameson, then leaned over the table and touched her fingers to the carnations. "They are exquisite."

"I arranged them myself," Mary said. "I too love fresh flowers."

Cook had set out the bottles of wine in the new burled walnut cellarette and put slivers of ice in the tin lining. Jameson and Sir Francis hovered for a moment to look at the evening's offerings, all of which Sam had selected himself from the vintner's best hoard. They had cost a pretty penny, but he noted with satisfaction the Governor's nod of approval.

"Your girls are well educated, Mr. Jarvis," Mrs. Jameson said. "I applaud your enterprise in providing them with such a superior governess."

"Excellent pea soup," was Mrs. Robinson's comment as she passed her bowl to Mary for an additional ladle-full. "Perhaps your cook could give my staff the recipe?"

There was a pause, punctuated by the sound of genteel slurping. Some more wine might liven things up, thought Sam. He motioned to the footman, who filled the glasses, then took the ham-and-egg pie from the rising cupboard and set it in front of Sam.

"Cook finds the rising cupboard so convenient, such a saviour of her poor arthritic knees," Mary said, no doubt to impress the Robinsons who, she told Sam, had a very old-fashioned kitchen.

"What are the serving classes for, but to serve?" was the Chief Justice's response.

"Excellent pie," Mrs. Robinson said. "Perhaps your cook might also include the recipe with the one for pea soup?"

Sam stifled a yawn behind his napkin.

Mrs. Jameson spoke up. "The viands served here in your elegant dining room are indeed excellent, Mrs. Jarvis, but sometimes the best meals are those that come to us totally by chance in the most primitive of circumstances. Do you agree, Mr. Jarvis?"

My god, thought Sam, she saw me yawn and has come to my rescue. He smiled at her. "Indeed, Mrs. Jameson. The best fare I have had this twelvemonth was a campfire meal in the wilderness with my Chippewa friend, Jacob Snake. It was roast moose kidneys, a hard biscuit, and a tin cup of strong tea and sugar."

"I remember Jacob Snake well. We had such fun that day on the lake with the snowsnake. Unfortunately, I have had no opportunity to practise since then."

"That was the day the Governor and I had our race on the lake," the Colonel said to the Robinsons, "and Mrs. Jameson shot out of my sleigh into the snowbank, just like a ball from a cannon and—"

Sir Francis leaned forward. "I must say that *my* best meal was taken in one of my gallops between Buenos Aires and the Andes. I stopped atop a mountain peak, and by the light of the moon dined royally on iguana roasted on a spit."

"Iguana, sir?" Mrs. Robinson asked.

"A huge native lizard, my dear." Robinson, like Sam, had heard the story before. "Very much like roast chicken, so the Governor says."

The footman removed the first course and set a side of beef with roast potatoes in front of Sam. He took up his carving knife.

The guests let the Governor drone on, until during a lull, the Colonel turned to Mrs. Jameson. "Do tell us, ma'am, about your favourite meal."

She told them about the overturned sleigh on her trip to Niagara Falls with her husband, and about the meal served up to them by the old woman at the Beamsville Hotel. Looking down at her plate, she concluded, "Yes, Mrs. Jarvis, because I was frightened, tired and hungry, it was as good as the excellent fare in front of me tonight."

Mary smiled. "I do understand, ma'am."

The hired footman set the third course in front of them. "Well," Mrs. Jameson said, as she leaned forward to look at it, "perhaps my old woman's offerings would be eclipsed by these." She pointed to the array of tarts: gooseberry, butter with raisins and nuts, and blackcurrant, accompanied by bowls of whipped cream within everyone's reach.

"Mmm," the guests said, almost in unison. Then from belowstairs came the heavy tread of someone climbing the steps to the dining room. In a moment, Cook entered, face flushed, snowy apron tied about her ample waist. On a huge Derby platter that she set down in the space near the red chrysanthemums was a jellied cream cut into the shape of a giant heart and sprinkled with red cinnamon candy.

Cook stepped back to admire her masterpiece. "Can't entrust this to that newfangled rising cupboard."

"Made with maple syrup from my own trees," Sam said as the guests applauded.

Even Jameson smiled and said, "Well done, indeed."

Later, over port, nuts and cigars, the Governor said to his male listeners, "You have all warned me of the danger of the reptile Mackenzie, and I know you will lend support in any action I may soon be forced to take."

He hooked his thumbs inside the pockets of his waistcoat, let loose a puff from one of Sam's fine Cuban cigars, and continued. "I must say of myself, however, that I am well fitted to assume charge of warring interests in Upper Canada, where both firmness and resolve are equally required." He paused, looked around the table, awaiting the murmurs of approval from his toadies.

Perhaps you can roast Mackenzie on a spit, like the iguana, Sam thought. Astonishing, really, how someone who had been in Upper Canada for a mere—what was it?—five months, had all the answers. Sam had lived all his life in the country and knew too well that simple solutions to complex problems did not work.

"Indeed, sir," Jameson said, picking up his cue. "Before you arrived in Toronto, I read in the English newspapers of your vigorous administration of the new poor law, how you protected your officers from enraged paupers who found the workhouse no substitute for the dole. All such insubordination, especially when it comes from the lower orders, must be suppressed."

Sam suspected irony here, but Jameson spoke in measured tones, and Sir Francis smiled, showing his brown teeth. He poured himself another glass of port.

Sam, as he looked down at the empty cellarette by his chair, remembered his bills. Time to be thankful to the Governor, who had given him a promotion that offered a partial solution to his problems. "You will be the man of the hour, Sir Francis," he said.

Robinson made a non-committal sound in the back of his throat. He was, after all, Chief Justice. One does not have to be obsequious when one has reached the summit. He cut himself a huge piece of Stilton and dipped the edge of it in his glass of port.

"There is one other matter, gentlemen, to which we must address ourselves before we join the ladies. Sir John Colborne left behind some details in his files about the Inspector General of Public Accounts."

"George Herchmer Markland, sir?" Sam asked.

"Him. Perhaps you can give me an opinion of his worth. I shall be interested in what you can tell me."

"A good fellow. He has been my friend for years." Markland had testified for Sam at the murder trial. While he and Sam had been walking arm in arm along King Street, Ridout had come out of the tavern and attacked Sam with a cane. "Dead drunk he was," Markland had told the jury, and he had given compelling evidence of how badly Sam's wrist had been injured by this act of violence.

"Why do you ask, sir?" Sam continued.

"Apparently my predecessor received rumours of...er... improper letters sent by Markland to a law-student named"—Sir Francis took a piece of paper from his waistcoat pocket and looked at it—"Frederick Muttlebury."

What on earth was the Governor talking about? "Improper letters, sir? I am at a loss as to what you mean. Markland is entirely honest. He was a classmate of mine at the Archdeacon's school in Cornwall and has always enjoyed an excellent reputation. He could surely not be involved in any financial skulduggery."

The Governor took a handkerchief from his vest pocket and coughed into it. "It was skulduggery of another sort. He gave a nervous laugh. Unnatural relationships, that sort of thing."

Robinson spoke up. "Markland is a good fellow, as Jarvis has said, very friendly—but now that I think of it, rather *feminine* in his speech and action."

"I will not involve myself in conjecture," Sam said. "I know from experience the damage done by scandal-mongering. If a viper like Mackenzie got hold of the rumour, it would sweep the town."

Fitzgibbon put in his penny's worth. "And really, Sir Francis, it's a tempest in a teapot, is it not?"

"Hardly. You surely know that sodomy is punishable by death."

"If everyone were punished for sodomy, our hangman would not have a day's rest. You have never lived in a barracks, Sir Francis, so you have not seen first hand what we seasoned veterans call 'Greek love.'"

"Greek love? What do you mean?"

"One of my men served under the captain of a British ship that sailed to Cyrene to plunder relics for the Prince Regent. There in the ancient ruins they found several statues of Apollo, all of which had identical faces, unlike anything the collectors on board the ship had ever seen before. Someone in Cyrene told them that a Greek had hired a sculptor to put the head of his lover onto the body of the god. Hence, 'Greek love.'"

"I see what you mean. But Cyrene is one thing. Toronto, another. We cannot have such goings-on here in a respectable outpost of which I am in charge."

"But these 'goings-on' are commonplace, Sir Francis. Two lonely men in a garrison far from congress with their wives may well turn to sodomy. I do not judge them. Indeed, when I reflect on it, I feel that the seduction of innocent young women by the Don Juans of the regiment is a far worse crime."

The Governor turned to Jameson. "We've heard nothing from you, sir. Do you know Markland?"

Jameson seemed preoccupied with the dregs of port at the bottom of his glass. "I've met him, of course. Everyone here knows the prominent men of our town. But I know nothing about his private life."

"I think, Sir Francis," Sam said, "that if Governor Colborne did not pursue the matter, you may take that as an indication of Markland's innocence."

From the drawing room came the sounds of the pianoforte, played in a manner equal to Miss Siddons's best performances—perhaps better. It certainly wasn't Mary. Or Mrs. Robinson, who had one number only in her repertoire, something she called "The Happy Farmer". Perhaps Mrs. Fitzgibbon? But then Sam remembered her blue-veined, arthritic fingers. So it was Mrs. Jameson.

"Shall we go to the drawing room?" he asked.

They entered just as Mrs. Jameson finished playing—something from *The Beggar's Opera*, was it?—and at the same moment, the yellow cat which had been lying by the fireplace jumped up on the back of the pianoforte. As it landed, it knocked off Sam's valentine, and the card fluttered down onto the keys, hitting the back of Mrs. Jameson's fine white fingers.

"Oh my," Mary said, blushing, "that is my dear husband's poem. He wrote it for me." She picked it up as it fell from the keyboard to the floor and held it for an instant to her cheek. "Do look at it, Mrs. Jameson. You are a writer, after all, and will appreciate its excellence."

Their guest took the card, admired the roses on its cover and looked briefly at the words on the inside. She turned towards Mary. Sam could see the raised eyebrows and the small smile that hovered on her lips for an instant, then disappeared. "So—Mr. Jarvis's poem. Very pretty." She set the card back on top of the pianoforte.

She knows, thought Sam. Will she say something?

"And now," Mary said, "while you are still at the pianoforte, will you and Mr. Jameson sing for us, if you please."

Jameson moved to the pianoforte, leaned over and whispered in his wife's ear. A soft chord, then he launched into the first line of the song: "Drink to me only with thine eyes..."

"And I will drink with mine," was her answer.

And so it went to the end, each taking a line, perfect tenor voice linked to sweet soprano. Sam moved close to Mary; and on the sofa, the Colonel held Mrs. Fitzgibbons's hand; Robinson and his wife turned in their adjacent chairs and smiled at each other.

The Jamesons seem so in love, thought Sam, as he listened. It's strange. Her face is so expressive and his so expressionless. Not a line in his cheeks or forehead, though he must be over forty. How do they get on together? She would be passionate, I believe, but he's such a cold fish.

The Governor rose to take his leave. They all stood up and bowed. Sam followed his guest into the hallway, where the corporal helped him into his coat and handed him his gloves and walking stick. He put on his beaver top hat, took a peek at himself in the mirror, adjusted his hat, and departed.

The other guests were now moving into the hallway. Sam noticed Mrs. Jameson looking towards the dining room. On impulse, he went straight to the table, plucked the carnations from the bowl, wrapped them in his linen handkerchief, and presented them to her.

"My dear Mr. Jarvis," the lady said, "I shall keep these in my bedchamber as a reminder of your kindness." She turned towards him then so that the other guests were behind her, and said in a low voice. "You may not be a poet, but as a gentleman, you are *sine qua non.*"

"What was Mrs. Jameson saying to you a moment ago?" Mary asked, when all the guests had left.

"One of her fancy Latin expressions. Don't know what it means, but I think it was a compliment. She liked my giving her the carnations." In fact, he did know. It was a phrase Robinson liked to throw around.

"She's so clever. And pretty, too, though you don't notice it at first. She and Mr. Jameson make a fine couple."

"He's lucky. In many ways. On his way up, so I hear. Rumour has it that by the month's end, he will be Vice-Chancellor of the new Court of Chancery. An extra twelve hundred pounds a year in addition to what he's already raking in. And his wife, undoubtedly she will settle in, perhaps become another Emma Robinson—though I can't see that—and live happily ever after as the Chancellor's lady. No children to support and no burden of debt to struggle under. I should be so fortunate."

"You sound bitter, Sam. Do you regret your children?"

He thought of Ellen and Emily and their performance of the sonnets, of little Charlie banging on the dinner gong, of the other children, of his pride in them. "No," he said, "I do not regret my children."

And, he added to himself, most of the time I do not regret Mary...

SIXTEEN

Anna heard the door of Robert's bedchamber shut behind him.
Well, that was that. She would spend St. Valentine's night
alone in bed. For an hour or two, she had hoped, that maybe the
music of their duet had touched him, that maybe he would feel
sentimental. But that performance had been pure theatre.

She put back into her trunk the contraceptive sponge she had
taken out earlier in the evening. She had been stupid to hope for
anything. The Niagara trip should have quenched any wayward
yearnings. But did a woman ever stop hoping to be loved? She
looked at herself in her mirror. Good skin still, red hair that set it
off, a narrow waist and full bosom.

Robert didn't give a damn.

She poured water from her pitcher into a vase and arranged the
lovely red carnations that Mr. Jarvis had given her. She folded the
linen handkerchief he had wrapped them in. She held it to her face
and breathed in his scent, an agreeable mix of fine burgundy and
imported cigars.

She put on her nightdress and climbed between the covers,
but before she closed her eyes, she heard the dreadful clang of an
alarum.

She ran to the window of her bedchamber and saw, perhaps
two blocks east of their residence, red flames against the black sky.
She rang for Mrs. Hawkins, but there was no answer, and when
she went to the head of the stairs and looked down, she noticed
that the fire buckets were not in their place in front of the main
doorway. Her housekeeper must have seen the fire even before the
alarum. She ran to Robert's room.

"Fire! Get up, Robert, we must go and see what we can do."

He sat up in bed. She could just make out his white nightcap in the gloom. "What are you shouting about?"

"Fire! Down the street. We must dress and go out and see if we can help."

"Nonsense. There are fires every other week in this place. What do you expect of a town made up of log houses? If I went out to them all, I should never get my rest. And I have an appointment with the Governor for tomorrow morning." The nightcap bobbed downwards.

She shut the bedchamber door then ran to the window again. In one direction, a full moon looked down upon the snowy landscape, and the icy bay glittered like a sheet of silver. Clouds of smoke and spires of flame rose into the sky. Far off, the garrison was beating to arms. Church bells tolled.

She threw off her nightgown and pulled on a dress and her heavy coat. She took her sealskin muff from the hook by the front door then made her way through the snow-heaped streets crowded with running, shouting people, and into a kind of court or garden at the back of the blazing houses.

A pitiful pile of furniture, bedding, pots, bottles and viands stood like a hillock in the midst, and a poor woman kept guard over it, nearly up to her knees in the snow. In the flickering light from the flames, her face seemed pale and wrinkled. Her figure was thin; a man's overcoat hung loose on her shoulders. She held a baby in her arms.

Anna climbed up onto a bedstead, on which was a feather mattress. "Come up here with me," she said to the woman. "You will freeze if you stay in the snowdrifts." But there was no response. "Hand me the child, then. I have a fur muff it will just fit into."

The woman looked at Anna, assessed the sealskin muff on her left arm, and passed the babe to her. He was a tiny, squalling bit of a thing with stick-like arms and spindly legs barely covered by a tattered nightshirt and a bit of cloth that looked as if it had once been a towel. He had soiled himself, and his legs were wet. Anna laid the infant on the mattress and took the muff from her arm.

She pushed the baby's legs into its aperture and tugged the length of it up over the tiny chest. His head she cradled in the sleeve of her coat. Warm now, the infant stopped his wailing. In a moment, he fell asleep.

So Anna stood on top of the bedstead, infant in her arms; the woman stood in the snow. Thus they remained till suddenly, with a terrible thud, part of the row of buildings fell in.

"This must be dreadful for you," Anna said, "to have to stand by and watch while your home is destroyed!"

"Yes, ma'am; but it's God's will, so they say. And now Jemmy's safe, I don't care for the rest. Jemmy's sister burned to death." She pointed to a small wrapped body, lying in the snow, over which Archdeacon Strachan and a sobbing woman kept guard.

"Is Jemmy your baby?"

"My sister's. Her man died yesterday of the fever, and now she has lost her little girl, only two years old."

Anna looked down at the frail bundle in her arm. If there is a God, she prayed, may he guard and protect this mite.

There had at first been a scarcity of water. Now she saw the bucket brigade in action. Holes had evidently been made through the ice on the lake. A double line of several hundred people had formed. Both lines extended from the lake to the buildings. One column passed water towards the burning rubble, and one column passed the empty buckets away from the fire back to the holes in the ice. In the lineup close to the burning buildings, she saw Mrs. Hawkins and her husband. They were swinging the buckets to people who stood so close to the flames that their clothes must have been singed.

"Here's Jemmy," Anna said to her companion. "Keep him warm in the muff. I don't want it back. I must go now and help the bucket brigade."

She ran towards the lineup and wedged herself in place behind her servants. "Lordy, lordy, it be you, ma'am, come to help us," her housekeeper said. "We surely can use all the bodies we can muster."

The pails of water came thick and fast. Soon Anna's shoulders ached from swinging them forward, but there was no stopping. At first, she tried to use her right arm, but then she learned to grab the pail with both hands, and move it to the left with one smooth motion, spilling nary a drop in the process. "Got the trick of it, ma'am," Hawkins said, as she swung a pail into his hands.

A sleigh went by her at full gallop. In the moonlight she could just perceive the extended form of a man with his hands clenched to his head. Dr. Widmer was beside him.

It was almost morning when the fires were finally extinguished. The bucket brigade began to disperse. "Go back home," Anna said to Mrs Hawkins, "and get into bed. I'll be along soon."

Through the smoke, she watched the crowd turn away from the charred and broken buildings, their faces smudged, their posture weary. It reminded her of a painting she'd seen, "The River". Where was it, Milano? In a room filled with pretty Madonnas and pretty Venetian landscapes, she'd come upon it, her attention caught by the brutality of the depiction. A hopeless, desperate crowd running from some long-ago disaster. Time to go to safety myself, she thought, but first I must check on Jemmy.

But the babe and his guardian were not where she'd left them. She could hear the Archdeacon's voice calling through the smoke. "Everyone into the church who needs help. You may sleep in the pews until we get lodging for you." His wife and some of the women from the congregation trudged by with kettles, probably of hot soup.

There was surely more she could do. She paused, uncertain of where to go next.

"Mrs. Jameson!"

It was Mr. Jarvis. His face was blackened with soot, and she might not have recognized him in the gloom, had it not been for his square, athletic body and the cut of the fine formal suit that he had worn—was it only a few hours ago?

"Can you help at St. James? I fear there will not be enough women to dispense the soup."

"Willingly."

There was a shout from nearby. Mr. Jarvis took her hand in his. "Thank you. And now I must help the sheriff. We have to carry people's belongings into sheds and taverns for safekeeping." He was off at a run.

At the church, she and Mrs. Strachan dragged tables from the vestry and put the kettles of soup upon them. Several women had brought a supply of crockery and ladles, and they turned to serve the dazed, stricken people who had begun to line up. Anna noticed the decorum of the crowd: no pushing, no angry words, though surely most of them had lost all their worldy possessions.

She was relieved to see Jemmy's guardian in the lineup for soup. In one arm she held the baby sound asleep in the muff, and her free hand clasped the shoulders of the sobbing woman Anna had seen earlier. Jemmy's mother: the poor soul who had lost two of her family in as many days.

Anna ladled soup into cups and put them on a small tray. "Follow me," she said, leading the little family to a choir stall. "Sit here, out of the crowd." She handed them the broth. "Drink it, even if you don't want it. It will help you."

"Oh, ma'am, you must not fash yourself. We are fortunate. Mr. Jarvis put our belongings into the horse shed at the tavern. And he give me a slip of paper so as we can claim them when this ree raw gets sorted out." The woman fished the precious bit of paper from deep in the muff, showed it to Anna, then put it back, safe with Jemmy.

Back behind the tables, Anna and two other women ladled out endless bowls of soup while Mrs. Strachan took offerings of food from people at the door of the church. Anna had no idea how much time had passed until she heard the Archdeacon's wife urge her to go home. "Nothing more can be done now, Mrs. Jameson. They have all been fed. And very soon, my husband will have enough billets for the most needy. The tavern keepers and gentry have been generous. Even Mrs. Powell has opened her doors."

Before leaving the church, Anna looked in on the trio in the choir stalls. Jemmy's mother was asleep, her tear-stained face smudged with dirt, her breathing ragged. Her sister had laid

Jemmy down on the bench, and when she saw Anna, she waved and put her fingers to her lips.

Anna trudged home. Her arms ached from swinging the buckets of water. Her feet were two blocks that she pushed forward. The stink of smoke hung in the air and pressed down on her lungs so that she could scarcely breathe. She thought of her first day in Toronto, of her dismay at finding that the house Robert had promised her was not completed. Now as she came in sight of the solid brick building he had provided in its stead, she could only feel thankful.

Almost at the door of her house, she saw Mr. Jarvis. "Just coming to inquire about you," he said.

"Safe and sound, as you can see. But what will become of the dispossessed?"

"Already—look over there—some of them are starting to clear away debris. Fortunately, there are plenty of trees ready to give up their lives to the rebuilding process. This block of houses will rise again."

"And were there many injuries?"

"Your husband's associate, poor Mr. Bedwell, had his leg so severely burned that Dr. Widmer had to cut it off."

"I think I saw the doctor in his sleigh and the unfortunate man stretched out upon it. I could hear his screams."

"Ten people died of burns and smoke inhalation, and of course, the living must contend with grief and trauma." Mr. Jarvis sighed and rubbed a smudgy finger across his brow. "I fear our jail will have its fill of the insane in the weeks to come."

What had the prison to do with the insane? Anna wondered. But she could not ask. Mr. Jarvis seemed utterly weary. "Good night, sir," she said and extended her hand.

"Dear Mrs. Jameson, you might have stayed here in your lodgings safe and comfortable, but you—a stranger in our midst— chose to help. I thank you from my heart." He hesitated for a moment, looking down at her. Then he leaned over and kissed her forehead. In a flash he was gone, lost in the haze of smoke.

Mrs. Hawkins appeared in the front hallway to take her coat. Her face was clean, and she had put on a fresh apron over her

soot-stained clothes, but the stink of smoke clung to her. "Oh
ma'am, I wondered where you be. I just filled the tin bath in your
bedchamber with hot water. Please to get in it right now."

"You go first, Mrs. Hawkins. And take your time. That is a
command. I shall be in the dining room."

Her husband was at the table, finishing the writing of a letter.
He had just blotted the page. When he saw her, he looked startled.
"I did not hear you, Anna." He folded the paper, and in his haste to
get it sealed, he dripped wax across the table's glossy surface. Then,
with the letter clutched in his hand, he strode to the mantel to
press the button. She could hear the bell jangle belowstairs, and in
a moment, Hawkins appeared. Like his wife, he had not had time
to change his clothes, and though his face and hands were clean,
his waistcoat and trousers were smeared with soot.

"Good god, man, you stink," Robert said. "Take this letter to
the legislative building at once, and when you return, change your
clothes."

"We must excuse Hawkins. He has been up all night hauling
water from the lake in an effort to try to save the dwellings of
those unfortunate people." Hawkins smiled, thanking her without
words. Then he bowed and departed with the letter.

"Really, Robert, what was so important that you could not leave
the poor man for a few minutes to tidy himself?" She looked at the
sideboard where Mrs. Hawkins had managed to supply an urn of
hot coffee and some oatmeal and raisin muffins. "Let's sit down
and eat."

"I gather, my dear Anna, from the aura of smoke that hangs
about you, too, that you were at the scene—as the writers in those
vulgar daily papers would say." He took the cup of coffee she had
poured for him.

"Oh, Robert, it was dreadful!" She spooned sugar into her own
coffee, drank it down in a gulp, and told him about the horrors of
the night.

"There is one good thing that comes from these terrible fires."

"What? I can think of nothing but the screams, the tears, the flames that devoured everything the poor wretches had in this world, the smoke, the—"

"Yes, yes, individuals suffer. But a fire is always a *public* benefit, is it not?"

She stared at him. Was the man mad?

"For every wood house that burns in this city, in time a good brick house is sure to rise in its place. Where this very block of five solid houses that we now inhabit stands, there was once, I am told, a miserable string of log huts. If these fires persist, we shall soon find a town of fine brick residences standing before our very eyes."

He took a sip of coffee and buttered a muffin.

"I cannot bear to think that any public benefit can be based on individual suffering. I hate the doctrine and am not convinced by the logic." She rose, shoved her chair against the table with a thud. "And now, Robert, I shall leave you. I have to wash and sleep. And you will want to enjoy another cup of coffee."

"A good idea, my dear. All the alarums kept me awake, and I must get myself into a calm frame of mind and think of what I shall say to the Governor at our meeting later this morning. Wish me good fortune, Anna."

The bathwater was tepid and smelled of ashes, but Mrs. Hawkins had left a fresh cake of soap and clean towels. Anna climbed into the tub. It was a small receptacle, and she had to bend her knees to fit into it. But the water made her feel better instantly. She got into her nightdress and crawled into bed.

She slept until she heard the case clock strike twelve o'clock. Heavens. Time to stir herself.

She dressed quickly and sat down at the table that served as her desk. She wanted to write while the horrors of the night were still vivid in her mind. She pulled the inkwell towards her.

She had got as far as the baby and its aunt when a knock came at her door.

"Excuse me, ma'am. I need to empty the tub. But I did not want to disturb you if you be sleeping."

Mrs. Hawkins went to the tub with her bucket and slopped

some of the water into it. But instead of taking the water belowstairs, she stopped by Anna's desk and set the bucket down on the floor. Her face was flushed. Her fingers picked at the fabric on her apron.

Anna put down her quill. "What is it?"

No answer. The housekeeper looked beyond Anna's table to the window behind her.

"Well? Speak out, please."

"The letter my husband took to the legislative building, ma'am."

"Yes?"

"It be to George Herchmer Markland, ma'am." More plucking of the apron.

"Well? What if it were addressed to…Samuel Taylor Coleridge? Really, Mrs. Hawkins, I cannot see that my husband's correspondence is anyone's business but his own."

"I don't know Mr. Cold Ridge, ma'am. But I do have tidings of Mr. Markland."

Anna pulled out a chair, motioned to Mrs. Hawkins to sit down, and said, "Something troubles you about Mr. Jameson's letter. Tell me about it."

The housekeeper sat on the edge of the chair. She had stopped plucking at her apron. Now she wrung her hands. "It be a story Hannah Pike told me, ma'am. She cleans the west wing of the Parliament, and she says there be some queer doings goes on in Mr. Markland's office most evenings."

"Yes?" Whatever was her housekeeper talking about?

Mrs. Hawkins had now placed her hands on the tabletop and was rapping the fingers of her right hand against its surface. Her top row of teeth gnawed her lip. She seemed unable to continue.

"Queer doings? Please explain."

Now it all came out in a rush. "Hannah Pike listened at the office door the other night. She said she heard such movements and such noises, the nature of which as convinced her there be a woman in the room." Mrs. Hawkins's face turned from pink to an alarming shade of magenta. "You take my meaning, ma'am?"

Anna took her cue from the woman's blushes. "Yes, on the whole I think I do. But what business was it of this Hannah Pike to listen at keyholes? And why would she care if Mr. Markland had a woman in his office? Perhaps she should attend to her mops and slop pails." Prostitution was evidently a commonplace in Toronto, just as it was in London. Someone had written a letter to the *Canadian Freeman* a week before about the "wretched and shameless depravity" of certain women "in our infant town".

"Oh, ma'am, the person who come out that door fifteen minutes later be no woman. It be a drummer from the garrison. Hannah recognized his white band uniform. And from what Hannah be telling me, there be others too, the Archdeacon's manservant and—"

"I believe I have heard enough, Mrs. Hawkins. And now I must ask why you are telling me this story?"

"Because you be a good woman, ma'am, and Hawkins and me thinks you should warn the master of the goings-on in that office."

"Thank you. But I must also warn you that it is unconscionable to engage in sordid gossip that may have no basis in fact and may harm the reputation of innocent people. Mr. Markland is the Inspector General of Public Accounts for Upper Canada and has, so far as I know, carried out his duties conscientiously and without a hint of scandal." Anna stood up, and her housekeeper rose at the same time, scraping her chair against the floor. "Go now, please, and focus your energies on household affairs."

"Oh, ma'am, I be sorry, so sorry. I didn't wish..." Mrs. Hawkins took the bucket of bathwater and moved towards the door, muttering apologies all the while.

Anna picked up her quill, but as the door closed, she threw it down again. Well, nothing could be proved. Robert might simply have had some pressing government business with Markland that required a letter to be sent at once. But she remembered his annoyance at her entrance to the dining room just as he was finishing it, the hasty way he had sealed it, and his desire to get it out of the way and into the hands of Hawkins for delivery.

And then she remembered the strange love sonnet that Hartley Coleridge had once written to Robert and his anger when he found her reading it.

All in all, she reflected, Mrs. Hawkins's news was not a surprise. Now she understood better her husband's lack of sexual interest.

"Wish me good forture," he'd said to her this morning. Perhaps today he would get his promotion. If so, she could leave him with a clear conscience.

She looked down at the notes in her journal and sighed. What a night. What a morning. She pressed her hand against her forehead. And touched the spot where Mr. Jarvis had kissed her. For a moment, she forgot the horrors and breathed in the cinnamon scent of red carnations.

SEVENTEEN

Mrs. Hawkins came into the drawing room, where Anna was putting the finishing touches to a sketch of the fire which she had drawn from memory.

Anna looked up. Her housekeeper had decked herself out in a pale blue cotton dress under an embroidered apron. "You look pretty, Mrs. Hawkins. What is the occasion?"

"Oh, ma'am, three o'clock it is, and if I'm not mistook, I believe the doorknocker will get some use this day."

"You think I'll have guests, do you?" Anna put her sketchbook and pencils down. Her housekeeper had a sixth sense about these matters.

"Sure, they'll all be along to have a chinwag with you now that the master be Chancellor. My man cleaned the silver trays and urns this morning, and I red up the house from stem to stern. Best put on your silk frock, if I may say so." As she spoke, Mrs. Hawkins knocked two cushions together and set them dead centre in the middle of the sofa.

Anna had barely got into her gown and straightened her hair when she heard a buzz of voices from the front vestibule. Taking a glance at herself in the mirror, she wiped a smudge of pencil from her cheek and made it to the head of the stairs in time to greet her visitors: Mrs. Powell, her daughters Eliza and Mrs. Sam Jarvis, and Mrs. John Beverley Robinson, wife of the Chief Justice.

"We come to pay our respects, dear Mrs. Chancellor, if I may call you that," Mrs. Powell said, shaking Anna's hand. "I heard the news last evening from the Archdeacon." She took a chair that offered her a clear view of the living-room, the hallway, and the dining room, while the others settled on the sofa. "We are, of course, not surprised at Mr. Jameson's promotion. He is universally respected."

Anna poured sherry from the decanter on the Pembroke table near the fireplace. Everyone sipped. There was a moment's silence.

"My husband mentioned your extraordinary help with the fire," Mrs. Jarvis said.

"I am seriously considering becoming a member of the volunteer brigade, now that I have mastered the delicate art of swinging a pail." As Anna thought of Mr. Jarvis's goodbye, she hoped that his wife did not notice her blush.

"I do not think that sort of volunteering would be advisable," Mrs. Powell said. "In his new position, your dear husband will now have an increased claim upon your affection, friendship and duty, and you must be the instrument to promote his comforts. You will be busy administering to his needs. You might, if you have any free time, consider some involvement with our main charities, the Society for the Relief of the—"

"Oh, Mama, Mrs. Jameson was making a joke." Mrs. Jarvis turned again to Anna. "And I am to tell you, so my dear husband said, that the mother whose poor little girl died in the fire is now in the jail."

"Jemmy's mother? What has she done, poor soul, that would send her to jail?"

"She has gone quite mad from grief, apparently, and her sister fears she may take her own life."

Ah, thought Anna. Now I understand why Mr. Jarvis said the jail would be full. "So, if I understand rightly, there is no institution for the insane in this town?"

"None. The mad go into the prison for safekeeping."

While they were talking, Mrs. Hawkins had come in quietly with the maple tea poy, and now she brought cakes and set them in front of Anna, who took a look at the array of baked goods. There was the usual excellent gingerbread, but today her housekeeper had tried something new. "Why, Mrs. Hawkins, what have we here? Derby cakes, to be sure. How...extraordinary."

Having made sure the guests had everything they needed, Mrs. Hawkins left the room, winking at Anna as she passed her chair.

Anna mixed the tea and poured boiling water over it. There was another silence while they all waited for it to steep. Then came sipping and nibbling.

Mrs. Robinson took a bite of one of the Derby cakes, chewed carefully and set the uneaten portion back on her plate. "Now that you are the Chancellor's Lady," she said, "you will undoubtedly find yourself presiding at a good many tea parties. May I respectfully suggest that my housekeeper send your Mrs. Hawkins her recipe for Derby cakes?"

"And may I respectfully ask what is wrong with Mrs. Hawkins's recipe?"

"Please do not take offence at this suggestion, but I recommend an increase in the amount of butter. And the raisins," at this point she touched her napkin to her mouth, "must be sultanas."

"If, as you say, the cakes need more fat, we have an excellent soap factory nearby. Perhaps they could supply a quantity of sheep's tallow. It would certainly be more economical than butter."

Eliza, who had helped herself to a second sherry from the decanter, giggled.

"Good recipes make for good living, Eliza," her mother said. "Your laughter is unwarranted."

There were footsteps on the staircase, and a few seconds later, Mrs. Hawkins's announcement: "Mrs. Widmer to see you, ma'am."

In the woman came, calling over her shoulder, "Please ask your man to bring a nosebag of oats to my horse." She was wearing a dust-coloured riding habit with large sleeves gathered at the wrist and a beaver hat trimmed with feathers.

Anna got up to greet her. "You have been out for exercise, I see."

"Along King Street East—past dear Mr. Jarvis's offices and the church. So exhilarating." She pulled up the short skirt of her habit to reveal in full a pair of white trousers and black half-boots. "Unlike the other ladies in this town, I do not ride side-saddle. I want full control of my steed." She let her skirt flop down again and moved into the room. "And now, Mrs. Chancellor, please be so good as to give me a cup of tea."

Mrs. Jarvis rose from the sofa, giving Mrs. Widmer a perfunctory nod. "Please excuse me. Mama, you and Eliza and Mrs. Robinson must stay if you wish, but I have a pressing engagement." She took Anna's hand, speaking to her in a low voice. "Will you come with me to the door, Mrs. Jameson? I have something to tell you."

At the bottom of the stairs, Mrs. Jarvis took her mantle and muff from the coat tree. "Dear Anna, I may call you Anna, mayn't I? I must explain why I'm running out. I cannot stand that woman. Well, you saw her in action at our Christmas party. She pursues my husband relentlessly. She rides up and down King St. every afternoon, her little white legs on full display, waiting for him to emerge from his offices."

"I suppose there is nothing you can do...Mary?"

"Nothing. Sam is indebted to Dr. Widmer in so many ways. He holds the mortgages on our land and supplies Sam with..." She broke off here, her face becoming very red.

"If I may say so, I saw nothing in Mr. Jarvis's deportment that would indicate he has the slightest interest in Mrs. Widmer."

"Oh, my dear, thank you for that." Mary pressed Anna's hand and opened the door. "I gather you do not have to worry about some hussy pursuing your husband, Anna?"

"No." Not a hussy, at any rate. Anna waited while Mary's coachman helped her into the carriage. As she waved goodbye, she thought about the Christmas party and wondered why Mary would worry about the Widmer woman. At the same time she remembered herself leaning over to put on her boots at the Jarvis's front door, and the fleeting glimpse she'd had of her host looking down at her legs. And there had been his kiss...

With a sigh, she mounted the stairs to rejoin her guests. With some effort, she hoped to get through the afternoon without pouring scalding tea down their ample bosoms.

EIGHTEEN

March and still not the slightest sign of spring. At the foot of the staircase, Anna donned her winter armour: coat, scarves, boots and the pattens she now found so necessary for her tramps through the snow. She put her hand on the door latch to go out, then paused. "Mrs. Hawkins," she called.

The housekeeper came to the head of the stairs. "What is it, ma'am?"

"I thought I could do what I have to do by myself, but I think I need you. Can you possibly put aside whatever you're doing and come with me to the jail?"

"The jail, ma'am?"

"To visit Jemmy's mother. You remember that Mrs. Jarvis said she'd gone mad and been incarcerated? It's bound to be a difficult visit, and I've never been in a jail before. I would be so glad of some moral support."

A few minutes later they set out, walking east along King Street. When they got to Toronto Street, Mrs. Hawkins pointed to a substantial, two-storey red brick building. "There it be, ma'am."

Anna noted its façade, topped by a pediment like that on a Greek temple, and the pilasters of cut stone on the front and sides of the building. "I suppose I should be impressed that Toronto's finest architectual achievement is a jail?"

They mounted the steps to the front door, passing the stocks—fortunately unoccupied—and just as Anna was putting up her hand to bang on the knocker, the door opened, and a man burst forth. He was an ugly little person with an ill-fitting red wig and a jutting chin, the bottom of which was fringed with a ragged beard. His cheeks were wet with tears.

"Oh ma'am, look. Mr. Mackenzie."

He did not hear Mrs. Hawkins's quiet remark. He was wiping his nose with a crumpled handkerchief and seemed oblivious to their presence.

So this poor man was the evil reptile so despised by everyone she'd met. She stepped aside to let him pass, and then, aware that she might never have another opportunity to speak to him, she said, "Good day to you, Mr. Mackenzie. May I introduce myself? I am Anna Jameson."

He looked at her fleetingly, his face contorted. "I'm sorry, ma'am, that it is not a time for making conversation. As you can see..." He ran down the steps.

The jailer, a man with a face that drooped like a bloodhound's, held the door open and watched his visitor depart.

"Whatever is the matter with Mr. Mackenzie?" Anna asked.

"He's been visiting the poor lad who's to be hanged tomorrow. Used to work in Mackenzie's print shop. Stole a horse he did. And Mac's been hoping for a reprieve from the Governor. No luck, though. Fine folk such as His Royal Highness got no time for the likes of a printer's apprentice."

"You call him 'Mac'. You know him well then, do you?"

"Everybody knows Mac. He stands up for the likes of us, and..." He seemed suddenly to remember that she was not one of his ilk. "And what is your business in this place, madam?"

"I've come to visit a young woman who has been incarcerated here because her sister thought she might take her own life."

"Mrs. Sykes, you mean. A sorry case." He motioned towards a staircase which led down to a place below the ground floor. "We keep the lunatics in the dungeon separate from the criminals and debtors in the main areas."

The explanation seemed scarcely necessary. Even before Anna and her housekeeper followed the jailer downstairs, they could hear incessant howling and groans. "Keep up quite a caterwauling, so they do," the jailer said. "I'm glad when Doc Widmer comes with the opiate. Shuts them up for a few blessed hours."

Anna put a perfumed handkerchief to her nostrils. She could scarcely breathe.

"What is that dreadful smell?"

"Privy's stopped up. Hope to see to it in the next day or two. But this jail is no place for a fine lady like yourself. Good enough for the scallywags that bide here."

"Mrs. Hawkins and I live in a clean, well-aired house. Perhaps the poor mad people here deserve something as good. Mrs. Sykes, as you must know, lost a husband and a child in two days' time. Surely she deserves compassion."

The jailer made a noise in his throat that came near to being a guffaw. "Tell that to the powers that be. I just do what they tell me." He gestured towards a corner of the dank, evil-smelling room they had just entered. "Take your time. Just come back up the stairs when you've had enough."

Coming from the bright sunshine reflecting on the snow, they took a minute or two to adjust to the gloom. The moans and screams led them towards two crib-like cages placed on a bed of straw. They were the size of the lions' cages Anna had seen long ago at a circus. Two women were chained to the bars at separate ends of one of these, and Mrs. Sykes was in the other. Her curly brown hair was matted and her face streaked with sweat, dirt and tears. Though she was not tied down, she could not stand up, the height of her cage being just enough to allow her to kneel and peer at them in the dim light.

"Do you know who I am?" Anna asked. There was no answer. "I talked to you and your sister the night of the fire —"

The poor woman's cries grew louder. She banged her head against the bars of the crib.

"Best sing something, ma'am," Mrs. Hawkins said. "Songs always soothe. Something they know." She thought for a minute, then began, "Rock of ages, cleft for me." Her voice was untrained but true.

Anna joined in. By the time she and Mrs. Hawkins got to the second stanza, the room's inmates had stopped howling. By the final stanza, they had formed a chorus, their voices loud and ragged:

> *While I draw this fleeting breath,*
> *When mine eyelids close in death,*
> *When I soar through tracts unknown*
> *See thee on thy judgment throne,*
> *Rock of ages, cleft for me,*
> *Let me hide myself in thee.*

"Again," Mrs. Sykes said. And the other two caged women had already begun the first stanza.

So they sang the hymn again and again and again. By the time Anna was wondering if she might go mad herself from the grimness of the lyrics, the three women, one by one, had fallen asleep. She and Mrs. Hawkins finished the last lines of the hymn, waited a few minutes to make sure all was quiet, then crept upstairs, where the jailer was waiting for them by the front door.

"What can be done for poor Mrs. Sykes?" Anna asked.

"Nothing. Lunatics is lunatics. I try to keep them from harming themselves and each other. That's it."

"Is their food wholesome?"

"It is what the town budget allows me. Nothing fancy. Water and three half pence worth of bread daily. Porridge on state occasions."

Mrs. Hawkins and Anna set out for home. For several blocks they said nothing, the only sound being the thump of their pattens in the snow. Then Mrs. Hawkins said, "I recognized Mrs. Sykes, that I did. Not more than a year back, she be making shrouds for the undertaker, Mr. Ross, just along the street here. The poor woman and her husband had put away enough to get on without Mrs. Powell and her do-gooders butting in. But now her man's gone, and what can she do? Shroud-making with her wits so scrambled? It don't bear thinking of."

"No. But if she has skills as a needle-worker, there's hope. Surely we can find something for her to do when she gets able to handle the grief of her losses. Meantime, I'm going to stop at that coffee house we passed earlier...what's its name?"

"The British Coffee House, ma'am."

"I'm going to order ale, some good roast beef, and fresh scones to be taken to Mrs. Sykes and the other two women each day. Once they've had good nutrition for a while, I'll see what can be done further." Anna had just that day received a few pounds in royalties from her British publisher. She would not have to ask Robert to fund an enterprise he would neither understand nor condone.

"I fear Mrs. Hawkins's fare is not up to its usual standard," Robert said that evening, looking down at his grilled lamb chop. "No mint sauce."

"My fault. I insisted on her accompanying me to the jail this afternoon."

"My god, Anna, what will you do next?"

She told him about her visit. "Does it not seem to you, Robert, that the justice system is skewed? I have had very little to do with the laws of the land. But now I have plunged with both feet into a mess. This very day I saw three insane women locked into cages in a dungeon. And I heard that a man is to be hanged for stealing a horse—"

"While murder among gentlemen goes unpunished. Only yesterday I met a member of the King's Bench who four years ago murdered a friend in a duel, and is now cock of the walk. And of course you know Sam Jarvis's story. But that duel happened in 1817, and one would like to say that things have changed. They haven't." Robert shook his head as he put a piece of the lamb chop into his mouth.

"And sodomy is punishable by death. I heard that from someone. Does that not frighten you, Robert?"

His knife and fork clattered onto his plate. "Why do you bring up sodomy? Sometimes I find it hard to keep track of your *non sequiturs*."

"You sent a letter in February, just after Valentine's Day if I remember correctly, to George Herchmer Markland."

"And what business is that of yours?" He tried to pick up his fork again but stopped. She watched his trembling hand.

"Markland's office is, so I am told, the place of meeting at night for young men of the lower classes: a drummer boy, a private from Fort York, and one of the Archdeacon's servants."

"*Who* told you this?"

"You gave the letter to Hawkins to deliver. Naturally, he remembered what he had heard about Markland, told his wife, who also had heard rumours about the man, and she told me. It took considerable courage for Mrs. Hawkins to speak on such a subject."

"Ah, servants' tittle tattle."

"No doubt, but I tell you this merely to caution you to be careful in your dealings with George Herchmer Markland."

"Point taken." He gave up his attempt to eat, pushed his plate away, the lamb chop half consumed. "I agree with you on the whole, Anna. The justice system is skewed. Why should Markland—if he is a sodomist, and mind you, I am not saying he is—fear a death sentence while murderers go unpunished? But my public responsibility is to uphold the laws of this land, whatever my private views may be. I am not a crusader. It is my conservative approach to law that has won me the most prestigious appointment in Upper Canada."

"'Forward with the status quo.' That must be your battle cry, Robert."

"Very funny. And now, if we can get onto another topic, let me give you some news you may find welcome. Our lease on this place runs out in three weeks. But no matter. The carpenters are finally back on the job after an extended break for things they considered more important than my needs. So—three weeks from today, we move into that pleasant little house I promised you when I wrote asking you to come here. "

It was her turn to push her food away. "This isn't news. This is a ton of bricks you've just dumped on me. You expect me to move into this place with you?"

"Now that I am Vice-Chancellor, it is even more necessary to maintain appearances. You must stay by me through the period when I am getting established in my new position."

"What about all the money wasted on making this place livable?"

"That was your bright idea, was it not?"

"And now you want me to put this new place in shape? You surely do not believe that I have settled into my Mrs.-Chancellor-happily-ever-after role?"

"For the sake of the money I give you, if for no other reason, I expect you will stay. If you leave, you will have nothing but the money you make from your books and your etchings. And may I remind you that under law, I could take every cent of that, too."

Anna stood up. Remembering the servants belowstairs, she strove to keep her voice controlled. "I shall stay for a while, Robert, but do not for a moment think that your threats have in any way influenced my decision."

It was true. If he seriously thought of taking her small income to add to his own immense salary, she could make things unpleasant for him. But she doubted that he meant anything much by that remark. He had more than enough money for his needs. Of greater import at the moment were her own inner wishes. She needed his money, yes. But everything considered, she had no great desire to leave Upper Canada immediately. Mrs. Sykes would need her ongoing attention for a while at least. And there was that great wilderness to the north of Toronto that she wanted to explore. It would be splendid material for her book. And...well, face it, there was Sam Jarvis, someone she wanted to know better.

NINETEEN

On his recent walks along King Street, Sam had noticed piles of neat birchbark baskets of maple sugar in Job Crimshaw's store. "Mokuks," Jacob Snake called them, and they signalled the probable arrival of Jacob and his Chippewa band at the stand of sugar-maple trees not far from the garrison. Each year, about this time, they travelled from Snake Island in Lake Simcoe to this spot for the weeks of sugaring-off.

He thought of Mrs. Jameson's research into Indian customs. She might be interested in a trip to the bush. She would never before have seen the sugaring-off process. Mary was visiting her mother for the day, Mrs. Siddons had taken the children skating on the lake, and he had time on his hands.

He looked at his pocket watch: there were still several hours before sunset. He left a note for Mary then pressed the ivory button on the drawing room mantel. Cook's helper came clattering up from belowstairs. "Tell the coachman to be at the front door in half an hour."

He had just time to change into a knee-length woollen coat, the buckskin leggings that Jacob's wife had once made for him, and moccasins. He took two pairs of snowshoes from the armoire in the back hall, and he was ready. "Drive to Bishop's Block on Newgate Street," he told John. The town gossips would note the destination of his sleigh, but what of it? If challenged, he would point out his need to keep in touch with the Indians and talk of Mrs. Jameson's research for her book.

He sent in his card, telling the manservant about the visit. In a minute, the man was back to say that "madam" was anxious to come along. Sam sat in the sleigh and waited, resigning himself to whatever length of time it would take the lady to get ready. He was used to female dithering. To his surprise, Mrs. Jameson was ready in a quarter hour, dressed in enough layers for an excursion to the North Pole. As the coachman helped her into the sleigh beside him, he noticed her footwear.

"And where did you get those moccasins, Mrs. Jameson?"

"The Indians come regularly to our door. Thanks to them, we have had a supply of fresh salmon all winter. And they're always ready to barter other things as well. I asked my housekeeper to swap a pound of butter for these. Pretty, aren't they? And so comfortable."

She poked her foot out from under her long coat. He looked at the moccasins and at the heavy stockings she wore and remembered the slender leg he had glimpsed at the Christmas party. He also thought of Mary's legs, always encased in elegant boots.

At the garrison, he gave his driver some coins. "Get yourself a drink in the mess, and keep warm there till we return." Then he strapped on his snowshoes, showed Mrs. Jameson how to attach hers, and they set out along the lakeshore.

She caught on to the technique quickly, saying only, "They're a bit like the pattens a giant might wear." After half an hour of slogging through the damp snow of late winter, they smelled the Indians' campfires.

"What on earth is that delicious scent?"

"It's burnt sugar. Isn't it wonderful? I remember it from the time I first went into the sugar bush with Jacob's grandfather. I must have been five or six at the time, and I had a little buckskin coat and breeches which the grandmother made for me. I was so proud of myself, I wanted to be an Indian in those days, and my mother tells me that she paid someone to do a drawing of me. She doesn't know exactly what happened to it in their move from Niagara to Toronto. I wish I knew, it would be amusing to see it."

Mrs. Jameson started to say something, but Sam's attention strayed to the Indian encampment close at hand. "Here already," he said, pointing.

As they came towards the first wigwam, Sam saw a familiar figure carrying an iron pail. At the same instant, one of the sled dogs barked, and his friend looked towards him.

"Nehkik!"

"Jacob!"

Jacob set down his pail and grasped Sam by the arm. "And you, Mrs. Jameson. I am glad to see you in the dark bush." He took her hand. "How do you like the snowshoes?"

"Not as much fun as the snowsnake, though they get me through the snowbanks well. But I've got very thirsty from all this exercise."

Jacob unhooked a tiny birchbark cup from a braided buckskin rope around his waist. "Then I offer you refreshment." And he dipped the cup into his pail and held it towards her.

She drank deeply, seeming to savour the clear liquid. Then she said, "Wonderful. It's so cold and sweet, just like the freshness of the woods and the scented air." She handed the cup back to Jacob, who filled it a second time and gave it to Sam. Sam had always loved the taste of sap, and here and now in this setting, it seemed better than the finest Spanish sherry.

"Please," Jacob said, "you come now to my wigwam and see the old lady." He led them back along a well-trodden path through the bush. They came to the centre of a grove, where the sap was boiling in a huge copper kettle, suspended by a chain attached to a low branch of a pine tree. Piled-up logs burned away under the bucket, and a dozen children ran back and forth heaping branches on the fire. From all sides of the grove, men and women carried sap pails to a large store-trough at the boiling place.

Behind the grove, they arrived at Jacob's wigwam, built of a triangle of upright posts covered in skins. They propped their snowshoes against the exterior, Jacob pulled aside a blanket over the opening, and they entered. The interior was dark and sparsely furnished. There was a covering of hemlock boughs over the ground, and on a reed mat, a little girl was playing with a corncob doll. Beside her, on another mat, an old woman boiled soup in a small cauldron suspended from a cross-pole.

"My mother," Jacob said to Mrs. Jameson. Sam had met her long ago. He bowed, removing his fur cap. "And my daughter," Jacob continued. "I tell you her Indian name—" Here Jacob pronounced five incomprehensible syllables which he translated as "sunbeam breaking through a cloud".

In one corner of the wigwam was a small painted chest beside a birchbark box filled with tin dishes and wooden spoons, and someone had pegged a pretty embroidered shawl of deerskin against the vertical posts. Sam counted seven neatly folded blankets piled on another mat. He knew Jacob had four children. The other girl and the two boys were probably outside somewhere gathering wood for the sugaring-off fire. And then there would be Chief Snake, Jacob's father, and the old woman whom he had introduced as his mother. Seven people in this small space. Yet everything was clean and well ordered.

It was warm in the wigwam. Sam and Jacob removed their moccasins and coats. Sam pulled two pipes from his pocket and offered one to his friend. "Would you like one, too, Mrs. Jameson?" he asked.

"No, I thank you."

They all sat crosslegged on the hemlock boughs, and the men smoked in silence for a few minutes. Jacob's mother smiled as she hummed a song and stirred her pot, and his daughter crept over to him and snuggled onto his knees. She had bright brown eyes and a merry face.

"I understand why you call her a sunbeam," Mrs. Jameson said, smiling at the child. She took a peppermint from a reticule hidden beneath her coat and gave it to the girl. Then she settled again beside the men. Sam liked the fact that she seemed completely at ease. It was hard to imagine Mary fitting in so well in these alien surroundings.

He noticed that Jacob no longer had black daubs on his face, but his eyes were sad. "You miss your wife, Jacob."

"Yes, Nehkik, man without woman is not a whole man. But we manage. When the spring comes, I marry again. A fine young woman, sister of my friend, Elijah White Deer."

"I am happy for you."

"A wedding in the spring," Mrs. Jameson said. "How pleasant to start a new life when nature, too, renews itself. And do you have a ceremony like ours?"

"I do not know about white man's ceremonies." Nor care to, seemed to be his unspoken comment.

"I shall not go into the whole affair," the lady said. "But I wonder if the Indians swear as we do 'to have and to hold, for better for worse, for richer for poorer, in sickness and health, to love and to cherish till death do us part.'"

"We cannot promise to love our wives until death. Such an oath we may not be able to keep, and Indians do not make promises we cannot keep."

"Very wise, indeed. I wonder how many white men love their wives for more than a year or two beyond the oath-taking. But perhaps you are better fitted to judge that than I am, Mr. Jarvis?"

Sam felt himself blush. "I cannot comment. It is impossible to conjecture." What was the woman getting at? Was she making some judgment on his own marriage, about which she knew nothing? He turned to Jacob. "Now tell me, friend, are your people somewhat better off now that you can sell your mokuks?"

"We barter maple sugar for flour and butter, sometimes for money. And yesterday, we shoot two fine deer, so we have plenty to eat." Jarvis paused, as if to consider what to say next. "But all is not better..." His voice trailed off. Sunbeam put her small arms around his neck and rubbed her face against his cheek.

"Tell me what's wrong, Jacob."

"We give white man a cure for scurvy. We show him how to make canoes and snowshoes. We teach him to tap trees, to grow pumpkin, squash and tobacco. And what does white man give us in return? Alcohol."

Sam had heard about drunken Indians all his life, but never from Jacob. "Why are you telling me this?"

"You are a friend. You are not like that dirty dog, Crimshaw."

Ah, the King Street merchant who bought the mokuks. Sam knew him well. He himself was in debt to Crimshaw for the imported wines he liked so well. He was a mean rascal who drove a hard bargain. Sam had heard rumours of how he plied the Indians with cheap liquor. Drunk, they gave him their furs, fish, and maple sugar for next to nothing. Still, the man was not all bad. He had only last week given Sam an extension of two months on substantial debt. Perhaps he had been impressed by the news of Sam's promotion.

Sam reflected that "drunken savage" was one of the favourite epithets for an Indian among Toronto's upper classes. And yet most of his white friends also drank to excess. He was about to confess something of this nature to Jacob when the lady said it for him. "Alas, alcoholism is the scourge of both the white and brown races."

The old woman tending the fire said something in her native tongue.

Jacob replied, then turned back to Sam. "Elijah White Deer is sick. Perhaps later this day, I show you the evil that Crimshaw does. But first, my mother wants to give you and Mrs. Jameson a cup of broth."

It was an excellent soup of venison and Indian corn, followed by a chunk of maple sugar sliced from a mokuk which the old woman kept in the painted chest. And there was tea too, strong, hot and flavoured with maple sugar. They all ate with a hearty appetite, and Jacob seemed to put aside his cares and enjoy it too. His mother sat with them by the fire.

At the end of their meal, the old woman put some pieces of dried salmon into a bark packet, which Jacob put into his deerskin pouch. "Food for Elijah," he said.

Then Jacob took them outside into the snow. Mrs. Jameson stopped at a large maple tree. Sam waited for the inevitable question. "Will you show me how the Chippewa tap the trees?"

"See," Jacob said, pointing to where a pine trough had been placed directly under the drip. "First we make a hole in the tree with this. I do not know white man's name for it."

"Auger," Sam said.

"Then we drive this into the hole." Jacob indicated a round spile, hollow in the centre. "Better always to tap on the warm side of the tree. Warm days, frosty nights, good syrup."

They watched Jacob's strong hands touch the tree bark gently. "You told us that the Indians showed white settlers how to tap trees," Mrs. Jameson said. "I gather they did not at first have the Indians' skill?"

"Long ago, my grandfather tells me this story. He says white man takes axe and gashes tree, starts sap flowing, then tree dies from pain." He shook his head as if he could not believe such ignorance.

"There is nothing a Canadian settler hates more than a tree," Mrs. Jameson said, and she told Sam and Jacob of the devastated bushland she'd seen on her trip to Niagara Falls.

"You have a flair for reducing complex issues to a simple sentence," Sam said. He knew his voice had an edge.

She did not respond, perhaps sensing his sarcasm. Jacob intervened. "Let us go and meet Elijah White Deer." They tramped back past the collection grove and deep into the bush. There were no footprints now, only the ones made by their own moccasins. They came to a wigwam, the door of which was covered by a filthy blanket. Jacob pulled it aside, and they entered.

Every part of the habitation was dark and wretched. There was not a single article of furniture, only a dirty blanket on the muddy floor, on which was sprawled a sleeping man, arms flung out, as if he had fallen on his back. His snores were loud, and from his open mouth came the unmistakable stink of cheap whiskey. A mound of excrement lay in one corner.

"And Crimshaw is responsible for this?" Sam struggled not to put his handkerchief over his mouth and nose.

"Two weeks ago," Jacob said, "my friend goes to town with the dogs and sled full of mokuks. Crimshaw gives Elijah tobacco and offers glass of whiskey. 'No,' Elijah says. So he leaves him alone and talks to his customers. Then he says to Elijah, 'Have a glass of cider.'"

Sam sighed. He knew what was coming.

"Elijah drinks. But it is not cider, really. It is cider mixed with strong alcohol, and Elijah has had no food. His mind goes crazy. He has two and three, maybe more. Crimshaw takes all of Elijah's mokuks and gives Elijah ribbons and a bottle of whiskey. He does not come back to camp. I go look for him, find him stone cold on the shore of the lake, sled upside down, empty bottle beside him." He set the birchbark packet of salmon beside his sleeping friend and arranged the blanket around him more securely. Then they went back into the camp.

The sun was sinking. "We have to get back to the garrison," Sam said. "But first I must buy some of your excellent maple sugar."

"I, too," Mrs. Jameson said. "My housekeeper makes a delicious maple sugar pie. I have never tasted anything better."

Jacob and another Indian put the mokuks of sugar into two slings for carrying. Then Sam and the lady strapped on their snowshoes, and Jacob accompanied them to the lake's edge. In the distance they could just see the garrison. "Before I say goodbye, my friend," Sam said, "I ask you to be steersman of my canoe when I go to Manitoulin Island this summer for the gift-giving ceremony. It is an important time, and I want you to be part of it."

For the first time that afternoon, Jacob's smile broke through. "It will please me, Nekhik. And may the Great Spirit guard and protect you this day and forever. And you, too, Mrs. Jameson." He grasped their hands.

They plodded in silence through the melting snowdrifts along the shore. Mrs. Jameson had insisted on carrying one of the slings, and the added burden slowed their pace.

"You are angry with me, I think," the lady said as they paused for a moment to lean against a tree and shift the position of their slings.

"Angry? Well, perhaps I am. You are a newcomer to our land, yet you take pleasure in making judgments on us. 'There is nothing a settler hates more than a tree.' 'Alcoholism is the scourge of both the white and brown races.' And what was the other thing? Oh yes,

'How many white men love their wives for more than a year beyond the oath-taking?' For Jacob to make judgments on us, that I can understand. His people were here long before the white settlers arrived. But you... After two months you have all the answers. You—"

"But I am right, am I not? Look at the drinking at those parties I've attended. Are any of your friends sober by the end of the evening? Are *you* sober, for that matter? The only difference between a drunken Indian and a drunken white man is that the Indian has to drive his own dogsled home while the white man has his coachman to steer him in the right direction. And the devastation of the trees, why Mr. Campbell, who has lived here all his life, agrees with me. You should go oftener beyond the confines of your smug little town, get out into the settlements, see what is happening to the forests." Her words lashed his face along with the snow that had started to fall.

"And what about the broken promises of marriage?" Sam replied. "What makes you an authority on that, you who can afford to look down on the rest of us from your perch as the Chancellor's Lady? You understand nothing about the demands of child-rearing, the stresses of debt—"

"Oh, Sam, if you only knew... I'm sorry. I've spoken rashly. Don't be angry with me. Please."

"Sam, you called me Sam." He stopped in his tracks, put out his hand and touched her sleeve. "Dear Anna, I am not angry. It's just that what you say strikes too close to home. I confess that I no longer know the meaning of love. It is so buried under the burden of family life, of expenses, of unfulfilled needs and aspirations. Do I love Mary? Does Mary love me? If you asked me that point blank, the answer would be 'yes', but what would I really mean?" He paused, trying to sort his thoughts. "To have and to hold, for better for worse, that part is clear. The rest of it—that stuff about loving and cherishing—too high-flown for me."

She smiled then. "Don't worry about it. The scholars who wrote *The Book of Common Prayer* liked the sound of their own words. As a writer I understand that. Like them, when I come up with a felicitous phrase, I'm so happy, I can't bear to throw it away—even when it's not exactly *a propos*."

"Not sure what you're getting at, Anna." Now that he'd come out with her name, he couldn't say it often enough.

"Listen to the rhythm." Slowly she intoned, "'To love and to cherish till death do us part.' They've followed up the iamb—"

"The what?"

"I-a-m-b. It's followed with three anapests, a-n-a-p-e-s-t-s, a perfect rhythm to show rising emotion. The literal meaning is totally subordinated to the sound."

"No idea what you're talking about. I'm as lost as any drunken Indian who has no coachman to steer him home."

Doubled over now with laughter, they tipped forward, grasping each other's arms to stay upright. He was so close to her. He could feel his prick rising. Then Anna pointed into the distance, through the falling snow. "The garrison doesn't seem to be getting much closer. Dear Sam, I suppose we'd better get moving before this idiocy goes any further."

So they set out again. As they plodded onward, he found himself making a confession. "You know, Anna, perhaps this new posting which I have—this Chief Superintendent of Indian Affairs—is not suited to a white man. My friend knows my language, you have heard how well he speaks it, but I know nothing of his. And today I have seen first hand the sordidness caused by white man's treatment of his people. It will not be an easy job to build bridges."

"But surely today Jacob has given you a start for that bridge building."

"What do you mean?"

"Job Crimshaw has mistreated Elijah, and I think we can believe what Jacob tells us. So perhaps..."

"Perhaps I should speak to Crimshaw and chastise him for giving alcohol to a vulnerable man in order to gain a profit for himself?"

"Exactly."

They had reached the garrison, where the coachman awaited them. No further discussion was possible as they set off towards town. It was pitch dark by the time they reached Anna's house. "Thank you for showing me the Indians at work in their sugarbush," she said as he helped her down from the sleigh. "It was an enjoyable outing, the last I shall probably have before I give myself over to things domestic." She leaned in towards him, lowering her voice. "I know you will do what's best in regard to Crimshaw. One more thing. You accused me of easy judgments. And now I caution *you*. Do not be too quick to judge *my* married life."

What did she mean, Sam wondered as the sleigh turned east towards Hazelburn. He tried to remember what he had said to her in his anger. Something about looking down on his married life from her perch as Chancellor's Lady? Did she mean that her own married life was not as perfect as it seemed?

Probably he was reading too much into her comment. And yet...she had called him Sam. And had not rebuked him when he'd said, "Dear Anna".

The servants had lighted the oil lamps, and the warmth from the fireplaces was welcome. Miss Siddons and the children had already had their supper, so Sam and Mary sat down alone to poached salmon with butter sauce, served on pretty green-patterned stoneware.

Mary passed him fresh rolls wrapped in a linen napkin. "Cook tells me the Indians were around this afternoon with fresh fish," she said. "Hence this excellent supper." She put another bit of salmon onto her plate.

"And what does Cook trade in return?" Sam asked. He was thinking of the packet of dried fish which Jacob had left in the mud and stink of Elijah's wigwam.

"For six large salmon, she told me they got flour and some freshly churned butter."

"It sounds fair enough." Then he told Mary about the bargain

Job Crimshaw had made with Elijah White Deer. "Tomorrow I intend to see that swine and set him straight. He gives all of us a bad name. In fact, with every mouthful I eat, I think of that poor Indian lying there in his piss. One thing I know, I will serve Jacob and his people to the best of my ability. If Crimshaw does not stop the abuse of the natives, I personally will make him into mincemeat."

"But surely there is nothing we can do about drunken savages. Give them one drink, then they will have another and another. If they don't get drink from one source, they'll find another. You must think this through carefully. You have debts with Job Crimshaw. If you get into a quarrel with him now, about what is really none of our affair, what will be the result? He may decide to call in the amount you owe. And then what will you do? Mortgage some more land? Get into more debt? At least wait a few days and think it over. Promise me. Please."

"I will give no promises."

With a sigh, Mary left the room without finishing her dessert. He could hear her climb the stairs. He lit a cigar. Its fragrant scent soothed him. Perhaps, he thought, Mary is right after all. It might in fact be a good idea to wait before I speak to the scoundrel. He does have the power to make matters difficult for me if I take him to task at this moment. Better not to stir the pot too vigorously until I'm well established in my new position.

He inhaled his cigar and reached for the bottle of port.

TWENTY

The "pretty little house" that Robert had offered as an enticement in his letters was certainly pleasant, or at least it would be when the weather was less cold and comfortless. It was simple in design, and its best feature was the southern frontage where four large windows overlooked Lake Ontario. Better fitted than the windows in their rented row house, these had no collection of snow on the inner sill. But the scene outside reminded her of the ninth circle of Dante's *Inferno*, where Judas and Brutus and other traitors are totally immersed in ice. If spring ever comes to this frozen world, she thought, I will plant a flower garden. I will, like Dante, climb up to "look once more upon the stars".

As a consequence of the move, she was forced to put aside her translations, etchings and writing. "If I have to undertake the stitching of one more set of curtains or the measurement and placement of one more carpet, I will do something quite unbefitting my role as Chancellor's Lady," she said to Mrs. Hawkins.

"Oh, ma'am, there be two more sets of curtains to hem, but before you and me both go barmy, I have a suggestion."

"Out with it."

"Why do we not try Mrs. Sykes?"

"Mrs. Sykes? What a splendid idea. She has improved so much with good food and the comforts we provide on our visits. But how would we arrange—"

"Easy, ma'am. We take the goods to her along with the needles and thread, and we arrange for a body, perhaps her sister, to keep an eye on her so that she not be harming herself with the needles. And we bribe the jailer to let her upstairs to sit on a chair and stitch—"

"And we pay her for her work, if she can do it. Perfect. And can you set it up, Mrs. Hawkins?"

In two days, Mrs. Hawkins came back from the jail with the curtains. Mrs. Sykes had hemmed them with tiny perfect stitches, and though they were a trifle dirty from the dirt on the floors in the jail, all in all, the plan had worked well. "And now, ma'am," Mrs. Hawkins said, "I be getting to work with that herbal bath I made up from the soapwort, good for delicate fabrics it is, and all will be well."

Though Anna liked the house on the whole, its size bothered her. Robert had made no arrangements for friends. The dining room was small, and there was no space for dancing or for musical evenings. She thought of the Jarvis establishment with its conservatory, spacious reception areas, library, and—so Mrs. Powell had told her more than once—six bedchambers.

As she and Robert ate their supper, she tried to draw him out on the subject of space. He had been in a foul mood before their meal. The front of the house was so completely blockaded by ice and mud that to reach the door was a matter of some difficulty. A stone walk would be laid in the spring, but for now Hawkins had put down planks to give access to the front door. This evening Robert had slipped off a plank into the snow and mud. His boots and fine striped pants were as filthy as his humour. He had stamped his boots all over the new carpet. Now, however, Mrs. Hawkins's excellent meal of pork chops and roast potatoes, completed by her maple sugar pie, brought a rare look of contentment to his face.

"Where will we put visitors who might stray this way?" Anna asked. "You have built only two bedchambers."

"There are hotels, my dear. I understand the Black Bull & Drovers' Arms is quite a respectable establishment." Robert put down his napkin.

"Oh, very respectable, no doubt." Anna had seen the place, a frame building with a creaking sign showing a black bull. In front was a wooden horse trough. "All the best farmers from the north and west stay there. I am quite certain that our friends would enjoy the stink of cow manure and the ale spilled upon the floor. And I understand there is always room for one more in the place. Colonel Fitzgibbon told me that one of his military friends stayed there—"

"Well then, my dear, if one of the Colonel's friends recommended it, I am sure you can have no higher accolade—"

"Let me finish, Robert. You don't understand much about Toronto hotels. The man was sound asleep when he was awakened by two young girls who appeared in the room. 'Please, sir,' they said, 'we be the innkeeper's daughters, and Papa has lent you our room, the inn being so full up this day. So you must make a place for us, sir.' So how were the three of them to sleep in one bed? According to the Colonel's friend, they had to position themselves crosswise along the length of the mattress in order to have enough room for three bodies."

"Well, there's the solution to our problems, don't you see? If your dear friends—let us say Ottilie von Goethe and Henry Burlowe—should arrive at the same time, could they not lie crosswise with you in your bedchamber?"

She had a sudden vision of Sam Jarvis and Jacob lying crosswise with her on her bed. She laughed out loud.

"I'm glad you enjoy my small joke, Anna. Now, how about some music?"

She played the piano and sang "Casta diva" from *Norma*, which she and Robert had seen together at Haymarket, London, in 1833. She turned the pages of her music and watched her husband drain the dregs from his wineglass. Mrs. Hawkins was right. Songs soothed—not only insanity, but her own sorrow.

For the next two weeks, the ice in the Bay of Toronto stayed four to five feet in thickness, though the snow had begun to disappear and the flocks of snowbirds with it.

"Perhaps spring will come," she said to Mrs. Hawkins one morning, "and this long winter's imprisonment will end."

"Sure, it will come. There be a large sky this day." Her housekeeper pointed out the front window at the expanse of blue which made the white-covered lake so dazzling that Anna had to cover her eyes and turn away.

"And the savages—beg pardon, ma'am, the Indians—come this morning to swap a brace of quails for a pound of butter. A sure sign of spring. And I be plucking them birds now for your dinner."

"And I see that Hawkins has just finished laying the oak planks in the dining room. Truly, without his help, the joiner would have taken at least two more days to do the room. Now, the house being ready, I shall be able to get to my etchings."

It was a profitable day, and she had one etching finished by the time Robert came home from his office. "You must entertain yourself after dinner," she told him. "My apologies, but I must have a good night's sleep."

But as she lay in bed, fearful sounds roused her from slumber. Creakings and howlings. What on earth...? She lit her candle and saw that the mantel clock said two o'clock. She got out of bed and looked out of the window but could see nothing in the darkness. She tugged on the bell pull beside her bed. In a minute or two, Mrs. Hawkins appeared in the doorway, her grey hair askew, hands clutching a shawl which covered the top of her nightdress. She rushed to Anna's side.

"What is that infernal noise, Mrs. Hawkins? It sounds as if the house foundations are breaking up."

Mrs. Hawkins laughed. "Oh ma'am, not the house, the ice."

"The ice? What do you mean?"

"The ice in the lake breaking, ma'am. Sure, it happens every spring. Go back to sleep. You scairt me. I thought you was taken with the ague."

Unable to rest, Anna lay awake and listened to the moan and the crack of the ice. She simply could not imagine this Canadian world without winter. Soon, to the sound of the breaking ice was added the roar of a tremendous gale from the east. In the early morning light she rushed to the drawing room window and saw that the ice had indeed disappeared just as her housekeeper—admirable woman!—had predicted.

"Spring here is so different from England," she said to Mrs. Hawkins mid-morning. "I have given some thought to the contrast and written what I call 'a set piece' for my new book."

"And what do you say, ma'am?"

"'In England, Nature is a sluggard. When she wakes from her long winter, she opens one eye and then another, shivers and draws her snow coverlet over her face and sleeps again. At last, slow and lazy, she drags herself up from her winter slumber.' Do you like it?"

Mrs. Hawkins considered and gave a nod of approval. "And what about Canada?"

"'Here in Canada, no sooner has the sun peeped through her curtains than up she springs, like a huntress for the chase. She puts on her kirtle of green and walks out of her winter chamber in full-blown life and beauty. And everyone basks in her smiles.' What do you think, Mrs. Hawkins?"

"Hmm, a bit fanciful, that one. 'Kirtle', no one wears them things these days. Why not 'apron'?" She put her finger to her chin, and said, "'She puts on her apron of green.' But then, ma'am, there be no green aprons. Maybe just 'She puts on her apron.' Yes, I think that be best."

Well, I asked, didn't I, thought Anna. The English servant would bob a curtsy and say something agreeable, even if it wasn't what she thought. I suppose, on the whole, I prefer the truth. "I shall get my pencils, Mrs. Hawkins. Drawings, not words, must describe this moment."

She sat the rest of the morning at the window sketching. Every moment the lake changed its hues. Shades of purple and green passed over the water. Then a streak of silver light divided the colours. Clouds tumbled over the horizon; and graceful little schooners came curtseying into the bay. And then there were the wild geese, and great black loons, skimming, diving and sporting over the water. A dinghy ventured as far as the King's Wharf. She put down her pencils and sat enjoying it all. Aloud she said, though there was no one around to hear her, "Today, in spite of myself, I begin to be in love with this beautiful lake, and look on it as mine."

Two days later, as she came into the dining room for breakfast, she found Mrs. Hawkins at the window, staring at the horizon. "Look, ma'am, do look!" She pointed towards the lighthouse. A huge steamboat had just rounded the spit and come into the bay. Black smoke belched from its twin stacks.

Anna tugged at the strings of her housekeeper's apron. "Let's get rid of this kirtle. No work this morning. This is a day worth a king's ransom. We shall go to the pier and watch it come in."

They arrived at the wharf in time to see the boat sweep into the bay, flags and streamers flying. There were already a hundred people assembled to cheer it on. Among the crowd, Anna spotted Colonel Fitzgibbon, in full dress uniform, with his portmanteau. With him was Sam Jarvis, whom she had not seen since her visit to the sugarbush.

"Good day, Mrs. Jameson," the Colonel called out to her, and Sam waved a hand in greeting. She ran up to them. "Oh, gentlemen," she said, laughing, "what a wonderful, wonderful morning."

"Indeed it is, ma'am," the Colonel said, "and Jarvis and I sail this day to Queenston for an important awards ceremony with the Indian troops from the War of 1812."

"May I go with you?" She felt so light-hearted, she could not stop herself from being ridiculous. "If I have a few minutes before the steamer departs, I shall run back home and get my portmanteau and my Spanish guitar and entertain you on the way."

The men laughed. "Come along, ma'am," the Colonel said, and he seemed to mean it. "We shall do a flamenco that will pound the ship's boards into the hold."

"I fear my knees will collapse long before the ship's boards," Sam added, "but my scarf will be a nice accessory for the occasion."

He took it from his neck and made a feint or two with it in the manner of a toreador confronting a bull.

The Colonel pulled out his pocket watch. "You have an hour. If you can't make it by then, I fear you will have to swim."

Hoist with her own petard. And she was aware that their laughter had attracted the notice of several onlookers, including a young man from her husband's office who would no doubt report everything to him. She didn't care. "If we run, Mrs. Hawkins, I think we can find a carriage, get home, pack and be back here in time. If you will help me."

"Oh, ma'am, sure I'm glad you be going, but what will I say to the master?"

"You'll think of something. Tell him it's research. But right now, let's save our breath for running."

TWENTY-ONE

Colonel Fitzgibbon had led the Indians to victory against the Americans at Beaver Dams in August of 1813. He had often told Sam that without his Caughnawaga warriors, the battle would have been lost. Sam was glad to have the Colonel along for this first major official engagement. Not only did he welcome his friend's knowledge of the Niagara Indians, he was relieved just to have someone to talk to on the long steamer trip to Niagara.

Of course, now he had Anna as well. Sam made a mental note to call her Mrs. Jameson in front of the Colonel. She was standing at the stern of the steamer, waving goodbye to her housekeeper. She had indeed brought her Spanish guitar and a very small portmanteau, so it would all be manageable—at least, the luggage part of it. As for the rest of what might unfold in the next two days, well, he'd have to see.

"Your knowledge of the Indian bands will be an asset, Colonel," he said as Fitzgibbon poured whiskey from the silver flask he always had with him. "Mohawk, Chippewa, Mississauga, Caughnawaga, it sounds almost like the first line of a children's rhyme, doesn't it? I know something of the Chippewa people. Jacob Snake has told me about them and introduced me to his relations, but I have to sort the rest of them."

"Especially now you Big Indian Chief." They both laughed.

Anna joined them. "How long will it take to get there?"

"Four hours, I expect," the Colonel said.

"Then I can surely provide some fun en route. Apparently there is an Irish American troupe on board who are making the circuit around the Great Lakes."

"They have just come from the Theatre Royal," Sam said. "They did some comic songs and dances there this week. I heard a good deal about it, and I wanted so much to go, but...there just didn't seem enough time to take it in." He remembered Mary's comment that there would be too many of the serving classes there, and he had caved in to her disapproval.

The next minute, it seemed, Anna had found a bench near the pilot's cabin, taken out her guitar and begun twanging away with some Spanish music. The theatre troupe improvised a flamenco, and the deck cleared so that people could stand at the sides and watch. It was a comical performance—Irish step-dancing overlaid with Spanish hand-clapping and twirls, and Sam did a few feints with his scarf, hoping he didn't look too ridiculous.

"Your toreador skills are sadly wasted in this part of the world," Anna said as the audience clapped in appreciation of the impromptu performance.

"Not really. I intend to try them on the next bull moose I meet."

"I have not had a chance to ask you about Job Crimshaw. But I'm sure by now you have things well in hand."

"It's not that simple. You, coming from Europe, cannot understand how dependent all of us are on Crimshaw's merchandise. If I upset the man, where am I to get what I need? I intend to do something, but not now."

He turned away. Would she bring up the subject again? To escape further questioning, he found a quiet spot below deck to look over the notes for his speech.

In Niagara, they rented a carriage to take them to Queenston Heights, where they alighted at a spot not far from where General Brock had died. There they were to receive the Indians in front of his monument, a massive column that towered one hundred and twenty-six feet into the sky. In the vault below were the bodies of Brock and his aide-de-camp.

Sam could see the birchbark canoes down in the river. Two hundred Indian veterans of the battles of 1812 and 1813 had

already climbed to the Heights and were waiting on the knoll.
As Sam looked over the assembly, he thought, "How aged they
are, though surely they cannot be much older than I." Some were
dressed in filthy trousers and ragged double-breasted frock coats.
Perhaps they, like Elijah White Deer, had suffered the abuse of the
white trader. Others wore eagle feathers in their braids, deerskin
leggings, and shirts decorated with strings of wampum.

He and the Colonel moved to the folding table flanked by
two chairs, which had been placed at the head of the crowd. He
fumbled in the left-hand pocket of his waistcoat and pulled out his
watch. Time to get on with it. He cleared his throat, and the gabble
of native dialects ceased.

"Please sit down." He gestured towards the grass, which on this
sunny day seemed dry enough for sitting. When he looked down
at the assembly, he could see no one he recognized except Anna.
She sat in the front row near an old chieftain with plumes in his
headband. He and Fitzgibbon had provided a chair for her, but she
had elected to sit on the grass with the Indians. When he caught
her eye, she smiled and made a clapping motion with her small
white fingers.

He waited while they settled, then continued. "All of you fought
along with me and my friend here in the war against the Yankees.
The Great Father across the sea recognizes your contribution to his
new nation." A Mississauga Indian named Blackbird translated his
words. As the translation spun out into the open air, Sam heard a
murmur from the crowd.

"What's the matter?" he asked Blackbird.

"That phrase 'his new nation', your Honour. Your Honour
forgets that we Indians consider this land our land. Did we not
fight to keep it from the hands of the Yankee scoundrels?"

Not an auspicious start. Best to rush on, skip most of it, and get
to the point. "The Great Father has medals for you this day, but he
will reward your loyalty further at a grand ceremony on the Island
of Manitou this summer. I hope to see you all there where there
will be gifts of blankets, pots, cloth and tobacco for everyone."

Applause was polite but subdued. No one seemed to remember him. He had been a young man in 1812, scarcely twenty years old, and dressed in the uniform of the Third Regiment. Now he was forty-five and fitted out in a frock coat and striped trousers.

His next duty was to give each of the veterans a medal. He reached towards the box on the table. "Good lord, man," Fitzgibbon whispered, "let me put some heart in it." He rose from the chair where he had sat during Sam's little speech. As soon as he stood up, applause broke out. He'd had the foresight to wear his battle uniform from those long-ago days: white pants with a sash, a sword attached to his belt, and a red jacket with epaulets. This was someone they remembered

"My brothers, you were responsible for the important victory at Beaver Dams." His voice rang clear across the Heights. "Though you were greatly outnumbered by the American troops, you scared the breeches off them." There was much laughter as Blackbird translated. "You beat the Yankees into a state of terror; and the only share I claim in the victory is that I took advantage of a favourable moment to offer them protection from your tomahawks and scalping knives. They threw down their weapons and surrendered. I and the Great Father will ever be indebted to you." He laid his hand on his heart. "We will never forget your bravery."

Cheers, then a shout from a deep voice at the back of the crowd. Everyone grew quiet. An old chieftain with eagle plumes, his cheeks painted vermilion and pea green, stood up and faced Fitzgibbon. "Yankee general miserable squaw," he said. More laughter. "Him fat dog, acted proud, but dropped tail between legs when he heard Caughnawaga war whoops."

Fitzgibbon laughed with them. "I had my own name for that Yankee dog. I called him General Jackass."

Sam could hear a pause in Blackbird's translation. Probably there was no Indian equivalent for the word "jackass". The Indians waited while Blackbird struggled to come up with a word they would understand. There was a spate of Indian lingo, then came the phrase—in English—"General Pisspot". This the Indians

found so funny that it was a couple of moments before the
assembly came to order.

Sam rose and called the crowd to come forward to the table
behind which he stood. He shook hands with each of them and
gave out a medal with an inscription: "Brave Hearts: The Great
Father Thanks You". The Colonel stood beside him, offering
congratulations and embraces.

The Indians had brought gifts—pouches, baskets, rifle slings,
moccasins—and they lay in a pile at the base of the monument.
They would find a ready acceptance among the folk in Archdeacon
Strachan's congregation at St. James.

"I am glad that I spoke," Fitzgibbon said to him when the
ceremony was over. "I meant it when I said I would ever be grateful
to those men."

"And I am grateful to you, my friend. You saved the day. I'm
afraid I will never be a public speaker." Sam wondered if he had
looked a fool in front of Anna. She now stood talking to the
old chieftain. There was much gesturing, but they seemed to be
communicating on some level.

"Didn't you enjoy Blackbird's translation of 'jackass'? Those
men from the deep dark forest soon found out all about pisspots
from their white comrades."

"We shall not mention that particular moment to Sir Francis.
He takes a dim view of the 'savages', as he calls them, and anything
he construes as lack of respect on their part for the white man. And
if he decided to discharge Blackbird from his duties, I don't know
what I'd do on Manitoulin." Sam looked at his pocket watch. "And
now what? Shall we take Mrs. Jameson to a respectable hotel in
town, then go to Fort George and knock back a few rounds?"

"You will not be rid of me with ease, gentlemen," the lady said.
She had come up behind them. "And before you try, I must tell
you, Colonel, that your speech was compelling."

"Thank you, ma'am. And since you have paid me a pleasant
compliment, I have a suggestion I think you'll like. Instead of
abandoning you while Jarvis and I knock back those drinks,

why don't we visit my old friend, Mrs. Secord? She will give us tea and excellent scones." Fitzgibbon thought a minute, then added, "But while that might be a compliment to the ladies we know in Toronto society, it doesn't do justice to our friend's real accomplishments. It would be like saying that General Brock knew how to put a good shine on his boots."

"I don't know anything at all about Mrs. Secord," Anna said as they walked down the hill towards Queenston.

"She overheard important news about the American plans for attack and walked for a whole night to tell it to me when I was in charge at Beaver Dams. Because of her, the scoundrels did not take us by surprise."

"Amazing."

"And there's more, much more to tell about her. Jarvis knew her once. Right, my friend?"

"Yes, I first met her after the slaughter at Queenston Heights." Sam said no more. He felt down in the dumps. So far, with the exception of a few laughs on the steamer, it had been Fitz's day. And now, for Anna's ears, Mrs. Secord would surely relate the story of her famous walk to Beaver Dams, and the Colonel would be front and centre once more.

TWENTY-TWO

Mrs. Secord lived in a plain little house set on a pretty lawn covered in tiny blue spring flowers. "Goodness me," she said as she opened the front door. "Lieutenant Jarvis and Colonel Fitzgibbon. I heard you were coming today, and I made scones—just in case you wanted to see an old woman. And here you are." She had the strong nose and strong jaw Sam remembered, and her deep-set eyes took in every detail of her guests. "And this lady is your wife, Lieutenant?"

Sam set her straight, and they all sat down to enjoy her generous tea of cheese, ham, and scones with whipped butter and maple syrup. She served it in her kitchen and made no apologies for the heat of the hearth and the homely smell of onions and cabbage that wafted from one of the boiling cauldrons.

"We had medals for the Indian braves, and we should have had a gold one for you," the Colonel said. "No one deserves it more."

"Indeed, sir, I did what I had to. I have always done my duty. Yet the British government and the colonials have done little over the years to help my man or me. In spite of your letters and petitions, sir. But now, at last, we make some headway."

"Ah, yes, ma'am. I heard that your husband is a customs collector? And does that go well?"

Mrs. Secord laughed. It was a guffaw that came from her belly and shook her body. "My man came in last night and said, 'Laura, tonight I intend to arrest three smugglers who will try to get some arms across the water under cover of dark.'

"'James,' says I, 'don't do it. It will be dangerous, and you have a crick leg.'

"'Never you mind that,' he says, 'I have my deputy.'

"'Two against how many?' I ask. 'Three, six?'

"So off he goes, determined to be a fool in spite of what I say. I think about things, then I put on James's breeches, boots, and long overcoat, smudge my face with ashes, pull a cap over my ears and set off for the river. I also take a mean-looking rifle with me, unloaded, of course, and I show up in the dark, alongside James and the deputy. And when those scoundrels, there were four of them, get out of their boat, I say in my deepest growl, 'Your weapons or your life.' And they handed over everything. Even stood quiet while my husband put the cuffs on them."

Sam laughed. "You haven't changed a bit, ma'am."

"'Till death do us part', that's what I vowed all those years ago. And if it hadn't been for you, Lieutenant, my man would not be here today for me to take care of. And all these years would have been a wasteland that doesn't bear thinking of."

"Please tell me what Mr. Jarvis did, ma'am," Anna said. "I have not heard the story."

"It was the day of that terrible slaughter at Queenston Heights. James was part of the militia. He always came home for his evening meal, said he liked the peace and quiet of this place with his wife and kiddies. Especially after the noise of the cannon and muskets, even though it was just practice most days. Well, Mrs. Jameson, it got on for five or six o'clock, and he still wasn't home, and I'd been hearing the artillery all the day long, so I knew something awful had happened.

"So I set out to find him. I took a tablecloth with me. You see, at the back of my mind, I had the thought, 'If he's dead, this will serve as his shroud.'

"So I went to the Heights where the battle had been. Oh ma'am, the horror of that sight. Hundreds of dying and dead stretched out before me as far as I could see. And the moans, the stench..." She broke off for a moment. "Well, Mrs. Jameson, I started my search. I turned over a dozen bodies, and then... Well then, I had to stop, I had no more stomach for it. But Lieutenant Jarvis saw me from afar and came up to me. That man you see before you in his fine suit—he was but little more than a lad then—went with me across the battlefield, turning over those bodies one by one. And after ever so long, we found James. Almost dead he was, but the Lieutenant took two flag poles and my tablecloth, fashioned a pallet, hoisted my poor man up on it and helped me carry him home. So there it is, ma'am. Because of him I have a husband today to love and to cherish."

Suddenly—with no warning—Sam felt his eyes water. Anna squeezed his arm. "What a wonderful story, Mrs. Secord, but I fear it has brought back too many memories for Mr. Jarvis."

"Memories, memories—if only one could drown the bad ones." Sam shook his head sadly. "But the Battle of Queenston Heights still haunts me. That charge up the Niagara escarpment, General Brock just ahead of us... I can hear the pop of bullets that showered the sky, smell the stench of blood and gunpowder. I see Brock's tall figure in red coat and white breeches fall to the ground without a word, without even a moan. I feel the thud of the Yankee cannonball slicing one of the soldiers in half. And then, the final horror of the bloodied corpse falling on top of the General's body. Oh, Mrs. Jameson, I pray nightly that my own sons will never know war."

"I too will never forget our General's death," the Colonel chimed in. "He was the best of men. I had little education when I came to this country. It was General Brock who taught me how to write a letter. In spite of his many and great responsibilities, he took time to help an ignorant Irishman." He wiped his eyes on his sleeve. "I fear, dear ladies, we are a couple of sentimental fools."

Anna turned to face him. "And what is wrong with sentiment, Colonel? I grow angry when I think of the way men define 'manliness'. I believe that the best men in this world are those who have tender hearts, who have sensibility as well as courage, who will speak freely to a woman of the thoughts that lie within them."

"Hear, hear!" Mrs. Secord banged the palms of her hands on the tabletop.

"And how are the doubloons, ma'am?" Fitz asked.

Mrs. Secord laughed heartily and pointed to the cauldron filled with the boiling onions and cabbage. "I do still keep the cauldron, sir, but the doubloons are long gone. They made good soup once, they did, but they also educated my children and paid the landlord."

"Now, ma'am," Anna interjected, "either my hearing is faulty, or my wits have turned. You say that doubloons make good soup?"

"Better tell her the whole story, if you please," Sam said.

Mrs. Secord's mouth was filled with scone. They waited while she chewed and swallowed. "Well, Mrs. Jameson, I had a collection of Spanish doubloons. Given to me by my dear father, who fought the Yankees in the Revolutionary War. When he came north with the Loyalists, he brought the coins with him, and on his deathbed, he says to me, 'Laura, my girl, this is your legacy. Guard it well.' And he hands over the doubloons.

"Well, I kept them safe against a rainy day. The years passed, and there they were, still safe and sound, in that jar there." Mrs. Secord pointed to a pretty blue piece of crockery on the mantel. "Then one day, it was June of 1813, and I heard the Yankee louts come up my path. A foul noise they were making, too, as if they'd been long in the tavern. I just had time to grab up that jar and throw the doubloons into a pot of potatoes and carrots and lamb shank I had boiling on the hearth.

"They burst through that door, and they say to me, 'Oh, missus, we hear in the tavern you've got doubloons.' And they go straight to that blue jar and look inside. Then they get nasty, real nasty. Their language should not have been heard by anyone decent, least of all my kiddies who were in the kitchen with me."

Sam shook his head. "Dirty scoundrels. I wish I'd been there."

"And I'm that worried about my little ones—and my husband upstairs in bed with his crick leg—so I say, 'Sit you down, and have some of my good soup. I long ago spent my doubloons, it takes money to feed my kiddies, sirs, but I can offer you the hospitality of this house.' Oh, I almost choked on that last little bit, I did."

"Dear Mrs. Secord, I am impressed," Anna said. "In spite of attempted robbery and verbal abuse, you offered them the best you had. Have you ever heard of such stellar generosity, Mr. Jarvis?"

They all laughed.

"Well, it softened them up, it did. So they sit down. I put my ladle into the pot, careful I am not to scrape up the bottom, and I give each of them, five there were, the potatoes, the carrots and the lamb shank.

"'Best soup we ever ate,' they say. 'And one of them, the corporal, he says, 'Write down the recipe for my missus.' So I go into the pantry," she pointed to a small room off the kitchen, "to find my recipe book, it's really a collection of my dear mother's favourites—"

"And you added, no doubt, 'one heaping ladle of the finest Spanish doubloons' to her recipe?" Sam smiled.

"And while I'm there, they're talking, see, talk talk talk about their plans to surprise the Colonel on the morrow. The brass of those louts. They know I'm in the pantry, but to them I'm less important than the trivet or the clock jack. So I sit down on the stool, and I listen to every word and I write it in my memory. And that's my story of how I got the information to pass on to the Colonel." She pushed the pitcher of maple syrup towards Sam. "Now have some more syrup on that scone, please do, Lieutenant."

"Mrs. Secord is too modest to mention the details of the walk she took to warn me. How she set off at dawn, talked her way past the Yankee patrols, walked a day and a night through swamp and bush, past wolves and rattlesnakes..." Fitzgibbon stretched one of his long arms across the corner of the table and clasped Mrs. Secord's hand. "I will not forget your part in the Beaver Dams Victory, ma'am."

They left the Secord homestead in the late afternoon for their short ride to Niagara. "My ideal woman, that one," Anna said, as she waved goodbye from the carriage. "She has courage, resourcefulness and a tender, constant heart."

"It is remarkable, is it not, how wrong we can be when we call woman 'the weaker sex'?" the Colonel said.

"And it is remarkable, is it not, Fitz, that Mrs. Jameson believes the ideal man and the ideal woman have the same qualities? I think of my wife as courageous. She has surmounted the tragedy of two dead children. She has buried her sorrow deep inside her and gone on. But somehow, I do not believe she would find Mrs. Secord her ideal woman. She would say that dressing as a man and carrying a rifle is singularly unfeminine."

"But what do you yourself think of the lady?" Anna asked.

"*I* find her singularly praiseworthy."

The minute he said it, he felt himself blush. Was his comment disloyal to Mary?

"It has been a good day," Anna said as they reached the town. "I have gained information for my book. And I have learned new and commendable things about two of my best friends."

"There are a number of respectable hotels," the Colonel said. "May I suggest one?"

"I believe I shall spend the night with the Almas, if they agree. My husband and I stayed with them when we made our trip here in January. They have a pleasant dwelling."

So they dropped the lady at the Almas' house just off the main street. Then they made their way back to Fort George. There, in the officers' mess, they settled into comfortable chairs, and a corporal, earning extra money for the night, brought them glasses of whiskey.

"A strange day of ups and downs," Sam said. "At first I could think only of my failure as a speaker, but after Mrs. Secord's kind reminiscences, I feel better."

"I wonder if Mrs. Jameson's praise has affected you as well, friend. I noticed how the lady squeezed your arm right in front of Mrs. Secord and me. Watch out. If she decided to engage in amorous combat with you, I wager she'd be more difficult to defeat than the Yankees."

"I think you've taken too much whiskey, Fitz. You not only insult the lady, but you impart a poor opinion of me as well."

"I just mean to warn you, that's all. She's a damned attractive woman, but you've got enough on your plate without that one for dessert."

It was late when they made their way into the clear night air. Around a corner and down toward the river was the small dwelling for officers, where they had taken a room for the night. Later, as Sam listened to his friend's snores, he thought about Anna. If she had been in a hotel, he might have been able to find some pretext for a visit in the early evening. As it was, he could only think about what might have been. Which was, perhaps, just as well. If Fitz had noticed Anna's response to him, he'd better guard his flank.

TWENTY-THREE

It was early afternoon when the steamer returned to the wharf at Toronto. Freeland's Soap Factory, just to the east of the pier, emitted its usual stink of tallow, and Fitzgibbon bade Anna and Sam a hasty goodbye, pinching his nostrils with his left hand while he hailed a carriage with his right.

John was waiting with the coach and horses. "Let me give you a ride home," Sam said to Anna.

She pointed to a figure coming along the street at the end of the wharf. "Mrs. Hawkins is here. She will carry my portmanteau, I'll carry the guitar, and we shall have a pleasant walk along the waterfront in the opposite direction from that stink."

"Do you remember that it was here we first met?"

"Yes, Sam, it was on this very wharf. I was so alone, so lonely, and you came to my rescue. And now I have something to give you as a token of our friendship. You mentioned it on the day we went to the sugarbush, and now..." Sam watched her set her portmanteau on the boards of the wharf and kneel to undo the buckles. From the top, she took a small, square package, which she handed to him.

He took off the paper wrapping. It was a drawing of a small boy in a buckskin suit. For a moment, he wondered... Then it came to him. It was surely the long-ago picture of himself that his mother talked about. "Oh my god, dear dear Anna, where...who...?"

"I saw it first in Mrs. Alma's bedchamber in the winter when we visited. She likes it, but she parted with it."

"What a wonderful gift. My mother will be so glad to see it back among the family possessions. But how can I pay you for it? Please, please, let me pay."

"Mrs. Alma and I have a mutually satisfactory agreement. I have agreed to give her two of my sketches. You see, she has some new household acquisitions that she is especially proud of—a commode chair in the bedchamber and a Franklin stove in the drawing room. I made sketches of both rooms when I was there last night, and I shall finish them within the week and send them to her."

He drew her close to him and kissed her hand. "My dear friend, how glad I am that I found you here on that snowy day not so long ago."

"Let us meet soon. I intend to strike out for the northern wilderness when summer comes. Do you think—would it be possible—-for me to follow you to Manitoulin Island for the Indian ceremonies?"

Mrs. Hawkins was almost upon them. "With all my heart, I would welcome you."

Sam's carriage swung north to King St. and began the drive east towards Hazelburn. He held the drawing in his hand, absorbed in the delicate, finely drawn details. It was so nicely framed, too, ready to hang, perhaps in the dining room, though he would have to give it to his mother if she wanted it badly enough. What a first-rate time he'd had with Anna, and what a wonderful gift. And now, perhaps, he could repay her by putting himself to a task he'd avoided too long.

"Mr. Jarvis, Mr. Jarvis!" He glanced up to see Mrs. Widmer waving at him from the board sidewalk. He motioned to the coachman to stop.

She rushed from the sidewalk and placed herself so close to the wheels that moving forward was impossible. "Dear Mr. Jarvis, my horse is lame today, and I have had to walk. Would you be a lovely man and drive me home?"

"With pleasure, ma'am," Sam said. "I have some business to attend to, so I shall get down now, and John will drive you wherever you wish." As he said this, he hopped down and hoisted the lady up into his vacant seat. "John, I shall walk home when I finish my business. You are to put yourself entirely at Mrs.

Widmer's service. Good day, ma'am." He bowed and made his way into the street. He waited till the carriage had moved off, then went into Job Crimshaw's store.

The jangling bell brought Crimshaw to the front of the shop. "Mr. Jarvis, sir, a pleasure to see you! Let me show you some bottles of Bristol's finest, just arrived, sir." Without waiting for an answer, the merchant snapped his fingers, and a lad in a striped apron took a bottle of cream sherry from a shelf and placed it on the counter in front of Sam.

"Very nice," Sam said as he looked at the rich blue of the bottle. In a flash, Crimshaw had removed the cork and filled a sherry glass to the brim.

"The best, sir, for my best customer. Now, tell me what you think."

It was a golden brown. Sam took a sip, another, and another. "Excellent." Crimshaw refilled his glass.

"My man will deliver it this very day, sir. How many bottles shall I put you down for?" Another snap of the fingers, and the lad produced the account book. Crimshaw flipped it open to a well-thumbed page. "Fifteen, sir? Twenty?"

"Make it ten." Sam took another sip. "Actually I came here on another matter entirely."

"Indeed, sir? What can I get for you? Perhaps some Madeira? Cuban cigars?"

"The Indians."

"Indians, sir?" Crimshaw's face settled into a half smile. The lad in the apron bowed and disappeared to the back of the store.

"Indians. That's what I said." Sam paused. Set down the glass with a thud. "You have no doubt heard of my promotion to Chief Superintendent of Indian Affairs. In that role I have come here today to..." Damn it, what were the words he wanted..."To talk to you about...about your unfair dealings with the natives."

"Unfair dealings, sir?" A bead of sweat appeared on Crimshaw's forehead, but the smile remained in place.

"I'll come to the point. You give cheap liquor to the Indians and take from them furs, fish, venison and maple sugar. You get them so drunk they can't do a thing about your robbery of their goods."

"Robbery, you say? Fair trade, I'd say. Though maybe a Chief Superintendent don't know nothing about fair trade, not being a businessman. So let me put it this way. The savages give me what I want, and I give them what they want. Fair trade...sir."

While he spoke, Crimshaw moved his dirty, misshapen forefinger slowly down the page of the account book until it rested on a figure at the bottom. From where he stood, Sam could not see the exact amount. He didn't need to, he knew only too well the three-digit total.

"The way I see it," Crimshaw continued, "is like this. Trade with the savages is more like fair trade than my dealings with some nobs I could mention." He tapped his finger on the account book. His voice grew louder. "I give nobs what they want, and they don't give me nothing in return. But then, as I say, some nobs don't know nothing about fair trade."

Sam laid down ten notes on the counter. "Put that on my account and shut up about fair trade. You have as much notion of the phrase as...as..." No words came to him.

Crimshaw's smile returned as he scooped up the notes. "No offence taken, sir, and none given, I trust?" He sidled after Sam as he moved towards the front door, holding it open for him to pass through. "And shall I send along the new sherry today, sir?"

"Go to hell," Sam said under his breath as he went out into the street. He took some comfort from this remark, though he could not summon the courage to cancel the order. Where was he to get his sherry and cigars if he had a final break with the swine? Well, at least he'd made his point about the Indians. He felt better that he'd gone that far at least.

He was eager now to get back to the fresh smell of his pinewoods. Perhaps the hazelnut trees would be showing more green, and there would be trout in the burn now that the ice had melted.

As he turned into the path leading to Hazelburn, he stopped on the little bridge of logs that he had built one summer over the stream at the foot of his lot. The water was clear, and in the shallows he could see minnows darting about and occasional flashes of silver as the larger fish swam over the pebbles. Once he'd given Mary the news—or some of it, anyway—he'd get into his old coat and breeches and see if he could catch some speckled trout for breakfast. There would be no time to arrange a fishing excursion on Lake Simcoe with Jacob before the trip to Manitoulin.

He'd be saddled with Sir Francis on the journey north, of course. He imagined the endless hours of self-congratulatory remarks which the Governor would make, while he and Jacob and the voyageurs would be forced into silence. No songs, no jokes. And just enough fishing allowed to provide the Gov with fresh catch to put upon the Derby china he'd probably bring along with him. But Anna would be there at the end of the journey. And in that great northern landscape far from Toronto's gossips, what might happen?

He heard voices from the front of the house that made him smile. Quickly he broke off some hanging catkins and stuck them under his top hat. They came down to his shoulders and curled outwards, so that he looked, he hoped, like some ancient god of the forest. A few minutes more, and Charlie and Caroline came scampering down the path with Miss Siddons following. He got behind one of the hazelnut trunks. When they were a few feet away, he leapt out. "Buh, buh," he cried, "who is here in my forest? Two small children for my fricassee, I wager."

The children shrieked. "A monster! Save us, Miss Siddons!"

The governess raised her parasol and took aim, as if she had the enemy in her sights.

"It's only Papa," Charlie said. "Oh, Papa, you scared us! You look like a monster with those things hanging out of your hat!"

"How brave you are, Miss Siddons," Sam said. "It's not often a monster confronts such a formidable foe in the depths of a hazelnut forest."

Laughing, the four of them scrambled up the steps of Hazelburn. Mary was seated on an oak bench on the porch. "Oh,

Sam, do remove those ridiculous catkins from your head." He took off his top hat and threw the branches over the porch railing into the tulip bed below. As he did so, he had a fleeting memory of Anna's laughter as he played toreador.

Mary rose and took his hand. "Let's go into the drawing room. I'll pour you a sherry, and we'll have tea." She turned to Miss Siddons. "Surely your time could be better spent in teaching Caroline her alphabet. I can send the maid with the children if they want to play in the shrubbery."

"This very afternoon, Mrs. Jarvis, Caroline learned to spell and write her name, and Charlie does an excellent capital 'C'. So with those accomplishments behind us, I allowed my scholars a break from their studies."

"And Miss Siddons deserves our gratitude for her courage in saving the children from the Monster of Hazelburn Woods," Sam said. "She must be praised." Charlie and Caroline giggled, and Mary shrugged and headed for the front door.

"Not sherry," Sam said to her in the drawing room, as he put his hand over hers on the decanter. "I'll have beer. Got to wean myself from the sherry."

Cook answered Mary's summons, bringing the beer from the servants' quarters belowstairs. Sam settled into a comfortable armchair. Mary sat on the sofa in front of the window. She wore a deep crimson bodice and skirt that looked well with the pink flowers on the upholstery that framed her.

"Dear Sam, just in time, as I hoped you'd be. Cook has a new recipe for scones seasoned with oregano. You must try one with this liver pâté." She put a dollop onto the scone and passed it to him. "And now, tell me about the Indians. I want to hear everything."

"Colonel Fitzgibbon was a great help—"

"I want to hear about you, Sam, not your friend."

"They liked my speech. I was generous in my praise of their military prowess. I told them the Beaver Dams victory would have been impossible without their help. Yes, I laid it on with a trowel. They like a bit of humour, so I called their Yankee opponent

'General Jackass', and that got a laugh. And when I wound up with my invitation to the summer ceremonies on Manitoulin Island, they applauded loudly."

"Oh, Sam, I'm glad you did so well." She reached for a plate on the table. "Now have a lemon square, and tell me about Mrs. Jameson."

"Mrs. Jameson?"

"Yes, Mrs. Widmer came by yesterday afternoon on her horse. She said she watched the boat go out of the harbour yesterday and saw her standing against the railing with a guitar and a portmanteau. At first I wondered why she was aboard. But I expect she was doing some research for her book?"

"Yes, I think she got lots of material. She was with the Colonel and me at the ceremony and went with us afterwards to Mrs. Secord's house for tea."

"Probably got an earful from that one. I hope Anna doesn't write her up as a sterling example of Canadian femininity. Tell me, does she make notes while people are talking? Or does she scribble it all down later?"

"The latter, I expect." Then he showed her the drawing Anna had given him.

She smiled as she studied it. "You were such a pretty little boy, Sam. Can you see how much Charlie resembles you? It's so pleasant to have this. I'll thank Anna—we are now on first-name basis, as you may have noticed—when next I see her. Mrs. Widmer seems disappointed that I like the lady. You know, I think her real purpose in dropping by yesterday was to stir up trouble. She wanted me to think there was something going on between you and Anna. She is such a little troublemaker, and of course, her one aim in life is to alienate you and me and have a go at you herself."

"On that score, my dear, you need have no worries." And he told her how he'd got rid of the woman when she pressed him for a ride home. But he decided to say nothing about his visit to Job Crimshaw.

TWENTY-FOUR

In Anna's first weeks in Toronto, she had grown accustomed to Robert's solitary evening walks—rain, sleet or snowstorm— "for his constitution," so he said. Probably, she realized now, his "constitutional" had ended in Markland's office in the Parliament Buildings.

But in those days, at any rate, she had been free to work on her journal and translations without interruption. Now, since his comment about "servants' tittle-tattle", he stayed home every evening, perhaps in an effort to quell any rumours. Certainly, if Mrs. Hawkins were to meet her spy at the Parliament Buildings, she would have nothing to talk about except her employers' seeming marital harmony.

On the night of her return from Niagara, Anna was in her usual place at the pianoforte. She had just finished Donna Anna's aria from *Don Giovanni*, 'Or sai chi l'onore'—and a demanding piece of singing it was—when Robert cleared his throat. She looked up from her sheet music, surprised to hear anything but the crackling of his newspapers and the clink of his wineglass on the table.

"Did you play that one on your guitar for Sam Jarvis?"

"Is there some innuendo in your remark, Robert? What is it all about? I played some Spanish music for Mr. Jarvis, Colonel Fitzgibbon and one hundred other passengers on the steamer. But no doubt your informant told you that the Colonel accompanied Mr. Jarvis?"

"My informant, as you call him, was Campbell, our guide to Niagara. He saw you going aboard the steamer with your luggage and said to me that he hoped you would find the landscape more appealing in springtime. If one can judge by your response, however, it appears that I have struck a nerve. Have you something you need to get off your bosom?"

"I am certain that Mrs. Hawkins told you about my need to research. You must surely understand that I cannot write a book on Upper Canada without getting beyond Toronto. In fact, Robert, I may as well tell you now that in the interests of further research, I intend to strike out this summer for the western and northern reaches of Upper Canada."

"And who is to accompany you on this wilderness journey? Sam Jarvis?"

"I feel insulted to have such a question addressed to me."

"It's just vulgar curiosity, my dear."

"I shall travel alone for most of my journey. I may meet Mr. Jarvis on Manitoulin Island. It is one of my several destinations. I don't want to miss the Indian ceremonies in August. Mr. Jarvis will be there, of course."

"I have another informant who told me what she saw on the wharf today."

"It's all beginning to sound like one of Mrs. Radcliffe's bad mysteries. Who was *this* spy, may I ask?"

"Mrs. Widmer. I tipped my hat to her as I was coming from my office. 'Sir,' said she, 'your good wife this very day was on the wharf near the soap factory where I went to strike a fair bargain for my potash. With my own eyes, I saw Mr. Jarvis kiss the lady's hand.' She then came up so close to me that I could smell the onions on her breath and added, 'Look to the lady, as they say.' She seemed angry, no doubt because from what I've observed, she has designs on Jarvis herself. But speak up, Anna. Explain yourself."

"He kissed my hand because he was surprised and happy that Mrs. Alma had given me the little picture she had of him as a child. You remember that I pointed it out to you in the bedchamber? And they offered me their kind hospitality on this trip, too, though why it is necessary to explain all this, I do not know."

"You are a loose cannon, Anna. At times, I fear the damage you may cause to my reputation by your waywardness."

Anna moved to the mantel and took down an invitation that Mrs. Hawkins had placed there earlier in the day. "We are invited to a ball at Government House, the occasion being to introduce Lady Head to society. I shall be happy to accompany you, Robert, and I promise to be the Chancellor's Lady *par excellence*. No waywardness, no stray cannonballs. And afterwards, you must give me an independent income of three hundred pounds a year and set me free."

"And if I refuse?"

"Well then, Robert, I must think about what to do. I have a good deal on my mind. I have held it all back in deference to your exalted position in this community. I have given you, in the eyes of the world at least, a respectable married life. I do not hold myself accountable for Mrs. Widmer's perverted views. I have put this new house in order and, to the best of my ability, promoted your happiness. But enough is enough. I know one thing. You cannot take an oak sapling, and prune it, and twist it into an ornament for the jardinière in your drawing room. Better to let it grow as it will—under the free air of heaven!"

"Hmm. Quite the metaphor. Now tell me, is there a threat implied in all this, Anna?"

"I counter with a question of my own. Will you set me free?"

"I make no promises."

"Then I too make no promises."

Next morning being bright and sunny, Anna walked along King Street, heading for Rowsell's to buy material for the vice-regal ball. As she passed Crimshaw's establishment, she heard a tap at the window. Looking in, she saw Mary Jarvis waving at her, motioning to her to come in.

"My dear Anna, are you shopping for the same reason I am?" Mary said as she stood in front of a broad table on which rolls of cloth were spread out.

"Quite a crowd, is it not? I suppose we all have but one

purpose." Anna gestured at the women flitting among the reticules, vinaigrettes, lace mittens and dance cards on offer.

"So exciting, a vice-regal ball. I do not know Lady Head well. I have met her at St. James, of course, and at our charity bazaar for the Relief of Poor Women in Childbirth, but this is her first big social occasion. It will give us an opportunity to..."

"See how she handles herself?"

Mary laughed. Then she unfurled the edge of a roll of pretty pink silk. "Do you like this?" she asked, pulling enough of it loose so that Anna could see the colour against her complexion.

"It suits you perfectly."

"My dear husband told me, 'Buy what you want.' Bless him. And there's a fine French dressmaker newly come to town. She has a small house on Market Street and charges 'a pretty penny', as Sam would say. But she has the latest patterns, and I've already picked out the one I want. It won't show my ankles, alas, since the French woman tells me that hemlines have dropped in Paris. Oh, Anna, I'm babbling, but it's all so exciting." She turned to Crimshaw, who stood nearby, an obsequious smile revealing a mouth of crooked teeth. "I'll take ten yards of this." She moved to the counter, where the merchant laid down the roll for cutting.

"And are you about to pick out some material too, Anna? There's a fine silk in a bright green shade over there that would suit you."

"I prefer not to shop here."

"Really? Mr. Crimshaw has by all odds the best selection."

"I'm going along the street to Rowsell's."

At that moment, they heard a giggle from the back of the store. It came from Mrs. Widmer, deep in conversation with Mrs. Robinson. Mary looked at them, and said, "God only knows what that one is up to."

"No doubt serving up a dish of half-baked gossip for Mrs. Robinson to digest. And now, I'll leave you to finish your shopping, Mary. We shall certainly meet at the ball."

As Anna went out, the bell jangling behind her, she thought

with envy of her friend, a pretty woman with an indulgent husband. Imagine the pleasure of living with someone who said, 'Buy what you want.' Dear Sam. Even though she'd been disappointed to find out that he did not have the backbone to stand up to Crimshaw, she liked him nonetheless. She'd have to watch herself. Things between them had heated up a bit too much, and if they got more involved with each other, where could it go? She could not upset that pleasant woman she had just chatted with.

And thinking of Sam, she decided she didn't care a fig for Robert's parsimony. She'd just focus on getting something that made her look good. "Buy what you want," she said to herself. She loved the bright green silk which Mary had pointed out. It was the colour of the willows and maples that had burst into leaf on the front lawn of her new house. But she could not stomach Crimshaw, remembering only too well Jacob Snake's friend, drunk in his filthy wigwam.

Bright yellow daffodils in clay pots decorated the outside of the shop of Henry Rowsell, Stationer, Bookseller and General Merchant. Here was a decent shopkeeper from whom she had bought English wallpaper for the new house and who had also supplied her with books from his small but indispensable circulating library. He was the first merchant she had known in Toronto. He had befriended her in January by providing an envoy to take her engravings to New York.

Rowsell moved forward to greet her as she opened the door of his shop. "A fine day, Mrs. Jameson." He was a young man with pink cheeks and an abundance of brown curly hair. In contrast to Crimshaw, who smelled like the moldy interior of a beer keg, this man exuded an aura of sealing wax and ink. "I have just this morning received from Oswego a parcel of books by Sir Francis Bond Head, including *Notes Made During a Journey Across the Pampas and...*" He broke off, seeing her shake her head. "But these do not tempt you. Perhaps you have heard Sir Francis's account first hand?" And now his smile changed to a grin.

"Yes, indeed, Mr. Rowsell. I have had the complete story from the llama's mouth, so to speak." They both laughed. "But I have a great favour to ask of you today. I need ten yards of fine silk for the Governor's Ball. I need it soon, and I know you have contacts who might provide it for me on short notice."

He hesitated and cleared his throat. "Perhaps I might suggest Job Crimshaw, ma'am? I understand he has a large supply of materials in his shop at the moment."

"I must tell you that I will not give that man a penny."

Rowsell nodded and shrugged. "The steamer from Oswego is still in the harbour. I shall send a boy immediately with a message to my agent who is on board. He will contact a dry goods store in Oswego, and the silk will be here on the next steamer, that is, within a week. But what colour would you like, ma'am, and how will I know if it will be to your taste?"

"Tell your agent I want silk the colour of our sky today or the green willows by the water. Or the daffodils in the pots on your front stoop. In fact, dear sir, I shall rely on your judgment."

"And since you have been so obliging, ma'am, allow me to present you with one of Sir Francis's books. If I may say so, they are not likely to be popular." Smiling, he wrapped it for her.

TWENTY-FIVE

When Anna's material was delivered a week later, she looked at the paper-wrapped bundle with some trepidation. It had come with a note from the Oswego merchant:

> *Dear Madam: I have the honour to provide for you ten yds.*
> *of my best silk. Mr. Rowsell described you as an elegant lady*
> *with fine red hair and white complexion. After much thought, I*
> *have selected this colour, and hope it is to yr. liking.*
> *Yr. obedient servant,*
> *Wm. Woxton*

"Mrs. Hawkins," she called. "Please, come and help me."

Her housekeeper hurried in, wiping her hands on her apron. "What is it, ma'am?"

"Open this package, please, and tell me the worst. I'm too much of a coward to do it myself. I shall look out the front window while you cut the string."

She heard the snip of the scissors, then... "Oh, ma'am, it be the most beautiful silk. It feels like...like cat's fur."

This was good. Mrs. Hawkins had a huge tabby that she loved. It followed her about all day. "But the colour, what is the colour?"

There was a pause. "Out with it, Mrs. Hawkins. Bile green? Pus yellow? Dirty-sheet grey?"

"Oh no, ma'am. Do look for yourself."

Anna forced herself to turn. Mrs. Hawkins had rolled the silk out on the table. It was not what she would have picked herself. No, because Job Crimshaw had nothing so beautiful. It was the colour of an oak leaf in October, a burnished golden brown. She held it against her face. "Oh, Mrs. Hawkins, what do you think?"

Her housekeeper's broad smile was answer enough.

Ottilie had sent her a pattern of the "*robe de mariage de Seigneuresse Treadwell*", which had been adapted for the winter's ballgowns in Paris and Berlin. "Treat yourself, dearest Anna," her friend had written. "This is fashion, *comme il faut*. Make a splash. Let yourself go. Show the *paysannes* how to do it."

"But who can make a dress for me within seven days, Mrs. Hawkins? I know of no one. There is that French woman on Market Street, highly recommended by everyone, but she is up to her eyebrows in material at the moment. Of the people I have spoken to in the last week, six of them have hired Madame, and not one of them is at all certain that she will be able to finish their dresses in time." Anna laughed. "Oh, it would be fun to see Mrs. Powell swanning about with one sleeve missing and no buttons to close her bodice."

"We have a friend, do we not, ma'am, who might be able to help. She would be just as good as that frog."

"Mrs. Sykes? Do you really think she's up to it?" Anna ran into her bedchamber, returning with the paper pattern. "She did a wonderful job of the curtains. You think she could handle this?" Ottilie had warned her that paper patterns were new to many seamstresses.

Mrs. Hawkins looked at it. "Sure, she could do that easy. And her sister told me this week that she be coming out of the jail soon. The babe will have his mother back, and the sister can go about her business. There be but one problem, ma'am. Supposing she come here to sew, she would be needing to stay. Like an itinerant."

"An itinerant, Mrs. Hawkins? You mean she'd stay here for the duration of her task?"

Her housekeeper nodded.

"Well then, we could give her three good meals, a flood of tea, and...but we have no extra bedchamber—"

"If you be willing to buy a cot, ma'am, she could put up in the alcove by the kitchen, right next to me and my man."

"It shall be done. I'll go to the jail myself today and make the arrangements for her transfer. The jailer and I are quite friendly now. And he's introduced me to the magistrate, who has the final say in these manners."

"For sure, it will all work out, ma'am."

"I think it will. And if she does this job well, she'll have no problem getting work from the women of the town. It'll be a new start for her."

Mrs. Sykes was a small woman. She had thin, supple fingers and a dour countenance with a forehead creased, no doubt, by too much sorrow. But Mrs. Hawkins had insisted that she have a hot bath and a hearty meal, and Anna had provided a clean gown, and all seemed well enough.

"You will be comfortable at the dining room table," Anna said to her. "There is plenty of light from the bay window, and you can sew from the time the Chancellor leaves for work in the morning until he returns in the early evening. After that, you may spend the time as you wish. Mrs. Hawkins has a bed for you belowstairs and will provide you with food and drink whenever you request it."

Anna's skills had never included sewing. Her dear father, a skilled miniaturist, had taught her to draw. As a young woman, she had read books, written poems, practised on the pianoforte, taken singing lessons and become a governess at sixteen. Now she loved to sit for an hour each morning and watch Mrs. Sykes at work.

"What you do is very much like my writing," she said, as the woman gathered the upper arm into a series of puffs with quick motions of her fingers. "You start with vast amounts of material, you cut it down into manageable lengths, you sew the various pieces together into an approximation of what you want, you try it on someone for effect, you make final careful adjustments. And *voilà*, a finished dress or a polished memoir."

"Hm," was Mrs. Sykes's response to this flight of fancy. Her mouth was full of pins. It was clear she did not want to talk while she worked. Well, Anna could understand that.

Mrs. Hawkins took a keen interest in the creation. Looking at the drawing of the dress one morning, she said, "I declare, I never noticed before that bit of fiddle-faddle that goes down the skirt, right here." She pointed to an asymmetrically placed string of bows, buttons, and tassels on the skirt. "I know something would work better than them geegaws."

"Why what could that be, Mrs. Hawkins?"

"Let me work it out, ma'am. It be a surprise for sure."

Two days later, she showed Anna a strip of black grosgrain with a motif of beautiful beaded butterflies in a rainbow of colours. "How lovely, where on earth did you get it?"

"My Indian, the one that brings the fish, he tells me his wife can do a piece of beadwork. So I say, 'go ahead', and here it be."

It was the finishing touch for Mrs. Sykes's creation. Anna tried the dress on and looked at herself in the pier-glass in her bedchamber. "Perfect," she said.

Mrs. Hawkins looked over Anna's shoulder into the mirror. "Perfect," she echoed.

But the dressmaker shook her head and pointed at the gown. Anna took it off, and waited in her petticoats while the woman adjusted the busk of bone built into the bodice to keep the low front of the waistline in place. That being done, she handed the dress back to Anna, who put it on again. There was silence while she circled round and round, examining her creation from every angle.

Then she removed the pins from her mouth, put them into the pocket of her apron, and declared, "*Now* it is perfect."

"Oh, Mrs. Sykes, what a wonder you are." For the first time in seven days, the woman's thin lips parted in a small smile.

Anna modelled the gown for her husband that evening. He put down his newspaper and watched her while she hummed a waltz and twirled round and round in front of his chair.

"Very becoming, my dear, in both colour and style. So lovely, in fact, that I shall not even ask you how much you have had to take from the household accounts to pay for it all."

"I believe that I shall be like Cinderella at the ball, Robert."

"And have I been cast as the ugly stepsister? Or the wicked stepmother?"

Anna did not bother to respond. Into her mind came a vision of Prince Charming. He looked a lot like Sam Jarvis.

TWENTY-SIX

O n the carriageway in front of Hazelburn, John waited with
the coach and pair. It was a beautiful spring night. Sam and
Mary climbed up. As they moved at a fast clip west along Lot
Street, the oil lamps and candles from the McGill cottage lent a
soft glow to the full moon. They were just far enough north of the
lake that the stink from the soap factory and the miasma of sewage
from the swamp did not spoil the scent of lilacs. Sam looked
across at Mary, who sat facing him. How beautiful she was.

She put her hand on her neck and touched the pink topaz
necklace he had given her. He had asked Miss Siddons what would
be best with the new pink gown, and she had taken a small piece
of the leftover material and gone with him to the jeweller's to pick
it out. "It's lovely," Mary said, and her smile added its warmth to
the spring air. "But could you afford it, dear Sam?"

"Worth every penny," he said.

They turned south at Simcoe Street and headed towards King.
Two blocks away from Government House, they came upon the
carriages lined up on both sides of the road, their drivers calling
back and forth to each other in the darkness. John drove up to the
front door and helped them down.

Sir Francis and Lady Head greeted them at the top of the
staircase. Sam had not met the lady before. She was even
shorter than the Governor, a small fat woman with a "tolerable"
complexion, as Mary had once described it.

"Our new Superintendent of Indian Affairs," Sir Francis said.

"I hope you have something more rough and tumble for your
intercourse with the savages." Lady Head pointed at his white satin
waistcoat and black silk velvet breeches.

Sam laughed, but suddenly into his mind came the memory of Jacob's neatly appointed wigwam and the bright face of his small daughter. What did Sir Francis and his wife know about "savages"?

He could hear the sound of laughter and fiddle music from the ballroom. It was ten o'clock, and most of Toronto's élite had already assembled. Good timing. He liked to make an entrance when there were people about to notice his arrival.

He and Mary cut fine figures tonight, he knew. His tailor had made him new court dress for the occasion. He had a black silk velvet jacket with stand-up collar that nicely contrasted the rose pink of his wife's gown. Court dress had remained largely unchanged since the reign of George the Fourth, so his old jacket and waistcoat would still have been in style. But the maidservant had sprinkled black pepper over everything to keep out the moths, and he'd sneezed uncontrollably when he'd taken his jacket and breeches out of the armoire in the bedchamber. Better to get something new than to suffer.

They stood in the doorway of the ballroom for a minute while the assemblage stopped its chatter to look in their direction. Sam had never seen so many bosoms on display in one place. The orchestra—some of whom he recognized as soldiers from the garrison—sat behind the ornamental shrubbery at the head of the ballroom. There were loops of greenery everywhere and huge vases of lilacs and mock orange in the corners.

He felt Mary tug on his sleeve. "Come, Sam, we are just in time for the country dance." She led him to the centre of the floor, where they joined the rows of dancers—men facing women—for the beginning of the intricate set of figures. As they waited for the opening chords of the dance, Sam heard the footman announce "Vice-Chancellor Jameson and Mrs. Jameson." He had just time to look around and catch a fleeting glimpse of Anna's white shoulders, narrow waist and the striking red hair twisted to the top of her head and fastened with a bright ornament.

"Hurry, Sam. They're waiting for us to lead."

He grasped Mary by the waist and did a quickstep down the rows of partners.

As the dance ended, the Jamesons came forward to speak to them. They made a striking couple. Anna was beautiful, and her husband looked as distinguished as a Vice-Chancellor should, but when Sam looked more closely at his rig, he was pleased to see that though the man had on a new pair of black silk hose, his court dress was definitely not new. And was there a stink of black pepper?

As Sam spoke to Jameson, he noticed George Herchmer Markland standing, arms crossed, on the opposite side of the room under a painting of a former governor. "I'm glad to see Markland here," Sam said. "It's a bit of a surprise after what the Gov said about him earlier in the year. I thought perhaps he'd get the cut."

"No doubt the rumours have died out," Jameson said. He turned to Mary. "You are looking extremely well this evening."

Instead of stringing out the niceties, as she usually did, Mary was staring at Anna's gown. And Mrs. Widmer was right behind Mary, whispering to her husband from behind her raised fan. Something was definitely askew if Sam could judge from his wife's flushed face.

Then the penny dropped. Anna and Mary were wearing identical gowns. He'd often heard from his mother and his wife that such an event was a catastrophe. Just as he was wondering what he should do, Anna put out her hand and touched Mary's arm gently. She leaned over and spoke into her ear. Sam heard what she said.

"If you will give me a minute, I can put things right."

Without waiting for a response, Anna raised her voice. It was a low, melodious voice, but it carried.

"Dear Mary, I have always admired your sense of style. I believe I said once—and it has been held against me, I know—that though the women of this town have pretty frocks, they are invariably in the fashion of two or three years ago. You have always been the exception. And now, I look at you and admire you once more. Your beautiful gown is, I know, patterned after the *robe de mariage de Seigneuresse Treadwell*. It has, this spring, been the fashion *comme il faut* of Paris salons."

Mrs. Widmer closed her fan with a click, and the buzz of voices stilled. "My dear friend, Mme. Ottilie von Goethe, daughter-in-law of the eminent writer, sent me a copy of the design of the Treadwell gown and assured me that there would be no one on this side of the Atlantic who could aspire to such a creation. And I believed her. I have been duped. At some expense, I had this gown made." Anna fingered the bodice of her gown. "And then I come here tonight and find that you have trumped me." She sighed. "But I do not complain. I have only admiration and envy of your fashion *savoir.*"

How would Mary handle this? Sam wondered. He listened as she showed the savvy he so often admired. "Dear Anna," she replied. "Someone once said that imitation is the sincerest form of flattery. And I commend you for choosing a colour that shows to perfection your beautiful complexion."

"Allow me to take a liberty," Anna continued, leaning over and taking the band of rose-coloured bows, buttons and tassels into her small white fingers. "I love what you have achieved with this accent." She pointed now to her own band of black grosgrain with the beaded butterflies. "What is your opinion of what I have done with this feature of the gown?"

"Quite lovely, I assure you."

Catastrophe averted, Sam bowed to the Jamesons and took his wife by the hand. He found her a chair where she could watch the dancing. "Hold the fort, my dear. I'll be back in a minute." He needed to find a pisspot. He knew from previous occasions that there was one in a small chamber down a narrow hall near the games room where the older men often gathered to play billiards.

Having done the necessary, he emerged, and almost ran into Jameson and Markland on their way into the chamber. Markland's hand was caressing—yes, that was the word for it—Jameson's sleeve.

They sprang apart at Sam's appearance. Markland spoke first, pointing to a greasy smear on the sleeve where his hand had been. "Jameson just got a blob of wax on his sleeve from the candelabra, and I was suggesting spirit of turpentine. What do you think, Jarvis?"

"Should do the trick," Sam replied then made his escape back into the main hallway and the ballroom. It could be true—perhaps Markland was simply giving advice on the candlewax—but he doubted it. The way they had jumped apart, the dismay on their faces when he had emerged suddenly from the room: those things suggested something quite different. They had clearly expected to have a few minutes alone over the pisspots. And now he understood what Anna had meant when she had asked him not to make facile assumptions about her marriage.

There was a commotion in the ballroom when he returned. He could see Dr. Widmer in the middle of the floor and a crowd gathered around him. Mary, however, was still seated where he'd left her, and Anna was beside her. "What's happened?" he asked.

"One of Emma Robinson's daughters was dancing at such a clip that she slammed into another dancer and cut the girl's arm with her bracelet. There was a loud scream and some spurting blood, and as you see, Dr. Widmer is looking after things."

"Quite the diversion," Anna said. "Robert took the opportunity to go and play billiards in the games room."

In a few minutes, the musicians began to tune their instruments. Anna looked at her dance card. "I see you have written your name on my card," she said to Sam. "Shall we join the line?"

"Here's Colonel Fitzgibbon for me," Mary said, and the four of them moved to the floor as the musicians struck up a galop.

"I don't remember putting my name on your card," Sam said, grinning at Anna in the few seconds before they leapt down the lineup of dancers. And then they had no more time to talk until they both stood gasping against one of the windowsills. On the far side of the room, Sam could see his wife and Fitz mopping their brows.

"I noticed your husband with Markland a few minutes ago."

"Ah, yes." She paused and looked straight into his face. "I knew his exit for the billiard room was merely an excuse."

"I am truly sorry," he said, not knowing quite what line to take.

"Don't be. It's something I've known about for a while, and I'm reconciled to it. After I make my journey into the wilds of Upper

Canada this summer, I shall return to Europe and take up my own life again. It is a good life. I have many friends there. I need nobody's pity."

"You promised to join me on Manitoulin Island, do you remember that?"

"I always keep my word."

"I hold you to it." He took her hand and led her across the room to Mary and the Colonel.

"Supper downstairs," the master of ceremonies announced.

"Gives them time to make sure all the blood is cleaned up," Sam said to the Colonel, who was still panting from the dance.

Anna took Fitz's arm. "Would you agree, dear sirs, that the Battle of the Sexes is less gory than, say, the Battle of Beaver Dams?"

Sam and his friend laughed. "As deadly, perhaps, but certainly less bloody," Sam said. He looked about the ballroom. "I do not see your husband anywhere, Mrs. Jameson. Will you join Mary and me and the Colonel and Mrs. Fitzgibbon for supper? All this exercise has no doubt given us an appetite."

Supper was downstairs in the dining room. Damask tablecloths covered the sideboards and tables, and a hundred beeswax candles caught the sparkle of the starched linen, wineglasses and blue-and-gold china. Menservants—again Sam recognized men from the garrison, hired for the occasion—stood about awaiting directions from the steward.

"A good spread, better than the usual fare," Sam whispered to Mary. He always liked to compare the vice-regal meals with his own suppers at Hazelburn.

"Sir Francis needed a wife to set it up," Mary agreed. "You will no doubt find an improvement in the quality of the wine."

It was the custom at these events for the gentlemen to hold back while the ladies ate. So the Colonel seated his "little girl", as he called her, at a comfortable table near the buffet, and Sam placed Mary and Mrs. Jameson beside her. The women seemed in perfect amity. He was relieved that the crisis of the matching ballgowns had passed, and now that he thought about it, it seemed actually amusing that the two women in his life should pick the same dress.

He and the Colonel looked over the offerings on the sideboard, then heaped the plates with cold tongue, roast chicken and meat pie. "I only hope there will be something left over when we finish feeding the ladies," Fitz said.

As Sam passed the food over Anna's left shoulder, he noticed the startling whiteness of her skin against the oakleaf bronze of her gown. For a second or two he paused. He wanted to put out his hand and touch her shoulder; it would be so soft...

"Please watch what you're about, Sam," Mary said. "There's such a tilt to that plate. Everything is about to slide off."

He came to his senses, set the food down in front of Anna and went to get another plate for Mary.

While the ladies ate, the men hovered, allowing themselves only a glass of wine from the server's tray. "Much better," Fitz said as he took a sip. "Remember how we used to joke about the discount Sir Francis got for relieving the vintner of his dregs?"

By the time the ladies had eaten the mince tarts and cherries in syrup, Sam and his friend were ready to fill their own stomachs. There was still plenty of food—the servants kept replenishing the platters—and now the men from the games room had joined the diners, and the room was crowded. The noise level rose.

They had just loaded their plates with food—some excellent whitefish had been added to the selection—when Jameson and Markland approached the sideboard. "Where's my wife?" Jameson asked. A bit the worse for drink, Sam thought.

"Fitz and I gave her and our wives supper. She couldn't find you, and though the lady made no complaint, mind you, she needed an escort. Why didn't you tell her where she could find you?"

"'Scuse me, no offence intended. I thank you for your attention to her, sir." He turned to Markland. "Better get some food into us." Sam watched as Jameson put a large chunk of chicken onto his plate and waved away the servant who offered wine. Then Sam, the Chancellor and the Colonel sat down with the ladies while

Markland moved off to join Henry Boulton and some of the other men at another table.

Sam had barely tucked into his meat pie when he saw the Governor approach their table. "May I sit down?" he asked, pulling out a chair. Everyone rose in deference to the honour bestowed upon them, and waited while he seated himself.

"I am happy to sit among you, for it gives me an opportunity to hear your comments on the achievements of Parliament in this last session."

"Very commendable," Sam said.

"Extraordinary," echoed Jameson.

Sir Francis cleared his throat. In this tiny town, Sam said to himself, there lives a teeny tiny man with a position too big for his tiny brain, and now we shall have to listen to a tiny speech.

"I am proud of what Parliament has accomplished in this session, and I am happy to say that as the leader of this society, I have been the prime mover of important changes that will benefit all and sundry, from the distinguished gathering in this gilded chamber down to the lowliest savage in our far-flung forests." The Gov paused, patted his curls, and continued. "Drunkenness has been the curse of this country, and now the Act which imposes an additional duty on licences to vend liquor will put an end to degradation."

He puffed out his little chest, like a pouter pigeon, and waited for the response that came, rather weakly, "Bravo! Bravo!"

He had more to say, had even cleared his throat again, when from down the table came Anna's voice. "Please excuse me, Sir Francis, but as one who attended the proroguing of Parliament last month—albeit from the gallery—and heard the reading of this Act, may I be permitted to make a comment?"

"Of course, dear lady. I am always glad to hear an opinion from the distaff." He beamed upon her.

"The Act on which you pride yourself will do very little good in the present state of society here."

Sam heard a murmur of voices from behind. Anna's voice, though soft, had undoubtedly reached the next table. She continued. "The Act will do nothing to make criminal the wretched practices by which certain merchants in this town cheat the Indians. Nor will it raise the price of liquor enough to deter drunkenness among the general population. You might as well try to dam up a flood with a bundle of reeds, or douse a fire with a cup of water, as attempt to put down drunkenness and vice by such trifling measures as that Act you passed."

Mrs. Widmer's giggle punctuated this remark, along with a buzz of voices like a hundred wasps whose hive had been knocked down. "My god," Fitz whispered in Sam's ear, "listen to that. Never before in the history of this town has a woman dared to say 'boo' to the Governor."

With a barely perceptible pause, Anna swept on. "I suppose, however, that anything which is *attempted* here is better than nothing. But I do wish that you had made an attempt during this session of Parliament to address the plight of the insane."

"The insane, Mrs. Jameson? What have we to do with the insane?" Sir Francis's hands clenched. He made little punching motions.

"At present these unfortunate persons either wander about uncared for, or are shut up in jails. In the dungeon of our town jail, for example, female lunatics are locked up in cages. Their confinement is severe beyond that of the most hardened criminal. I know one of them. She lost a beloved husband and a small child within one week this winter. The affliction of grief struck her down. What did she do to deserve—"

"I must ask you to say no more, madam. This is neither the time nor the place... Please, Chancellor Jameson..." Sir Francis nodded at Jameson, who rose and went over to his wife.

"Anna, we will go home now. Kindly excuse us, sir." Jameson bowed, and Anna pushed back her chair and got up.

"I thank you and Lady Head for a fine evening, Sir Francis," she said. "If I have upset you by talking politics—a topic unfitting for a lady—I apologize. I fear I have upset my husband, and I must apologize to him as well. He is one of your staunchest supporters, Sir Francis."

In a moment they had gone. The Governor turned to Mary. "Dear lady, what an embarrassing interlude." His face very red, he rose and moved on to another table where, no doubt, he hoped for a warmer reception.

"Anna is a fine woman in many respects, Sam," Mary said as they drove back to Hazelburn. "I think of the lovely way she handled that embarrassment of our identical dresses. But I cannot think what prompted such an outburst this evening. It was most unfeminine."

"She was right in everything she said, you know. She's heard about Crimshaw's dealings with the Indians."

"So that is why she would not buy her dress material from him. I wondered about that."

"She hit the mark with that comment on the insane, too. When I was in prison, I remember not being able to sleep because of their incessant howling. And that was in 1817, and now, twenty years later, nothing has changed."

"You think she was right to speak up?"

"Brave, certainly, and I think she deserved more support from the rest of us. But I sat there like Sir Francis's spaniel, said nothing but 'woof woof' and wagged my tail."

"We are all so dependent on the Governor's goodwill, Sam. You thought of me and the children, and I love you for that. Anna has no dependents. Mama told me that she even makes enough money from her writing to support herself. So her rules are not our rules."

As the horses clattered on through the fresh night air, Sam thought over Anna's outburst. It was almost as if she had wanted to embarrass her husband, though she made it clear her opinions were not his. Aloud he said, "You're right. She makes her own rules. For that reason, I admire her, but she scares me." He couldn't say anything more to Mary. But he had plenty to think about. What if Anna had orchestrated this evening's outburst in order to free herself from Jameson? If that was the case, what would happen on

Manitoulin? What would she expect?

He must have sighed. Mary patted his hand. "Dear Sam, you are tired. It's been quite an evening. We both need a good, uninterrupted night's sleep."

In our separate beds, was the unspoken completion to that sentence. Well, so be it, thought Sam. Anna will undoubtedly be alone in *her* bedchamber too. Is she thinking of her escape from her husband? Looking forward to seeing me in the privacy of the northern wilderness?

"I can hardly wait," he said aloud. And remembered, just in time, to add a yawn.

TWENTY-SEVEN

Anna was thankful for the carriage ride home, for Robert would be unable to say anything to her in front of the coachman. She had a quarter hour to compose herself and think about the coming battle.

At last, in the privacy of their own drawing room, he pulled her around to face him. "Are you happy now that you have made a fool and a laughingstock of yourself in front of Sir Francis and everyone else who matters in this town?"

"There were truths that needed to be stated. I have longed to speak out. My only regret is that you interrupted me before I had a chance to remind Sir Francis that William Lyon Mackenzie petitioned the government in 1829 for the establishment of a lunatic asylum. I heard all about it from the jailer. Mackenzie must have some good points after all. Perhaps I'll write a letter to—"

"Stop right now. You will say nothing more, Anna. You will leave Toronto, take that damnable wilderness trip you keep nattering about, then return to Europe as soon as it can be arranged. I want nothing more to do with you." He went to the sideboard in the dining room and poured the contents of the whiskey decanter into a glass.

"Nor I with you, Robert. But if I leave, I must have the guarantee of an income. Only a short time ago, you refused me an annual stipend of three hundred pounds."

Robert whacked his glass on the sideboard with such force that its contents splashed across the polished surface. "You have it."

"And I must, of course, have some sort of formal document drawn up."

"I'll see Robinson tomorrow."

Anna glimpsed her reflection in the mirror over the sideboard. She composed her features into a smile of gratitude. Inside herself, however, she felt her heart thudding with excitement.

Anna's room was a mess. On top of her books and manuscript on the writing table lay the letter from Ottilie; on a chair, the strange vessel that her friend had sent in a separate packet; and piled on the bed, the assorted clothing and necessaries that were to go into a small trunk. Anna picked up Ottilie's letter and rubbed her cheek against the beautiful linen paper on which her friend always wrote. Yes, there was still a faint hint of her wild rose fragrance. For a moment, nostalgia surged through her as she thought of coffee and Viennese pastry and laughter with Ottilie on her tiny balcony overlooking Schönbrunn Castle. Then she reread the letter for perhaps the tenth time.

> *Vienna, April 2*
> *Dear, dear Anna:*
> *I intended to send this missive via a graceful little passenger pigeon I have trained for the purpose, but since your letter reached me today—after a mere six weeks—I have decided to entrust it to the mailboat.*
> *You tell me about your plans for summer rambles in the northern wilderness. I hope you will receive this letter and the packaged gift before you venture far from the meager amenities that Toronto has offered you. You may find yourself in a canoe in the middle of a bottomless lake. Or trapped in a wigwam whose only furnishings are scalps. Then you will take my gift from your portmanteau and say, "Enfin!"*
> *Even utilitarian objects like this one should be beautiful, and when I saw it at the Sèvres porcelain factory, I thought, "Expensive, yes, but of service in moments of dire necessity." So here it is. One cannot say, "Enjoy it." Ma per l'occasione...!*
> *Dearest friend, how I envy you! To soar free as an eagle over*

lake and hilltop—sans enfants, sans mari—quelle aventure!
And if you should be swamped in a bog or eaten up by a bear
or scalped by a savage—what a magnificent shuffling off of
these mortal coils! I shall immortalize you in a poem. What
think you of "La Mort d'Anna"?

Besides the training of my darling pigeon, I have been much
engaged in the care and nurturing of my newest amour—Gustav
Kühne. He is a writer of bad historical novels, as you undoubtedly
know, but as a lover... ! Sono malata d'amore, veramente!

How I long to hear from you again, dearest Anna! Write to me
from one of those beautiful lakes over which you will soon travel
avec tes voyageurs basanés. Don't forget to pack your sponges!

My love, always, always, always,
Ottilie

Anna had just put the letter back on the table when there was
a knock at the door, and Mrs. Hawkins entered. She clutched a
blue handkerchief in one fist, and her eyes were pink. Her other
hand encircled a slip of paper with a red seal. "Mrs. Robinson's
manservant brought this over a few minutes ago, ma'am."

Anna slit it open, glanced at it and laughed. "The silliness of the
woman! It's her recipe for Derby cakes. She actually thinks I might
carry it about with me over land and sea, lo, to the Western Isles?"
She rolled the sheet up, gave it a twist and aimed it at the hearth. It
fell into the ashes, where it gave a brief hiss and expired.

"Oh, ma'am, I never learned to make them things right, did I?"

"Thank goodness for that. Who would ever pine for a Derby
cake when she could have a slice of your good gingerbread? Now
there's a recipe I'd like."

The housekeeper dabbed at her eyes with the handkerchief.
Anna walked towards her and put her arms around the woman's
shoulders. "Please, please, do not grieve, Mrs. Hawkins. I shall come
back at the end of August and say goodbye to you before I set out for
New York and Europe. Think, do, of how much less work you will
have for the summer months without my clothes to wash and—"

"Oh, ma'am, it be the beginning of the end."

"It is an end of one life for me, certainly. And I shall miss you so much, dear Mrs. Hawkins. You have been a true friend throughout these long months. But I need to think about new beginnings. And you must stay where you are and help Mr. Jameson. Haven't you noticed how he looks forward to the comforts you offer—his Sunday tea, his lamb chops with mint sauce? He's come a long way since those desolate winter days when I first arrived. And now, will you please help me to look over these things on the bed and decide what may be left behind? I expect to have to fend for myself most of the time, and I do not want to be burdened with a heavy trunk."

Mrs. Hawkins stuffed the handkerchief into her apron pocket. She studied the items laid out. "Oh, ma'am, I love that shawl. Them pink flowers are perfect against your lovely face." She held it next to her own red cheeks. "And so soft and warm, too." She put it back on the bed and looked over the other things again. Then she took up the guitar and set it to one side. "Now, ma'am, sure, you do not need this."

"It was a partial payment for my first major book, you know, and I have never gone anywhere without it." As Anna looked at it now, she remembered how she had played it on the steamer to Niagara and how wonderfully silly Sam had been in his role of toreador. And now there was Manitoulin to look forward to. She moved the guitar back into the centre of the bed. "Perhaps I shall be in far places where there is no piano, but I shall still have my music."

"Now, this knife be a good idea, I do say." The housekeeper ran her finger along the edge of the stiletto. "I will get my man to sharpen it this day. Out there"—Mrs. Hawkins gestured towards the window and the expanse of Lake Ontario—"be savages and white folk worse than savages."

"Not to mention bears and rattlesnakes and cougars and shopkeepers who overcharge." She was relieved to hear Mrs. Hawkins's laugh. Then her housekeeper spotted Ottilie's gift. She picked it up and turned it round and round in her hands. "A vase, ma'am? Sure, and you don't be needing *that* on your trip."

"Not a vase, Mrs. Hawkins, but something far more useful. *Una vasa da notte.*"

"Now, ma'am, none of them frog languages for me, if you please. Just tell me straight out in the King's English what this be."

"Chamberpot."

"Chamberpot?" Mrs. Hawkins shook her head in disbelief. "I never seen a chamberpot like this one."

Nor had Anna. It did, indeed, look somewhat like a vase. In fact, she had read Ottilie's letter over several times before she got the right idea. Her friend's phrase "in moments of dire necessity" had been the clue. Unlike the usual chamberpot, round and deep with a lid, this one was deep, narrow and lidless. Anna could see how, in an emergency, she could place it between her legs and relieve herself without having to retreat to the cover of woods.

Mrs. Hawkins had taken hold of the idea. "Useful it may be. If you be short-taken in the back of a wagon, ma'am, think how—" She broke off, stroked her chin as she thought further. "But adjustments must be made. Yes indeed." She looked over the items on the bed. "I be taking your drawers away now to put slits between the legs. Just to make things more convenient, like." There was not an ounce of embarrassment in her manner as she gathered up Anna's undergarments and made for the door.

"Oh, Mrs. Hawkins, you are a wonder, you are. And for such a wonder, this shawl seems far too small a gift. But here it is." She took the wool-and-silk oblong scarf that her housekeeper had admired and draped it around Mrs. Hawkins's shoulders. Then she pulled the housekeeper towards her and gave her a hug.

After she left, Anna picked up the *vasa da notte* and looked again at the scenes with which it was decorated. No mere container for urine, this was a masterpiece of the porcelain-maker's art. On its outside and inside surfaces were naughty—indeed, lewd— scenes from the *commedia dell'arte*. Anna's favourite showed a bedchamber and two lovers in the throes of intercourse, oblivious to the old man (undoubtedly the husband) who listened from under the bed.

She had also received gifts from three of her Toronto acquaintances. Mrs. Powell had sent a bar of scented soap, and her daughter Eliza a hand towel. And Mary Jarvis's servant had dropped off a small sachet of dried rosemary. With it was a note that said, merely: "Rosemary, that's for remembrance." She was pleased with the little gift and the quotation, surprised that Mary had studied *Hamlet*, given Mrs. Powell's views on the uselessness of formal education for women. Perhaps the governess had helped her. She put the sachet in her trunk then took from her shelf *Characteristics of Shakespeare's Women*. It was one of her most successful books, and she enjoyed rereading her thoughts on Ophelia. Poor mad Ophelia, deranged by the unhappiness of her love. She had not had the strength of character to get on with life.

But much as she was touched by these small gifts, it was the chamberpot she liked best. So different from the staid pots in staid bedchambers, it would go along with her as a sort of symbol of her new way of life. She must tell Ottilie all this in her thank-you letter. She sat down at her table, took up her pen, and smiled to herself at the thought of how Ottilie would laugh at her wayward fancies.

Part Two

Summer Rambles

TWENTY-EIGHT

In the June sunshine, Sam walked down the main street of Kingston. His second major meeting with the Indian bands had gone better than the first one in Niagara. Not through anything, really, that he had done. Its success had been due to the contribution of a Chippewa missionary.

"Don't even try to pronounce my Indian name," he'd said. "Call me George Copway." He'd given Sam an eloquent message for the Governor. "The pale faces have taught the Indians to drink, to steal horses, to curse, and now it's high time to give them spelling books." And he'd followed up with a document on the need for Indian schools, with excellent suggestions on how to proceed. If Sir Francis would only pay attention to it...

And the Indians hadn't seemed to mind the meeting place at Fort Henry, that citadel of British superiority.

And now, before he treated himself to a well-deserved drink, he had an errand to carry out. After thinking hard about the matter on the steamer from Toronto, he had decided to pay a visit to Mary's niece and her lover, John Grogan. Or, if they weren't at home, at least to have a look at the place they lived in.

He walked to the end of town, turned off the main street and stopped at a small frame dwelling behind a freshly painted brown fence, the gate of which opened with a squeak. The front yard was planted in beds of late spring flowers: narcissi, grape hyacinths, daffodils and red tulips. He had not gone more than a few steps down one of the pebble paths when a stout, bright-eyed young woman launched herself at him, crying, "Uncle Sam! Uncle Sam!"

He kissed Elizabeth and turned to greet the tall man in red coat and epaulets who had come down the path behind her. "My god!

Sam Jarvis! What are you doing in town?"

Sam tried to explain while Elizabeth and Grogan—one on each side of him— pulled him towards the house. "You will have tea with us, won't you, Jarvis? It would cheer us up tremendously." Grogan looked down at Elizabeth, whose cheeks were streaked with tears. "Elizabeth feels so isolated in this place. But how did you know we were here?"

"Mary's mother mentioned that you'd moved from London, and I got directions to your house from a sergeant at Fort Henry."

"London got too hot for us, so Elizabeth and I escaped here till things cool down a bit. Of course, if that devil Mackenzie kicks up a fuss, I'll be posted to Toronto, and Elizabeth will have to stay behind until things get sorted out."

Grogan pulled at one of his large ears, looked embarrassed, and blurted, "I say, Jarvis, you've always been a decent chap and...I appreciate this..." His voice trailed away.

Sam remembered his own days of unhappiness after his trial and release from prison. "I've needed kind words and friendship myself."

"Dear Uncle Sam, let us sit on the back porch."

The back stoop overlooked the St. Lawrence River. Elizabeth pulled forward a comfortable Windsor chair for Sam. Grogan took a handkerchief from his white breeches and wiped the tears from her flushed cheeks. He kissed the tip of her nose. "And now, my dear, let us have a good tea. Your Uncle Sam needs sustenance."

"In five minutes it will be ready. The merchant's boy delivered some pickled lobster today, and I have just made Grandmama Powell's lobster pâté. It will be the best tea in the annals of Kingston tea ceremonies, and think—oh think—how fortunate that dear, dear Uncle Sam should come on such an occasion." The tears had given way to giggles, and Sam found himself suddenly happy to be with his niece and her lover.

"Some sherry while we wait?" Grogan took a decanter from a small table on the porch and poured three glasses. From inside the house, they could hear the clink of teacups and Elizabeth's chatter to the maid.

"I must tell you at once, Jarvis, before Elizabeth comes back, that I expect the worst from Stuart. He is in a rage, and my friends in London tell me that he plans to file for divorce and sue me for a thousand pounds 'for the destruction of his marital bliss'. *Marital bliss.* But he has always been a successful barrister, and even if he does not get what he wants, I fear he will be awarded a substantial sum."

"Good god, man, how will you pay it?"

"By selling my commission."

"And that will be the end of your military career. What then?"

"Why then, we will be married and move to England. My family have promised to help us, but they have little to spare. I fear it will be a rocky road."

Elizabeth came through the back door with the teacups and tea caddy, followed by the maid with the urn. Elizabeth took the tea leaves from the pretty floral tea caddy, put them into a pot, poured water from the urn, passed the lobster pâté on small rounds of oatmeal biscuit, offered more sherry—all in the grand manner of her grandmother. But Sam noticed that her cheeks had been touched with rouge, and her hands trembled.

She closed the lid of the tea caddy with a bang. "Oh, Uncle Sam, I know that I will never see Papa again, nor Grandmama, nor my aunts, nor my daughters...but I could not go on. I...could...not... go...on." Grogan set down his cup and pressed her hands into his.

"It was as bad as all that?" Sam asked. "I'm afraid I've mostly heard the story that Mrs. Powell tells." How this "volatile and vulgar" granddaughter had "abandoned" her husband and small daughters and taken up with a "low-class" British officer of the Thirty-Second Regiment, posted to Upper Canada. How Elizabeth had disgraced the Powell family and must evermore be banished from it.

Suddenly a shadow seemed to engulf Elizabeth's round, pleasant face and bright eyes. "He kept quoting that judge who came after Grandpapa..."

"He" was obviously her husband. "You mean the judge who replaced your grandfather on the King's Bench?"

"Him. My husband would sit there, staring at me through those thick spectacles—Four-Eyed Stuart, people call him—and then, out of the blue, he'd recite the judge's creed, 'Men as lords of the creation have a right to chastise rebellious dames, as long as that chastisement does not endanger their lives.' And I'd say, 'What have I done now?' And he'd say, 'Time for chastisement.' Just as if I were a fly on the wall that needed swatting. And then, then..." Her face went so white that the blobs of rouge stood out grotesquely.

"He beat her," Grogan said. "With a riding whip. Where it wouldn't show. I saw the bruises on her back and legs."

"I suffered in Hell for three years, and then I met John, and suddenly the world was new again. Suddenly I was Eve in the Garden of Paradise, and he was Adam."

And look what happened to them, Sam reflected. Aloud he said, "Your grandmother has never mentioned the beatings, though Mary has said things. It's horrible. And the laws of the country being what they are, this abusive man will get custody of your little girls. My god, what will become of them?"

Fresh sobs from Elizabeth. "I know, I know. I've...I've blown up the powder keg, as Grandpapa used to say, and now I have no ammunition."

"But we have each other, dear Elizabeth," Grogan said tenderly.

"Yes, my darling, we have each other. You know, Uncle Sam, I never, ever, loved my husband. In fact, I scarcely knew him before we married. He used to wink at me in church, and I suppose I was flattered. I was a stupid little girl, I had no education, and everyone wanted to be rid of me. So I went along with it. Women have no choices in this world." She sat up straight, blew her nose and wiped her eyes. "What I should say is, women have *few* choices in this world. I've taken one of those choices. But oh, Uncle Sam, it's been hard..."

"Yes, my dear niece, you've chosen love above subjugation. Above motherhood. Above gossip-mongering and scandal. You have faced the realities of the world we live in and weighed the consequences. You've been brave, braver than any of us could know." Sam rose from his comfortable chair, made a deep bow and kissed Elizabeth's hand. "I wish the both of you much happiness."

He sat down again. "And now, I must have three or four more of those excellent oatcakes and lobster pâté."

They stayed on the stoop for some time, feet propped on the stretchers of their chairs, and watched the schooners and steamers move up and down the river. Then Sam noticed the sun dipping into the west. He rose. "I had better get to my hotel."

"Will you not stay with us for the night, Uncle Sam?"

"No, my dear. I thank you, but my hostelry is booked and my luggage delivered there." He had seen enough of adulterous bliss to know that he needed peace and time to think. "Goodbye. God bless you both."

Elizabeth wrapped three leftover biscuits in a little white napkin and tucked them into the pocket of his waistcoat. She kissed his cheek. As he walked through the front gate onto the roadway, he turned round. His niece and Grogan stood on the pebble path, among the tulips, waving.

He did not go directly to his hotel. He walked back and forth along the harbour, thinking of those little girls in the hands of a monstrous father, of the sacrifices made by their mother in the name of love, of his own children, of Mary. And Anna.

TWENTY-NINE

Sam and Mary waited together on the pier while Colonel Fitzgibbon superintended the unloading of Anna's small trunk from the wagon and its placement in the hold of the steamboat which would leave for Niagara in a half-hour. Anna herself stood near the log hut at the end of the pier. She was saying something to her housekeeper—whom Sam recognized from the New Year's levee—and another woman who held a babe in her arms.

"Who's that one?" Sam asked. He remembered her from somewhere. The night of the fire, was it?

"Oh, she's the seamstress who made the gown that Anna wore to the ball. Anna tells me she charges half what I paid to that French woman, so I intend to give her some work soon."

Anna came towards them holding a small portmanteau. She wore leather gloves and a plain, dark green gown with long tight sleeves. Not a glimpse of those beautiful shoulders and hands. But her smile was in place. "How lovely of you to come here to see me off."

"But where is the Chancellor, Anna?" Mary posed the question Sam could not summon courage to ask. "I assumed he would be here with the rest of us."

"He's gone to the government offices. We said *adieu* at breakfast."

There was a long silence. Sam watched the passengers stream onto the pier. "What's after Niagara?" he said.

"Across the province by coach and wagon. First to the Talbot settlement. I knew Colonel Talbot's family in the Old Country. Then it's off to Windsor, by steamer to Detroit, across Lake St. Clair, and up Lake Huron to Mackinaw. Then, if my luck holds, by bateau to Sault Ste. Marie. And afterwards to the gift-giving—"

"Jarvis, Sam Jarvis!" Sam turned to see a young man in clerical rig come alongside. A handsome man with a Roman nose, patrician jaw, and a head of thick dark hair.

"Mac McMurray? It's been years."

"Far too long. We've just been here overnight. On to Niagara now for the day." He smiled at Sam's companions. "And here we have your good wife. And Fitzgibbon. Lovely to see you both. And this is my wife, Charlotte." He nodded towards the young woman holding his arm. She had brown skin and dark eyes, her hair gathered into a neat braid. In spite of her European-style dress, she was undoubtedly Indian. McMurray turned to Anna. "I have not had the pleasure...?"

In a flash, without waiting for Sam's intervention, Anna introduced herself and mentioned her "summer rambles".

"Unaccompanied, ma'am?" McMurray said. "Oh, you and Charlotte have much in common. She is Chippewa, you know, and thinks nothing of paddling a canoe miles along the Ste. Marie's River on a summer's day to bring home a fine catch of whitefish. We eat whitefish morning, noon and night."

"You are from Sault Ste. Marie? It's my last stop before I head to Manitoulin Island for Mr. Jarvis's Indian ceremonies."

"Then you must stay with us," Mrs. MacMurray said. "Many Indians from Mac's congregation are going to the Island, and we thought we'd go ourselves in a bateau. You could look around the Sault for a day or two, then we could certainly find room aboard for you."

"Wonderful!"

"Well, there will be the mosquitoes, Mrs. Jameson. You will not find them wonderful, I assure you. In fact, this country has the biggest, most bloodthirsty mosquitoes in the whole world. But we Chippewas have remedies, and I shall be only too happy to cover your fine white complexion with goldenrod ointment. It's messy, perhaps a bit smelly, too, I warn you. But effective." Mrs. MacMurray seemed positively gleeful as she imparted this information.

For a moment, Anna looked stricken. "I had no idea about these...these...mosquitoes."

Everyone laughed. "There's still time to change your mind," Sam said. "If you haven't heard about mosquitoes, I fear you are ill-prepared for this journey."

"Yes," Fitz said. "Bad roads, bad inns you will undoubtedly encounter—if, in fact, there *are* roads or inns at all. Not to mention the human riffraff—black, brown, and white—that you will come upon at every bend in your path. But there will be nothing as bad as the mosquito, believe it."

"I believe you are trying to frighten me," Anna said. "So I shall change the subject. You are from Toronto then, Mr. McMurray? That is how you know Mr. Jarvis?"

"I lived here for several years. I shall not forget Jarvis's attention to my family at the time of my dear father's death. It was in 1832, the time of the great cholera epidemic."

"Your father was one of its victims?"

"He was taken ill with the cholera in the early morning and died the afternoon of the same day. Funerals were hasty events in those days, badly attended, everyone in the town terrified to be out and about. But the good Reverend Strachan did the honours with great dignity. There were five mourners, and one of them was Sam Jarvis." McMurray put his hand on Sam's arm. "I appreciated that."

"Mr. Jarvis was a close friend of your father, was he?"

"Not at all. My father was a shopkeeper. You must know by now, Mrs. Jameson, that Toronto is filled with toffee-nosed gentry who look down on shopkeepers, though they depend on them for all the things that make them gentrified. So that's one of the reasons I remember Sam Jarvis's presence at my father's last rites. And I remember his kind words to my mother."

"I must set the record straight," Sam said. "McMurray's father was a decent man. He did not make my own father's last days a misery by plaguing him about his unpaid bills. Attendance at the funeral was a small gift of respect to such a man."

"I say, Jarvis, why don't you pay us a visit, too, when you're in the neighbourhood? Sault Ste. Marie is not far from Manitoulin. Three days there, three days back, and you'd meet some fine Indians who'd give you an earful about their problems. Now that you've got this new posting, you need to inform yourself."

"Listen, Mac. The only information I'm likely to get on my journey north is from the Governor. He'll keep me in a straight line for Manitoulin, and he'll talk at me all the way. Not a chance of a diversion, I'm afraid, much as I'd like it."

The steamboat's bell summoned the travellers. "Since we'll have four hours together, Mrs. Jameson," Mac said, "we shall have a good opportunity to know you better."

Anna was already taking out her notebook. "If I ask too many questions, just push me overboard."

Handshakes all around, and Sam and Mary and Fitzgibbon trailed behind the McMurrays and Anna as they moved towards the steamboat. She stopped for an instant at the log hut, where she kissed her housekeeper goodbye and shook hands with the seamstress. Then as she stepped up to the ramp, the buzz of voices gave Sam his opportunity.

"Your marriage, Anna?"

"Finished."

"What were you and Anna whispering about?" Mary asked as John drove them back to Hazelburn.

"I don't remember, really. Nothing of import."

"Did you notice how she latched on to Mrs. McMurray, practically inviting herself to camp on their doorstep?"

"Probably wants to get some tidbits on the Indians, from a female viewpoint. She'll never meet another Chippewa woman who speaks such perfect English."

"I've been glad to be Anna's friend, goodness knows. But really, sometimes she is too forward. It's so...so—"

"Unfeminine. Isn't that your favourite word for a woman you can't understand?"

"You think I'm being critical. But have you ever thought about what she might get herself up to when she's at Manitoulin—far from the restraints of white society?"

Sam did not answer immediately. What could he say? That, yes, he had thought long and hard about Anna alone—or practically alone—with him on Manitoulin?

"Sir Francis will be there, my dear, plus the Indian agent—Major Anderson—and the McMurrays. Not to mention five hundred braves with tomahawks. No doubt we can gang up to restrain her if the need arises."

Mary laughed.

THIRTY

It had been nine hours since Anna had eaten. She had had a good dinner at the last wayside hostelry: slices of dried venison, broiled; hot cakes of Indian corn, eggs, butter and a bowl of milk. Her companions at table had been two backwoodsmen, tall and strong, bronzed and brawny, shaggy and unshaven. "Two bears set on their hind legs" was how she'd described them in her notebook. Unlike bears, they had at least been civil.

Right now, in her rented wagon, she concentrated on staying alive. There was an iron bar in front of her, and her hands were swollen and blistered by continually grasping it with all her strength to prevent herself from being flung out. She could never have imagined such roads. Everybody had told her that the roads of Talbot country were better than elsewhere. Perhaps it was true, but only in the sense that Beelzebub was a better fallen angel than Lucifer.

Her driver was a young lad of fifteen or sixteen whom she'd hired at the hostelry. From Glasgow, he told her, and his mother and baby sister had died of the cholera on the way over.

"They threw Mama into the sea. And then Lizzie, only nine months old, died, because there was nobody to take care of her. Me and Father tried our best, but we couldn't do nothing. So they threw Lizzie into the sea—poor wee thing."

The lad wiped his cheeks with the back of his sleeve. "There was a man called Martin on board. He had fought in Spain with the Duke of Wellington and sold his pension to come out here. And he had a wife and nine children with him, see. Well, first his wife died, and they threw her into the sea; and then he died, and they threw him into the sea, and then the rest of 'em, one after t'other, till only a girl, twelve year old, was left."

"And she survived?" Surely there would be one morsel of happiness in this tragic tale.

"She had nursed 'em all, one after another, and seen 'em all die. And then..." He took a hand from the reins again, and again wiped his cheeks with his sleeve. "Well, *she* died, and then there was nobody left. Nobody out of eleven of 'em.

"Nothing but splash splash splash all day long—first one, then t'other, then another." There was a long silence. "Splash splash splash," he repeated.

On this note, they struggled onwards, over a road—a mud slough really, with trunks of trees laid across its worst abysses— taking so many bends, and sweeps and windings that the journey stretched out into eternity. If only there were someone seated beside her on this leather strap, someone who might cry with her or even smile at the *reductio ad absurdum* of that pathetic refrain, "splash splash splash".

The shadows from the trees and underbrush fell deeper, and soon she could not see a yard in any direction. Once or twice a deer bounded across the path, its antlers defined against the moonlight. An owl sent forth a prolonged shriek.

The boy called to a man who was trudging along with an axe on his shoulder. "How far to Colonel Talbot's?"

"About three miles and a half, straight afore you!"

Darkness fell more deeply. Clouds covered the moon. They jolted onwards.

A whistle in the darkness signalled another traveller. "How far to Colonel Talbot's?" the boy called again in the direction of the sound.

"About seven miles. You'll never get there tonight, boy. Sleep by the wayside and start fresh in the morning." The disembodied voice was that of a gentleman. Anna decided to place her faith in the woodsman's estimate.

The lad evidently shared her thoughts. "There's an inn hereabouts, ma'am. But it's not for the likes of you. If you've comed across the sea to visit Colonel Talbot, best we keep moving."

"I'm grateful for your resolve." She had already lain awake in too many flea-infested beds, listening to drunken laughter from the bar.

More jolting. Her teeth ground together and her head ached. They went slower and slower, fearful of overturning in one of the unseen ruts in the path.

Finally, when she thought her fingers would never again open, nor her brains ever settle, they ran almost headfirst into a cantering horse. There was a wild whinnying and snorting, and the cart lurched to a stop. "Watch where you're going, you bastard!" its rider yelled. "Or I'll have you before the old bashaw on charges."

"Colonel Talbot, do you mean?" Anna asked, rising from behind the slender form of her driver. "How far are we from his house?"

"Why, who have you got there, boy?" cried the man in surprise, poking his head forward to look.

"A lady that's comed a long way to visit the Colonel."

"I beg your pardon, ma'am." The man brought his horse to the side of the cart to peer at her in the gloom. "You must be the lady that the Colonel has been expecting this week past. Shall I ride back and tell him you're here?"

"No, I thank you. My driver here will take me onwards."

"Straight ahead then, you bast...boy. Follow your nose." The man slapped his horse on its neck, and they plunged into the darkness.

She knew that Colonel Talbot had built his house high on a cliff overhanging the lake called Erie. Another hour, straight uphill, and they came at last to a group of low buildings. She could see little but the whale-oil lamps that burned in the windows, and as the cart pulled up to a door, a man emerged. In the darkness, Anna could just make out a smiling face and a small, neat figure. "My dear Mrs. Jameson," the man said, "It is delightful to meet you. I have looked forward to this visit." He bowed and took her arm to help her down from the wagon while over his shoulder he gave instructions to a manservant. "Take the

boy to the kitchen, Jennings, give him a good supper with beer
and put him to bed."

With Anna's hand still on his arm, the Colonel led her into
a vestibule where a stink of animal hides and grain assailed
her. He steered her past sacks of wheat and piles of sheepskins.
"A mite different from the old home in Ireland," he said, and
Anna had a moment's memory of the gilt tables, marble floors,
and family portraits she had once seen in the front hall of his
ancestral castle in Ireland.

She had gone there, long ago, with her father to see a woman—
the Colonel's mother? aunt?—who had wanted a miniature
painted of a dead baby. The lady had taken them into a small
nursery where the baby lay in a tiny wooden box. She remembered
the pinched, grey face of the infant against the white ruffles of the
pillow, the swish of her father's pencil on sketch-paper, and dust
motes floating in the sun's rays through a window. The butler had
served them stale cakes while they sat beside the corpse.

"Sit here, madam," Anna's host said, as they came into a simple
room with a huge chimney and hearth and a long wooden table,
flanked by two chairs obviously made from the forest she had
passed through.

He poured her a glass of wine, and the servant put in front of
her a huge steak and cornbread. "Do tell me how you liked my new
roads. I take great pride in those roads. Think, there was nothing
here a generation ago but the forest paths made by the savages."

"Truly, sir, I longed for one of those quiet paths leading to a
wigwam, a piece of maple sugar and a soft bed of balsam boughs."
She looked down at her plate, took a bite of the cornbread and
thought of the effort required to saw through that piece of ox flesh.
She set down her fork. "I fear I can neither speak nor eat, sir. I have
been hours on the road, and though it was no doubt an excellent
road, I am now so weary that I ache in every bone and nerve." She
was also cold: she had felt the wind whistle across the hilltop as she
climbed out of the cart.

In a minute the man Jennings ushered her to the open door of a comfortable bedroom. A cheery fire blazed, and in front of it, a large-bosomed woman poured hot water into a ceramic pitcher. She helped Anna strip off her clothes, sponged her aching back and pulled the quilted wool coverlet over her after she'd climbed into the sleigh bed, obviously made by a local craftsman. "Such comfort, thank you," she managed to say before she passed into oblivion.

A hum of voices and smell of tobacco wakened her in the morning. She opened her eyes to find a white-headed chubby little child staring at her, perhaps the son of the angel who had assisted her the night before. The clock on the shelf above the hearth said it was almost noon. The child was gone before she could say, "Off with you," and she hastily dressed herself and went out into the hall. Along the rough log walls, five ragged, bearded men lounged. Four of them were smoking clay pipes, and the fifth was pushing a wood splint through the spaces between his teeth.

"Good morning," she said to the man with the splint. "May I ask why you are here?"

"To see Himself." The man pointed towards the open door of a room, where Anna could see her host seated behind a desk. "No need to sit," the Colonel was saying in a loud voice to a man in riding clothes who stood on the other side of the desk, "I take no fine gentlemen in my settlement. I want no dandy here who stays by the fire while hired labourers do his work for him. I need men prepared to fell and plant, to sow and reap, to build roads. I give no one a land grant until he has cleared the land and thrown up a cabin with his own hands. Such a man only will appreciate what I myself have accomplished in the thirty-five years I have been in this wilderness."

"In other words, sir, you want inferiors and dependents. You are the Great Poobah. You have your own kingdom here, and you people it with serfs."

"Get out. You waste my time."

Anna thought she recognized the voice. It was the gentleman

she and her lad had met the night before, the one who had so greatly exaggerated the distance to the Colonel's house. His face was flushed and his stock dishevelled. One brass button hung loose on his coat.

She moved quickly past the waiting men and found her way to the dining room. The capable woman who had assisted her the night before was there, pulling a handwoven cloth over the long table. "Sit you down, ma'am," she said. "I will bring victuals directly."

It was the best room Anna had seen so far in the Colonel's chateau. Here the logs had been plastered over and the walls papered. There was an elegant maple sideboard with a bowl of roses upon it and a mahogany box for the silverware. The Windsor chairs were plain but comfortable, and in a very few minutes, the woman appeared again with cheese, cornbread and hot milk in a pitcher.

"You are Mrs. Jennings?"

"Yes, ma'am, the only woman master will allow in his house, and that only because my man wanted a wife and a child and took me, the woman nearest at hand, though master swore at him for a fool." Anna looked at her blotchy complexion and crooked teeth, and thought yes, no doubt he chose her for her proximity, certainly not for her physical attractions.

She had just put some butter on her cornbread when the Colonel burst into the room. "Look here, woman, keep your brat from my audience chamber, if you please—" He broke off, seeing Anna at the table. "Excuse me, Mrs. Jameson," then continued to rail, "How can I deal with those land-pirates if he keeps climbing on my knee? It completely destroys my stature with the lower orders." He shut the door with a bang.

"He is an old bear," Mrs. Jennings said, "but my man has worked for him for a quarter century and will hear no evil of him."

"Indeed, Mrs. Jennings, the Colonel gave me a kind welcome last night, though we arrived at midnight, as you know."

"Oh, he is a nice old bear. Sometimes."

Anna wandered into a covered porch littered with shovels, mortars and pestles, bed slats, axes, a copper-lined bathtub and a hundred other objects. She looked upwards and gave a scream. Suspended from the rafters was the pelt of an enormous cougar. Its face leered down at her, ghastly and horrible. "Master killed it when it attacked the pullets," Mrs. Jennings said.

"I'm going outside to get away from the thing."

"Look over there, ma'am, you'll see the log hut which master built when he first came to these parts four-and-thirty years ago." It was a crude structure, but she noticed that the chinks between the logs had been carefully filled.

There were, in fact, a dozen or more outbuildings of all shapes and sizes, scattered here and there without the slightest regard to order or symmetry. Near one of them, obviously used to shelter geese and poultry, Jennings had just whacked the head off a hen. The *pièce de résistance* of dinner, undoubtedly. With cornbread, undoubtedly.

Beyond these buildings were the cliffs overlooking the wide blue expanse of Lake Erie. She counted six schooners with white sails. Then she wandered through acres of orchards and on her way back to the house came upon a rose garden.

"You have found my favourite place." The Colonel had come up behind her. He took secaturs from a bench and cut a bouquet of pink and crimson buds, which he presented to her with a flourish.

"You have no idea how much I have missed English roses," she said, breathing in their fragrance.

"I brought cuttings myself from England when I was there three years ago. They have done well. Let us rest here awhile and enjoy them." They sat down on a pretty seat under a tree. "I often come here to meditate."

She took a good look at him as they sat side by side. He was, she knew, about sixty-five years of age, though he did not look as much, and still handsome. His dress was rustic: buckskin breeches, sturdy boots, and a loose shirt tied with a string at the neck. Yet no one would mistake him for anything but a gentleman. There was the accent, the air, the deportment, the *something* that stamped him as such.

He seemed anxious to talk about the people they both knew in Toronto. Her dear Colonel Fitzgibbon was "an Irish peasant with no small measure of courage." Mrs. Powell was "a biddy of immeasurable ignorance." Archdeacon Strachan had "the nerve to criticize me for taking two hundred acres of land for every fifty that I assign to settlers." And as for the new Superintendent of Indian Affairs, "I have heard about the infamous duel. And I remember his father, William Jarvis, whom I had the misfortune to know when I first came here with the Simcoes in 1792. He was a wastrel and an incompetent. But what is your opinion of the son, Mrs. Jameson?"

"I like him, sir. He has proven to be a kind and generous friend."

"Well, I'm out of touch with modern views. I have not yet learned to like a murderer."

"And if I may say so, sir, you have not yet learned to forgive one's trespasses."

The Colonel's face looked for a minute like that of the fearsome cougar. Then he said, "*Touché*," got up, pruned a rose bush or two and reseated himself.

A bell from the roof of the main building sounded at that moment, and the Colonel laughed. "My courtiers summon us. We dine early." As they walked towards the house, he continued, "I say courtiers because I am sovereign here. I have twenty-eight townships, six hundred and fifty thousand acres of land, of which one hundred thousand are cleared and cultivated. I think I have worked as hard as any monarch of the realm. Or harder."

Anna's host arranged the roses himself in a green and white earthenware pitcher and set them in the middle of the dining room table. He took a place at the end of the table and motioned Jennings to seat Anna beside him. Mrs. Jennings brought in green pea soup. "Everything is fresh," the Colonel said as he ladled the steaming contents of the tureen into bowls. "You cannot imagine how I longed for a garden and a poultry shed when I first came back to Upper Canada in 1802. But for five years, I had only a blanket-coat and an axe. I slept upon the bare earth, cooked raccoons and rabbits, squirrels if we could get them, for twenty working men, and cleaned my own boots." He finished off two bowls of soup and wiped his mouth. "And now let us see what Mrs. Jennings has prepared next."

Surprise. A roasted, stuffed hen and a basket of cornbread. But it was savoury and good. And there was a perfect dessert: fresh raspberries and thick cream.

Over the meal, the Colonel had finished a second bottle of wine. His speech was slower now but still coherent. "What do you think of the temperance movement in this province?" he asked as he uncorked a third bottle. Then, without waiting for her answer, "Damn cold water drinking societies."

"Many people would agree with you." Not the time to give her own opinion on the prevalence of drunkenness in Upper Canada. "It has been an excellent meal, thank you. I am grateful that squirrels did not become a permanent item on your menu."

"Squirrels were a favourite item at Mrs. Simcoe's dinner parties in Niagara. Just like lamb, she used to say, and she did use a good deal of mint sauce to season the carcasses."

"A remarkable lady, from all I hear. They say she adapted so well to life in the wilderness that she was broken-hearted when she went back to England."

"There was no place for the Simcoes to stay when they came to Upper Canada forty-five years ago. They had brought with them a tent that they purchased from Captain Cook's estate. I was a youth of twenty-one, the Governor's private secretary as you perhaps know, and I lived with them in that canvas home."

"Close quarters, I imagine."

"Well, it was not an average tent, I assure you. It had room for their bedchamber, a dining and reception area, and a small corner for me. But I knew everything that went on in those quarters. I was closer to that dear lady than to any other being on this earth."

The Colonel downed a glassful of wine from the third bottle. He wiped his forehead, which had become flushed. "The Governor was often absent on official business, and he left me to look after her. I arranged her dinner parties at Navy Hall, I paddled her back and forth across the river to Fort Niagara in the sunlight and the moonlight, I rode with her in rainstorms and gave her my cloak to keep her dry, I held her in my arms when her baby died..."

"You were fond of her."

"I loved her. But she never knew. I never told her." He sat, silent, staring at the tablecloth. "I wish now, oh how I wish that I had said something. But I used to hear her say to others, 'Dear Mr. Talbot provided these sandwiches for tea,' or 'Dear Mr. Talbot made sassafras tea for me when I had the ague,' or 'Dear Mr. Talbot is such a comfort to me.' I made myself believe that she would not have said these things so freely if I had been more to her than an upper servant."

He leaned toward Anna, and took her hand in an iron grasp. "You must never repeat this to anyone."

"And this is why you have never married?"

"I have never loved, nor could even tolerate, another woman. Though I have enjoyed your company, Mrs. Jameson. Indeed, you are the first lady to cross my threshold in a quarter of a century."

"Perhaps you have accomplished in your lifetime what you could never have achieved with the cares and burdens of a wife and large family. You have planted civilization in this brave new world, and that must make you happy."

"Why, yes, I'm happy here," and then the old man sighed and reached again for the wine bottle.

"He is not really happy being alone," she said to Mrs. Jennings the next morning, as she ate her solitary breakfast of poached eggs, hot milk and cornbread. Her host, as usual, was busy with his interviews of the "land-pirates".

"Perhaps not, ma'am, but he has made his choice."

"He has honour, power, obedience, but where are the troops of friends, the love which should also accompany old age?"

"I'm thankful, ma'am, I don't have to make cornbread for the troops."

No newspapers came to the chateau during her six-day visit, but Anna found plenty to do when her host was occupied. She revised her book about Toronto. She had decided to call it *Winter Studies*, and now she got started on the first chapters of its sequel, *Summer Rambles*.

And she explored the Colonel's vast acreage. One morning she looked over the high cliff on the east side of the house and saw a precipitous descent through a wild ravine, along the bottom of which was a stream that led into the lake. It would be a wonderful place to sketch, but how would she get down?

"I have an idea," Mrs. Jennings said when Anna broached the problem to her. "Come with me."

They went into the covered porch where the fearsome cougar reigned. The housekeeper threw aside a pile of farm implements to find an ancient chest. It had once been covered with fine leather, and the Colonel's family crest was still discernible under its lock.

Mrs. Jennings rummaged for a minute or two. "Here we are." She produced from its depths a pair of short trousers in the style of thirty or forty years ago, gaiters and shoes, a crumpled smock.

"Perfect," Anna said, and thought of Mrs. Sykes's same comment on the ballgown she had worn on the fateful night that had freed her from Robert and launched her into a new life. "Perfect," she repeated.

In her host's old clothes and with her hair tucked up into a low-crowned hat belonging to Jennings, she was ready. A satchel over her shoulders, she made her way down into the ravine, clutching at small branches to keep herself from sliding.

Soon she was on the lakeshore, where she found trunks and roots of trees half buried in the sand. She sat down on one of the trunks and took out her sketchbook and graphite pencils.

The most surprising object in her landscape was a huge tree that had fallen headlong over the cliff. Its long roots remained attached to the cliff above, so that its position was reversed. The top hung downwards, dead, bare of leaves, but the upturned roots formed a platform on which new earth had accumulated, and new vegetation sprang forth. Tall green shoots flourished, fresh and leafy.

If Heaven can do so much for a dead tree, what can it do for the human heart? I will not be like Talbot, she vowed. I will not live a solitary, blighted life. I have plenty of work, but I want love, too. And why should I not have it? Why should I ever despair? If I have a chance at love, I'll take it. *Carpe diem.*

She ate the cornbread, cheese curds and peas in pods that the housekeeper had put in her satchel. She did her sketches. She waved at the Indians who paddled by her on the calm waters of the lake. It was mid-afternoon when she scrambled up the ravine again, dirty and dishevelled from grabbing at small tree trunks to hoist herself upwards.

The next morning, the Colonel put her trunk into the back of the vehicle he had ordered and introduced her to her Irish driver and guide. As the cart began the long ride down the hill, she waved goodbye to her host. They turned into the main road, and she looked up again to see Mrs. Jennings and "the brat" waving at her from another part of the cliff.

As she waved back, a wayward line strayed into her mind. "I have measured out my life with cornmeal cakes," she murmured. It sounded like the line of a poem, but she'd leave someone else to write it. At the moment, she needed to ready herself for the road ahead.

THIRTY-ONE

Sam and Sir Francis had left the steamer at Kempenfeldt Bay in Lake Simcoe. There they piled Sir Francis's belongings into an oxcart for the journey to the barracks at Penetanguishene, where they would embark in a canoe for Manitoulin Island.

"Oh, my god, my god." The Governor held his hands to his head. His once-perfect curls were messed and greasy. "How much longer, Jarvis, how much longer?"

Sam gritted his teeth. He had heard these phrases, five hundred? a thousand times? since they had disembarked six hours earlier. And that didn't include a count of the moans and groans on the stagecoach between Toronto and the Holland Landing. Or the cries of anguish and the pukings into a pail on the steamship from the Landing across Lake Simcoe.

"Easy, man," Sam said to the stocky, red-faced driver as the oxen sank into another rut, and the occupants of the wagon struggled to keep from being thrown out and crushed by the wheels.

"Oh, my god, my—"

"Here, Papa, have a chocolate." Henry Bond Head pushed a tinselled box towards his father. "There's one of those ginger-filled ones you like so much. You always say ginger is good for the digestion."

Sam had at first thought the boy might be a copy of his father. He certainly looked like him, though at fourteen he still had teeth that had not become brown from cigar smoking. To Sam's surprise, the lad had actually been a great help. On the steamer, for example, he had provided a diversion just at the point when Sam had seriously contemplated throwing His Majesty's representative overboard.

"Look, look, Papa," Henry had said. "The Lake Monster has just leapt from the water. You can still see the ripples from his tail if you look hard. It's something you can put in your memoirs." And while "Papa" left off gagging into the bucket and ran to the stern of the steamer, Henry had actually winked at Sam.

Sir Francis popped two of the chocolates into his mouth as the driver negotiated their passage over a bridge of logs that covered a narrow riverbed. "Bit of a wrong'un, that Gov of yours," the man said to Sam, who perched on the box beside him. Fortunately, his words drowned in the snorts of the oxen as they heaved their burden up a small incline.

"How much longer, Jarvis?"

"Hang on, sir. I believe that we're about—yes, look!" Sam pointed to a low stone building just visible through a partly cleared grove of pine trees. "It's the Officers' Quarters."

They lurched to the front door, the bundles of luggage heaving perilously forward as the driver pulled the team to a halt. A British captain rushed out to help Sir Francis down from the cart. "Bring on the brandy, I think every bone in my body is broken," the Governor said, falling forward into the officer's outstretched arms. He had unbuttoned his fancy waistcoat during the journey, and his thick cravat—the size of a small tablecloth—had come loose. Supported and held upright by the captain, he made for the front door of the building. Over his shoulder, he said, "See to my luggage, Jarvis, and get those savages and frogs of yours busy. We'll embark as soon as I can get my aching back and my digestion in order."

A couple of hours without the complaints. Hallelujah. But there was plenty to do. Sam noted with pleasure that behind the Officers' Quarters, two long birchbark canoes were pulled up onto the sand, ready for loading. Jacob Snake and a band of voyageurs stood on the pier. He had asked Jacob to hire them. Some of them were smoking, and the others seemed to be enjoying a joke.

Sam was always a bit wary of voyageurs. They were usually half-breeds, and they had their own language, a mixture of Chippewa and French dialects. They also had their own kingdom, the expanse of Lake Huron glimmering in the early afternoon sunshine. Once the canoes got under way, they would be masters of their universe. As Sam strode onto the pier, his Indian friend moved forward to greet him. "Jacob," Sam said, "I'm so glad to see you again."

"And I to meet you, Nehkik." Jacob pressed Sam's hand with his strong fingers. His long black hair was tied back with a red cotton kerchief. His face had filled out since Sam had seen him in the maple bush in early spring.

"You have been well, Jacob?"

"Yes. I marry again, Nehkik. My new wife is a good woman. My children like her. She likes them. And we plant corn again on Snake Island. Good harvest means food for the winter." He pulled from his skin vest a small corncob pipe and a deerskin packet of tobacco. "For you," he said.

"I need that, my friend." He and Jacob sat on the edge of the pier and inhaled the fragrant smoke while they basked in the sunshine. It was lovely to be silent for a few blessed moments.

"And now, Jacob, to work." Sam called out to the other men. "Lend a hand here."

It took six voyageurs along with Jacob to unload the baggage from the oxcart. The Governor had brought a cumbersome walnut travelling stand with a tin-lined compartment to hold water for his daily ablutions. There was a wine cooler set on four sturdy mahogany legs, and with it, a block of ice, for which they'd made a stop at a Kempenfeldt Bay ice-house. There were three dozen bottles of champagne and cases of assorted brandies and sherry. There was a set of Duesbury Derby china, each piece of which had been wrapped separately in velvet. And a huge epergne in silver, "to impress any savage chieftains we may have to entertain at table," Sir Francis had told Sam on the steamer from the Holland Landing.

Finally, Jacob wrestled from the bottom of the cart a huge sloping circle of tin, painted a delicate sky blue, with a small round indenture in its middle. "What is this, Nekhik?" he asked as he struggled to pull it from the cart.

"A bathtub. You see them sometimes in a white man's house, usually in the bedchamber. A servant will carry hot water upstairs and pour it into the middle, then the master will sit on the edge of the tub and put his feet into the water."

Jacob shrugged and laughed. "Why would white man wash in a blue dish when there is a whole blue lake to wash in?"

"Good question, for which I have no rational answer." Sam grabbed one side of the bathtub, Jacob took the other, and the two of them struggled with it to the luggage canoe. The craft was already full. And they would still have to find room to wedge in eight paddlers, a bowsman and a steersman. "Absolutely no way we can get this thing into that space," Sam said. "Let me be the one to tell Sir Francis. It will give me pleasure."

Sam put his portmanteau and fishing equipment into the canoe on top of the Governor's belongings, then checked out the willow poles, rifles and tents that were stowed in the bow. Everything was in readiness.

Their job done, Jacob and the voyageurs drifted off for a snooze in the shade of a huge oak tree. Sam left the tin tub on the sand beside the baggage canoe and sat down again on the pier.

Out in Georgian Bay, a heavy-built schooner had stopped, probably becalmed. A bateau manned by five rowers moved toward shore, perhaps to pick up some wine or other provisions from the Officers' Mess.

He watched Henry Bond Head run up and down the beach with one of the Indians, a swarthy man, more than six feet tall, with a red and green embroidered band tied round his head, the ends falling in two exactly matched swaths down his back.

They had started an impromptu lacrosse match. Henry had obviously not played the game before, and the Indian was showing him how to pass the cedar ball by means of a stick made of green wood with a deerskin web just big enough to catch the ball from either side.

"Come, play with us, Jarvis!" Henry called to him. "It's a ripping game! What do you call it?" he asked. And seeing the Indian did not understand, Henry pointed to the ball and stick and tried again. "What is it?"

"Baggataway."

Sam had always fancied that he was pretty good at lacrosse, but when the Indian flipped the ball from his stick towards him, he managed to catch it only half the time. When it fell on the sand near Henry, the man scooped it into his web and tossed it to the boy, who lunged at it and missed. Finally, with a shrug and a muttered comment in his own language, the Indian ran off to join the voyageurs under the oak tree.

The sun had moved a bit to the west, and the lake was perfectly calm, excellent for paddling. It was time to go. First, Sam had to get Sir Francis aboard. He moved from the pier towards the Officers' Mess. He had just put his hand on the latch when he heard a cry from the lakeshore. The bateau had landed, and its crewmen were running up the shore to where he stood.

The first man to reach him was a sunburned, lean young man, scarcely more than a boy. "Sir, sir, we have an urgent message to pass on to the men stationed here. An Indian canoe intercepted us an hour ago and..." He stopped, out of breath, while his comrades overtook him.

"Calm, calm, man," Sam said. "Take your time, take your time. Not another war with the Yankees, is it?"

That got a weak snort of laughter. Then a stout man, mopping his forehead, gasped, "King William is dead, sir."

Some of the Penetanguishene officers who were outside ran into the stone building to tell Sir Francis. He came out immediately, one hand inserted between the buttons of his waistcoat, the other extended palm up as if he were about to make an important point before the Legislature.

"I am Sir Francis Bond Head, Lieutenant-Governor of Upper Canada, Royal Emissary of King William—"

The stout man interrupted, "But, your reverence, King William ain't with us no longer—"

The young man who had arrived on the scene first cut in. "What he means to say, sir, is that—"

Five people began talking, all at once. Sam turned to Sir

Francis. "They say that Victoria is now Queen of the Realm."

"A girl of eighteen? I cannot believe it."

"They say that King William died on the thirtieth of June, sir, and therefore, our new Queen, young as she is, appears to have been in charge of the Empire for more than a month." Sam took off the low-crowned, broad-brimmed hat that had once belonged to his father, and which he often wore to shield himself from the sun. He swept it across his chest, and bowed his head. "Long live Queen Victoria!"

Sir Francis took his cue. Hand over heart, he repeated, "Long live Queen Victoria!" And then, "Unpack the canoe, Jarvis, I must get back to Toronto. There must be a memorial service for King William. And an official reception to pay tribute to the new Queen. And speeches to prepare. My country and my countrymen have placed their trust in me. I must honour it. I shall be off to Toronto within the hour."

"But the gift-giving ceremonies at Manitoulin, sir?

"No time for the savages now. You travel on by yourself, do what you can without me." Sir Francis looked at his pocket watch, shook his head and wagged his forefinger at Sam. "For god's sake, Jarvis, don't stand around twiddling your thumbs. Where is that confounded rogue with the oxcart?"

Sam dispatched Henry on a borrowed horse to chase down the road after the oxcart and its driver, who had departed ten minutes before. Then he, Jacob, and the voyageurs staggered up from the beach again with the Duesbury Derby china, the travelling stand, the tin bath, the boxes of spirits and the wine cooler. They had it all piled neatly in front of the Officers' Quarters just as Henry returned, followed by the oxen and their driver.

"Can't stand to drive that'un again," the man said to Sam, ignoring Sir Francis's agitated gestures. "Begging your pardon, but that's the way it is. 'Oh my god, oh my god.' I heard that ditty sung too often. As if I'm responsible for them ruts. Enough is enough. I got plenty other jobs that put food on my table." He wiped his nose on the back of his hand, then shook the reins.

But before he could say, "Giddap," Sam intervened. Since the driver had come back, he obviously expected persuasion. Sam reached into his pocket, extracted a gold coin, and held it in front of him. "Think of it this way, man. It's one day out of your life. Keep a civil tongue in your head, and you will be the richer for it." The driver took the coin and turned it over between his fingers. He chewed the edge of it for a full minute, then dropped it into one of his big leather boots. Without speaking, he backed up his team, turned the wagon around and waited while Sam and the voyageurs loaded the Gov's belongings into it.

King William couldn't have died at a better time, thought Sam. He waved a cheery goodbye to Sir Francis and his son as they jolted down the road. Now he would have the show at Manitoulin Island all to himself. He would write his own speech, hand out the gifts to the tribal chieftains in his own way and try to bridge the gap that had grown between the white man and the Indian. It would be the first major achievement of his new position as Chief Superintendent of Indian Affairs. Yes, he would make his mark. It would be a chance to drown forever his shameful past in a glorious present.

He had plenty of money at hand to fund whatever was needed. The government had provided him with a generous discretionary fund for distribution to those chieftains who had served the nation well. But he could foresee other uses, too, for the funds. To start with, there was the driver's bribe. No reason that it should come from his own pocket. And, come to think of it, he'd have a quick drink at government expense before he embarked, perhaps stow a couple of bottles in with his luggage while he was at it.

In half an hour, twenty crew members embarked in two birchbark canoes. Each vessel was over thirty feet in length and had a bowsman, steersman and eight middlemen. Sam's canoe was decorated with the profile of an Indian chieftain's head, complete with feather headdress, carved into the bark. The baggage canoe had a four-petalled flower cut into the rear.

Sam sat near the stern, the lower part of his body resting on the bottom of the canoe. He propped himself up with a cushion that he laid against one of the thwarts. His back was to Jacob, who stood upright in the stern, and ahead of them, the eight paddlers and bowsman cut through the clear, still water. As they moved into the bay, Jacob began to sing an old French ditty that Sam had heard many times before. Though he couldn't understand the words, he hummed along. The paddlers joined in, keeping time with their oars to the steady beat of the song.

Sam wished that there had been an opportunity to learn French at his school in Cornwall. He envied Jacob, who could make his way not only in his Chippewa language but in English and French. He wished he had not joined in the general dislike, in his Toronto circle, of anything "frog".

There was still plenty of sunlight. Perhaps I should get started on the damned speech-making, he said to himself. He reached for his satchel where he kept his pencils and paper. But the song lulled his senses, and the sun was warm on his face. The satchel remained closed. In a moment, he had pushed himself down farther into the bottom of the canoe, so that his head rested on the cushion. Another round of the song, and he was asleep.

He awoke to the gentle bump of the canoe's prow against the sand.

"Where are we, Jacob?" He pushed himself upright.

"Christian Island, Nehkik. We make stop for the night here. Still enough daylight for fishing. Then a good supper afterwards."

"And while we fish, my friend, we shall have a pipe. It will keep us happy, and the mosquitoes unhappy." Sam turned to the paddlers. "Well done. We have made good time." They began the task of lighting fires and setting up tents.

From the baggage canoe, Sam took his favourite rod. It was made of the best Calcutta split bamboo with a tough fibre and long growth between the joints. Job Crimshaw had ordered it specially for him from Scotland, and no doubt the exorbitant price he'd charged for it could still be found in the list of Sam's ever-mounting debts.

He put on an artificial fly, also from Crimshaw's Scottish

supplier, stood near Jacob on a rocky outcropping, and spun his line into the deep pool just below them. Jacob set up a smudge on a nearby rock and handed Sam a pair of gloves for further protection against the mosquitoes. Then he, too, cast his line. In a split instant, Jacob's rod curved into a shallow U.

As Sam watched, his friend's pole bent even more until the tip of it was almost at right angles to the water. The fish, realizing its predicament, had dived farther towards the bottom in the hope that the hook would jerk from its mouth. That failing, it shot straight to the surface, leapt into the air, and with its tail gave a whack at the line in a desperate effort to snap it. That too was futile. Next, in rapid sequence, came the turning from side to side, the shooting into the rock cavern, the effort to cut the line on a piece of sharp rock.

But after five minutes of struggle, it gave up. Jacob flipped it onto the rock, and grabbing a short, stout stick, whacked it once over the head, putting an end to its agonized efforts at escape. It was a beautiful trout, perhaps ten pounds in size, its scales a silver grey with a delicate pink cast.

"Well done," Sam said, though not with much enthusiasm.

Jacob took the hook from its mouth. He stowed his catch safely back from the edge of the rock. Then he picked up a piece of something and baited his hook again.

"What have you there, Jacob? Not an artificial fly, is it?'

"No, Nehkik, I tell you before. I do not use white man's bait. Use piece of dry leaf." He cast into the water again. Sam's line drifted with the current. Another strike at Jacob's rod. Another large trout lined up beside the first one.

At last Sam landed a trout. He was pleased to note that it was slightly bigger than either of Jacob's two. His envy dissipated, and he gave himself up to the magic of the early evening: the brilliant sun sinking towards the lake, the scent of pine trees, the gentle lapping of the water.

He wished only that he had someone with him who could duly admire his Calcutta rod, his fine hand-tied flies, his impressive catch, which Jacob was now putting into a tin pail with his own fish. Jacob never complimented Sam on his rig. He seemed totally satisfied with his simple, green-branch rod and his dry-leaf "fly".

Yes, how pleasant it would be to have someone with him now from his own society, someone to whom he could speak from his heart. He thought of Anna.

"Would it be far out of our way to detour along the St. Mary's River to Sault Ste Marie?" he asked.

"Not now, Nehkik. Later, maybe. Maybe after Manitoulin. Not possible now."

Well, he knew that, didn't he? "Three days there, three days back," was how his friend McMurray had described the distance of the Sault from Manitoulin.

"Not possible," as Jacob rightly said. He imagined explaining to the Gov how he had missed the gift-giving altogether!

On their third day, as they moved into the channel that separated Georgian Bay from the main body of Lake Huron, a canoe of Chippewa Indians from Sault Ste. Marie hailed them. There was much talk between the Chippewas and Sam's men, little of which he understood, though he did comprehend that part of their conversation was about the Great White Mother who had replaced the Great Father as ruler of the realm. And then, as his attention began to wander, he heard clearly the word "Jameson", followed by a spate of Indian lingo. There was much waving of hands, and loud exclamations of "Hah!" from the tall Indian brave who had whipped him at lacrosse on the beach. Jacob had once told him that "Hah!" was a word of approbation, a substitute for clapping of hands.

Could it be Anna they spoke of?

"What were those Indians talking about just now, Jacob?" he asked as his men waved goodbye to the strangers in the canoe.

"They talk of Mrs. Jameson, call her 'Lady of the Bright Foam'. I tell you the story soon," Jacob said. "Now I must watch. Big rocks in water."

The Lady of the Bright Foam? What did that mean? Why would they make such a comparison? Something to do with her beautiful white skin or blue eyes? There was more to it, surely. It had been a long story that those Chippewas had told. And their tone had been excited but respectful. She seemed to be the centre of some major Indian speculation. Once they got around these confounded rocks, he'd know what it was all about.

THIRTY-TWO

The bateau which Anna had hired at Mackinaw Island deposited her on the Canadian side of the river at Sault Ste Marie. "There, madame," the rowers said, pointing up the hill to a large stone house. "That's where the McMurrays live."

It was eight o'clock in the morning, an unconscionable time to come calling, so Anna left her luggage on the pier and walked along the waterfront where there seemed to be much activity. She watched as an Indian family took apart its wigwam, packed it neatly into a canoe and embarked. What pleasure to be able to dismantle one's house in an hour, travel with it wherever one wished to go and set it up again in a trice.

"Where are they going?" she asked one of the rowers who had lingered near the pier.

"To Manitoulin Island for the gift-giving ceremonies, madame."

"I'm going to Manitoulin, too," she said. "I know Mr. Jarvis, the Superintendent of Indian Affairs." And how pleasant it will be to see him again, she reflected, after all these weeks of travel—and without the never-ending surveillance of those Toronto women.

But the rower seemed more interested in lighting his pipe than in her conversation.

At nine o'clock, she climbed the hill to the stone house and banged the impressive brass knocker, an almost life-size replica of a lion's head.

The door swung open. Mr. McMurray himself, barefoot. "Who the hell?" He took another look at Anna. "Mrs. Jameson, please excuse the language. Come in, come in."

"I fear I have disturbed you, sir. My bateau from Mackinaw dumped me on the pier at eight o'clock. I have spent an hour making sketches, and I shall be glad to go back to the waterfront and make some more. I can easily return later."

"I didn't recognize you at first, ma'am. That was the problem. Your face..."

Anna caught a glimpse of herself in the hall mirror. It was the first time she had looked at herself in the forty-eight hours since she had left Mackinaw Island. Her face was covered in red blotches, and there were scratch marks where she had clawed at the itchiness.

"You warned me about mosquitoes, sir, when we talked on the pier at Toronto. But I fear you did not do them justice. I have met mosquitoes in Italy, but their assault is a jest compared with the torture inflicted by these Canadian devils. My blood has provided a rich banquet for them."

The front hall gave way to an impressive curved walnut staircase, down which Mrs. McMurray was now descending, buttoning her bodice as she came. "Dear Mrs. Jameson, how happy we are to see you. I fear we have had a late night and are just now readying ourselves for the day." She shook Anna's hand. As she did so, she said, "But your beautiful white hands, Mrs. Jameson—what has happened?"

Anna looked down at her red, roughened fingers. "I must acknowledge that I had no idea of the realities I would meet, though my friends in Toronto tried to tell me. I had to help get a fire going because the rowers on the bateau needed my assistance. One of the men and I tugged at a dead bough almost as big as ourselves and managed to move it forward to the fire pit. After an hour of this, I'm proud to say we had a pile of driftwood almost as tall as St. Paul's Cathedral...but I'm rambling. Fatigue, I fear. It was a sleepless night hunkered down under bearskins to keep out the mosquitoes."

"Come in, come in, sit down." Mr. McMurray gestured towards a comfortable settee in a well-appointed drawing room.

"What a lovely house!"

"It belongs to a wealthy old miller who rents it to us along with all his furniture. I warn you about the beds. You have to climb into them by means of a stepstool. He thinks beds high off the floor allow for healthy circulation of air. As if the air in this place could be anything but fresh." He massaged his ankle. "Fell out of the damn bed this morning." And turning towards the door into the adjoining breakfast room, he added, "I'm going to rouse Cook now to get us some coffee."

"And I'm going to raid my supply of herbal remedies," Mrs. McMurray said.

She was back in a minute with a jar of bright yellow ointment. "First of all, ma'am, you must put this on your face and hands and rub it in well."

Anna did as she was told. "This is the goldenrod ointment you mentioned when I talked to you in Toronto? It is so soothing. I no longer want to tear my face apart with scratching."

"The same. An Indian remedy, tried and true. My mother uses it on all occasions for insect bites. My father was a white man from Ireland, and when my mother first saw him here in this remote corner of the world, she said he was a perfect spectacle of deformity from mosquito bites. She made him an ointment of goldenrod, his bites healed, they married, and lived happily together for thirty-six years."

"I wish all marriages could be sealed with so simple a panacea."

"And what would you like now? A cup of coffee?"

"First, if you please, a nap of several hours on any flat, stable surface you can provide. This one is so comfortable."

The Indian maidservant put a snowy sheet over the sofa and covered Anna with a pretty patchwork quilt. Mrs. McMurray looked down at their guest. "And when you wake up—whenever it is—we'll give you blueberry pancakes with the maple syrup my mother makes on Sugar Island."

The McMurrays retired to the nearby breakfast room for coffee. Anna shut her eyes. As she drifted into sleep, she heard muffled laughter as Mr. McMurray said, "'We had a late night and are just now readying ourselves'... That was a good one..."

"Well, I didn't tell any lies, did I? And fortunately my dark skin doesn't show blushes."

More laughter, then Anna heard no more.

At noon, she awakened refreshed and ate her pancakes and syrup. Then her hosts took her to the little frame Church of England chapel that was the heart of their missionary work. Here in the tiny vestry at the back of the church, Mr. McMurray showed her the catechism his wife had helped him translate into the Chippewa language. "Without Charlotte," he told her, "the mission could not have been successful. Together we have achieved sixty-six communicants, thirteen marriages, more than a hundred baptisms, and seven Christian burials. And though I speak the Indian language well enough, I like to have Charlotte stand beside me to translate my sermons each Sunday."

"If the Indians are to be assimilated into white culture, and I suppose that's inevitable," Mrs. McMurray said, "they must come in contact with decent white people whom they can respect."

"Not those goddamn traders and merchants, excuse my language."

"My Chippewa friends respect my husband. He encourages them to cultivate potatoes and corn, and he gets them a fair deal for the catch they sell to the fisheries. Because they recognize his worth, we now have thirty children in school."

"And Charlotte is my right hand. She noticed that the women were constantly tipsy, so she drew them into the singing of sacred music, and now she has a fine choir which has achieved renown in this part of the world." He smiled at his wife and gestured at the open door of the vestry, through which they could see the women who sat quietly in the pews nearby, talking among themselves as they did their beadwork. "Instead of drinking cheap whiskey in their wigwams, the women come here for hours every day."

"Dear Mrs. McMurray, would you have them sing something now? I should so like to hear them. I have always enjoyed good music."

Anna's hostess went to the front of the chapel. She said a few words to the women in Chippewa, and in a minute they began to sing "Fairest Lord Jesus" in their own language.

Anna moved forward to stand beside Charlotte. As the Indian choir sang, she listened, then joined in the last verse, singing it in the familiar words she knew. Then she went along the pews, smiling at each of the women as she said "Bojou". Several of them touched her swollen face gently, talking to her about the goldenrod cure while Charlotte translated for them.

The next morning, Anna looked at herself in the pier glass in her bedchamber. The swelling around her eyes had receded, and scabs had formed on the red blotches on her cheeks. She went down to breakfast carrying the goldenrod ointment, which she placed beside her napkin.

"Whitefish from the Ste. Marie's River," her host said as the servant put a platter on the breakfast room table. "I eat it three times a day for most of the year. But Cook could fry you an egg, if you'd like."

"No egg for me, thank you." Mrs. Jameson slid a large portion of the fish onto her plate. She ate in silence, helped herself to a second piece, then said, "I have had tuna from the Gulf of Genoa, anchovies from the Bay of Naples, and salmon from the highlands of Scotland, but there is nothing in the world better than this whitefish from the Ste. Marie's River."

Mr. McMurray smiled and passed the apple vinegar. "Even better with a splash of this."

"And what would you like to do today?" Mrs. McMurray asked as she collected their coffee cups and stacked them on a tray.

"My greatest wish is to visit the rapids and see how the fish are caught. But I know that you must have parish tasks which cannot be postponed, so—"

"We do need to travel downriver for several miles to visit one of the chiefs."

"Why don't you come with us?" Mrs. McMurray said. "Then we can spend the rest of the afternoon at the rapids."

At that moment the knocker on the front door banged. "Oh, I

know who that is," Anna said, getting up to follow Mr. McMurray
into the hallway. At the door was a young half-breed dressed in a
buckskin suit tied at the waist with a blue sash from which hung
a beaded pouch. He carried a red paddle. When he saw Anna
and her host, he swept off his *capote* and bowed. "Here for Mrs.
Jameson, your Honour."

"And right on time, too, my boy. Good for you," she said. "May
I introduce Fanchon? He was one of the voyageurs who rowed me
from Mackinaw Island. He lives here in the Sault, and I engaged
him to paddle me about in his little canoe."

"But Charlotte and I intend to—"

"My dear sir, I will not interfere with the many tasks of
your daily life. Turn me loose with Fanchon to sketch those fair
meadows and woodlands we sang about in the chapel, and I shall
be back just before sunset—"

But before she had finished speaking, Mr. McMurray had thanked
Fanchon, given him a coin and closed the door on him. "You are ours
for the day, ma'am. Now get yourself ready, and we'll be off."

"Chief Shingwauk is one of our star converts," Mrs. McMurray
said as she and her husband paddled down river, Anna sitting
between them. "It was a year ago. Mac offered up prayers in the
chapel for his son, who was gravely ill. The boy recovered, and the
chief became a Christian."

"Now he tells his band, 'I once lived in a dark forest, and now I
can see a blue sky,'" added Mr. McMurray.

They beached their canoe near the chief's wigwam, and as they
approached, they saw him talking to three men.

"Goddamn traders from the Hudson Bay Company at
Michipicoten," Mr. McMurray said to Anna. They had bottles of
whiskey in their hands, but the old man was shaking his head
vigorously.

"When I wanted it, you would not give it to me without a pile
of furs into the bargain," they heard him say. "Now when I do

not want it, you try to force it upon me. Drink it yourselves!" He turned his back on them and went into his lodging, closing the skin flap behind him.

"Damn you scoundrels!" Mr. McMurray said as the traders headed for the shore. "Tell your factor to leave the man alone. Or better still, tell him to learn something about fair play. Furs for money, not whiskey. Let him learn that—if his thick skull can comprehend such a complicated message."

"Stick your Bible up your arse, preacher," muttered one of them, an unshaven, coarse-featured brute with a red nose. He gave Mr. McMurray a punch on the shoulder as he passed.

Anna picked up a heavy stick from the path. But Mrs. McMurray put her hand into her husband's and said softly, "Leave them alone, Mac. You cannot reason with curs."

The interior of Chief Shingwauk's wigwam formed a good-sized room. It was like Jacob Snake's abode, neat and clean. The floor had been levelled and trodden to smoothness and was covered with mats of varying attractive patterns, woven from corn husks.

"You are welcome," he said to them in his Indian dialect, while Anna's hosts provided translation for her. "Please sit down." He pointed to the raised couch which circled the birchbark walls of his home. When they were settled and had spent some minutes talking about the catch for the fishery, he passed them tea in tin mugs and got down to business.

"I shall dictate a letter to the Governor. Then I entrust it to you. You will present it to him at the Grand Council on Manitoulin Island. My letter will deal with the Governor's refusal to carry out what the former Governor promised us."

"I have with me a tablet on which I shall record your words exactly as you tell them to me," Mrs. McMurray said. "But since the Governor does not speak our language, I must transcribe what you say into the white man's dialect."

"Great Chief," Shingwauk said as she took down his words, "your predecessor made promises to me and to my band. He promised log houses, but nothing has been built, though five years have passed. I am now old, and to judge by the way you and the former Great Chief have used me, I shall be laid in my grave before anything is done. Better that such promises were never made than that they were made and not carried out.

"Great Chief," he concluded, "it may be that I do not see clearly. I am old, as I have told you, and perhaps you have indeed carried out the promises, and I cannot see those log houses because of my failing eyesight. If you visit me here, I shall give you a plate of whitefish, and we shall go together into the countryside, and you will show me that you have carried out those promises."

Anna, the McMurrays and Shingwauk laughed together. It was a fine piece of irony. "We leave for Manitoulin at sunrise tomorrow," Mrs. McMurray said as they parted from him, "and my husband will see that your excellent letter is placed directly into the Governor's hands."

"Alas," Anna said as they got back into the canoe, "I do not know that Governor Bond Head will be any more sympathetic to the Indians than his predecessors."

"But what about Sam Jarvis? He is a decent man. Surely he can bring pressure to bear on the Governor?"

"I hope so." But as Anna spoke, she thought of Sam's reluctance to deal with Crimshaw.

True to their promise, the McMurrays took her to the rapids in the afternoon. They stood for a while on the Indian burial ground at the top of the falls and looked down at two little canoes dancing and popping about like corks in the midst of the boiling surge of water. In each, a man sat in the stern, steering with a paddle, while on the prow, a fisherwoman placed herself, balancing a log pole with both hands, at the end of which was a scoop-net. With each dip into the water, she caught a fish or two.

"Amazing, amazing," Anna said. "I have never seen anything so wonderful. The passage between the rocks is so narrow, and yet they manage to keep their footing."

"Not all of them." Mr. McMurray handed her his telescope. "See those tall wooden crosses on the landing place at the foot of the falls? They speak for themselves."

"You have not been here long enough to understand the full danger that awaits those people," Mrs. McMurray said. "Even if they can keep their footing, their canoes are so light and fragile that a large wave might break them in two. We have had to read 'The Burial of the Dead' over two corpses recently. There is no need for such daredevilry, you know. There is a portage that connects the navigable parts of the strait. Voyageurs—they are generally men of good sense—would rather carry four hundred pounds on their backs over this two-mile portage than face the terror of the falls."

"Voyageurs, perhaps, but these are Indians, and look, they seem to be managing. With a good canoe and an experienced steersman, there would surely be little danger. It would be a glorious sensation, would it not?" Anna stood a few minutes in silence then looked straight into Mr. McMurray's eyes. "I intend to descend those rapids."

"Forget it. It's madness. A burial ground above and crosses below, you can see it's a perfect setting for calamity."

As he spoke, a tall Indian appeared behind them. He wore a dirty blanket coat, but he'd taken time to paint one eye with a red circle, and the knots in his hair held feathers from an impressive variety of birds. "Ogima-quay, Ogima-quay," he said, bowing from the waist.

"What is this word he keeps repeating?"

"It means 'fair English chieftainess'," Mrs. McMurray said with obvious reluctance.

Anna listened to the spate of Indian dialect and pieced together the meaning from his gestures towards a small birchbark canoe which lay nearby. "He has a proposition for me, does he not?" she said. "He wants to take me for a ride down the rapids. Tell him I will go."

"No," the McMurrays said in unison.

But the Indian had already read Anna's intent. With a flourish he readied the canoe in the shallows beside the rapids and held it steady while she settled onto a mat at the bottom of the craft.

In a minute they were into the heart of the falls. "It's as buoyant as a bird on the waters," she said loudly, trying to drown out Mr. McMurray's cry of "Goddamn pigheadness!"

The water poured over them in a surge of white foam. Her steersman with astonishing dexterity kept the head of the canoe to the breakers, and somehow they danced through them. Though she was soaked from head to toe by the spray, she could just see that the passage between the rocks was sometimes not more than two feet in width. One miscalculation on the part of her steersman, and it would indeed be "calamity".

But the Indian managed to turn in sharp angles to avoid the rocks, and after a few seconds, Anna had not the slightest sensation of fear, only a giddy, breathless, delicious excitement. She was aware of everything, even the tiny blue kingfisher that dived into the foam at the bottom of the cascade.

They plunged more than a mile in five minutes, and suddenly they were at the landing place. Her steersman helped her alight, and she found herself in the midst of a group of Indians who took turns clasping her hand while shouting "Hah!" in unison.

Then she heard over and over a polysyllabic word, "Wah,sah,ge,wah,no,qua! Wah,sah,ge,wah,no,qua!"

What did it mean? Seeing her incomprehension, one of the women said, "Lady of the Bright Foam, that is what we call you. You are first European lady to come down the falls."

"And who is my steersman?" she asked the woman, pointing to the Indian whose expertise had provided her with this accolade.

"Camudwa."

"Please tell Camudwa I thank him for his skill. He has given me the best experience of my life."

All this was translated, and Camudwa clasped her in his arms as he said, "Bojou, Wah,sah,ge,wah,no,qua!"

More shouting of "Hah!" and Anna found herself back in Camudwa's canoe. "Now he takes you home to reverend sir," her helpful Indian translator told her.

A short trip along the Ste. Marie River, and she was again in front of the McMurrays' stone house. Camudwa seemed reluctant to leave her, and it was only when the McMurrays hove into sight, coming from the burial ground, that he stepped on shore and helped her out of the canoe.

She remembered a word she had learned when Mrs. McMurray had praised her Indian choir in the chapel. "Minno, minno," she said, and a smile spread across Camudwa's handsome face. Anna turned to meet her hosts.

"I suppose we must congratulate you," Mr. McMurray said, "but what you did was sheer idiocy. Did you think about this Indian who steered the damn canoe? Did you think about anyone but yourself?" He took a deep breath. "I apologize, ma'am. That last comment does not befit a gentleman. My only excuse is that my nerves are shot."

"You may chastise me if you wish. But nothing you say really affects how I feel at the moment. I am as tipsy as if I had drunk two glasses of champagne." Anna laughed and waved at Camudwa, who waved back and shouted "Hah!" as he steered his canoe out into the current. She turned back to her friends. "It was Camudwa's decision to take me along, was it not? He is a man, not a child. And I am capable, too, of making independent decisions."

"So we'll forget the burial service," Mrs. McMurray said to Anna over their whitefish supper in the early evening. "Perhaps something could be done now to adapt the 'Service of Thanksgiving for Women After Child-birth'?"

"Yes, indeed," Anna said. "Something in the line of 'O Almighty God, we give thee humble thanks that thou hast preserved this woman in the great peril of Ste. Marie's Rapids'?"

"I could work it out, I suppose. And Charlotte could translate it into Chippewa for the congregation. But right now, why don't we just break open that bottle of good sherry we've been hoarding?"

The sherry being produced by the Indian maid, Anna's host

rose and gave a toast. "Wah,sah,ge,wah,no,qua, 'Lady of the Bright Foam', you are undoubtedly the first European woman ever to have risked life and limb in those rapids. And though you are responsible for the white hairs that have sprouted on my head this day, I must commend you on your feat." He bowed and sat down.

"I recommend it as an exercise before breakfast." Laughter bubbled from Anna like water from a geyser. "But I take no credit unto myself. Had it not been for Camudwa, I'd be a bloody corpse fished from the rapids and put into a pine casket. I'd like to see him and thank him, now that I've had time for sober reflection on his great skill in keeping me alive."

"He is already on his way to Penetanguishene, so I understand," Mrs. McMurray said. "The Department of Indian Affairs has hired him to paddle the Governor and Mr. Jarvis to Manitoulin."

The servant came in again with dessert. "My favourite," Mr. McMurray said.

Anna put three large spoonfuls on her plate. "What is it?"

"A recipe from Charlotte's mother. 'Indian pudding' is what she calls it, and it's made of Indian corn flour, milk, an egg or two, and spices, and always served warm with maple syrup."

"The best fare I have had since I left Toronto," said Anna, settling in to enjoy it. A group of Indians came into the dining room as the pudding was being passed around. There was plenty to offer these uninvited guests, and they sat crosslegged on the floor and ate it from their own tin plates with the carved bone spoons they had brought along with them.

As dinner ended, there was a final toast from the Indian woman who had spoken to Anna at the landing place. This time she spoke in Chippewa, and Mrs. McMurray translated. "Wah,sah,ge,wah,no,qua, it is with pleasure that we now adopt you into our race. Indian women for centuries have descended the falls, but you are the first white woman to do so, and you have proved yourself worthy of becoming our sister."

"Hah!" Sounds of approbation from all present.

It was late when the guests left. "Try to sleep," Anna's host said as the three of them mounted the stairs. "Everything is in readiness for an early departure for Manitoulin Island. We are going by bateau instead of canoe, because we shall be encumbered with baggage and provisions. The distance is about one hundred and seventy miles, and there is scarcely a settlement or a habitation on the route, nothing but lake and forest."

"I recommend that you apply the goldenrod ointment liberally," Mrs. McMurray added.

"And I warn you, there is only one small tent for the passengers. We are taking two of Charlotte's nieces with us, so there will be no privacy."

"And our crew, sir?"

"Four rowers, one of them being Fanchon. I thought you might like him to have a job, after my summary dismissal of him this morning."

They parted for the night. Anna scrambled up the side of her enormous bed and left the curtains open so that she could watch the moonlight through the window and listen to the roar of the rapids.

She drifted gradually into sleep amid flickering images that brought back the urgency and passion of her day. The fretting, fuming waters pounding over the rocks had been like a beautiful woman in a fit of rage. That image had compelled her, pulling her close in spite of the danger.

From the bedchamber next to hers came muffled thumps and cries. The strange exhilaration of the day had evidently affected Mr. and Mrs. McMurray as well.

Later she awoke to see that the light through the window had changed from black to soft grey. They would soon embark. Three days' journey and more. And three nights of communal sleep in the confines of a small tent. How would it all work out? She smiled. Nothing that might befall her could lessen the glory of her epiphany.

THIRTY-THREE

Anna leaned over the side of the bateau and strained to catch a last glimpse of the white spray of the rapids and the black dots of the fishing canoes. But the voyageurs—Masta, Content, LeBlanc and Fanchon—took to their oars with gusto, and soon they were into the main channel of the river, heading south east. The McMurrays seemed tired, and the two pretty Indian nieces had little to say.

In mid-afternoon they stopped for dinner near St. Joseph's Island, where they climbed up to a rocky ledge overlooking the channel. Masta took the sail from the bateau, and Mr. and Mrs. McMurray threw it over some bushes to form an awning. No scrabbling for firewood this time. The crew did the work necessary to get the fire up and going. Then Masta fried some pork, and Fanchon made a *galette*, "a flat cake made of flour and water and dirt from the cook's hands and fried in grease," as Mr. McMurray described it.

They stayed close to the campfire to avoid the mosquitoes, and as they ate these delicacies topped off with some fresh-picked wortle-berries, Anna said, "It's like an outdoor café in—"

"Why not just enjoy it all without the comparisons?" Mr. McMurray said.

"Actually, dear sir, I meant to say *better* than dining out in Vienna. No obsequious waiters. No stink of horse manure."

After dinner, they got back into the bateau. A stiff wind enabled the voyageurs to put up their sail, and the boat moved with ease along the north shore of St. Joseph's Island. At dusk they came to another rocky island where they pitched their little tent and had tea. The sunset was glorious, and the stars and the fireflies came out together. But the mosquitoes swarmed too.

"Into the tent," Mr. McMurray said, grabbing a cedar bough, "and let the slaughter begin." The passengers obeyed readily. Mrs. McMurray closed the curtain of the marquee, and her husband smacked the buzzing devils into silence with the bough. Then he shed his jacket and waistcoat while the women made do with some unbuttonings of bodices and loosening of stays, and they all lay down.

Anna positioned herself to the right of Mrs. McMurray. Her husband placed himself on the left side of his wife, and the two Indian girls lay crosswise at their feet. Notwithstanding the closeness of bodies about her, Anna found that the mats and blankets spread on the floor of the tent formed a comfortable communal bed.

She lay awake for a long time, thinking back on her descent of the falls and forward to her meeting with Sam. No such excitement seemed to disturb her friends, whose chorus of snores and deep breathing punctuated the stillness of the night. Just before dawn, there was a tremendous clap of thunder, then lightning blazed through the sides of the tent, and torrents of rain pounded down.

Beside her, Mrs. McMurray stirred and said softly, "You are awake, Mrs. Jameson? Don't worry. These summer storms are over soon, and the men had the foresight to throw an oilcloth over the tent. We shall be safe and dry."

The sun shone brightly the next morning, though the lake was still swelling and heaving from the recent storm. The bateau rode the waves into a bay, where they stopped for breakfast on a grassy little lawn surrounded by high trees. "Watch out for rattlesnakes," Mr. McMurray warned as the passengers and crew dispersed for morning ablutions.

Anna took her small bag of necessaries with her as she walked along the lakeshore. She gripped her stiletto in her right hand. If she met a snake, she would deal with it in summary fashion. As for the mosquitoes, no battles were necessary. They had disappeared, dispersed by the early morning storm. Two hundred yards or so along the water, she came to a small creek running into the bushes, and there, feeling perfectly secure, she took off her clothes, washed, brushed her teeth, and arranged her hair.

She placed Ottilie's *vasa da notte* on a fallen log, but when the time came to use it, she decided just to squat in the fragrant green junipers nearby.

Back at the breakfast fire, she took several minutes to make a rapid sketch of the scene before her. The voyageur Content was washing plates; LeBlanc and Masta were cooking fresh-caught fish; and the Indian girls had just spread a tablecloth on the grass. Under a tree sat Mrs. McMurray, the very image of the Madonna in "Repose in Egypt". Nearby, Mr. McMurray had wedged his shaving glass between two branches of a pine tree, and was in the process of scraping off the stubble on his chin while he sang an air from *Le Nozze di Figaro* in a loud, slightly off-key baritone.

"I have never before seen such a strange combination of the graceful, the wild and the comic," Anna said to Mrs. McMurray as she drew close to the campfire.

"I suppose you include my husband's singing with the comic. But when I hear him happy in this way, I'm happy too, even though my ears are assaulted."

"My friend, I hope you intend no rebuke, because I intended no slight. I am envious of you and your husband."

They set off again after breakfast, and as the channel widened, the wind moaned, and the waves rose higher. Anna began to be sorry she had eaten so much for breakfast. She was not alone, evidently, in her uneasiness. As they crossed a wide, open expanse of about twenty miles, all her fellow passengers became gradually silent. Then, their faces pale and contorted, they vomited their breakfast over the side of the boat. Only the voyageurs remained well. They increased the volume of their singing, so that the retching of their passengers could not be heard over the splashing of the waves.

"Rattlesnake Islands coming up soon," Mr. McMurray said as he clutched his stomach. "We'll be protected there from the swell of the main lake, and things will be better. Hang on, mateys," he added, trying to smile.

He was right. The roiling waves subsided, and they were able to land on a mass of rock, where the crew lighted a fire under the pines and sycamores. "We must eat something," Mrs. McMurray said, "or we'll feel worse in the long run."

So her husband heated port wine and water, into which he broke some biscuits, and they all drank it from the same slop basin. But it had its effect, and soon Anna and the others felt better. Before embarking again, they took what Mr. McMurray called a "bush break". This time Anna did not bother looking for her *vasa da notte*. It seemed easier just to find a quiet corner and do the necessary without fuss.

The afternoon voyage was better, with a fresh, fair wind and no huge waves. At dusk, they beached the boat at a small Indian settlement. Anna felt well enough to take out her notebook. "By evening," she wrote, "we entered the Missasagua River"—she would check the spelling later—"which means 'river with two mouths'. Here we found a small tribe of Indians belonging to the Chippewa nation. Most of them had gone down to the Manitoulin Island for the gift-giving, but some poor wretches remained inside three or four filthy bark wigwams. The settlement is in the service of a fur company, and it is not surprising to encounter—"

"Drunkenness, poverty, degradation." She turned to find Mr. McMurray looking over her shoulder. "That will complete your sentence, Mrs. Jameson. It's what I have waged war against in my mission at the Sault. But when I come to villages like this one, I feel that the battle is hopeless."

Nevertheless, the inhabitants were friendly and invited them to take their night's lodging with them, but the wigwams were so abominably dirty that they all preferred the shore. When they pitched the marquee, Anna stood for some time watching the antics of a little Indian boy in a canoe about eight feet in length. The craft seemed alive beneath him, as he shot backwards and forwards, made circles and whirled himself round and round in pirouettes. "What fun," she said to Mrs. McMurray. "He's like one of the boys I was governess to long ago. He used to play just as many tricks with his pony."

Given the surroundings, it seemed almost inevitable that their dinner that night was doomed. The voyageurs had prepared a large piece of fresh whitefish ("Sturgeon, ma'am," one of the Indian girls said, correcting her) and suspended it over the fire by a cord affixed to three sticks. As the smell wafted into Anna's nostrils, making her realize that her earlier malaise was over, there was a shout from Content and Fanchon. One of the mangy curs from the Indian encampment pounced into the flames, grabbed the piece of fish and ran off into the forest. "I hope its toes are well cooked," Fanchon said in his French dialect.

In addition to the meal *manqué*, the mosquitoes had by this time descended in great buzzing clouds, so they retreated to their tent, chased the winged incumbents out with boughs, closed the curtain, and passed around the dry biscuits that Mr. McMurray rummaged from his satchel. They also shared a small bottle of port wine left over from lunch, passing the bottle from mouth to mouth. "It's rather like the celebration of the Eucharist," Anna said, "without the prayers."

"I'll spare you those," Mr. McMurray assured her.

Their third day of travel presented no difficulties, only an endlessly beautiful passage through countless islands of all shapes and sizes. They made eighteen miles before stopping at one of these islands for breakfast, and as Anna sat on a rock to eat some fresh-caught fish, Fanchon came towards her carrying a vase of pretty wildflowers.

"*Pour vous*, madame," he said, setting the container of bergamot and daisies next to her on the rock.

"*Merci*, Fanchon. How lovely." Then she took another look. "And where did you get this beautiful vase, my lad?"

He giggled. "I found it near the lake the morning after the storm. Perhaps you know who it belongs to, madame?"

Anna blushed, than laughed. "It's yours to keep, Fanchon. Make good use of it." Then she looked at the McMurrays, who were smiling.

At five o'clock they saw in the east the high ridge called the mountains of La Cloche. "Just a fast bush break at La Cloche, then we take off again," Mr. McMurray said. "I have no intention of lingering."

"Why not?" Anna asked, seeing a large log house come into view, surrounded by sundry small dwellings.

"It's a fur traders' post. Bigotry is rampant here. I want nothing to do with them."

They landed a good distance away from the settlement. Nevertheless, when Anna emerged from the forest, she saw a man talking to Mr. McMurray.

"Do stop a while and visit us, sir," she heard him say as she came close. "Have your meal with us and spend the night in comfort. Your half-breeds," he gestured at the four voyageurs, "can hobnob with their like down in one of the huts on the shore. And the squaws," here he pointed to the Indian girls, "no doubt will find one or two of the men in the factory keen to give them a night's pleasure." The man turned to Anna. "And this is your wife, sir?"

"My friend. Here is my wife." And he gestured towards Mrs. McMurray, who had just come from her part of the bush.

There was a long pause, during which the trader appeared to be absorbing the fact of Mrs. McMurray's Indian heritage. "Good day, ma'am," he said finally.

"We cannot stay longer, I thank you." Mr. McMurray nodded at the man. "We must press on while the crew is willing. There is so much daylight yet, and time is valuable. As for my nieces, they will not be *taking a night's pleasure*—do I have the correct phrase?— with anyone here."

"Apologies, sir, profoundest apologies. I fear I have given offence."

Mr. McMurray gave a perfunctory glance at his pocket watch. "We must be off."

The fur trader bowed and headed in the direction of the log house. Anna's entourage got into the bateau. But Masta had evidently met someone he knew and was deep in conversation on the shoreline. "We'll wait," Mrs. McMurray said. "I know how pleasant it is to meet a friend in this remote wilderness."

So they waited, and eventually Masta said goodbye to his friend and resumed his place at the oars. As they were about to push off, the trader rushed towards them. In his hands he held a large packet covered with newsprint. "Broiled fish," he said, "and cornmeal bread. And two bottles of wine. Take them with my good wishes." He thrust the lot into Mr. McMurray's arms, bowed and ran back up the shore.

In a few minutes they had pushed off in the bateau. Out in the bay, the voyageurs shipped their oars, and passengers and crew alike ate the viands with their fingers, passing them up and down the length of the craft until every bit of fish and every crumb of bread had disappeared.

"All this should stick in my craw," Anna's host said, "but it doesn't. I relish it, knowing that for once a fur trader made an apology for his rudeness and tried to atone for it."

Just after sunset, they reached an island which sloped up from the shore in successive ledges of rock, fringed with trees and bushes and a species of grey lichen, nearly a foot deep. While the voyageurs made their campfire and put up an awning, and the McMurrays pitched the tent, Anna gathered a quantity of lichen and spread it under the mats to make a comfortable pillow on the rocky surface. Then, utterly conquered by fatigue, she slept in peace.

Daylight had just crept up the sky when they set out again to the southeast on the last leg of their journey. In a very few minutes, they saw the dim outline of Manitoulin Island. As they rowed in its direction, they could just discern a huge black hull, with masts and spars rising against the sky. It proved to be a great heavy-built schooner in progress up the lake against wind and current. They soon overtook it and saw a man in the bow waving an immense oar at them.

"What news?" Mr. McMurray called.

"The King is dead! Long live the Queen!" came the answer from the bow.

"Is the Governor at Manitoulin, or did he have to leave?"

"Gone back to Toronto for memorial services!"

"And the gift-giving ceremonies?"

"Today! The chief officer of the Indian Department is in charge!"

So, very soon, she would see Sam again. And without the surveillance of the Governor. That would be pleasant. As for the new Queen—Anna strove to recall what she knew about her. Only eighteen years of age! Her father had painted a miniature of her two years before, and she remembered wide-set eyes, an underslung chin, and a lace handerchief clutched in a small hand.

"Do you think this queen will care about our land?" Mrs. McMurray asked her.

"I believe that her youth and gender are absolutely in our favour. If she has a true heart, the quick perceptions and kind instincts of a woman, and a fine moral sense, she will do better for our world than the officials who run it now."

"Like Sir Francis Bond Head and others of his ilk," Mr. McMurray said with a downturned lip.

The bateau had at that moment entered a little bay within a bay. Here the water was perfectly calm. The shores sloped upwards from the margin of the lake, like an ampitheatre, and here the Indians had set up their wigwams amid the trees. Smoke from bonfires curled into the air. Beyond the dwellings, a tall pine forest crowned the settlement. Some hundred or more canoes darted about on the water or glided along the shore, and a beautiful schooner lay against the green bank, its white sails half furled, and half gracefully drooping.

The voyageurs pulled the boat up upon the shore. Anna stepped out.

"Bojou, Wah,sah,ge,wah,no,qua," came the cry from the Indians who had watched the landing. A crowd of them swarmed down to the water's edge. She saw Camudwa emerge from his wigwam to join the group.

"Bojou," she replied as she clasped the hands of her greeters and found herself in the warm embrace of Camudwa's arms.

"And I too shall say 'Good morning, Mrs. Jameson.'" It was Sam, emerging from behind the tall warriors. "Or should I call you Lady of the Bright Foam? Your fame has preceded you."

Anna looked over her shoulder. The McMurrays and the girls were a few paces behind. "I would love to hear you call me 'Anna,'" she said in a low voice.

Sam smiled and moved forward to greet the rest of her party. "Welcome to Manitoulin, which my Indian friends tell me means 'dwelling of the spirits'. I hope you will be happy here and find kindred spirits among us. We have a busy schedule planned. Please, all of you, join in the fun and come to the ceremonies afterwards." He turned back to Anna. "I have waited for this day," he said quietly.

"I, too. Here I am in Paradise."

THIRTY-FOUR

As Sam greeted Anna and the McMurrays, he noticed that the lady's blue eyes were as bright as ever, but two or three red blotches had appeared on the beautiful white complexion.

"I see you have met our winged scourge."

"I have come to accept the mosquito as part of the Canadian experience. In fact I have devoted an entire page of my journal to a description of its proboscis—"

"Its what?"

"Proboscis. Like an awl, I say, and it bores into your veins and pumps the life-blood out of you. But I am fortunate to be still alive to enjoy this island and my time with you."

"We can put you up in the government log house at the top of the hill," Sam said to the McMurrays, "but it will take a while to make things ready. Perhaps you would like to pitch your tent here in the meantime? And while you are doing that, I shall take Mrs. Jameson to look at the wigwams and meet some of the folk here. We'll have breakfast on the way."

Sam offered his arm to Anna, and they set off for the encampment. They had gone three or four paces when Jacob Snake opened the flap of his tent and hailed them.

"Join us, Jacob," Sam said. "No doubt Mrs. Jameson is hungry, and you can persuade one of your friends to let us have some porridge."

So the three of them walked up the hill among the wigwams, stopping from time to time at the campfires, where the Indians filled wooden spoons with their porridge and passed it to their visitors.

Anna put the mixture into her mouth while Sam handed her

a handkerchief to wipe away the surplus that dripped down her chin. "What is in it?"

"Indian corn and lard, part of the government food allotment for their five-day stay. But Jacob will give you the recipe."

"Fill a big tin kettle with water for ten men, put in one quart corn per man and big helping of pork fat. Boil all night in campfire. Daylight comes. Porridge now so thick, stick stands upright in the kettle. Add a pinch of salt. Very good, Mrs. Jameson. Now try it with black bass." He scooped the fish out of a frying pan with a spoon, set it on a leaf, and handed it to Anna.

"All a man can ask for," Sam said, "so I'm told."

"Indeed." Anna smiled at the Indian woman who was pushing another spoonful of porridge towards her. "But now, please tell your friends, Jacob, that I have had enough."

A din of voices drowned out her words. Hundreds of Indians were running towards the shore. "I think they've just announced the canoe race," Sam said. "I scheduled one for this morning and asked the Indian agent, Major Anderson, to supervise."

"Oh, do let us go and see it," Anna said, clapping. So down to the starting place on the shore of the lake they proceeded, through the throngs of men, women and children that jostled about them.

"For women only," Anderson shouted through his trumpet of birchbark. "With prizes. Twenty-four pair of silver earrings."

Thirty canoes were filling up, each containing twelve women to paddle and one woman to steer. "They are to go round the small island in the centre of the bay," Sam told Anna, "and the first canoe that touches the shore at the starting point is the winner."

Anna ran back and forth along the shoreline to get a better view of things. As she hiked up her skirts to avoid tripping, Sam, who was coming behind her, noticed her slender ankles and her small feet shod in a fine pair of beaded moccasins. He remembered those feet climbing up into the sleigh the day of their trip to the sugar bush. Only then, they had been covered in enough stockings for an expedition to the Arctic.

A hundred Indian men ran with her, urging their wives and

sisters on with loud cries, leaps into the air and clapping of hands. For a few seconds he lost sight of her.

"What is that wild white woman doing?" Anderson yelled at Sam. Anna was attempting to get into one of the canoes that seemed to be short one Indian paddler. "Get her out of there, damn it!"

"Anna, Anna!" Sam ran up to the side of the canoe. "You mustn't go with them. You'll only slow them down. Please, please get out."

But it was too late. The Indian women had handed her a paddle, and she waved it in the air at Sam as they pushed off into the water. There was a rifle shot, and all paddles dipped together with a burst of speed.

He watched the progress of the canoes until they disappeared around the far side of the island. Anderson stood beside him, cursing. "An almighty nerve that woman has, Jarvis. Why didn't you stop her?"

"Shut up, man. It's all about good fun, isn't it? And it wasn't as if the Indian women didn't want her. In fact, they encouraged her."

As the canoes came into view again, Sam could see that Anna was paddling as hard as the others in her craft. "By god," he said to Jacob, who stood beside him, "she's got the hang of it."

"Look, Nehkik! Canoe pulls ahead. Mrs. Jameson wins."

By now the Indians were milling about, yelling "Ny'a! Ny'a!" Anna's canoe splashed up to the landing place, and the men ran into the water to carry the winners out in their arms. Sam moved towards Anna, but the show-off Indian who had trounced him at lacrosse back at Penetanguishene was there first. He grasped her around the waist, threw her over his shoulder like a bearskin blanket, and sloshed through the water to dry land. The pinewoods rang with the shrieks of the onlookers and victors, and Anna was shouting as loudly as any of the Indians crowded around her.

Anderson handed out twelve pairs of earrings to each of the paddlers in the winning canoe and twelve to the second-place winners. As Sam noticed Anna giving hers away to the steerswoman, he recognized, belatedly, that they should have provided one more pair of earrings for each canoe. "Big white chief can't count" would be the assessment in every wigwam that night.

"You are not angry with me, Sam?" Anna asked as he walked with her through the crowds.

"No. I think perhaps I was envious of the fun you were having. But who was that fellow who carried you out of the water? I noticed him before on the shore. Puts himself forward a bit too much for my liking."

"He's Camudwa, my steersman from the Sault."

"The one who steered you down the rapids?"

"And covered me in glory. I will not forget him."

"Well. I'm not your keeper. But I must warn you against giving the wrong impression to these people."

"Don't worry about me. It's all good humour and fun. And no, you are not my keeper. If I had wanted constant surveillance and uncalled-for advice, I'd have stayed in Toronto with the Vice-Chancellor." She turned her back on him to wave at the McMurrays. "And now I must see what my friends are doing."

"You'd better watch that one," Anderson said as he approached Sam. "Here we are, two white men in charge of almost four thousand savages. I don't count those Catholic priests or that missionary friend of yours. They'd be useless if there was trouble. We don't know anything about the sexual urges of these men."

"They'll keep their distance, surely."

Anderson's square-jawed face grew stern. "Didn't you notice the getup of that one who pulled your friend from the water? Look at him." He pointed to Camudwa. "This morning, when your friends landed, he was a plain Indian, dirty blanket coat and greasy hair. Now he's got himself rigged out like some sort of stage savage in a bad European melodrama. Wants to be noticed, I'd say. And she seems crazy enough to be impressed."

Sam had not fully taken in the details of the Indian's costume. Now he took a second look. Yes, he was certainly splendid. Scarlet leggings, confined with bands of beads, strings and tassels.

Moccasins worked in a rainbow of dyed porcupine quills. Beaver helmet stuck with silver pins and bits of dyed green and red moose hair that matched his chest, painted in red and green stripes, and his face, half red and half green.

"Maybe he just likes to get dressed up occasionally. Why don't you get up to the storage shed and sort the gifts? We don't have that much time."

"Can't do it all myself." Anderson stalked off.

Sam broke into a run, catching up with Anna before she rejoined her friends. "I should keep my mouth shut," he told her. "It's got me into trouble many times in my life. But one thing I know: I do not want to quarrel with you. Forgive me."

"For penance, you can take me to look at the gifts," she said, smiling. "I've been wanting to see first hand the government munificence that draws all these people from the far-flung corners of this land."

Anderson had brought the gifts by steamboat from the Sault, and he and Sam had arranged them in piles in the storehouse. As Sam and Anna entered the large log house, Anderson was standing, arms folded, looking at the gifts. "About time," he said, when he saw Sam. "It's no place for a woman," he added, giving a perfunctory bow in Anna's direction.

"But how on earth, Major Anderson, do you get the right goods parcelled out to each of the thousands of Indians in the encampment?"

Waving sheets of paper under her nose, he said, "We have made a list of the number of braves, squaws and children in each of the seventy-five tribes present. We count out the articles for each person accordingly, then the chief collects the whole kit and allots the booty to tribal members. So, if there are any complaints about shortages, we say, 'Look to your chief.'"

Sam was amused at the lady's reply. "Brilliant organization, if I may say so."

And even more amused at the instant effect of those few words.

"Feel free, dear lady, to watch while we get the allotments out to each chief." Anderson moved over to the far side of the storehouse to begin the work.

Sam put his hand on Anna's sleeve. "It wasn't all that easy. To be quite truthful, I had to ask Jacob the best way of sorting it. I'm pleased with myself about that. There was a time when I would not have admitted my ignorance to an Indian."

Anna took out her notebook. "Now tell me exactly who gets what."

"For each man: three and three-quarter yards of linen and blue cotton; one blanket; some thread and four strong needles; a comb, an awl, and a butcher's knife, three pounds of tobacco; nine pounds of shot, three pounds of ball, four pounds of powder, and six flints."

"How do you keep all that in your head?"

"Practice. After I sorted piles of twenty or so, I scarcely had to think. At night, when I can't sleep, I usually count moose. But up here, it's government packets, infinitely more sleep inducing than moose, I may say."

"And for each woman?" she pursued.

"A yard and a half of calico; two yards of woollen cloth; one blanket; some thread and four needles; one comb, one awl and one knife." And forestalling her next question, he added, "For each child, bits of woollen cloth and calico."

"A veritable treasure, indeed," the lady said. "Well worth a week's trip and a hide bloodied with mosquito sores. No wonder the Sault Indians were so keen to leave home."

"What can I say, Anna? It is indeed a small return for so much travel. And yet the Indian Department decrees that no gifts will be given unless the people travel here to Manitoulin to receive them. In fairness to the Department, let me remind you that we give gifts even to those Indians who come here from American territory. Like the Chippewa bands from Mackinaw Island and the south side of the Ste. Marie River. But I will be telling the assembly this afternoon that we have to cut them off in the future unless they move to Canadian territory."

Anna listened to all this and said with a frown, "So much ado about nothing."

"The gifts are paltry, I agree, but it's a wonderful place for a party, isn't it? These people, as you yourself said a few minutes ago, are enjoying themselves." Sam noticed Anderson sidling over from the far side of the room in order to join in their conversation. "Please say no more now."

"You don't want that wretched man to hear you criticize the government. Is that it?"

"I'm dependent on the government for my wages. And I don't trust Anderson. He wanted my job, and he's quite capable of repeating anything I say to Sir Francis. Think about my position for a minute. There's no gift-giving ceremony for a debt-ridden white man like myself. I have to keep this job and the five hundred pounds annually that come with it."

"I suppose it's my turn to apologize." But the tone of her voice contained no regret. She turned to the agent, who was now within earshot. "Major Anderson, I know that you and Mr. Jarvis must now give your full attention to your work. I shall keep out of the way."

Sam heaved the bundles of gifts onto wooden trolleys, cursing inwardly. Two arguments in the space of fifteen minutes. His silly dream of a romantic idyll had flown away like a puff of wind through an open window. What could a free-spirited woman like Anna understand of his multiple responsibilities?

THIRTY-FIVE

Anna looked with pleasure at the tiny room and narrow bed that had been alloted to her in the government log house. It was hers alone, and she would have the luxury of reading by candlelight for as long as she wished. A maid had left a pitcher of cold water and a cake of soap on a pine table, and she unbuttoned her bodice in order to wash her neck and arms. A shadow obscured the sun that streamed through the little window, and she turned abruptly. Seven small brown faces peered through at her.

Smiling, she took a blanket from her bed and placed it over the glass. Really, there was no rudeness in their stares, only curiosity.

She remembered her dismay earlier in the summer when she'd found herself in a room with no lock on the door. She had told the innkeeper her concern; he had been grumpy but had put a nail lengthwise over the latch. Now, after these days of sleeping in tents and bateaux, it seemed almost normal to have company.

From the shore, she could hear shouts and drums beating. She finished her wash and took the blanket from her window. She threw up the sash and poked her head out. The children who had been at her window a few minutes before were now running down the slope. "What's happening?" she called after them. No one stopped to answer.

There was a knock at her door, and Mrs. McMurray entered. "What's happening, you ask? Several of your Chippewa fans plan a dance in your honour. They've sent me with the official invitation."

"How exciting! I am honoured. What will it be like? What should I know about it?"

"I won't tell you. Wait and see. Let me only recommend that you have a few minutes' quiet rest before you come down to the shore. You will need it. But, please, do be down on the waterfront in half an hour."

Anna lay down as suggested but could not sleep. In a short time, there was a loud banging on her door, and a host of small voices yelling, "Come, come, come!" She got up immediately, pulled on her moccasins, gave her hair a hasty pat, and along with the crowd of excited Indians, ran down the hill.

A row of fallen oak "sofas" had been arranged around a circular expanse of sand. Anna seated herself beside the McMurrays, the Catholic priests, and a number of Indian chiefs. Beyond the shore, the slope of land covered with wigwams rose high like a wall and formed a backdrop for the "stage". Above was the sunshine of a cloudless summer's day.

Just as the fun was about to begin, Sam Jarvis came running from the storehouse, and Anna squeezed over to make room for him on her log.

Two drums, two rattles and a chorus of male and female voices formed the accompaniment for the dancers: two dozen braves fantastically adorned and painted in a manner to which they had evidently taken much thought and attention.

They had thrown aside their leggings and blankets to display their painted bodies to full advantage. They all had slender, agile figures, with shapely legs and small feet, but no two men were alike in their accessories. One had the feathers of a crane on his head; its long beak stuck out from his forehead. Another had the shell of a large turtle suspended from a cord around his neck. Yet another wore the skin of a bear, paws intact, draped over his chest.

Camudwa was most picturesque of all. On his chest was an expertly drawn white hand. ("Some symbolism in that?" Sam asked Anna.) He had added red bars to his right leg and green lines to the left. Over his skull he had fitted the head of a cougar so that his own face was scarcely visible behind the ears and the fiendish teeth of the creature. He pranced up so close to Anna that she could not avoid seeing his muscled chest and forearms, his shapely legs, and the bulge of his genitals.

A year before, she had been seated in a box at the opera, spellbound as she watched Carlotta Grisi and Perrot flying through the galop in *Benyowksy*. The juxtaposition of that memory with this reality seemed unreal, but simple as this dance was, it was equally entrancing. It consisted of the alternate raising of one foot, then the other, while the performers swung their bodies back and forth and flourished their clubs, tomahawks, and javelins. There was an intensity in their movements that was hypnotic. Anna felt herself pulled into the frenzy of the dance.

"Why are you laughing?" Sam said. "Because it's so grotesque?"

"No, no. In fact...I didn't realize I was laughing."

"Well, they've taken it as an expression of your enjoyment. Look at them."

The drums now beat louder and faster, and the dancers quickened their steps to a frenzy. Camudwa pranced closer and closer until Anna could see the sweat smearing the white hand on his chest and smell the stink of stale tobacco. He swept off his cougar headpiece and smiled broadly, while a series of grunts emerged from the back of his throat.

"Sounds like a rutting moose," was Sam's comment.

"Please, oh please, Sam, let me just live in this moment. All too soon—for both of us, surely—the wonderful dress and wild dance will metamorphose into trousers and the waltz."

"You are enjoying it, then?"

"It's like a plague of fiends breaking into paradise! But there is something so compelling..."

The dance wound down. At the end, Anna clapped her hands as loudly as any of the Indians and shouted "Hah, hah!" with the rest of the crowd. Then she went up to Camudwa, pressed her hands around his, and congratulated him, saying "Minno, minno!" over and over. He spoke to her in Chippewa, then pointed towards his wigwam, but at this point Mr. McMurray intervened, saying something in the dialect that stopped the flow of the Indian's speech. He bowed in European fashion and went off with the rest of the dancers.

"I think his intent was clear," Sam said to Mr. McMurray. "Most

Indians have an unwritten law that keeps them from overstepping the boundaries of proper decorum. Not that one, it appears."

"I suppose I must thank you for stepping in, but it really wasn't necessary. I am not a member of the weaker sex," Anna said, adding, "And now, if you will excuse me, I shall go back to my room and get ready for the awards ceremony."

"And I'll come along with you, if you don't mind," Mrs. McMurray said.

In Anna's room, they combed their hair and washed their faces with the cold water in the pitcher. "Come and sit with me, my dear." Mrs. McMurray patted the side of the bed. "And let us call each other by our Christian names. Surely we have become friends and can take this liberty."

"Dear Charlotte." Anna took her friend's hand in hers.

"I apologize for Mac's intrusion. He meant well. And you restrained yourself from saying, 'please, oh please, let me run my own life.'" Charlotte gave an embarrassed laugh. "I suppose you understood what Camudwa was suggesting?"

"Of course. And do you know, Charlotte, that I was—well, not tempted, exactly—but flattered? The European men in my literary entourage appreciate my mind. Toronto men will not acknowledge that I *have* a mind. To them, I'm just an appendage to my husband. I don't know exactly what it is about me that Camudwa likes. It can't be my mind, since we don't speak each other's language. Perhaps it's my body. It's been so long since a man has accorded me that compliment. I remember once being in the Doges' Palace in Venice. There were two Italian men behind me, and one said to the other, '*La signora inglese, che seno magnifico!*' They didn't think I understood Italian, you know, and were quite abashed when I turned around and said, '*Grazie*.'"

"I don't know Italian, but I get the gist of what you say. But there's more to Camudwa's admiration, I think. He admires your courage, your spirit. The white women he has met in his life have undoubtedly been as tightly laced into their attitudes as they are into their corsets."

"As I was, too, not so long ago. But I hope I have changed."

At three o'clock, Anna and the McMurrays went into the council chamber. Two Catholic priests were already seated. One of the priests rose when he saw the women. "Dear ladies," he said, fingering the cross on his soutane, "I have never before seen the weaker sex at such a gathering. Perhaps you might find other pursuits more to your liking?"

Anna ignored this bit of presumption and kept moving towards the empty places on the bench, but she heard Mr. McMurray say, "Look after your own flock, father, and I'll look after mine." They seated themselves close to the platform on which Sam was to make his speech. It was a wooden plank raised on trestles. Near the plank sat Major Anderson and the translator, Blackbird.

Then into the council chamber sauntered the chiefs of the Menomoni, Ottawa, Pottowattomi, Chippewa and Winnebago tribes. They moved quietly and with no fuss. There seemed to be no particular order or ceremony, unlike the bigwigs Anna had seen once with her father at the opening of the British Parliament.

There were men with hair in fringes hanging on their shoulders or tied on top with a single feather; men with faces painted in vermilion and eyes circled in black or white; men with belts of wampum from which hung pouches and scalping knives—and horrors, even a scalp—men in embroidered leggings and headbands ringed with eagle feathers; three chieftains in mourning with faces blacked with grease and soot. "Look at Two Ears," Mrs. McMurray whispered, pointing to a chieftain who had large clusters of swansdown hanging from both sides of his head.

Then in the midst of all these strange and wonderful figures, Anna spotted Jacob's father. He saw her at the same moment, came towards her and held her hand for a moment in his strong fingers.

"Bojou, Wah,sah,ge,wah,no,qua," he said. He wore a surtout of fine blue cloth, under which Anna could see a bright red shirt. Round his head was an embroidered band, in which were stuck four eagle feathers. Though he held a tomahawk in his hand, his face was mild, as Anna remembered it.

"Who is he?" Charlotte whispered as he followed the other chiefs.

"Chief Snake. He had breakfast with me in Toronto in January."

The room was hot, and by this time dense with smoke. Every door and window was filled with onlookers, so that the fresh air from outside was stifled. The Catholic priest who had dubbed her and Charlotte "the weaker sex" brushed by them and headed towards the outdoors, a handkerchief over his mouth and nose.

"Sorry you can't take the heat, father," Anna said. "But we'll give you a summary later."

When all were assembled, there was a pause, then Sam came into the chamber. The Major and Blackbird stood up, ready to hoist him up onto the plank, but he quickened his pace at just the right moment and vaulted onto the platform without their help. As always, Anna noted, his clothes were beautifully tailored, and his neat figure set them off to advantage. Really, for a man who professed to be "debt-ridden", he spent a good deal on his appearance. Today, for this important occasion, he wore a cream linen frock coat, strapped trousers, a waistcoat and a brilliant red silk cravat.

"Nice," Anna said to Charlotte, gesturing at Sam. "But I wonder if his clothes seem as fantastic to the chiefs as theirs seem to people like me."

"I'll ask."

Charlotte spoke briefly to a chief sitting behind her then turned back to Anna. "He says the Great White Chieftain has a good body, would look better in leggings."

Anna laughed. Yes, she thought, the Great White Chieftain does have a good body. It might look even better *without* leggings.

She hoped Charlotte didn't notice her blushing.

THIRTY-SIX

Sam stood on the trestle like a treed lynx, feeling that he would never get through what he had to say and come down from his perch. The room was unbearably hot and crowded, and he became more nervous when he saw Anna and her friends only a few feet from his platform. He knew his limitations as a public speaker. And this time, there was no Colonel Fitzgibbon to bail him out.

Then he heard Anna laugh. He caught her eye, and she smiled at him, and flipped her fingers at him in an encouraging wave. He felt better immediately.

He'd given this speech a lot of thought. Sir Francis had left him notes, but they were of little use. The man had actually suggested starting each section of his speech with the words, "Children!"

That'll get their attention, he'd written in the margin of his notes.

But Sam knew that this epithet would be as offensive to the Indians as "the weaker sex" was to Anna.

"Friends!" he began, and with this one word, the assemblage quieted and everyone looked towards him. He told them of the death of the Great Father on the other side of the Great Salt Lake and of the accession of the Great Mother. He complimented them on their quiet, sober and orderly conduct in the camp during their stay, and urged them to take their gifts directly home without dealing with the traders and their firewater.

As he heard his own words, the doubts poured in. Was he being condescending? Too late to revise now. He stumbled on, forcing himself to stop at the end of every sentence so that Blackbird could put his words into the principal languages of the assembly. There was, in fact, more translation than speech. Blackbird's voice was loud and high-pitched, accompanied by much hand-waving. Sam had no idea of the accuracy of what the Indian was saying— translators always had the upper hand—and from time to time he thought he heard suppressed laughter from the chieftains. Was Blackbird mocking his delivery?

But when he looked down at the people he knew—the McMurrays, Anna, Chief Snake—he saw that they were polite and attentive. And Anna kept smiling at him as if she were enjoying what he said. He took a deep breath and moved into his conclusion.

"My friends, the Governor warns that no more gifts will be given henceforth to our brethren from the American side of Lake Huron. In order to receive the generosity of the Great Mother at the next council, they must move to Upper Canada."

He waited while Blackbird translated this last bit, noting that a buzz began immediately before the translation. A good many of them understood English, though they might not let on. He looked down at a handsome chieftain signalling him imperatively from the crowd.

"Speak."

The chief rose to his feet, waving Blackbird aside with a dismissive hand.

"Great White Chieftain, we have always ranged freely without regard to the false boundaries set by the Great Father and the Long Knives. Whether we consent to live on one side or the other of these boundaries is a matter on which our chieftains must deliberate. Why should it be necessary to live within the white man's boundaries when this land has belonged to all of us for centuries before the white man came among us with measuring tools and paper documents? Our chieftains will ponder on what you say and bring an answer when you come again among us."

"Point taken," Sam said, abandoning the stilted diction he'd grown tired of. "I'll speak to the Governor about your objection. And now, sir, while you are still standing, I give you, on behalf of the white man's government, the new flag of the Empire."

It was a beautiful specimen of heraldry—the British lion side by side with the Canadian beaver—and the chief who had spoken out seemed, for the moment at least, mollified.

It was a relief to come to the next item on the agenda. The Governor had given him a discretionary fund from which to buy brass kettles, silver gorgets, medals and amulets for chieftains whose conduct merited them. He now distributed these, making sure that Jacob's father, Chief Snake, received a medal and a gorget.

As a final gift, he had intended to give Blackbird something extra for his work as translator, but now he decided to put the expense of a brass kettle into his own pocket. No one from the government ever asked for an accounting of the money spent from this fund, and he knew he had come upon an unexpected nest egg. He would take just enough from his stash to pay for his new clothes for this occasion. Business expenses, they were called, and surely he could not get into trouble over such an outlay.

At the end of the assembly, everyone plunged out into the open air. Sam stood with Anna, Major Anderson, Jacob Snake and the McMurrays, enjoying the sunshine.

Blackbird ran up the slope towards them.

He spoke to Sam in his rapid but fluent English with flourishes of his hands and a series of small bows. "Come, come, quick, quick. Trader from Toronto hides in cove near entrance to bay. Trader's boats filled with firewater."

"We must get off at once, Anderson," Sam said. "Come along with us, Blackbird. And you, Jacob, find ten or so strong men you can trust. We must dump the rogue's cargo into the bay."

Anderson cleared his throat. "But what if he—"

"Get on with it, man. We've got to deal with the swine before the natives come upon him. Go, go."

Sam set off at a run, Jacob beside him, picking up braves along the way in their dash to the shoreline. In five minutes, they were into a long canoe with Jacob as steersman. They saw Anderson plodding towards the shore. "Push off without him," Sam said. "No time to lose."

Another minute, and they had made progress along the bay. Five minutes more, and with Blackbird's direction, they found the trader's bateaux hidden in a secluded cove. The man had tethered the two boats with long ropes to a tree near the water's edge, and he was seated on a log enjoying his pipe.

"Shouldn't be too difficult," Sam said to Jacob. "The crew seems to have disappeared."

The paddlers threw down an anchor, jumped from the canoe and ran to shore. Seeing them come at him, the man rushed towards the forest. But Sam caught up with him, grabbed him by the back of his collar and brought him down. As he tried to struggle to his feet, Sam landed a punch that knocked him back onto a pile of brushwood.

He looked at the bloodied face of his victim. "Good lord. Crimshaw."

The trader launched into a string of curses.

"Shut up. Stay where you are while my crew finds a market for your firewater."

The Indians climbed onto the bateaux, each brandishing a heavy stick from the shore. They smashed the barrels and tipped gallons of cheap whiskey into the lake.

"You call this a market for my whiskey, do you? By god, I'll see you swing for this." Crimshaw wiped his bloody nose on his sleeve and tried to rise. But Sam kept a foot planted on his chest.

"The bass and whitefish will enjoy it, I assure you," he said. "But if you want restitution, apply to Sir Francis Bond Head. He'll be glad to hear of your plans to stock your shelves with the government's gifts."

"Just wait, you bugger. I'll throw those unpaid bills of yours before the courts. You'll rot in debtors' prison for the rest of your goddamned life."

Sam leaned over Crimshaw and spat in his face. Then he took his foot from the man's chest and turned towards the Indians who had come up on shore, having finished their work. Together they waded to their canoe, climbed in and paddled into the channel. Crimshaw's curses followed them.

Sam felt a rush of excitement. Of all the impulsive things he'd done over his lifetime, this one at least had been right. He'd settled Crimshaw's hash, once and for all. The Indians would be able to make their way home without his treachery. Anna would praise him. Great White Chieftain. Maybe he deserved that title after all.

Then, slowly, the euphoria passed. He sat, morose, staring into the depths of the water.

"It is a good thing we do this day," Jacob said, breaking in on his reverie.

"Was it? You know, I'm glad we wrecked Crimshaw's profits. But part of me is ashamed that we have treated the Indians in the encampment as children."

"I do not understand, Nehkik."

"Let me tell you something that happened earlier. You may know about it anyway. That Indian, Camudwa, made an improper suggestion to Mrs. Jameson. McMurray—with my approval—told him to take a hike. The lady was angry. 'Do not assume I am a member of the weaker sex,' she said. She was right, you know. And now, here I am, making the big decision to control the lives of hundreds of Indians."

"Big decision?"

"To destroy the whiskey they might want to trade their gifts for. Hell, Jacob, I like a glass of firewater myself, and I wouldn't want anyone—you, for example—to decide I shouldn't have it. In fact, it's my bills for firewater that keep me in thrall to Crimshaw. When it comes to drink, I often feel as helpless as any Indian."

Jacob dipped his long paddle into the water with a twist that sent the canoe towards the shoreline and the encampment. Then he said, "Sometimes, Nehkik, people do not know when they need help. Sometimes they need someone to speak for them. I think of Elijah White Deer. Remember, I tell you in the spring about him.

He does not have me beside him when he goes to Crimshaw. He takes drink. Now he is—what do you call it?"

"A drunkard?"

"Yes, a drunkard." Jacob gave a deep sigh.

"It's true, friend, what you say. Sometimes we do need someone to push us in the right direction, even if we don't acknowledge we need their help." Yes, he reflected, feeling hopeful again for a moment, Anna had given him good advice about Crimshaw, and he had finally taken it.

But he'd had a lot of bad advice in his life, too, and he'd taken that as well. He thought of the duel. Damn it. If he hadn't had Boulton and Small pushing at him to take his shot, would he have done what was right? Fired in the air? Maybe not. Still...

"You frown, Nehkik. Something is wrong?"

"Just thinking some more on what you say. Sometimes people can push us in the wrong direction, too."

"Yes. But today we do the right thing."

That evening, Sam entertained the priests, the McMurrays and Anna at dinner in the council chamber. He was both relieved and annoyed in equal parts when Major Anderson said to him just before the guests arrived, "Sanctimonious clergy or an opinionated blue-stocking, I don't know which would be more injurious to my digestion. And I can't deny I'm hopping mad at you, Jarvis. You paddled away and left me standing there, looking like a fool, so you alone could take the glory when you smashed that trader's stash of firewater." He paused to wipe his flushed face with his handkerchief. "So excuse me from dinner. I shall take it alone in my room."

The plank on trestles did duty this time as a dinner table, and the cook, wife of one of the voyageurs, served excellent fried sturgeon and steamed blueberry pudding. In a recess in the magazine, Sam had found some bottles of sherry, which he smuggled in a deerskin sling for his walk from storehouse to council chamber.

Sam gave his guests an account of the raid as they refilled their sherry glasses and ate their sturgeon. "Well done, sir," Anna said. "Crimshaw has finally had his comeuppance."

"If only every goddamn trader in this world could be dumped into the lake along with his booty!" Mac said. He paused, then mumbled, "Excuse the language."

"Did you know the devil when you lived in Toronto, Mac?"

"Yes. He was just starting up in business then. Not doing that well, from all we heard. But my father's sudden death left a dearth of merchants and gave Crimshaw his golden opportunity. My father was a decent man, but Crimshaw appears to be an unmitigated scoundrel."

"There is no one the Lord loves more than the sinner," one of the priests said, a smarmy fellow with bloodshot eyes. Sam couldn't remember his name.

He was grateful that Mac let the remark pass.

But the peace was short-lived. The priests seemed determined to pick a fight. The other one, Father Crue, spoke up. "We Catholics have been much more successful than you Protestants in stamping out polygamy among the Indians."

Mac had just asked the serving girl for some maple syrup for his pudding and did not hear the comment. It was Anna who replied. "But, father, that is because the Catholic Church allows a man the choice of which of his women he wishes to bear the title of 'wife'. The Church of England is stricter—and justly so—in this matter. Mr. McMurray told me something about it."

Mac took his cue. "We have an Indian in our community at the Sault who wanted to become a Christian. He had three wives, and he wanted to keep the latest, a young and beautiful woman, and put aside the other two, and—"

"Perhaps it's time to tell Mrs. Jameson—Anna—that his name was Camudwa," Mrs. McMurray said in an aside.

"We informed him, of course, that the woman he had taken to wife first was to be the permitted one. And he stomped off in anger and has not since mentioned becoming a Christian."

Anna gave a loud laugh. The priests looked at her. "Whatever is funny about this heathen story, ma'am?" the smarmy one asked.

"Forgive me, but..." Anna's giggles changed to coughing as she choked on her pudding.

Sam gave her a slap on the back. "Take a moment, Mrs. Jameson, and drink some of this water." He passed the pitcher to her.

Father Crue's face folded into a frown. "I don't understand."

"Oh...oh..." Anna got control of herself. "It's just that this very day Camudwa made a proposal to me. Think of it, I could have been Wife Number Four." She dissolved into giggles again, and the McMurrays and Sam joined in her laughter.

Father Crue turned to Sam. "I suppose that since there is no drawing room in this place for the weaker sex to go to, we must feel ourselves privileged to hear their comments, however ill-conceived."

"It *is* funny when you think of it," Sam said.

The servant at this point removed the cloth from the trestle, in the manner of faraway dinner parties in Toronto.

The conversation went on and on, and Sam found himself slipping into a stupor as the sherry began to play havoc with his reason. He was dead tired. He had been up since the crack of dawn. There had been the ear-splitting dance and the long speech on the trestle. And he had had time to reflect again on his dealings with Crimshaw that might culminate in disaster if the wretch carried out his threats about the unpaid bills.

Seeing him look at his pocket watch, Anna leaned over and whispered into his ear. "You are tired, Sam. Have a good night's rest. Tomorrow you leave for Toronto, and I want to go with you."

At least that's what she might have said. He didn't think he could have heard her right. So he nodded and smiled at her. That's what a well-bred host did when a lady spoke to him.

He rose. "I must be up early for our getaway, so I bid you goodnight. If we do not meet again, I thank you for this most interesting dinner conversation."

He shook hands with everyone, including Anna. She smiled and said, "I shall see you on the pier in the morning. Thank you for agreeing to my request."

Had he agreed to take her with them? One woman with twenty-one men? He didn't remember giving an outright assent. But he'd been half asleep, and four people had been talking loudly at the time.

When he finally got into his narrow bed, he made up his mind to straighten matters out in the morning. If Anna came with them, it would be pleasant. But then...what would she expect from him? How far was he prepared to go? He thought of Mary's niece and her lover, John Grogan. They had thrown away their lives for love. That was courageous, as he had told them. But was it courageous or just plain crazy?

THIRTY-SEVEN

Sam went down to the quay at daylight to supervise the loading of the gear for the trip home and found Anna already settled there with her baggage. She was surrounded by four Indian children, who were turning over cards from a pack she had evidently given them. "I'm teaching them to play *vingt-et-un*," she said. "And a good morning to you, sir. My bags are all ready as you can see."

"You're sure about this, are you? Think about it once more. You will be travelling down Lake Huron in a birchbark canoe with twenty-one men as your companions. You might be more comfortable with the McMurrays until a more suitable escort can be arranged."

"I should not dream of inconveniencing you, but my friends must travel back to the Sault today, and I myself need to return to Toronto, where I must make a few immediate decisions."

"About what?"

"Do I stay in Toronto? Do I go on to New York and thence to Europe? My husband would like to see me leave, and now that I have achieved a settlement of money from him, there is really no reason to stay." She paused, looked directly into his eyes. "Is there?"

"I can't advise you," he said. "I wish only for your happiness."

She smiled, and even in the dim light of early morning, he noticed again her beautiful white teeth and bright blue eyes. "Well, at any rate, though I would willingly spend the rest of my life in the beauty of Lake Huron, I must face the necessity of returning to Toronto."

"It's not a trip I'd recommend for a woman of refinement. Or am I implying 'weaker sex' again?"

"I think you are merely warning me about the realities of our voyage. You have treated me with such kindness, dear Sam, that I foresee no difficulties in our travelling arrangements."

He stepped gently into one of their two thirty-foot canoes tied to the side of the quay. He rolled up Anna's blankets and night gear to make a comfortable seat and gave her a pillow for her back. As he was reaching for her parasol, she took it herself, picked up her notebooks, sketchbooks and travel basket and put them within easy reach of her seat. "Please, let me look after myself," she said, hoisting up her skirt. For a moment, she looked as if she would hop off the quay into the craft.

"No, no," he told her, trying to ignore the grins and winks of the voyageurs, who had moved closer. "You must wait. The bark canoe is much more fragile than a bateau. It is so easy to break off bits of the pine-gum that hold the thing together. And then we would have to waste time caulking the seams. The crew and I will get in once we have loaded, then we shall assist you."

Leaving her on the shore, he ran back up the hill to the magazine. In a dusty corner, he found a marquee to protect her in case of heavy rain. Dragging the roll down the hill after him, he put it into the second canoe, where it added to the load of tents, guns, provisions and baggage. That done, one of the voyageurs in the passenger canoe helped the lady down from the wooden pier into the craft. She made a light, graceful descent, to everyone's relief, and Sam ceased to worry about the pine-gum caulking. He even managed to enjoy another glimpse of the lady's slender ankles.

Jacob Snake, as steersman, and eight paddlers soon got the canoe moving into the bay. In order to make room for their guest, Sam had to leave the bowsman behind with a few pounds to cover his unexpected dismissal. He and Anna sat facing each other in the middle of the canoe.

"What a glorious pink canopy!" she said, pointing at the morning sky. Sam nodded without speaking. He hoped she did not intend to rhapsodize the whole way down the lake to Penetanguishene. One of the delights of travel in the wilderness was the absence of the need for polite conversation. Old Solomon, who was on board to act as translator, so that Jacob could concentrate on his steering duties, had learned to sit absolutely silent until called upon to speak.

Sam was pleased that Jacob had hoisted the British flag on the stern of the canoe. It lent an air to their leave-taking. As his official party pulled away from Manitoulin Island, there were cheers from the Indians on shore and a firing of muskets in salute. "And isn't that your husband-to-be?" he asked Anna, pointing to a green-and-red figure waving from the dock.

"Alas, I fear that is now an opportunity lost."

Already there were a hundred canoes ahead of them, embarked on their homeward voyage. The water was crystal clear, and he could see shoals of black bass. The voyageurs plied their paddles and chattered among themselves in their French and Indian dialects. The trials and tribulations of Toronto seemed remote. He began to think about the journey. Three days and three nights with Anna. Anything could happen.

"Look, monsieur!" The voice came from the baggage canoe.

"What is it?"

Then he saw what had happened. "Damn, damn!"

Above them, into the blue sky, soared one of the two young hawks he had purchased from an Indian on the island.

"Whatever is wrong?" asked Anna.

"I had a pair of hawks in a basket in the other canoe. They were gifts for my oldest boys," Sam told her. "I thought they could train them like falcons to scare off the rabbits that eat my lettuce at Hazelburn."

"And now one of them has escaped." She looked up into the sky. "It's so beautiful. Look how it floats on the air current. Oh, to be a bird, to break free, to soar."

Sam shrugged. "Perhaps it's for the best. They'd be difficult to train. One might be enough of a handful."

They made headway, and he was surprised to realize, several hours into the trip, that Anna was capable of long periods of silence. She took from her basket a portable inkwell and quill and began to scratch notes in her book. Her attention seemed focused on Jacob. She wrote rapidly, paused from time to time to glance up from her book, then down again to make amendments to what she'd written.

What was it all about? He turned around to look at Jacob. There was nothing unusual that he could see. His friend wore loose leggings and a cotton shirt with rolled-up sleeves, and his long black hair was tied back with a cotton handerkerchief. It was the typical garb he wore when he was steersman.

"You find something remarkable about Jacob. What is it?"

"Haven't you watched the way he turns and twists? How the beads on his sash catch the sun like the scales on a snake? I've been trying to get it into words."

"Let the lady get her words right," Jacob said, smiling.

Sam looked again at his Indian friend. As steersman, he had a paddle twice as long as the others, and the manner in which he stood, striking the water first on one side, then on the other, was indeed picturesque. "You're right. I've never before really noticed the beauty of his movements. They're almost hypnotic. But will you read me what you've written, please?"

"Later. As Jacob says, when I've got the phrases exactly right, or as nearly right as I can get them."

After a few more scribbles and scratchings, Anna put her notebook aside and took out her sketchbook.

"And now, Jacob," she said. "I'll make a sketch of you in action. With your permission, of course."

He smiled. "It is my first...first...picture of myself."

"Your first portrait," Anna said.

As the sun climbed the sky, she finished her sketch. Then, as they glided between the rocky cliffs of the islands, she busied herself with sketches of the white water-lilies and the dwarf pines in the clefts of rock. Sam remembered how Mary prided herself on her drawing ability and often showed him sketches of Toronto harbour, but her art had none of the sureness of Anna's pencil.

Looking down at her work, he saw that she caught to perfection the flow of the water, the careening gulls and the scudding clouds.

"*Allumez!*"

At Jacob's sudden cry, the voyageurs laid their paddles inside the canoe and rested their shoulders against the thwarts. Then from the wide sashes around their waists, they took out small pouches of tobacco and lit their pipes. Anna put down her sketchbook.

"I almost wish I could have a pipe myself," she said to Sam, as the men exchanged jokes in their dialects. "You remember that night at the Governor's when I sat with the gentlemen and that stuffed-up butler offered me a barley stick instead of a pipe? I was quite disappointed."

Jacob must have heard her comment, for a minute later he passed a pipe along the ranks of paddlers, tobacco tamped down and lighted, ready to smoke. "For you, Mrs. Jameson," he said.

"What now?" she asked Sam as she looked at the wreaths of smoke around her.

"Put the end in your mouth and gently, gently, draw in just a bit of smoke. Then puff it out quickly."

The fine English lady with the pipe was the subject of much merriment among the crew, and Anna's laughter was heartiest of all. After a few coughs and splutterings, she got the hang of it.

"You know," Sam said, "I thought I might have to ask them not to smoke in your presence. I'm glad you can play along. It makes our voyage easier if the men can stick to their old ways."

"They measure their distance in pipes, do they not? And they have had *trois pipes* this morning. How many more this day?"

"Hard to say. I leave it to them. I'd say we've come twelve miles thus far. So much depends on the heat, the hunting and fishing they do along the way, and the light of late day. In these long canoes, we do not travel when the steersman cannot see into the depths of the water. If we scrape the bottom on a rock, we're in trouble. Though you've probably noticed we have those birchbark buckets in the bow for bailing. Each of them will take a quart of water in one swipe. And there's a bucket for each man in the canoe."

"Or woman?"

"We'll call on you, don't worry."

When they stopped an hour later for a midday meal on a rocky island, they tethered the canoe just off shore, because there was no beach to pull it up on.

Without preliminaries, old Solomon grabbed Anna about her waist and slung her over his shoulders. Then he waded through the water, carrying her. After an initial cry of surprise, the lady took all this in good part, even Solomon's side-of-the-mouth comment to the paddlers as he set her down on the rock where they were to build a fire.

"Do you know what he said?" she asked Sam, laughing.

"I don't speak French."

"He said his back was broken."

"Such impudence."

"But are broken backs necessary? When I came to Manitoulin with the McMurrays, the rowers pulled the boat up on shore. Then we all got out."

"If there's no beach, Solomon is expected to carry a lady—or a fine gentleman, for that matter—ashore. He's done it before. It's part of the drill. I'll speak to him about his comment."

"No, no, please, say nothing. I shall handle it in my own way."

As they sat around the campfire a half-hour later, eating fried black bass, Anna put her hand on Solomon's shoulder. She said something to him in rapid French, her brow wrinkled into an expression of intense sympathy.

The voyageurs laughed heartily as Solomon's face turned bright red.

"What on earth did you say?" Sam asked.

"I merely said that I was sorry about his back. That if it was truly broken, I should be glad to carry *him* to the canoe."

Now Sam too joined in the laughter. But Anna put a finger to her lips. "Please do not laugh at him. Now that I know the drill, as you call it, I shall never again break the poor man's back."

The cat was out of the bag, and Anna knew they would all be
more careful in their speech during the days to come. Which was
a pity. She had heard them brag about their exploits at the Sault
and Mackinaw, where they had spent many a *piastre* on wine and
food and bright sashes to impress the dusky maidens, as they called
them. For Anna, it was all interesting, easy research.

But it was surprising that they had said nothing untoward
about her. Though their descriptions of their female conquests had
been unsparing, there had been no ribald comments about her
own figure.

She turned her attention back to the landscape. They had a
most delightful run among hundreds of islands, sometimes darting
through narrow rocky channels, so narrow that she could not see
the water on either side of the canoe; and then emerging, they
glided through vast fields of water-lilies.

"Sheer delight," she said to Sam. "Such a day cannot be long
enough."

There was no response, just a nod.

So she concentrated on her note-taking and had just finished
describing the water-lilies when the voyageurs began to sing in
unison, marking the time with their paddles. She had hoped for
this. She remembered how much she had enjoyed the songs of the
crew in the McMurrays' bateau. These paddlers had several new
ones that they sang over and over, and she soon learned the words
and the melodies. Each man had his favourite song. Jacob always
led them in "En roulant ma boule, roulant" while Louis liked "La
belle rose blanche" and LeDuc's voice drowned out the others in
"Trois canards s'en vont baignant".

"*Et vous, madame,*" said Louis when they had finished their
repertoire, "*que voulez-vous?*"

"I have not heard paddling songs before," she said. "Please, let
us sing them all again. And you, Sam, must sing along with us."

"I probably won't get the words straight," her companion said,
"but I'll hum the tune."

By this time, the second canoe with the provisions had pulled alongside, and now there were twenty-one men singing in full voice along with Anna. And when they had worked through their repertoire of six or seven *chansons*, old Solomon sang a new one that only Jacob seemed to have heard before.

It had a word in it Anna was unfamiliar with, but not for long. "*Les maringouins*," she said, spelling the word out for Sam. "Solomon's song says that they sting your head and deafen your ears with their buzzing, but you must endure them patiently, for they show you how the Devil will torment you if you don't look out for your soul."

"Only in Canada could there be a song about mosquitoes. I imagine that one day, if we ever leave off singing 'God Save the King'—excuse me, 'Queen'—it will be the national anthem of this new land."

They both laughed. Anna took up her quill again. "I must write down what I remember of the words of Solomon's song."

Sometimes the voyageurs sang at double or triple speed, at which time they would paddle towards a wall of rock with such extreme velocity that Anna held her breath, expecting to be smashed to pieces. Then in a moment, they would all, with a simultaneous backstroke of their paddles, stop with such a jerk that she thought her head would fly off. After the second repetition of this game, she learned to brace herself with her knees pressed against the thwarts.

At each *pipe*, some of the men took up their rifles to shoot wild ducks or catch fish. There was a growing pile of catch in the canoe as the day wore on. Once, when LeDuc had caught a particularly large pickerel, he took the hook from its mouth and threw it on the floor of the canoe where it lay gasping.

With one smooth stroke, Jacob took his paddle and whacked the fish on the head. "Great Spirit's creatures must die without pain. That is what Great Spirit tells my people."

"I confess that I do not understand the pleasure the paddlers take from barbarism," she said to Sam.

"Barbarism?"

"What would you call their killing of that water snake for no good reason? Or the way they lure those gulls to a bloody death with biscuit crumbs? Or the shooting of that mother duck and the leaving of her six fledglings to fend for themselves? Or—"

"I take your point." He turned to Jacob, "And you, friend, I think you understand what Mrs. Jameson is talking about?"

"Chippewa people do not let creatures suffer. But the paddlers are not Chippewa. Half French, half Indian. Perhaps they do not understand."

"They will listen to me. After all, it is the Indian Affairs Department that is paying their wages." He turned around and spoke to the old man slumped behind them on the floor of the canoe. "Wake up, Solomon. Time to translate. Tell the crew that from now on they must shoot on land, if possible, rather than from the canoe. And if they catch fish, they must kill them instantly rather than leave them gasping to death."

Anna soon had an opportunity to see the effects of Sam's commands. As the canoes passed through a bed of reeds, a cry went up from the cargo canoe, "Otter! Otter!" But just as the voyageurs started beating the reeds with their paddles, Sam shouted, "Stop!" and they changed their minds. Quickly they moved out of the reeds back into the main channel between the islands.

"Thank you, sir, for giving that poor creature another day of life."

"I think I have a special feeling for otters. Don't I, Jacob?"

He smiled. "Yes, Nehkik. You swim like the otter."

Anna thought for a minute. "Ah yes. Now I understand. 'Nehkik' is Chippewa for otter, is it not? You know," she leaned towards Sam and touched his knee, "it is so pleasant that you have a Chippewa name. I love mine, too, though I know it is not given with the genuine affection that Jacob accords to you. In fact, as Mr. McMurray pointed out to me, I could have killed Camudwa in my race for glory."

Just at sunset, they landed on a flat ledge of rock. The men pitched the marquee and set up Anna's tent at a respectful distance from the rest of the group. Sam made her a soft bed of boughs, over which he spread a bearskin and over that, blankets. She put on a fresh pair of gloves and covered her head with mosquito netting. Then she walked along the cliff to enjoy the strange blending of rose and amber light in the western sky. The lake was a bath of molten gold; the rocky islands nearby were a dense purple except where their edges seemed fringed with fire. While she stood there, the purple shadows darkened, and the crescent moon rose.

Sam came out from his tent to stand beside her. "Beautiful, beautiful."

"'My spirits as in a dream are all bound up,'" she replied. "I have such a deep respect for the power that created this beauty that..." She paused and turned to him. "I am so suffocated by it all... I cannot find words."

She noticed the blush under Sam's tanned cheeks.

"In Toronto, I seldom have to search for the right word," Sam said. "A loud voice—sometimes, even a fist or a pistol—usually fills the bill. But now I remember some words that seem exactly right." He cleared his throat. "Would you like to hear them?"

And without waiting for her answer, he began to sing:

The spacious firmament on high,
With all the blue ethereal sky,
And spangled heavens, a shining frame,
Their great Original proclaim.
The unwearied sun from day to day,
Doth his Creator's power display,
And publishes to every land
The work of an almighty hand.

"Lovely," she said. "It is one of my father's favourites. And you sing it so well. It was only this morning—in the canoe—that I realized you have a fine baritone voice."

"Until today I didn't realize how much I enjoy singing, though I have always liked listening to songs. But in Toronto, it's the tenors that rule the roost."

The smell of the campfire cooking wafted upwards, making Sam's mouth water. He gave his canoe partner his arm with a bow and a flourish, and they descended to the campfire for an excellent supper of fish and pigeons, wild gooseberries and a good glass of madeira.

He was glad to see Anna's response to the meal.

"Yes," she said, seeing him look at her tin plate piled with roast pigeon. "I acknowledge my hypocrisy. Though I inveighed against the massacre of these helpless fowl, I am thoroughly enjoying them now. I fear the fresh air and excellent food have played havoc with my morality. No doubt you despise me." She laughed at him through her mouthful of pigeon.

He thought of his own ill-fated resolutions to deny himself Crimshaw's best imported sherry. "Not at all. We all have our hypocrisies."

She lingered after her meal, seeming to enjoy the fireside and the companionship of the voyageurs. At one point, she went back to her tent for a minute. Call of nature, he assumed, but when she returned to the campfire, she carried with her the instrument that had been the subject of much conjecture in Toronto and so much pleasure on the Niagara steamer.

"Your Spanish guitar," he said.

"One of my favourite things. When my first book came on the market some years ago, I said to the publisher, 'If it is a success, I want nothing more from you than a Spanish guitar.' And it has been with me ever since."

She struck a few chords of "En roulant ma boule, roulant" and soon they were all singing. They went through the day's repertoire, then came the finale, Solomon's tribute to the mosquito.

Anna rose, walked over to where Jacob was seated, and handed him the guitar.

"Very pretty," he said as he stroked its shiny surface. "I keep it safe for you until morning?"

"No, indeed. You must keep it forever. It is my gift to you and the crew. I wanted to part with something that is precious to me, something that would say to you all, thank you, thank you for this voyage, for your kindness." In the darkness, Sam saw tears shining on her cheeks.

Soon afterwards, she left. Later Sam went to his tent, closed the flap and drifted into a sound sleep. He wakened at midnight. The voyageurs were still up, dancing and singing on the rock below his tent. It was their relaxation from the hours of hard paddling. At last the noise subsided. He knew the men would be lying now on their blankets and bearskins between the upturned canoes and the fire, not minding at all the smoke that served to dispel the mosquitoes. He fell asleep again.

THIRTY-EIGHT

Just at dawn, Sam wakened, hearing a splash. He took his hunting telescope and opened the flap of his tent. He knew where the sound had come from: a pool in the secluded cove just behind the rock where the voyageurs had pitched Anna's tent.

First he looked down at the shoreline. All the men, including Jacob, were busy caulking the canoes with pine gum, applying it to the seams with torches. At least once on every voyage, they did this to keep the crafts watertight.

Telescope in hand, he crept along the rocky height and looked down on the pond, his body hidden by the juniper bushes fronting the water. Anna had left her garments over one of the bushes and was now stroking her way across the pond's breadth. He followed the progress of her white shoulders as she swam, feeling the same excitement as when he stalked a moose.

She turned at the far side of the pond and came back towards him, her arms pushing the water aside in steady strokes. Glass trained on her, he watched her step out of the water onto the rocky shore. Her figure was an hourglass, with large breasts and wide hips, and her waist was narrow, her legs long and shapely for such a short woman. He became conscious of his stiffening prick.

She turned her back to him and walked into the pool again. "Come and join me," she called over her shoulder. "The mosquitoes can't get us under water."

Down went the telescope onto the lichen. Off with his clothes and into the water. "How did you know?"

"I saw the glint of your telescope."

His prick now at full alert, he pressed against her. The water was deep, and she grasped him about his waist, while they both kicked their legs gently to stay afloat. He ducked his head under water and nibbled her breasts, feeling the nipples grow hard.

He took a gulp of air and dived down again, seeking her pubis. She managed to keep herself upright, using her arms and legs to tread water. But just as he was about to touch her, he saw a huge reptile swimming towards them. His erection collapsed.

"We must get out of here," he said, surfacing.

"What is it?"

"A snapping turtle. A big one. Swim, swim."

A minute later, they scambled up onto the rocks where they lay, panting.

"What is this creature you fear so much?"

He took a few seconds to catch his breath. "A two-foot mass of hard shell...with a scaly tail like an alligator's and hooked teeth that sink into your flesh and remove a finger or a toe without trouble. One of my classmates at school lost half his hand in the jaws of one of the brutes."

"Why are you laughing all of a sudden?"

He couldn't tell her. He'd just had the thought that his lost member might have solved some problems for Mary.

They got back into their clothes. "Perhaps it's as well that the critter brought us to our senses," he said. "There's so much to think about before we get into something we can't get out of."

"What specifically are you thinking about, dear Sam?"

"All my life, in all the important moments of my life, that is, I've acted without thought or reason. Just fallen into one mess after the other. Time to grow up. Time to think about...about an unwanted child, for instance."

"Forget that. I have sponges. But..." She laughed. "I wasn't prepared this morning. I didn't expect you with your glass. So, yes, perhaps the turtle saved us from that worry."

"And our marriages—"

"Mine is over, I told you that."

"But mine—"

"I know, I know. You would give up so much more than I. And

frankly, I don't know if you're able to take a step that would sever you from Mary and your children. And do I want you to? That's a question that—at the moment—I can't answer."

"Can you understand—"

"Your responsibilities? Of course I understand. And I have a fair idea of what you're thinking right now. That I, unlike you, am a free creature, without responsibilities. You're wrong. I work hard to survive. Do you think it's easy writing books?"

"You have a settlement from the Vice-Chancellor, so you said."

"Three hundred pounds a year. If he gives it to me. He's not a bad man, and I hope he will live up to his agreement. But that stipend does not cover the expenses of my father, who has suffered a stroke. And I also support my mother and two unmarried sisters." She got up. "So I have responsibilities. Now let's go back to our tents and try to act as if nothing has happened."

When Sam got into the canoe an hour later, Anna was already seated, making sketches of the men as they waded into the shallows with the baggage and provisions. "Look," she said and pulled up her petticoats to show bare legs and wet moccasins. "I waded out on my own this time. Solomon had only to hold the canoe steady while I got in. There will be no more complaints about his back."

He was relieved that she could talk normally.

As the paddlers got under way, she showed him the pages of her work, asking from time to time, "What is this one's name?" So excellent were her drawings that he had no trouble identifying the men she did not know.

"I shall give each of them a pencil portrait when we reach Penetanguishene. It will be a way to say 'thank you', as I do not have much money at the moment. I have just enough to purchase lodgings and meals in the town, share the cost of the wagon for the portage to Lake Simcoe, and pay for the steamer.

"The men all have such well-muscled upper bodies," she continued, looking over her sketches. "Any of them could have served as models for Michelangelo's David." She leaned in towards him and whispered. "Including my swimming companion of this morning."

"How I wish I could draw. I'd do a picture of you. I can't stop thinking of you..." Sam broke off, afraid to say more, but thankful that she had forgiven his stupid innuendos about her carefree life.

Now she was pointing at the faces of the men she had drawn. "Look at that one with his nose bitten off. By a snapping turtle, no doubt. And that one with the huge nose and jutting chin, but no forehead. And Jacques, the boy whose features are wrenched ever so slightly to the right. Quite fascinating. And do you know why?"

"Was he born that way?"

"Not at all. He told me this morning that *he had been slapped on the face by a grizzly bear!*"

Sam tried not to laugh. It would be a good story for the lady's travel book, and her credulous European readers would probably swallow it. "It's the sort of thing foreigners think is typical of Canadian life. Do you believe it?"

"Of course. Don't you?" She laughed.

In the afternoon they landed on the Island of Skulls, an ancient Indian burial ground, so Jacob told them. Sam and his crew had at first decided to dine here on the shore, but the sight of two newly dead bodies wrapped in bark and laid upon a rock upset them.

"This is no place to eat," he said to Anna, holding a handkerchief over his face. "but I observe your notebook at the ready. Take a few minutes and see what you must see. Jacob will go with you and translate."

"Please come, too."

"If you wish it. The rest of the crew can perch here on the shore where they get a breeze from the lake."

They followed a narrow trail to the interior of the island. In a bark wigwam, they found an old Indian, alone, seated crosslegged on a bed of balsam. His face was smeared with the black paint of mourning. He rose immediately.

Jacob recognized the old man at once. He clasped the man to him, and they stood for a minute in a close embrace. "Father of my dead wife," he said. "Father of this dead woman and grandfather of child. Now he loses all his family."

"Jacob, we must not intrude," Sam said. "Let us leave the poor man to grieve. I cannot even imagine the pain of having all your children die before your own departure."

But the afflicted man seemed to welcome their visit. Perhaps he needed the company of the living. He led them back along the trail to the corpses on the rock and showed them the household items piled beside the bodies for use in the afterlife. Nearby a bonfire had been kindled. He spoke to Jacob at length.

"He tells us," their friend said, "that the fire shows departed spirits the route to land of the dead."

The stench was overpowering, but Sam managed to keep his handkerchief in his pocket. He looked at Anna. Her face was grey, she had put a hand upon a tall rock to steady herself, but she did not faint.

"Father takes us now to see important skeleton," Jacob said. One hundred yards away from the newly dead was the skeleton of a chief who apparently had died leading a war party against another band. "We do not bury Indian war chiefs," Jacob told them. The chief had been placed in a sitting posture, his back against a tree, with his head-dress mouldering on a grinning skull, and a tomahawk and scalping knife in his bony fingers.

Sam found a gold coin in his pocket. He knelt down and placed it near the skeleton. Perhaps the old man would consider it part of the treasure of the afterlife. But Sam hoped he would use it himself to lighten his own burdens.

It was a relief to return to the crew. On the sandy shore, two of the men skipped stones into the still water of the lake. "I won," old Solomon said to Sam, "fifteen skips to LeDuc's twelve." His watery brown eyes shone with the pleasure of his victory, and his wrinkled cheeks were ruddy. For Sam, it was an antidote to the horror of the past hour.

That afternoon, the canoe travelled onwards past a cape which Alexander Henry called Pointe aux Grondines because of the never-ending moan of breakers from the heavy swell. LeDuc told Anna that a fur trader and sixteen people in a *canot du maître* had been wrecked here upon the rocks.

They passed near the mouth of Rivière des Français and came again upon lovely groups of Elysian islands, channels winding among rocks and foliage, and more fields of water-lilies. But Anna could not put from her mind the memory of the corpses and the grim history LeDuc had related. "Even Paradise contains lost souls," she said to Sam. "I have had enough of death for one day."

A sudden rain came down later, accompanied by a brisk wind that lashed up the waves. The sky darkened, forcing the canoes to go ashore. Anna was grateful for the special attention the voyageurs gave to her. They pitched her tent high on a rock so that the water ran off on all sides. "Get inside quickly," Sam said, thrusting dry bearskins and blankets inside the flap. "Got to get the canoes unloaded and everything covered with a canvas," he told her before he ran off.

She arranged the skins and coverlets to make a comfortable bed, undressed, and lay in the shadows of her tent. Then she got up, rummaged through her portmanteau and found her sponges. Over the noise of pelting rain, she could hear the laughter and singing of the crew below. The rain seemed not to bother them one bit. It meant an early end to their day's labours, that was why they were so merry, and she lay still, enjoying the sound of happy voices. It was a far cry from her Toronto nights with Robert.

Sam in the meantime had pitched his own tent near Anna's on the height of land overlooking the shore. Everything in the canoes now safely under cover, he waited while the crew built a roaring fire, tipped the canoes over for shelter, and passed a bottle of rum from mouth to mouth. Then he heated a flask of madeira for himself, intending to drink it in the privacy of his quarters, and bade them goodnight.

He opened the flap of his tent, closed it again, and stood for a moment in the rain, holding the flask. Then he turned, walked a hundred yards, and stopped. He was a foot from the pegs of Anna's tent. He called softly, "Perhaps you are cold? I have hot madeira here."

"Come in."

He walked into the tent, stood while his eyes adjusted to the darkness, then saw her outline in the gloom. He moved towards her. A blanket covered her neck and shoulders. She motioned for him to sit beside her on the bearskin and stretched out her hand for the hot drink.

"There's enough for both of us," she said, as she took a sip from the flask and passed it back to him. He put the flask to his own lips, catching the scent of her breath on it. It was a clean, fresh fragrance. They sat in silence enjoying the warmth of the drink. Then, without preamble, she shrugged the blanket from her shoulders. She was naked.

"The madeira has helped to warm me," she said, pulling him towards her, "but I am still cold."

"Lie down beside me, my dear Anna." He encircled her waist—that waist he had dreamed of all day—and kissed her neck.

She laughed, a gurgle of sound in the darkness of their small enclosed world. "If you are my brave, you must get out of those clothes. Then we can be redskin to redskin."

He began to laugh too. He pulled off his shirt, kicked off the knee-high moccasins he wore in the canoe and threw his trousers aside. His body snuggled into hers, his prick stiff in the hollow between her legs.

"I am prepared for this moment," she whispered. She moved on top of him. "Love me, love me." Used to Mary's reticence, he responded as he had never done before, thrusting himself inside her and abandoning himself to the moment.

"Now," she said, as she rolled away from him, "it is my turn." She pulled his hand towards her body. She smelled of lavender and her nipples were hard. Between her legs was a wetness that drove him onwards.

He wakened just as the darkness of the tent was changing to the shadowy light of pre-dawn. Anna was still asleep. He kissed her ear gently. She stirred. "Goodbye, love," he said, and moved towards the opening of her tent. He looked out cautiously. All was still, and the only sound was the hoot of an owl in a pine nearby. He crept back to his own canvas home. Later, on his way down to the encampment, he picked a bunch of wild roses, still covered with raindrops, and laid them just inside the flap of her tent.

THIRTY-NINE

Breakfast that morning was a hasty affair, taken on a dining table of wet rock overlooking the lake. The voyageurs were anxious to get into the water and make up for the time lost by the rainstorm of the previous afternoon.

Anna arrived late, yawning as she arranged wayward strands of hair. She seemed to avoid Sam's gaze. He went to the campfire and piled her tin plate with food. Their fingers touched as she took it from him.

She looked down on the tangle of grey strands fried in pork grease. "What is it?"

"Wa,ac," Jacob said.

"*Tripe de roche,*" LeDuc said.

"A species of lichen pulled off this very rock," Sam said.

"Well, I am hungry, and since there is nothing else, I'll eat it."

"Try a pinch of salt." Sam passed a small shaker to her.

As they travelled, she lolled back in her seat. Instead of sketching and writing, she drifted into slumber, awakening only at midday when they came to the Bear Islands, so called, Jacob told her, because of the number of those animals found upon them. Along the shoreline of one island, the Indians had stuck a bear's head on the bough of a dead pine.

"An offering to the Great Spirit," Jacob said.

"Resurrection and new life," Anna said.

"Am I missing something?" Sam asked.

"The bear emerges from the hibernation of winter into the warmth of spring and summer."

"Sometimes I wish I'd paid more attention to the good Reverend Strachan when he tried to teach me literature."

"You know enough about resurrection, dear sir, without the formal training."

Sam blushed.

They paddled onward, and the sun rose high in the sky.

"On next island," Jacob said, "we make lop stick for Mrs. Jameson."

"What on earth is a lop stick? Some kind of new treat like this morning's grey moss?"

"A rare honour," Sam said, "given only to special people." He added in a low voice so that only she heard him, "Like you, my dear Anna."

They came to a small island on which was a tall pine on a promontory near the water's edge. Everyone studied it, the voyageurs back-paddling with their oars. "Perfect," they agreed after several moments, and in an instant, they had anchored the canoes offshore with a long rope.

Sam and the men splashed through the shallow water to the rocky shoreline. Anna followed. They ran up the slope to the pine they had looked on so intently.

But before Anna caught up, the youngest crew member, Louis, was already halfway up it, an axe strapped to his back. At the top of the tree he left a tuft of green intact, then he came down slowly, lopping off all the branches as he descended.

"So now you understand what a lop stick is?" Sam asked.

"But what is its purpose?"

"You'll find out soon enough. Let's move up close and see what Jacob is carving on the trunk."

She leaned in to look at the letters. WA-SAH—"It's my Chippewa name! But why—"

"Because ever after," Jacob said, bowing, "this island will be called Island of the Lady of the Bright Foam."

"Wa,sah,ge,wah,no, qua's Island," all the men shouted. Then they discharged their rifles and shouted again, "Wah,sah,ge,wah,no,qua's Island!"

As she made a quick sketch of the naked tree with its green

chapeau, Anna said to Sam, "My own island. Truly, this is an honour I could not have imagined in my wildest dreams."

They stopped just before sundown on a small island to the east of Christian Island. In the clefts and hollows of the rock were quantities of gooseberries and raspberries which the men set about picking as a special treat on this, the last night of their voyage.

Anna found a rock a few yards away from the encampment. She had some notes to make while the light was still good enough. What a book this would be, she reflected. It was sure to find a London publisher. Everyone wanted to know about the new land. As she sat on her rock, the fresh, scented breeze penetrated the mosquito netting around her face and cooled her cheeks. To the west was a sunset whose beauty even Turner or Canaletto would be challenged to capture. Yes, what a book this would be. More than an account of a physical journey, it was the chronicle of her move from death into life. An insensitive male critic might dismiss it as "female picaresque", or some such term, but the reality would remain. This journey had been her renaissance.

Would she name names in it? No. She would say what she had to say, but she would not betray her husband, Mrs. Powell or the other biddies of Toronto society, or—Sam. Dear, dear Sam. Perhaps sometime, somewhere, she would tell Ottilie about him. In the book, she would speak only of his kindness.

And now, she thought, tucking her quill and inkwell away, I'll wander about a bit, find a quiet pool to wash in, perhaps pick an herb or two for the cooks. And wait for the night to come.

To atone for the breakfast of lichen, the men were preparing an excellent meal: fried bass and a couple of dozen eggs which they had found in nests on the rocks. While Anna wandered off into the bush, Sam stayed near the fire and watched LeDuc crack the eggs into an iron skillet. Knowing that the men would sometimes eat eggs so nearly hatched that they could almost hear the chicks peep, he was relieved to see that these eggs had not been long in their nests. He hoped Anna would not inquire too closely into the source of this unexpected treat.

She came back in half an hour with some wild mint for the cook. "Eggs, what a delicious surprise."

"I'm sure there's some important symbolism I'm missing here?" Sam whispered, leaning towards her.

"Let's just enjoy them on the culinary level. And think about the fact that there are far too many gulls in this world."

So it was a happy meal. Sam brought out the bottles of wine he had removed from the government shed at Manitoulin and stowed away for this special occasion. He did not worry about the crew's consumption of alcohol. The Department of Indian Affairs paid them well, they wanted the money, and they were smart enough to regulate their intake. As the men washed the plates in the lake afterwards, there was a bird's cry over their heads. High above, a hawk hovered on the wind currents. Then down it came and perched on the bottom branch of a pine tree near where they were cleaning up.

"By god, I think it's the hawk that broke loose," Sam said. Jacob handed him a pair of deerskin gloves, and he donned them and walked slowly towards it. It made no attempt to take flight, so he put his hands gently around its wings and returned it to the basket with its companion. "I can't believe it," he said to Anna, "it's kept its mate in sight all the way. And now they are together again. Who would have thought a bird could have this commitment?"

The usual campfire songs began. Anna taught Jacob some chords on the Spanish guitar, and LeDuc marked the beat with tin spoons. Voices were loud, no doubt the influence of the wine, but everyone sang in tune.

"I'd better get to bed," Anna said finally. "So much to be readied for tomorrow." She spoke one soft word to Sam as she left the fireside. "Later."

He was careful to stay with the voyageurs. It was well past

midnight when they put the guitar and spoons away, stoked up the campfire to keep the mosquitoes off, and tipped the canoes over for shelter. He climbed to his tent, waited a half-hour, then looked out. All was quiet on the shore. The paddlers were fast asleep.

He went to Anna's tent. She stirred when he pulled back the flap and sat up. They embraced, and he inhaled the lavender fragrance of her naked body.

"It's the last time, love."

"I know. You will go back to your nest with Mary and your fledglings, and I shall return to my brood in England. It must be so. But we have this night."

So he did his best to pleasure her, but all the while he felt as he had on that far-off evening when the sheriff and his men had marched him past the palisade of spiked poles and through the iron doors of the King Street jail. When their love-making was over, Anna tucked her body into his, and he held her close until her breathing deepened. Then he went to his solitary bed.

FORTY

The crew broke camp at dawn, and the canoes were afloat by six o'clock. At nine they sighted Penetanguishene, "place of falling sand", as the Indians called it. When Sam had set out from here—in another life, it seemed— it had been the launching-place for all things possible. He had come a great distance since then, but now, as the canoes approached the settlement, he knew that there on the high sandbanks the fragile structure of his happiness would collapse. He had soared for a few days. Now he must return to his family and his debts.

He doubted that Crimshaw would find a sympathetic ear with the courts, if he pushed for revenge. But he'd taken money from the Indian funds. How long would it be before someone demanded a tally? He could still put it back. Perhaps he could sell Hazelburn and the rest of his extensive property. Toronto was booming now, and there were sure to be buyers.

His immediate concern was to dispatch a sergeant to find Anna accommodation in the town. The men at the barracks would expect him to stay with them. Then on the morrow, several of them would make their way to Coldwater, and thence by oxcart sixteen miles across the forest to the head of Lake Simcoe, by steamer to the Holland Landing, and from there by wagon to Toronto. He and Anna would not be alone together again.

He stood by as the voyageurs unloaded the luggage onto the quay. Anna was among them, giving out the portraits she had completed during the voyage. There was much laughter as the men passed the drawings from one to the other.

Now she handed Jacob his likeness. It was Sam's favourite. Her other sketches were in pencil, but Jacob's was in watercolours. It showed him standing in the stern of the canoe holding his long paddle, a beaded scarlet sash on his doeskin breeches, and his long black hair tied back with a twisted handkerchief.

While Sam watched, Jacob suddenly grasped Anna by the waist, hoisted her aloft in his strong brown arms, and swung her round and round as if she were a small child. Then he set her gently down on the wooden planks.

As all this unfolded, Anna noticed him watching her and came towards him breathless and laughing. "Farewell, best of my *cavaliers*," she said, and she thrust into his hand one last sheet of paper.

He looked down at a portrait in charcoal of himself with the hawk in his hands. He'd had no idea... She must have done it last night while he waited on the shore to come to her. She had drawn him dressed in his knee-high moccasins and the buckskin shirt he wore when he travelled with Jacob. And at the bottom of the sketch she had written "Nehkik".

"It's the grown-up equivalent of the portrait Berczy did of me all those years ago," he said, trying to hold back his tears. "I'll frame it and put it on the wall beside the other."

Then he noticed that she'd written something below "Nehkik". He turned his back to the sun to see better. "What are these words?" he asked, and then... "Surely not, surely not..." He laughed. "Yes. Yes. You've written '*Carpe diem*'."

It was his turn now. He pulled a pair of beaded moccasins from the sling that he wore over his shirt. He'd bought them from an Indian woman on the day when Anna had come ashore on Manitoulin Island. They would fit, he knew. He had memorized the shape and size of those feet when Camudwa carried her out of the water after the canoe race. The woman who had made them had sewn a water-lily in white beads on each toe.

Anna sat down then and there on the quay to put them on. She removed the ones she had worn during her voyage, rubbed and damp from her splashings through the water. As she started to pull the left one on, she stopped. "Something in the foot," she said and reached in to extract a small piece of birchbark.

"There's a message I cut into it with my knife," Sam said. "Read it."

"*Carpe diem*." It was her turn now to laugh.

"The only Latin phrase I could remember from my school days."

And those were his final words to her. He wanted so much to say something eloquent, something she might remember for the rest of her life, but his heart was too full. He could not force out the fine phrases.

So he looked down at her bright face for the last time. Then he turned away in the direction of the barracks.

AFTERWORD

Anna Jameson returned to England in 1837 and never came back to Canada. To support her needy family, she churned out popular books on art and literary criticism. She also lectured on women's rights and the need for hospital reform.

She had a large circle of prominent friends, including Lady Byron and Robert and Elizabeth Browning. Friends obtained for her a small pension from Queen Victoria, but she was always short of money. She died in 1860. Her Canadian memoir is still in print.

Robert Jameson sold the "pleasant little house" he built for himself and Anna and speculated in land in the west end of Toronto. Jameson Avenue commemorates his name. After retirement from public office in the late 1840s, he stopped paying the yearly settlement to Anna.

He died in 1854 of consumption or alcoholism, leaving his estate to two Toronto friends. Anna did not contest the will.

Samuel Jarvis struggled with debts to the end of his life. He eventually retired in disgrace from the Indian Department, accused of defrauding the government of money. But in his insouciant way, he continued to enjoy hunting and fishing and his active social life with Mary. Eventually he subdivided Hazelburn in an attempt to settle his debts. A major Toronto thoroughfare, Jarvis Street, recalls his presence. He died in 1857.

The "viper" William Lyon Mackenzie, always popular with ordinary folk, led an unsuccessful rebellion in December of 1837. He lived in exile in the States until his return to Canada in 1849. He died peacefully in 1861, his funeral cortege stretching a half mile behind the hearse.

Sir Francis Bond Head was recalled to England following the thwarted Mackenzie rebellion and never again held public office.

First Nations communities continue to struggle against racism and indifference.

AUTHOR'S NOTE

I spent years researching this novel. Most characters are historical figures, and some of the events and situations are found in history books. I have, however, invented scenes and situations to bring characters to life. Because nobody appears to know why Anna Jameson and her husband were estranged, for example, I have made him a closet homosexual.

I thank the ghost of Anna for her 1838 memoir, *Winter Studies and Summer Rambles*. I also thank Clara Thomas for her biography *Love and Work Enough: The Life of Anna Jameson*. It allowed me to put Anna's brief time in Toronto into the larger context of her rich and colourful life.

Three books in particular gave insight into Sam Jarvis. Chris Raible's *Muddy York Mud: Scandal & Scurrility in Upper Canada* provided wonderful accounts of the duel and the Types Riot and trial. Katherine M. J. McKenna's *A Life of Propriety* described the stifling social life of early Toronto. Austin Seton Thompson's *Jarvis Street* outlined Sam's tenure as Superintendent of Indian Affairs and even provided the drawing of little Sam in his Indian garb.

At the Peterborough Canoe Museum, I bought Grace Lee Nute's book *The Voyageur* and got the inside story of life in a birchbark canoe.

When I moved from writing non-fiction to fiction, I needed help. Particularly I thank Richard Scrimger for his witty lessons and Barbara Kyle for her gentle insights into opening chapters. Gail Anderson-Dargatz offered rigorous commentary. And what would I have done without the support of my West Coast writers' group? Thanks so much to Laurel Hislop, Annette Yourk and Carolyn Gleeson for their helpful critiques of the book over many months.

I am grateful to Carolyn Thompson who gave information on period fashions, did an extensive copy edit and helped in a hundred ways.

Finally, my experience with Sylvia McConnell, Allister Thompson and Emma Dolan has shown me what a first-rate publishing house is all about.

Ann Birch has worked for a decade in Toronto's finest old houses as an historical interpreter. These places have given her a wide knowledge of nineteenth century domestic, social and political life. What she enjoys most is research into the journals and letters of early immigrants to Upper Canada. An award-winning educator, she was head of English at several Toronto high schools and an associate professor at York University and the University of Toronto.

Settlement is her first novel.